Chartile

Book I: Prophecy

Cassandra Morgan

Ordering Information:

www.authorcassandramorgan.com

www.amazon.com

First Printing: February 2015

White Whiskers Publications

ISBN: 978-0-692-40732-5

This book is dedicated to

Conor, Brenda,

Mr. William "Bill" Urban,

and Mr. Scott Carroll

Thank you for my childhood and for always
believing in me.

A special thank you to my dear husband, who
wouldn't let me give up on writing no matter what.

Julia,
Always follow your heart, And Never give up on your dreams, You are far more extraordinary than you could ever possibly imagine.

Love,
Bill

This book is co-edited by Little Ra, and occasionally the other furry
paws of Snowflake, Aila, Aster, Pharaoh and Pixie. But, mostly Ra
liked to sit on the keyboard and lick the screen.

Thanks, little ones.

Table of Contents

Chapter One

The Dream

Jayson Hill walked down a path he had travelled a hundred times before. It was the path to the fort he and his friends had built in the woods last summer. He knew he was dreaming, but it was unlike any dream he had ever had before. The summer sun was warmer and more real than any normal dream. The trees of the wood surrounding him were slightly hazy, which seemed to be the only normal thing about his dream.

Jayson spun around as a voice filled his ears. It called his name over and over again. The voice seemed to come from everywhere, but there was no one with him. Jayson began running full out, headed for the creek and the little drawbridge he and his friends had made to access their treehouse fort. With each step he took, the voice grew louder and louder. The sun was beginning to grow brighter, and still the voice called to him. He could barely make out the trees anymore.

He stopped running. There was a flash of white light, and Jayson woke with a start, lying flat on his back in his bed as if he had dropped straight through the ceiling. The pull chain on the fan above him swayed in time with his still rapid breathing. He rubbed his eyes and took several deep breaths. The haziness that had plagued his dream slowly subsided in the light of another typical Swansdale, Ohio morning. It was day break, and the sun had just peeked over the horizon, casting misty patterns of pink, amber and gray tones across the sleepy little housing community the fourteen-year old boy lived

1

in. It had rained that night, and the foliage seemed to be alive with thousands of twinkling Christmas lights as the morning sun hit the tiny droplets.

His Jack Russel Terrier, Jesse, quietly snored beside him. Jayson scratched behind the dog's ears as he turned to face his alarm clock. 7:02 AM.

"Crap!" Jayson flung his blankets off the bed entirely, sending Jesse to the floor. The little dog pranced around his feet excited as Jayson grabbed for pants here and a shirt there. He wasn't entirely sure whether his socks matched, and his thick red hair was sticking up every which way. He tried to flatten it as he raced down the hall to the living room skidding to a stop long enough to slip on his shoes.

"Good morning," said his mother from the kitchen table. She did not sound pleased with her son tearing through the house, and looked even less thrilled as she raised an eyebrow at him.

"Good morning! Love you! Bye!" said Jayson slamming the front door on his untied shoe lace. He opened the door again to free himself and smiled sheepishly at his family who sat together eating at the kitchen table. His little sister, Jessica, rolled her eyes at him and stuffed another spoonful of Frosted Flakes in her mouth.

Jayson slammed the door closed behind him and winced. He hadn't meant to shut it so hard. He leapt down the small set of porch steps in a single jump and took off for his friend, Leo DeHaven's house. He breezed past a jogger making her way around the block and barked back at the neighbor's dog as he ran.

He approached Leo's front door breathless and clutching at a stitch in his side. After a moment, he raised his hand to knock on the door. His knuckles nearly collided with Leo's pudgy face. Leo whipped back just in time, and his blonde hair fell into his blue eyes.

"Dude! You almost broke my glasses!" Leo cried.

"Sorry," said Jayson with a sheepish grin as he stepped past Leo and into the living room. "And sorry I'm late."

"For you, Jayson," Mr. DeHaven called from the kitchen, "late is right on time."

Jayson shrugged and ambled into the kitchen. He plunked himself in a chair beside their friend, Jack Mitchel. Jack sat staring into a cup of hot chocolate and coffee, the bags under his eyes more pronounced than usual. A copy of Shakespeare's Romeo and Juliet lay on the table beside him. No doubt it was his natural knack for poetry that had Jessica swooning over him. His perfect, wavy brown hair and towering height probably had something to do with it too. Despite Jack's slightly disheveled appearance that morning, he greeted Jayson with a wide smile that lit up his hazel eyes.

"Egg sandwiches!" sang Mr. DeHaven, and a steaming plate of sloppy egg sandwiches appeared on the table in front of the boys.

"Oh, you really didn't have to do that," Jack mumbled. His smile faded, and he looked from the plate of sandwiches to Mr. DeHaven with guilt.

The DeHavens had been rather well to do at one time, but now their financial situation was growing increasingly dismal, and so was the state of their rather bare refrigerator.

"Nonsense! You can't be gallivanting around those woods on an empty stomach! Eat." Reagan DeHaven demanded and turned back to the stove.

Quietly the three boys obliged.

"I'm not sure I want to go out there today," said Leo quietly. Jayson and Jack stopped chewing to stare at him. Jayson's grip on his sandwich faltered, and a piece of egg slipped from between the soggy bread and landed on his pants. "I just — I had this weird dream, and it kind of freaked me out."

"Wh-what happened?" Jack asked. He set his own sandwich on his plate and swallowed hard.

"Yeah," said Jayson. He sat up a little straighter and took another bite of sandwich. "What happened?"

Leo rubbed the back of his neck. "Well, there was this weird voice that said my name. And a funky light thing."

"A light?" Jayson asked, his mouth now full of egg sandwich.

"What did the voice say?" Jack asked.

"M-my name. That was it."

"It could be someone trying to send you a message," said Mr. DeHaven over his shoulder. He turned, his eyes wide with mystery and a small smile tugging at the corners of his mouth.

"A message?" Jayson frowned. "Well, does that mean we should go to the fort or not?"

They sat chewing their sandwiches in silence for a long time. Eventually, each had turned to stare at Mr. DeHaven's back. When he turned from the stove, the man threw his arms up in surrender.

"Don't look at me!" he laughed. "This is your adventure."

As one, Jayson, Jack and Leo scrambled out of their chairs and headed for the door.

"Sandwiches!" Mr. DeHaven called after them. They ran back to the kitchen, grabbed their half-eaten egg sandwiches and bolted out the door.

They trudged toward the wood behind their subdivision in silence. They were anxious and nervous, and Mr. DeHaven's egg sandwiches sat heavy on their stomachs. When they reached the path to their fort, they all hesitated. It was the same path from Jayson's dream, and he suspected it was the same for Leo too. But there was no voice, and no bright light. It was the same stretch of trees, game trails and dirt hills that had always been there.

"I guess it was just a dream then," Leo shrugged.

Jayson grabbed a rope slung over a tree limb and lowered their make-shift drawbridge. They crossed the little creek and sat on the dilapidated furniture inside the fort.

They had spent all of the previous summer building the two-story tree house. Jack had supplied the old, shabby furniture from a dump near his father's work. They had arranged an overstuffed arm chair and a futon beneath the large oak tree. In the boughs of the tree was their storage area, complete with a floor, ceiling, and tarps and shower curtains for walls.

Jayson climbed to the second level and tossed down three sticks to his friends.

"I call King!" he said, shaking off the unease that had plague his walk to the fort.

"You're always King," Leo protested. He caught the stick Jayson had thrown to him and rolled his eyes.

"Yeah, and you're always the wizard. You're the only one with powers, so I don't see you complaining," Jayson snapped back.

"Well, I want to do something different this time," said Jack. "I'm always the knight. I have to take all my orders from you, and I don't even have any powers to fight."

"But you get the damsel at the end. Remember, pretty boy?" Jayson made a kissy face at Jack and laughed.

"What if we started a new game," suggested Leo, "Three wizard kings —"

"No, I like this game." Jayson folded his arms before him.

"Yeah, because you get to boss us around. I don't think I want to do this today, guys." Jack turned and headed for the drawbridge.

"Come on, Jack!" called Leo, "Don't go!"

"He's just upset because he heard his crush from, like, forever, started dating Tanner Fulton, and he knows Claudia Benedict will never be his girlfriend." Jayson jumped from the second level. He landed with a loud thud and nearly lost his balance.

"I am not!" Jack shouted.

"Dude. Harsh," Leo said, glaring at Jayson.

"Don't you think we're just getting a little old for this?" Jack asked.

"No. And now you just sound like those jerks from school." Jayson shoved his stick into his belt so hard he nearly stabbed himself in the leg. "You're not going to tell anyone, are you?"

"No, I just —" Jack struggled for the right words. "It'd be different if this were real, or something, you know? I'm just tired of pretending to be something I'm not. I know that sounds so bunk, but — maybe it's time to grow up." Jack stabbed his stick into the ground, his face flush. "Time to stop believing in stupid dreams!"

He turned quickly and headed back across the drawbridge. He half expected Leo to chase after him, but he could hear him arguing with Jayson back at the tree house. He was glad. He just wanted to be alone anyway. Jayson's reminder that he didn't stand a chance at ever being Claudia Benedict's boyfriend hurt. But not nearly as much as discovering his dream hadn't actually come true.

Chapter Two

Chartile

Jack's eyes shot open. He had had the dream again. It was the same dream Leo had described the day before. But this time it was interspersed with screaming, breaking glass and a crying baby. His dresser was still pushed in front of his bedroom door. He pushed it aside and peeked into the hall. A broken beer bottle his father had thrown against the now cracked mirror littered the floor. He stepped over the broken shards and grabbed a trash bag from the bathroom. When he had finished, he picked his sleeping sister from the floor of his closet and set her in her crib in the next room.

Downstairs, his mother had fallen asleep on the couch. A melted ice pack had fallen to the floor beside her, and the cordless phone lay on the pillow. Jack picked up the phone and walked into the kitchen.

"Aunt Kiera?" Jack whispered and pulled the peanut butter and bread from the cupboard.

"Jack?" Said a sleepy voice on the other end.

"Hi, mom's sleeping now," he said, "I'm going over to Leo's house, so, is it okay if you stay on the line for when Dad comes home?"

"Of course, sweetie. I'll let your mom know, too. Are you alright?" Aunt Kiera asked.

"I'm fine. Amanda is still upstairs sleeping too. Thanks, Aunt Kiera." He set the phone back down beside his mother's head. He covered his mother with the afghan lying on the chair and looked at the bruise rising around her eye and cheek. When his father had refused counseling after this third relapse, his Aunt Kiera had told his mother to leave. But she had refused. Jack sighed and swallowed hard, putting a few peanut butter sandwiches in the pocket of his jacket. He kissed his mother on her forehead and headed out the door.

Jack was halfway up Leo's front lawn when he noticed a strange white Cadillac in the driveway. He looked up and saw Jayson and Leo sitting on the porch steps. Jayson looked up from his bowl of cereal and waved.

"Our glorious knight returns!" He cried, his mouth full. A line of milk dribbled down his chin. Jack smiled. Leo looked up from his copy of Popular Mechanics, frowning. His tangled mess of blonde hair was more untidy than usual.

"So, you didn't abandon us after all," snapped Leo.

"I'm sorry," said Jack, sticking his hands in the pockets of his windbreaker. "I— it was a long night. I know it's really not an excuse anymore, but…"

Leo sighed and went back to his magazine. "It's okay," he mumbled.

Jayson set his cereal bowl on the step and finally wiped his chin.

"What are you guys doing out here?" Jack asked. He sat in the grass and moved Jayson's bowl before it was knocked over.

"Well," said Jayson, "Some weird guy showed up and needed to talk to Mr. DeHaven. They said something about 'the project' and started pulling out all these boxes."

"It's the documentation from my dad's NASA project," said Leo. He put his magazine into the mailbox and sat back down. "It's the one that got cancelled before we moved out here. It's why mom moved to France and all that." Leo looked at his feet and pulled on the collar of his shirt nervously.

"You can have my mom," said Jayson punching Leo in the arm, laughing. "She likes smart kids the best."

"Shut up, man." Leo glared at Jayson. "She's coming back. She's just – busy."

"So, why are we out here?" Jack asked, breaking the tension that had risen between them.

"Totally kicked out," said Jayson. "As if we know anything about what they're talking about."

"The project was super top secret," Leo said defensively.

"But it got cancelled," Jayson countered.

Leo shrugged. "Whatever."

"You guys wanna go to the fort?" Jack shrugged.

"Sure," said Jayson, leaping to his feet, and still nearly upsetting the bowl on the ground. Jack nodded, and handed Leo one of the peanut butter sandwiches he had stuffed in his pocket. He held it out like a peace offering, but still wouldn't look at Leo.

Leo took the sandwich and punched Jack in the arm. "Thanks," he said, and followed after Jayson.

Jayson's sugary cereal had begun to kick in by the time they reached the tree fort. He lowered the bridge, and skipped across the little creek. Jack and Leo followed at a walk and watched as Jayson tripped and nearly fell. They stifled laughs together, their anger forgotten.

Cassandra Morgan

Jack flopped across the arm chair. "Hey, guys, I've been thinking," he said.

"Uh, oh," said Leo with a grin, "That could be dangerous."

"Hey, it's not like I'm Jayson," Jack teased. His wide smile had returned.

"And what's that supposed to mean?" Jayson jumped down from the second level of their tree fort. His arms flailed to keep balance, and he smacked himself in the head with his stick-sword.

"Well, I was just wondering if you guys might like to try and study martial arts or something. They have the Mortal Combat movies on a marathon this month, and I've been watching them, like, non-stop at night. You can practically teach yourself how to do this stuff." Jack jumped up and executed a mock kick and punch. "We could really take our game fighting to the next level."

Leo and Jayson glanced at each other uncomfortably. Finally, Leo spoke. "This wouldn't have anything to do with your dad would it?"

"My dad?" Jack took a step back.

"You're not gunna try to fight him, are you?" Jayson asked.

"Why would I do that?" Jack scowled at his friends and crossed his arms. He hadn't talked to anyone about his dad in years. He shifted side to side uneasily. How could they have known?

"Jack, we're your friends. We know what's going on," said Leo.

"And yesterday you were talking about being something you're not." Jayson blushed beneath his freckles. "We care, dude."

"Just because you have a perfect little family doesn't mean I have to try to act like I do!" Jack cried. His hands clenched into fists, and his face burned red. "So what if I want to do something change my life?" He jabbed his finger at Leo and Jayson. "You don't have any idea what I have to go through!" Tears filled his eyes. He tried to fight them off. His father's voice echoed in his mind. "Only babies cry."

"No, I don't know what you go through, because you won't talk to anyone!" Jayson yelled back. He threw his stick on the ground. "I've got my own stuff going on too, Jack! Why are you so special, huh?"

"Whoa, hold the phone," said Leo. He rushed between Jack and Jayson, forcing them apart. "Let's just take a chill pill. There's a time and place for everything. My mom used to say that."

"And how do you know this isn't it?" Jack shoved his finger into Leo's chest, then turned pointed at himself. "I make my own fate, Leo! I'll decide my destiny!"

The silence that fell was deafening. Not a bird sang, not a leaf shifted. Jack looked at the creek behind them. It had stopped in mid wave. He turned to his friends again. Their forms were becoming hazy and distorted. The sunlight was increasing and was close to blinding. He saw Jayson shaking his head in disbelief, the anger and rage turning to fear. The world went white, and Jack knew no more.

❧

Leo was the first to wake. He blinked in the bright sunlight and pushed away the dizziness that lingered. He got to his knees and saw Jayson and

12

Jack close by. They were still unconscious. He crawled to them, and gave each a gentle shake.

Jayson shook his head and sat up.

"God, what happened?" he asked.

"We must've...blacked out... or something," Leo said uncertain.

"Yeah, but where are we?" asked Jack as his eyes came into focus.

Where they sat was not their fort or any place in the woods they recognized. There was no wood. Just a sloping plane of craggy rocks before them, and a towering gray mountain behind them. The sun was shining, but the sky was a dreary, overcast gray.

"Do you think someone at school is trying to bunk us?" Jayson asked.

"More likely we were kidnapped," said Leo with a nod.

"Then why aren't we tied up?" Jayson raised an eyebrow and crossed his arms before him.

Leo shrugged. He opened his mouth, intending to give a scientific hypothesis, but was cut off.

"Hey look." Jack pointed to a line of smoke rising into the air in the distance.

"Where there's smoke, there's fire." said Leo with a grin. He always looked exactly like his father whenever he did so.

"And where there's fire, there's probably people," Jack finished excitedly.

"Maybe they know where we are!" Jayson jumped to his feet and nearly twisted his ankle.

"And how to get home," Leo added, taking no notice of Jayson.

The boys ran up the sloping hill, tripping occasionally on a loose stone from the boulders that littered the way. They stopped when they reached the top of the hill, panting and surveying the scene before them.

Below was a tiny village nestled between the hill they stood upon and another identical hill at least a mile away. The homes were small huts with thatched roofs. Dirt roadways wound between wooden structures that appeared to be bakeries, smithies and stables.

Jack nearly fell to the ground in disbelief. Jayson plopped down next to him.

"Come on, man!" he cried and pulled on his red hair. "No electricity? I figured a campground would have electricity."

"I don't think that's a campground, Jay," Leo whispered.

"It's gotta be! What else could it be? Like some stupid renn faire thing?"

"What's the last thing you all remember?" Jack asked them.

"Well," Leo folded his arms and grabbed his chin as he thought. "It was like I went deaf."

"Yeah, and everything just kind of stopped. It looked like the creek stopped in mid-wave," said Jayson.

"And the light," Jack added quietly. "Just like from my dream."

"Mine too," Leo whispered.

The boys fell silent, not daring to look at one another.

"Maybe this is one of those government tests, and they messed it all up," Jayson broke the silence. Jack and Leo looked at him but did not speak. "Maybe they're working on a way to control a person's mind, to make them see things. Like... a controlled and forced hallucination. Or..." Jayson paused, his eyes widening. "Maybe they were doing something with time and accidentally sent us back in time."

"Are you for real, man?" Jack interrupted. He narrowed his eyes and shook his head.

"What?" Jayson asked with a shrug.

Jack rolled his eyes and sighed. "Why us? Why Swansdale? That doesn't make any sense."

"It sort of does," Leo said. He sat down between Jack and Jayson. "No one would believe us if we tried to tell someone. We're kids. And Swansdale's a no-name little town. No one would ever look there for signs of government testing. And, if we tried to go public with it, well, everyone would just think we were trippin! No one would believe us. It's not a bad hypothesis."

Jayson's stomach grumbled loudly, making them all turn and look.

"Well, wherever we are, I hope they have something to eat." Jayson rose to his feet and headed toward the little village.

"Jayson, where are you going?" cried Leo, "We don't know where we are — Jayson! Come back! What if you're kidnapped?"

A sound like thunder made the boys stop. They could feel the ground shake beneath them. Jayson ran back up the hill and joined Jack and Leo behind a giant boulder. Carefully, they peeked around the edge of the rock and watched as s large company of men on horseback came rounded the mountain corner. They wore white and green gambesons emblazoned with a golden phoenix over chain armor. They carried swords and spears, and halted no more than fifty yards from the boulder. Jayson, Jack and Leo pulled back behind the boulder and crouched close together.

"Search every house, every building. Kill anyone who stands in your way. I will not tolerate this any longer."

It was not a man's voice that commanded the horsemen, but a young woman.

"Your Highness, this is the last village between our kingdom and Chamberlain Herodan. Wouldn't it be better served to... revitalize it as a major trade route?" a man's voice suggested.

There was the creak of cured leather, and the shifting of chainmail. Someone cried out in pain and a horse snorted.

"In case you have forgotten, Valar, you are only here because my father ordered it so. You would do well to remain silent." The young woman's voice rose above the clatter of the horses and their riders. "These people refuse to obey the law. They aren't turning over their portion of food or taxes, and they led a rebellion against us three winters past. Do you forget?" A murmur spread throughout the company. Jayson, Jack and Leo huddled closer together. "These sort of people cause pain and problem in a kingdom, and it must be stopped immediately!"

"The only pain and problem in this kingdom is you, Taraniz." Another female voice spoke, this time closer to the boulder the boys hid behind. The company of riders hushed into an eerie silence.

"Ah, Piper, the rebel leader herself. Not looking so good these days. I hear your village turned their backs on you after the attack. Yet, after all this time, you still defend them. Why?"

"I fight against the tyranny and injustice you have brought to all of Chartile, Taraniz. Unless you have an official order signed by the King and the Captain of the Royal army, you cannot touch this place. You would commit an act of near war against your own people, and yet call us rebels and traitors."

The men grew restless and spoke in whispers. One of the women screamed, and there was the clash of metal on metal.

"Stay your weapons," the man who had first opposed Taraniz said.

Jayson dared a peek around the boulder. A thin woman hair and furs fought a tall blonde in a long green dress. The horses stamped their feet as their riders waited with their hands on their sword hilts.

"Come on, we have to help," whispered Jayson as he whipped back behind the boulder.

"How? Throw rocks at them?" Leo suggested sarcastically.

"Good idea!" Jayson smiled and picked up a fist-sized rock at his feet.

"Jayson, are you nuts? Those people have swords!" Jack clutched at Jayson's forearm.

"You heard what that one chick planned to do to those people down there," Jayson protested. "We have to help them!"

"Jayson, we don't know the laws here. We don't even know where we are! We can't interfere!" said Leo. "Dude, we could die! This isn't a game!"

17

"I'm not gunna stand here and let some innocent people get — get slaughtered. Jack, you wanted this to be real. Well now's your chance to do something!" Jayson pulled his arm from Jack's grasp, shoved the rock in his pocket and began to climb to the top of the boulder.

Jack and Leo watched him go, then turned to each other.

"We can't be separated," Leo whispered. Jack nodded and picked up a rock. He ran out from the side of the boulder as Leo did the same on the left.

The sudden appearance of the three boys, with their jeans and brightly colored t-shirts, made the men on horseback point and murmur. Jayson, Jack and Leo now saw the two women fighting were not much older than themselves. They did not seem to have noticed the boys.

Jayson took aim, and threw the rock as hard as he could. He narrowly missed Taraniz by inches.

"Hey! Tar-bees!" Jayson called, "Why don't you go back where you came from and leave these poor people alone!"

The distraction was enough for the girl called Piper to disarm Taraniz. She kicked the blonde to her back and held her sword at Taraniz's throat.

"Your father is not dead, yet. Until then, his law still reigns," said Piper through clenched teeth.

Taraniz pulled a dagger from her belt and pushed Piper's blade aside to slice her across the cheek.

"Not yet, but soon," she said so quietly only Piper and the boys heard. She jumped to her feet as

18

Piper staggered back. She pulled a handkerchief from the pocket of her riding jacket and wiped her dagger clean. She glared for a moment longer at Piper before tossing the handkerchief at the girl's feet. They watched as she mounted her horse, nose in the air and dirt and leaves all over her embroidered dress.

"Back to the camp, all of you, until you can learn to defend your princess against rock-throwing peasants!" With one last glare at Piper, who stood at the base of the boulder clutching her face, the company rode back around the mountain trail.

Jayson, Jack and Leo let out a cry of victory.

"Ya bunch'a wusses!" Jayson taunted after them. He leapt from the boulder and gave Jack a high-five. Their celebration, however, was short lived. Piper stepped toward them and pointed her sword to Jayson's throat. Her green eyes were as hard as when she had looked at Taraniz.

"Who are you? Speak swiftly!" she demanded.

"Whoa, take it easy," said Leo, holding his hands up in surrender. "We were just trying to help—"

Piper pressed the blade against Jayson's skin now. "I asked, who are you?"

"My name is Jack. This is Leo and… that's Jayson. We're from Swansdale. Um, we really don't know how we got here. We just want to go home, so, if you have a phone around here or something…"

Piper narrowed her eyes, and slowly lowered her blade. Jayson sighed in relief.

"Where did you say you were from?" She asked.

"Uh, Swansdale. Ohio. Um, America?" said Jayson.

"Is that north of here?" Piper continued to furrow her brow.

"Uh… where is here exactly?" asked Leo.

"Chartile," she said, not bothering to hide the suspicion in her voice, "Kingdom of the Elves. Beyond that last hill…" She pointed to the far side of the little village. "There begins the territory of Humans. You are Human, are you not?"

It was the boys' turn to be confused. The idea of a government conspiracy was beginning to sound more believable by the minute.

"So where are we in relation to say, the Atlantic Ocean, or Russia? Australia, maybe?" Leo asked.

Piper did not answer. The group continued to look at each other in an awkward silence.

Jayson's stomach made a terrible gurgling sound.

"Sorry." He patted his stomach. "Do you have anything to eat?"

Piper looked back up the path Taraniz and the horseman had left by, and sheathed her sword. "Follow me," she whispered. "This is a conversation to be had under cover."

She headed down the steep hill toward the mountain, not the village. The boys looked longingly the cozy huts below, and trudged begrudgingly after her. She led them up and down steep and winding roads, narrow squeezes between large boulders and toe paths full of loose pebble under foot. She ducked beneath a low hanging outcrop and seemed to disappear. Jack, Leo and

Jayson followed and found themselves in a small cave. A stone fire ring lay in the middle of the room. A few natural shelves in the cave wall held a collection of bowls, utensils and two water skins. Another large natural shelf closer to the ground was covered in blankets and furs.

The boys stood just inside the mouth of the cave as their eyes adjusted to the darkness. Neither of them had ever been in a girl's room before. Piper moved to the back of the cave and pushed a large rock from over a hole in the cave floor. She lowered herself through until only her head and shoulders could be seen.

"Um... where...are we supposed —" Jayson stammered.

"I'll be right back. I'm getting some water," she said and disappeared.

They listened until they could no longer hear her. They stepped cautiously further into Piper's cave and sat around the fire ring. A few embers glowed from the charred logs in its center. Their eyes began to wander from the fire ring to the rest of the cave. An assortment of worn weapons sat in one corner. Jayson stood for a better look, but immediately turned back when he saw the dead game animals hanging from the ceiling.

"What have we gotten ourselves into?" he whispered and nodded toward his discovery.

Jack and Leo did not answer. This was definitely not Swansdale.

"You could have started the fire," said a voice behind them. They jumped and watched Piper push the boulder back over the hole. She slung a gigantic water skin over her shoulder and reached

21

for a large pot that had sat beside the hole. "Potatoes are in the rucksack over there." She pointed to the corner where the animals hung. The boys did not move.

"Uh, we'd love to help, but…uh — we," Leo stammered, "We make our food a bit different back home."

They all felt rather ridiculous and blushed. None of them had ever done more than heat a frozen Hot Pocket in the microwave. Piper furrowed her brow again. When the boys continued to do nothing but look at her with shame, she busied herself with preparing the meal.

Soon, a roaring fire blazed beneath a kettle full of stew. The boys ate as if it could be their last meal. Jayson sighed and leaned back, rubbing his now bulging belly. "So, why do you live here? Aren't your parents worried about you?" he asked.

"My parents are dead," Piper said.

"Oh," said Jayson blushing. "How?"

"It is a long story." she replied and tossed a bit of bone into the fire.

"We've got time," said Jack with a shrug.

Piper gave a small, sad smile and sighed.

Chapter Three

Piper

"My parents were not my birth mother and father." Piper stoked the logs in the fire with a long stick. She stared at the flames as she spoke, the light of the fire turning her green eyes golden. "I was less than a day old when a soldier rode into the village. He claimed he had found me abandoned in the forest. My mother said he was fearful and left in a hurry. In his haste to be rid of me, he never raised his helmet. My parents never saw the face of the man who gave them a daughter.

"My father was a blacksmith, and my mother was a healer. Outland Post is very isolated from the rest of the elven cities. Most of the people in the village knew my parents had taken me in, though I was never treated any different.

"When I was fourteen, a messenger from the palace came to Outland Post demanding all men, young and old, were to report to the palace. Princess Taraniz was organizing an army to drive all Dwarves and Humans from the kingdom. She sought to first take Mount Kelsii from the dwarves before bringing the rest of Chartile under Elven rule. She claimed to be doing so in the name of her father, King Aramor, who had begun to fall ill. She said it was for the good of all Elven kind."

Piper looked up from the fire and sighed. She leaned back and ran the ends of her hair through her fingers.

"My gran had worked at the palace as a scribe and errant. My mother taught me the laws of our kingdom as passed down from her. I knew that without an official order of mandatory recruitment, no one was obligated to go. I said as such to the messenger. He struck me and it roused my village into tumult."

"Wait a minute," Leo interrupted. He immediately blushed and swallowed hard before continuing. "Did you say dwarves? Like from The Lord of the Rings or something?"

Piper narrowed her eyes and studied Leo for several long seconds. "I'm afraid I do not understand your question."

"What do you mean by dwarves?" asked Jack. He did not want to offend anyone. "Like, little people?"

The scowl and confusion on Piper's face deepened. "There are many races in Chartile. Dwarves, Elves, Humans. Of course, the Merfolk haven't been seen for many centuries. Most certainly the dwarves are not little. They are a strong people who live in this very mountain."

"So, what are you?" asked Jayson.

"Me? I am elven, of course."

"Why aren't your ears pointy then?" Jayson smiled and raised his eyebrows.

Piper's expression relaxed and she sighed. "I have heard my people had tipped ears at one time, but this is a legend." she paused. "Have I answered your questions?"

"Yeah, sorry," said Leo. "Uh, go ahead. You were saying your village started to fight back?"

"Yes," Piper said, crossing her legs. She resumed staring into the fire and poking at the logs with the stick. "We drove the messenger and his soldiers back to the palace, but at a great cost. My mother and father, along with countless others were dead. Taraniz declared the uprising at Outland Post treason, and the remaining members of Outland Post turned me over to her as the instigator. I nearly lost my life that day. A man, a knight I presume, stopped Taraniz. He said would be a greater punishment to cast me out into the wild. Taraniz agreed, and here I have lived for the last three years.

"Outland Post is the last to still follow the ways of King Aramor and not the tyranny of his daughter. We pay only the taxes and portions of food that are dictated in the law as set forth by the King. The elven palace has very little farmable land. Each town is expected to produce a certain amount of food to be given to the palace as part of our taxes. However, since Taraniz has decided she does not wish to wait for her father to die in order to take his place on the throne naturally, she has been attempting to change the laws on her own, which she has no right to do. The other cities obey her out of fear. I hear rumors she has killed hundreds of people, and taken many prisoners on petty crimes or actions. But she won't touch this place. She fears me."

Piper drank from her water skin, and cast each boy a glance before returning her gaze to the fire. Jayson, Jack and Leo remained silent. None of what Piper had said reminded them of any video games they had ever played. They still held onto the hope that they were dreaming.

"What I can't understand is how you three fit into this," said Piper looking at them all again. "I find myself wondering why. Why today? Why can't I get the old stories out of my mind? Fairy tales about a prophecy. A fairy tale I haven't remembered in over ten years, until now."

Jack and Leo looked at each other confused as someone began to laugh.

"Us? A fairy tale?" Jayson sat between his friends, smiling. His laughter sounded like small hiccups as he tried to contain them. "Let me guess. We're some figment of your imagination and everything that has happened in my life up until this point was all part of a prophecy? I suppose there's some mystical reason I got a D on my last math test right?"

"You got a D on Mr. Harmon's math test?" asked Leo, furrowing his brow at the boy beside him.

"Jayson, stop it." Jack glared at his friend as Jayson continued to laugh.

"No, I'm done with this," Jayson said and rose to his feet. Jack and Leo stood and watched as he headed for the mouth of the cave. "Thank you for dinner, Piper, right? But I'm out. Peace, man." Jayson waved at the girl still sitting beside the fire before slipping out the entrance. Jack and Leo followed. They gave Piper an apologetic look as they hurried after their friend.

"What the heck are you doing?" Jack asked, running to catch up. Jayson was walking incredibly fast along one of the path, staring at the ground beneath his feet. Neither Jack nor Leo knew where he was going, and they suspected Jayson didn't have a clue either.

"If I don't give into their test, they'll have to send us back," said Jayson.

"What are you talking about, dude?" asked Leo. He was already panting and out of breath.

"The government, the military and the conspiracy, remember? If I refuse to give in to this world they've created, they'll have to send us back."

"Back? What do you mean back? Jayson, there is no back, just —" Jack stepped in front of Jayson. He grabbed his shoulders, stopping him short and pinched Jayson hard on the arm.

"Ow! What the —" cried Jayson and rubbed his arm. The sun was setting quickly, but even in the dim light of dusk, he could see the stern look Jack was giving him.

"This isn't a game, Jayson," said Jack "You're acting so bunk right now, it's not cool. Does that valley look like a made up conspiracy world? Or Piper? She was helping us, and you totally walked out on her! Not cool, man. Now what are we supposed to do?"

"Well I'm not going to lie down and accept it, if that's what they think!" cried Jayson, "Give me proof!"

"Proof?" Leo shouted throwing his arms into the air. A deafening roar broke through the darkness somewhere above them. The boys huddled together and stared up at the strangest creature they had ever seen.

Hunched as it was, it was taller even than Jack. Its front arms hung long like a gorilla's though the only fur it had was a small patch on the top of its head. Its entire body was covered in a thick, dark gray hide, and its orange eyes bulged out of their sockets. It stood to roar at them again, and the boys huddled even closer.

Leo whispered, "How much more proof do you need?"

"Shut up!" said Jayson. He edged toward the underside of the ledge the creature stood on. It roared again, and banged its fists on the ground. Jack and Leo pulled Jayson back, but he had managed to grab a large stick.

"I'll distract it. You go to the village and get help." Jayson whispered as the creature began edging its way down to them.

"Come on, man, enough with the hero crap. Let's just run!" said Jack. He gave a longing look back up the path toward Piper's cave.

"And what if it catches all of us? Better one dead than three," said Jayson.

"This isn't a game —" Leo stopped short, and gave a high-pitched scream as the creature leapt from the ledge onto the path directly in front of them. It lunged for them, swinging its long arms back and forth.

Jayson swung his stick and hit the creature squarely in the head. The creature shook its head and retreated a few steps back. Jack, Leo and Jayson began to inch back slowly when the creature let out a different sort of cry. It was louder, but still just as terrifying. Dozens of orange eyes glowed out of the darkness around them as more of the creatures emerged from the shadows.

The first creature lunged again. It pushed Jack and Leo to the ground with one swipe of its massive hand and grabbed Jayson by the collar of his shirt. Jayson screamed and struggled to break free from the creature's grasp as it turned, dragging him off into the darkness. The other creatures closed in around Jack and Leo. They watched from where they lay on the ground as Jayson disappeared from sight. They clung to each other as the other creatures shuffled closer, Jayson's desperate cries for help growing more distant by the minute.

Fire blazed into view high above them, and a figure stood silhouetted against the flame.

"Up here!" It was Piper. She tossed a sword and bow staff into the middle of the throng of creatures that had momentarily stopped at her call. Jack and Leo caught the weapons, and a pulse of warm, tingling energy flowed up their arms and through their bodies. Leo cocked his body into a box frame. He had never done this before, but it felt instinctual. Jack twirled the staff in front of him, opting for the flurry of an intimidation factor. He wondered where he had gotten the idea, but dismissed it. They couldn't place why, but the boys felt a strength and understanding as they handled the weapons. There were instincts and distant memories they were unsure were their own.

Piper had disappeared in her quest to rescue Jayson. Having made the advancing creatures retreat with a few well-placed attacks, Jack and Leo took off in the direction they had last seen her. They slid down a steep embankment and landed on an outcrop. They looked down to see Piper advancing on the creature carrying Jayson. It dropped Jayson and turned to face its new adversary with a snarl. Jayson rolled down the mountainside several yards before hitting a boulder. His eyes fluttered and then closed.

More orange eyes appeared out of the darkness around them. Jack and Leo leapt off the outcrop and hoisted Jayson up between them.

"Piper!" Jack cried, "Let's get out of here!"

Piper took a deep breath and closed her eyes. A ring of fire sprang up around them. It was close enough they could feel the sudden blast of heat, but it did not burn them. The creatures were blinded by the flash of fire light, and they fled with angry screams and roars. Piper grabbed Leo's sleeve and ran toward the fire. She held out her hand and flames parted before them.

Leo and Jack somehow remembered Piper's home being much closer when they weren't supporting the entire weight of Jayson between them. They were relieved when they finally ducked inside the dark cave. The blood rushed in their bodies and pounded in their ears, making the stillness of Piper's home deafening.

"Put him over there," Piper said, pointing to her bed.

Jack and Leo carried Jayson to the bed while Piper began rummaging through her rucksacks for linen strips and clean water.

It felt too long before Piper, Leo and Jack sat staring into the flames of a newly roaring fire once more. Jayson lay behind them on Piper's bed, bandaged, cleaned and resting. The cut on his forehead was the least of their concerns. The bruise rising around his ribs had them all worried. Jack glanced at the weapons in the corner as he chewed a piece of bread. The sword and bow staff he and Leo had used once more among them. He looked back to see Piper staring at him.

"You never finished telling us about that prophecy," he said to her.

Piper looked away, shaking her head. "It is nothing. A children's tale. A superstition. There is no historical indication it ever occurred."

"I don't know what happened back there, but when I held that sword in my hand," Leo pointed to the blade leaning against the side of the stone wall, "and I — I, like, wielded it, or something. It was like I had done it before. I don't know if I've ever believed in prophecies and stuff like that. Things like that only happen in movies, ya know? But it's got me wondering what this prophecy is, and what it's got to do with us."

The fire crackled and popped loudly in the silence that followed. Piper would not look at Jack or Leo. Her eyes had found their way back to the flames and to a distant memory only she knew. She rose and headed for Jayson who still lay unconscious. She knelt beside him and murmured.

"In times of old,
Of magic told,
When dragons ruled the skies,
Four kings there lived,
Four cardinal winds,
And peace on lands did lie."

She stood and frowned at the sleeping boy. "That is the beginning of a poem, a story allegedly of the history of Chartile, and the prophecy. I do not remember it all, but…"

She closed her eyes, wrapping her arms around herself and sighed.

"King Pasalphathe
Of Kingdom South

With courage of the Fire Sword,
King Florine
Of Kingdom East,
Who brought us law and word,
King Jenemar,
Of West Wood far,
Whose love brought peace to all,
King Kasmalin,
Of Northern Wind,
The high king great of all."

Piper turned back to Leo and Jack, but she would not meet their gaze. "It tells of how the four kings were fulfilling a prophecy of their own. Their ancestors had created Chartile, and they were to bring peace to the land once more. It tells of a world with unicorns and centaurs, and," she swallowed hard, "and magic. All the races of Chartile had their own unique magic. Then, one of the kings' brothers became hungry for more power. He felt the rule of Chartile should belong to one person alone, and it should be the person with the greatest power: him. All races should heed him, for his magic was so great, he was nearly a God himself.

"Great battles fought,
And bloodshed wrought,
Their magic failed us in the end,
And ere too long,
Their magic gone,
We wait and wonder when.

"Some say their magic simply dried up. Others say the Gods took their magic from them. Either way, the kings perished and Chartile was left in ruin.

"From stranger lands,

Return again,
Bringing to right the wrongs,
And then in kin,
Come back again,
Joining two worlds as one.

"Legends claim the lost descendants from the great kings would return to Chartile one day, guided by the spirits of the kings. They would bring peace and magic back to us." Piper bit her lip and swallowed again. "But there is no magic, and there are only three of you, not four. It is a story." She sighed and moved toward the entrance of the cave. Jayson caught her by the wrist.

"You," he whispered.

"What?" asked Piper.

"You," said Jayson again, "Fire... you've been... secrets...magic." He released her arm and slipped back into unconsciousness.

Piper stood frozen, staring down at Jayson. She turned, and took off for the mouth of the cave. Jack hurried after her and Leo stood to attend Jayson.

Chapter Four

Gran

Jack followed Piper and found her sitting quietly atop the overhang of the cave entrance. She gazed at the stars and paid little attention to him joining her.

"Do you see that constellation there?" she finally asked after several long minutes of silence, pointing to the sky. "Those four stars in a line, then those six that look like a hilt? That's called Pasalphathe's Courage." Jack could hear her steady, controlled breathing as she worked to keep tears at bay. "Jack, I —"

He could hear the strain in her voice. She fell silent, staring into the palm of her hand. Slowly, a soft, yellow glow formed in the center of her hand. Jack watched in wonder as a small flame danced in the light of the newly risen crescent moon. She closed her hand and the flame disappeared.

"Taraniz seems to believe the source of my magic is somewhere in the village. She has no true desire for more troops or any such nonsense. She is after me and my power. But she won't dare kill me or defy me until she learns my secret. If she only knew I was born this way, she may leave the rest of my village alone."

"Have you tried just talking to her?" Jack asked gently.

Piper turned to look at him, but her eyes remained unfocused. She turned away, shaking her head and swinging her feet back and forth.

"Much has happened today," she said, the strength back in her voice again. "I believe we should rest for tonight and see what tomorrow brings." She smiled at Jack, leapt from the outcrop and entered the cave once more.

Jack sighed loudly. Part of him believed this was all still just a dream. A glorious, wondrous, but terrifying dream. The other part of him wished it were real. His whole life he had dreamed he could do something to change his situation, to save his mother and little sister, to help his father. But in the real world, he was only a fourteen year old boy. He had no powers of magic and certainly not the courage to face the hardships in his life. He put his head down and lived his life day by day.

However, here in this incredible place, in Chartile, there was a chance he was somebody, that he was something. The only question was whether to accept it, to do something about the feel of that bow staff in his hands, or just follow Piper back into the cave, curl up and hope to wake in his own world in the morning.

When his eyes had readjusted to the darkness of the cave, Jack saw Piper and Leo tending to Jayson. They had wrapped him in more blankets, and Piper had changed the bandage around his head. Leo and Jack gave each other a brief, side long glance of concern then settled in around the fire with blankets and furs Piper had given them.

"You will need to stay here for at least a few days," she said. "I believe his concussion is worse than I first feared, and the troll broke a few of his ribs."

"What can we do?" Leo asked. He removed his glasses and set them on a rock beside him.

"There is a healing woman in the village I trust. I will go to her tomorrow. Now rest." Piper sat before the fire, silent once more, and added another log to keep the flames. Jack and Leo pulled the blankets over them, and feigned sleep. The memories of their day twisted with the words of the prophecy Piper had spoken to them. It wasn't long before Piper heard their breathing slow as they drifted into sleep.

When Leo opened his eyes, it was still dark. The only light in the cave was the fire that had reduced to little more than glowing embers. Piper lay across the fire ring from him, curled under a single blanket. She had buried her face in the collar of her shirt for warmth. Leo picked up the stick Piper had used as a poker and added some kindling to build the fire up. Jack stirred beside him and sat up. They were quiet for a while, then Jack whispered, "So, what do you make of all this?"

"I don't know, man. This is beyond me," Leo said. He stood to retrieve a log to add to the newly revived fire.

"I'd hoped when I woke up, this would all have been, you know." Jack shrugged.

"A dream?" Leo finished. He sat back beside Jack and crossed his arms. "Yeah, I know, me too. Obviously it's not. I just – I don't know what to do."

"We have to wait until Jayson's better," Jack nodded toward Jayson sleeping soundly behind them. "But, Leo, do you think we could be? You know, the prophecy and all that?"

Leo sighed. He looked from Piper to Jayson and back again. "I don't know, dude. None of this makes any sense. And, like, how did we know how to use those things?" He pointed to the weapons stacked innocently in the corner. "At this point, I think I'd believe almost anything, ya know?"

Jack nodded. He covered himself with the furs and blankets again, and looked at the stars outside. He thought he could see Pasalphathe's Courage hovering over the place he knew Outland Post to be. With the fire newly crackling, Leo settled back beneath his covers as well and drifted into sleep once more.

Piper had barely begun to drift off when she heard Jack and Leo whispering. She steadied her breath, pretended to sleep, and listened. Similar thoughts Jack and Leo discussed had been racing through her mind all night. She, too, had hoped when she awoke her encounter with the boys would have been no more than a vivid dream. Or nightmare. Her fears that Taraniz was becoming bolder about usurping the non-elven races of Chartile had been confirmed today. Had anyone else heard her words as they fought?

"Soon," Taraniz had said. Did she intend to kill the King, to kill her own father? King Aramor had done little to advance his kingdom during his reign, but he was a good king. He cared for his people and meant well for them. What little he had accomplished before falling ill was to build up the resources of the basilicas and chantries that helped the widows and orphans in Chartile. He did not deserve to die, especially at the hand of his own despot daughter.

Piper often wondered what had made Taraniz so wicked when Aramor had been so kind. The rumors said magic was to blame. Three years ago, she might have laughed at such things, but now?

Jack and Leo had ceased their conversation, and one was breathing loudly again. Piper rose and collected a dark cloak from the corner where her weapons were stored. Her eyes lingered on the sword and staff the boys had used only hours ago. She tore herself from her thoughts, smudged soot from the fire around her right eye and nose, and disappeared into the night.

Piper reached the top of the hill that overlooked Outland Post. She lowered herself flat against the ground and surveyed the tiny village. It was still. Thin lines of smoke rose from the chimneys of the thatched roof homes. Everyone lay asleep. She crept down the rock strewn hill and wound her way through the boulders, finally emerging onto the dirt paths that led to the heart of Outland Post. The home she sought was close to the outskirts, and she did not have to travel far.

She found the little house and looked up and down the street before approaching. She knocked softly on the window to the right of the door three times, then on the door itself twice, and finally on the little window again twice. Then, she waited. She sat on the doorstep, bundled in her cloak, with her face shrouded in the darkness of her hood. Her heart pounded in her chest as it always did when she came here for fear of being recognized and caught. The curtain beside the door moved faintly. A moment later, the door opened. Piper stood and entered without a word.

A candle was lit in the center of a scrubbed, wooden table. An old woman with a long silver braid of hair flung her arms wide to embrace the girl. Piper leaned into the woman. The cloak fell away from her shoulders, revealing how thin and worn she and her clothes were.

"Gran," Piper whispered. "How are you?"

"Better it appears than you, my darling girl," said the old woman, and she held Piper out at arm's length for a better look. "Come, I have some things for you." The old woman motioned toward one of the chairs at the table. Piper sat and watched as her grandmother busied herself at the stove. "What brings you so early?" Gran turned a questioning eye on the girl. "I was not expecting you for another two weeks."

Piper sat with her elbows on the table, pressing the heel of her hand between her eyes. She said nothing for a long time, but accepted a cup of herbal tea and drank deeply. Finally, very softly, she spoke.

"Gran, what do you know of the prophecy of the four kings?"

The old woman sat a bit straighter, and her eyes narrowed with curiosity. She leaned toward Piper and set her own cup on the table. "What do you wish to know, child? I thought I had taught you that story well."

"I do not remember it all, I am afraid. Gran, you will not believe– I scarcely believe it myself. I– I think it may be true. I believe it may be happening now. I met three boys yesterday. They are not of Chartile. I do not believe they are of this world. Their clothes, their speech. It is unlike anything I have ever seen or heard. And, when I am with them, my magic–" Piper stopped. She trembled, and looked fearfully at her grandmother. With a deep breath, she recounted the previous day's events: her fight with Taraniz, the sudden appearance of Jack, Leo and Jayson, the mountain trolls – even her use of fire and magic. When she had finished, what little tea was left in her cup was cold. She felt surprisingly relieved, and yet still trembled.

Gran sat quietly for several minutes. She took Piper's hands in her own, locking her blue eyes to Piper's green, and asked, "Piper, my darling, do you know who you are?"

Piper pulled her hands away quickly. The fear on her face could not be hidden by the soot smudging.

"I—I don't understand," she said.

"Yes you do," Gran said softly. "You have suspected for some time, I know. Your mother and father knew. I knew. And so do you."

"Why didn't you tell me?" Piper's eyes pleaded with her gran for answers.

"We never thought we would need to. No one could have foreseen Aramor's sudden illness. No one ever thought Taraniz would have been so…well. I cannot imagine what horrors befell that poor child to make her so. Spoiled and pampered, yes, but a tyrant? How she managed to convince the entire Elven army and the Noble's Conclave to follow her before Aramor's death, and at such a young age, is beyond me."

"If you never saw a reason to tell me, then why try to train me?" Piper crossed her arms before her, her voice turning haughty and defensive, "Why calligraphy and law? Why the etiquette, and dragging me all over Chartile? Why teach me to control my magic?"

"Precaution, child." Gran patted Piper's hand. "We couldn't have you losing control and draining someone's life, or burning –" She stopped and looked away, lost for a moment in tragic memory.

"I never wanted this." Piper stared at the table top, following the intricate lines of a knot in the wood. "I don't want it. I should have run away to Duneland. None of this would be happening."

Gran reached across the table again, but Piper pulled away.

"No, my child, I would not wish Duneland on anyone," she said and reached for her cup instead.

Piper looked at her grandmother, brow furrowed in confusion and anger. "Why? Because it is hot? Because it is full of sand where nothing ever grows? Never seeing a tree again would be worth the escape and freedom from…this!"

"Because Humans are slaves," said Gran rather coldly. "Had you gone to Duneland, you would have had orenite cuffs slapped on your wrists and been sold into the pleasure trade, or bought as a beck-and. Elf or Human, they can little tell the difference anymore."

"Orenite? I've never heard of such a thing," said Piper more calmly. She hated seeing her Gran angry, and curiosity had tempered her for the moment.

"Orenite is a rare metal found only in Mount Kelsii. Its discovery is what made the dwarves extend their settlement past the Tutarian Mountain

Range. Once inscribed with the ancient Draconian runes, an orenite item can keep magic from passing forth from a person. If they attempt any form of magic, the orenite holds the energy inward until the body can no longer contain it, and they perish."

"That's horrible!" cried Piper. "Who would do that? And why?"

"The prophecy, my darling. Duke Noraedin, brother to King Pasalphathe, wished the rule of all the races of Chartile to be turned to him. He was a very powerful man, and a great alchemist. He was a natural leader, but a cruel man. He killed many in his lust for the crown. It was King Pasalphathe's own proposition to use the new-found orenite to strip Noraedin of his magic. But orenite alone could not do it. If the orenite item was removed, the wearer's magic remained, if only temporarily suppressed. It was Kahiri, King of the Dragons that gave the Draconian runes to the Dwarves to make the orenite stronger – and permanent. King Pasalphathe would only allow this if all Humans and Elves agreed to have their power taken, so as to prevent such evil from ever happening in Chartile again. I am sure I have taught you this, my child."

"Perhaps you have, but I cannot recall it. I still have yet to see what it has to do with me." Piper drank the last of her cold tea, and rose to pour more from the kettle hanging over the fire.

"The four kings tricked the Duke by acting as though they were resigning their rule to Noraedin. They gave him an orenite circlet to show their defeat and acceptance of the new King of Chartile. During the crowning ceremony, Noraedin did not survive. A similar ceremony is how the

Elven Royals eventually eliminated magic from their bloodline. Most survived, but some still perished, even with the weaker orenite and Draconian rune magic. And through laws of selective marriages, the rest of the elves lost their magic over the centuries."

"What is this to do with Duneland, and why such practices are still used? There is no more magic. Or at least, there wasn't."

"Pasalphathe was King of the race of Humans. And though the magic of the Elves eventually perished, the magic of humans is far more resilient to the effects of orenite, and persistent in its survival. From only a few years of age, all humans are forced to wear some form of orenite. And all because one man decided he wanted more power."

Again, Piper stared at the knot on the table, everything coming together at once.

"And if the boys and I are the returned souls of the Kings, then Taraniz may be —"

Gran nodded. Piper closed her eyes, and held her head in her hands.

"I can't do this, Gran. I don't want it. Jayson, Jack and Leo, they are innocent in all of this. I cannot allow them to be hurt or killed, or to kill someone themselves. They are not even from our world. It would be wrong to place any burdens of Chartile, past or present, on them. What do I do?"

The old woman stroked Piper's hair. She swallowed hard, but her voice still cracked. "That is your decision alone to make. Only you can decide if you wish to take the path that has been laid before you, or forge your own. Either way, there is a young man back there who is still injured, am I right? Even if you are fearful of your own path, you have always been compassionate and selfless. If that is not the quality of a true leader, then may the Gods help us."

There was a small opening in the cave to the right of the main entrance that had gone unnoticed when the boys first arrived the evening before. Now, as the sun rose over the mountain, a shaft of light fell across Jayson's face from the opening. He raised his arm against the light and immediately gasped. He clutched at his side and gasped again. His entire body felt as though he had been hit by a semi-truck. His ribs were bandaged, but he couldn't remember why. Everything was a blur.

His eyes focused, and he took in his surroundings. He was in a cave. Jack and Leo were sleeping around what was left of a fire. He blinked a few times and memories began to make sense of themselves out of the fog in his mind. Their arrival in Chartile, Piper's story, and that strange creature that had nearly killed him. The thought of it made Jayson wish he had been hit by a truck. He attempted to turn to face the wall. The pain in his ribs was so intense it made his already dizzy head swim even more. He yelped and nearly lost what little was left in his stomach from the night before.

Leo was at his side in a matter of moments, a water skin in hand. Jayson took it and drank without a word. The cold water hit his stomach like a kick in the gut. He wiped his mouth and found a piece of bread in his hand that Jack must have placed there. He sighed and ate in silence while his friends looked at each other from the corners of their eyes. Occasionally they dared a glance at him.

He finished the flavorless hunk of bread and stared at the wall in front of him before finally speaking. "I'm so sorry you guys." His voice was barely whisper as his broken ribs made it difficult to even breathe.

"Well, it was bound to happen eventually," said Jack with a grin.

"There'll be plenty of time for apologies and pay back later," said Leo also smiling.

"I don't know, Leo. This could be a once in a life time opportunity. I mean, when was the last time you remember Jayson Hill apologizing for anything?" Jack patted Jayson's shoulder gently. Jayson grimaced and wondered how the pain he felt at Jack's touch could cause such a pounding in his already throbbing head

Leo laughed and said, "So true! But, you just rest. You're no good 'till you're no longer broken."

Jayson did not smile as his friends rose and went to tend the fire.

"Frickin', frackin' frookin'," he muttered to himself and gently laid back down, "I'm never going to live this down. Like, ever."

Piper returned to the cave just as Leo and Jack had figured out how to restart the fire. She had smeared soot across her nose and around her right eye, and wore a long, heavy cloak, though the weather was already warm.

"It was a precaution," she explained, "so I would not be recognized. I was fortunate. Few were awake and no one took notice."

She pulled two pouches of herbs and a thick leather cord from a bag slung over her shoulder. She, Jack and Leo gathered several long and thick sticks from the wood pile, and fashioned a tripod to hang a pot over the fire to boil water. Piper made a tea from the first pouch of herbs to help Jayson sleep and ease his pain. It smelled horrible and tasted even worse. She made a paste from the second pouch of herbs and applied this to the wound on Jayson's head.

"Ow! That stings!" cried Jayson. He pulled away only to grab his side and cringe in pain.

Piper did not reply or move from her poultice-applying position. She raised her eyebrows at Jayson and gave him a stern look with her piercing green eyes. Jayson sighed and leaned toward her slowly. A gentle smiled pulled at the corner of Piper's lips, and she finished wrapping his head. "You will like what I must do next even less." She reached for the leather cord at her feet. Jayson's eyes widened. Ignoring the pain, he held up his hands and cried, "Whoa! Hey! Look, I'm sorry, okay! It's just a lot to take in at once, you know? What are you—"

Jack and Leo each grabbed Jayson by an arm, despite his protests and helped support him perfectly up right.

"This is going to hurt," Piper said, silencing Jayson's struggling cries. "Your ribs move freely inside. We need to immobilize them while they heal."

With Jack's help, she pulled Jayson's shirt over his head. Even though Jayson knew Piper had already seen him without his shirt before, he still flushed red at the thought of her seeing his lack of abdominal muscle. She wrapped linen cloth tight around his ribs, then began wrapping the cord even tighter.

"The rope helps to keep you as still as possible, while giving you the freedom to use your arms and legs," she said, "We will loosen the tension over time as you heal. It also serves as a physical reminder to limit your movement, especially bending and twisting."

It took a few tries to get the tension just right. All the while, Jayson complained without reservation that a lady's corset would have been easier torture. In the end, he lay bandaged and roped, resting very straight on the bed.

Leo and Jack stood at the mouth of the cave, arms folded, and leaned against the cool stone while surveying their friend.

"It'll take weeks for him to get better," Leo whispered.

"So, what do we do?" asked Jack, squinting up and the sun.

"Well, we obviously can't leave him."

"Yeah, but we can't really go anywhere anyway. Especially not dressed like this."

Leo nodded, and kicked at the loose stone below his feet with his bright white tennis shoes.

Later, Piper helped Jack and Leo find their own small cave close by. It was just large enough for a small fire pit and space for sleeping. They came together for meals and hunting, but there was just something odd about sleeping so close to a girl that the boys couldn't seem to get over. Piper helped them modify their clothing with furs from the animals they caught and fabrics they acquired from Gran in the village. The mountain nights were chilly, and the fashions of 1997 Swansdale were not made for such. She taught them what plants to look for that could heal wounds or flavor their meals, and how to hunt with an arrow and spear.

By their third day in Chartile, Jayson had insisted he join them.

"I am so bored!" he whined. "You can't just leave me here all day."

They gave him his bow and quiver, and, to their surprise, found he was not only able to use it if he moved slowly, but that he was also a decent shot. Jayson shot two rabbits and some kind of small bird on his first day hunting. They used these for trade through Piper's Gran, and eventually had enough leather to fashion more appropriately styled shoes.

When they weren't hunting, Piper took the boys down to the base of the mountain where she had first met them. She taught them how to use the weapons they had used during the attack by what they now learned were mountain trolls. They learned to use them all, but each seem to find an ease and strange familiarity in the weapons they had first wielded that fateful night.

It was on their fifth day in Chartile that Jayson made a particular amazing shot by at what Piper called a diten mouse. Leo said it seemed to be a strange combination of guinea pig, gopher and chinchilla, but his friends ignored him. Jayson pumped his fist into the air and did not wince in pain. Piper looked at him a bit stunned and slightly concerned.

"Oh, yeah! One shot and down! Boo-ya!" Jayson fist pumped the air again before noticing his friend's stares. "What?"

"Dude, you broke your ribs, like five days ago. Did you forget?" asked Jack.

Jayson lifted his tunic and removed the cord and bandages. The bruising was gone. He twisted and turned, flexing his torso.

"No pain," he said and shrugged.

"Did the prophecy say anything about the kings healing really fast?" asked Leo turning to look at Piper.

Piper did not reply. She looked at the ground and frowned. They watched as she broke from the group to retrieve the diten mouse and headed back towards the mountain path. Jayson picked up the bandages and cord he had dropped and followed Piper and his friends back up the mountain.

The trip back to Piper's cave was long and uncomfortably quiet. Leo started the fire, and Jack cleaned the arrows while Piper skinned and prepared the diten mice they had caught for dinner. They had agreed not to think of home until Jayson was well again, but they hadn't expected it to be for another few weeks. Jayson's sudden recovery had sent their heads reeling.

"It does, doesn't it?" Jayson asked, staring into the flames.

"What?" asked Jack. He had finished washing his socks, and laid them by the fire to dry.

"The prophecy." Jayson looked at Piper. She had refused to look at them since returning from their hunt. She sat cleaning a pelt laid out across her

49

lap. "The kings had the ability to heal quickly, didn't they?"

She tried but could not ignore Jayson's eyes staring at her any longer. Wiping her hands on a damp cloth, she stood and turned to face him.

"I honestly do not remember, Jayson. I cannot recall the entire poem. But," she addressed all of them now. "Your abilities to use weapons, your healing, your unexpected arrival. I do not know what else to make of all of this."

"From stranger lands, return again, bringing to right the wrongs. Shnikies, could it be anymore vague?" Leo sighed loudly and shook his head.

"For real," said Jack, "How do we even know what we're supposed to do?"

Chapter Five
Dimitri

The next morning was warm and inviting. A cruel taunt, Jayson thought, as if the world was trying to act completely innocent. He was the first to wake, and sat up to watch the embers of their fire smoldering and hissing beside him. He didn't move, he just sat and thought. They had stayed the night in Piper's cave. No one would admit it, but they all feared that with Jayson's injury healed, something else would happen – though what they didn't know. They had talked all night, attempting to solve the riddle of the prophecy. Piper had tried desperately, but to no avail, to remember the rest of the poem.

"Was there ever a written record of the prophecy?" Leo had asked.

"Or maybe you know someone who knows all of it," Jack suggested.

Piper looked up from the fire she had been tending. "Gran had made a copy when she worked at the palace, and had given it to my mother. But it was destroyed during the rebellion."

"The original might still be at the palace," said Jack brightly. "We could go there, and —"

"Are you out of your mind?" Piper cried. "I am at large. They'll kill me the moment they set eyes on me. And not just anyone can walk into the palace and start sifting through the documents of the royal libraries. Some of them date back hundreds of years, and are extremely delicate. It is impossible. There must be another way we have not thought of yet."

"We're either stuck here until we can figure out a way into the palace, or we make an opportunity to get the heck out of here," Jack winced as he looked at Piper, "Er...no offense."

"How about both?" said Jayson. Leo Jack and Piper whipped their heads around to him. Any plan was worth presenting at that moment, but Jayson was the last person they had expected to hear from. "We go to the palace, steal some guard clothes, and then we can walk around, right? I mean, that's what they'd do in the movies...I think."

"And what of me?" asked Piper.

"We say you were pretending to be Piper, but really aren't her. We say we're on our way to take you to the dungeons for questioning." Jack smiled at his ingenious idea.

"It is impossible." Piper snapped and rubbed her temples. "You do not know any royal etiquette and your accents would give you away instantly. We would be walking into their hands with rope on our wrists."

"But you know all that stuff. From your mom and Gran?" asked Jayson. "I'll bet you even went with her to the palace when you were little. You can teach us. This is our only shot, Piper. We act now or never." He slammed his fist into his open palm, and Leo and Jack nodded in agreement. Piper closed her eyes and sighed in resigned defeat.

ᔆᕫᕫᕘ

Leo crouched low in a defensive position historians would have called The Plow. He had remembered hearing about it during a field trip to Fort Meigs many years ago. He wasn't sure how he actually remembered how to do it. His breathing was slow and steady, which belied the rapidly beating heart in his chest. Jayson and Piper sat with their backs to a half dead bush that had stubbornly grown amongst the craggy terrain of the mountainside. They were pouring over notes and diagrams, discussing the layout of the palace and the best locations to get inside.

Leo ignored them. He was focused. He was collected. All he cared about was the feel of the steel in his hands, the perfect balance of its weight, and the opponent standing across from him: Jack.

Jack advanced, the bow staff gripped in both hands. He swung, aiming directly for Leo's head. But the once over-cautious boy was ready. Leo blocked Jack's attack with an instinctive parry and lunged for Jack's heart. Jack, too, was ready for this, and the parry-repost continued up and down the rocky hillside.

As Jack and Leo fought, Jayson and Piper rolled up their maps, their discussion complete. The girl rose, brushing the earth from her backside, and stretching towards the sun with the faintest bit of a smile on her lips.

"Piper," said Jayson cautiously. He stared up at her from where he still sat on the ground. "When are you going to teach us how to use magic?"

Piper froze and stared blankly down at Jayson. He looked away, his shoulders drooping and his frown deepening. The silence between them was almost palpable.

"Jayson, I wish I could teach you, but I honestly do not know how. Most of what I know came after I was banished. I was alone, desperate, hungry, and frankly, bored. I cannot put into words how I do what I do. It just happens." She refused to meet his eye, as with every time Jayson had asked this over the last week.

"You could at least give us some tips, you know, like some magic words to say or something," Jayson continued to press.

"Jayson, I refuse to talk of this!" cried Piper, and she turned, storming back up the mountain, the parchment crushed tightly in her hands.

"Well, you're going to have to!" Jayson yelled at her. He leapt to his feet, and squeezed the grip of his bow until his knuckles turned white. "If we're supposed to fulfill a prophecy here, we need to have all sources of power and weaponry available to us. How else do we win?"

Piper rushed back down the hill to Jayson, stopping within inches of his freckled nose. She glared, but Jayson could see her eyes glistening with tears. He had never seen her this angry before, and his hands shook as he glared back.

"Power and weapons do not guarantee a victory, Jayson Hill." Her words came as a breathless whisper as she fought the emotion that welled in her. "It takes brains as well as brawn, perhaps even more so. If you are going to be a leader, you need to learn some humility as well." She took a step back and sighed, her voice softer. "Maybe you aren't the souls of the ancient kings. Maybe I was wrong. Or maybe, you just need to grow up more first."

She looked over her shoulder at Jack and Leo who had ceased their fighting in mid stance. Their faces fell with the same loss of confidence Jayson's had, and for a moment Piper felt a pain of guilt. But she knew she was right. These little boys were nothing more than that — at least right now. She had to be the strong one. She had to guide them.

She looked at the map still clutched in her hand. "This was a mistake," she said, and threw the parchment to the ground, "You aren't ready." She left the boys standing still as statues, and staring after her with pleading eyes.

"Piper, wait," said Leo, and started after her.

Jack grabbed his arm. "No, just let her be. Let's find out what Jay did this time."

Piper stalked up the rocky cliff side making far more noise than she normally would have. But she didn't care. She was angry, and confused. Above all else, she was afraid. Everything she had been taught as a child seemed as though it had been to groom her for this. No one else in her village knew about the laws of Chartile, or had been taught how to speak with confidence and humility. They did not know the difference in poise necessary when addressing a small or large gathering of people. They did not know which colors signified which rank within the royal army. She was different. She always knew this. From her bright green eyes, when everyone she knew had blue or gray. From the sharp defined jaw, to her natural ability to teach and lead. It had been easy for her neighbors to banish her. They had feared her.

Questions whirled in her mind. Surely her destiny was bigger even than usurping Taraniz. And the boys. How did Jayson, Jack and Leo fit into everything? She regretted those hurtful words. They made her stomach twist in knots.

At the base of the mountain, amidst the rock and dry earth, a lone beech tree had grown. There

Prophecy

were a few sparse and smaller trees that had tried and failed to grow in the desolate terrain. But this tree was special. It was tall, thin and weathered. Despite the sparse landscape, it had grown and survived. It was the place Piper came to think. She had found it after the riot, when her parents had died, and after she had been cast out. Like that day, she sat at the roots of the beech tree, her hands clutching at the gnarled white bark as she dropped to the ground. She buried her face in her arms, and cried.

She cried long and hard. She let every emotion she had ever felt for the last three years wash over her. Her tears, hot and salty, stung at the cut still healing on her cheek. She cried, and she cried, and she cried. She cried until she could cry no more. Then she just sat, trembling and hiccupping, and wishing she had remembered the water skin.

"Piper," said a gentle voice behind her.

She lifted her head at the sound of that voice, and slowly turned to look over her shoulder at the young man kneeling behind her. Her face brightened, and she leapt from the ground to embrace the man.

"Dimitri," she whispered, "What are you doing here?"

"I need your help." he said.

ঌও

"I have to admit, I tend to agree with Jayson. Even if he does have a lack of tact about it." Leo said taking a drink from the water skin Piper had left.

Jayson thrust his hands out before him and replied, "See? I'm not always insane, ya know."

56

"Yeah, but Piper might have actually listened if you hadn't had a tantrum about it. You could have said things differently," Jack suggested.

"Like how? It's never a good time to discuss magic with her. Never! I don't understand what she's so afraid of." Jayson accepted the water skin from Leo. He stopped mid swallow. Water dribbled down his front when he saw Piper coming around the path with a tall, dark skinned and muscular young man at her side. They stood to greet the newcomer, suddenly feeling very awkward in their gangly fourteen year old bodies.

"There has been a change of plans," Piper said matter-of-factly as she came to a stop before them. "We will be leaving for the Dwarvik fortress on the other side of Mount Kelsii." She gazed at each of the boys in turn. "Immediately."

Jayson, Jack and Leo looked at each other, but did not speak. The young man at Piper's side stepped forward, seeing the uncertainty in their faces, and smiled politely to them.

"My name is Dimitri. I am a friend of Piper." He gave a small bow. "I am a retainer and the royal liaison to the Empress of the Dwarves of Chartile. She has personally requested a meeting with all of you."

"With us?" asked Leo.

"Yes," Dimitri replied with a nod.

"But, we're just kids," said Jayson.

"I am sure all of your questions will be answered very soon," said Dimitri with another smile.

Silence fell. Jayson swung his arms at his sides while Jack contorted his mouth into several bored faces. Leo picked at a pimple on the back of his neck, and Dimitri turned to Piper, his eyebrows raised and a smile pulling at his lips.

"Well, I suppose we should gather our things, then." Without a look at any of them, Piper headed back up the narrow mountain path toward their cave homes. The boys were left standing in an uncomfortable circle with Dimitri until the young man finally broke ranks, and trudged after Piper.

"Anyone else get the feeling he's a bit more than her friend?" Jayson asked. Jack and Leo rolled their eyes at Jayson before turning to follow up the path. "What? You agree, don't you? You just don't want to say anything." Jayson followed after, bringing up the rear.

They must have been quite a sight, if anyone had cared to take notice. Dimitri, a strong, dark skinned young man with wavy dark hair, dark eyes and rippling muscles in the lead. Jack, Leo and Jayson, three dirty and lanky boys followed in the middle, and Piper, a tall, messy red-haired young woman brought up the rear. They made their way slowly up and eastward, around the craggy, desolate mountain. They had packed light, for Dimitri had said he would take them along the same path he had travelled to get there, and there was plenty of food, water and shelter along the way. It was hard going. The path narrowed and widened unexpectedly, or took sharp turns beside sudden vertical drop offs. The boys had decided to put their tennis shoes back on to give them more traction on their still untrained feet. Dimitri was fascinated with the shoes, and soon they were talking and exchanging tales. Only Piper remained silent.

They walked for hours, moving slowly along the paths. The vastness of the large mountain seemed less noticeable when they were living at its base by Outland Post. Gradually, the mountain began to turn greener and lusher with trees, flowers and moss. Little brooks bubbled from the rocks, only to disappear again a few feet away beneath the ground once more. They noticed birds they had never seen before, and the bugs were atrocious. With the craggy little foothills and sparse landscape they had been living in, it was hard to believe such an immense ecosystem lay only hours beyond where they had made their temporary home. They wondered why Piper had never brought them here to hunt. When asked, she simply replied, "I don't like to be far from my home," and she refused to speak more on the matter.

The boys realized their daily treks hunting and gathering food were nothing compared to hiking the entire mountain. They stopped often to rest and refill their water skins. Jack assumed it was because they were too slow and complained often of fatigue. Leo suspected Piper was stalling for time. She did not seem eager for what awaited her when they arrived at Fortress Kelsii. Jayson was just grateful, and heaved himself to the ground with great dramatics each time.

"Holy cramping legs to the max, Batman!" he cried after nearly eight hours of traveling. They had stopped at their third or fourth spring, and dusk was beginning to fall. "How much further is this place? You said you got to us in a day?" Jayson asked Dimitri, his eyes wide and staring in disbelief.

Dimitri smiled and laughed, his eyes kind. "Yes, but I did not need to rest as often. As liaison to the Empress, I often run messages from one side of the mountain to the other, and back again. We do have ponies some of the errants use for longer treks. The furthest orenite mines are miles away from the main living areas. But, the ponies are few in number, and they do not seem to care much for me."

"What are the mines like? How deep do they go?" Leo was fascinated with the sciences of something he once believed to be no more than myth and fairy tale. He questioned Dimitri every chance he could, and the young man answered him patiently.

"Oh, I do not know anything about that," said Dimitri. He wiped his sleeve across his brow and stretched his long legs. "We are always digging deeper and creating new tunnels. It is a great feat of engineering that only the most skilled are trained to do. They must work with precise calculations to ensure the tunnels do not collapse. They must account for the ventilation shafts, and even the kind of stone they are working with. This is why there are runes and jewels covering the tunnel walls. They serve not only as adornment but as markers to tell you where you are, and how to get to certain places of importance. Some tunnels have sharp turns every twenty feet for miles! But they are truly gorgeous. Human or no, I would never want to live anywhere else."

"If you work for the Empress," said Jack as he banged and scraped mud from his shoes, "who's the Emperor?"

Dimitri laughed a deep belly laugh unbefitting his age. It made Piper smile in a way the boys had not seen before.

"My apologies," Dimitri replied. "I forget you are not of this world. There can be no doubt of that now, I am sure." He wiped a tear from his eye and looked at the sky above him. It was growing darker by the minute. The shadows around them had lengthened significantly since they had stopped. "We should set up camp. I told the Empress I would be back by nightfall, but it is too dangerous to travel much farther in the dark."

"That overhang is probably as safe as we are going to find without exploring." Piper pointed at a location several yards away.

"That's why I'm here, my gem." Dimitri smiled at her again, and ran his fingers through his curly black hair, making Piper blush. "Just a little further is a small cave. It will be a bit crowded, but we will be safer there than out in the open." He scanned the area, squinting through the deepening darkness. "There are worse things than bumbling mountain trolls out here. Come."

They travelled only another quarter hour, yet it was so dark when they arrived, they could barely see the person in front of them.

"Night sure comes fast here," said Leo.

"It is the angle of the mountain," said Piper. "You will find morning comes too soon, and the dew seems to linger."

They built a fire with what little kindling and wood they could find in the dark. The threat of creatures that feared the flame was greater than those attracted to it. They took turns keeping watch.

Prophecy

Jack was too excited for sleep, and volunteered for the first watch.

"You never finished telling me about the Emperor," he said quietly to Dimitri. They had all settled into their respective nooks and crevices in the tiny cave for the night.

"Ah, yes," Dimitri whispered. Piper had already fallen asleep against Dimitri's chest. He carefully adjusted his arm and continued quietly, "Well, there is no Emperor."

"Did he die?" asked Jack.

"No, there simply isn't one. The Dwarvik society is mostly run by our women. Ladies are very rare amongst the dwarves. Women are the head of their House, and they can take up to four husbands. The first Hasana, or husband, to give her a daughter becomes Harasan, or the Head Husband. He is in charge of the daily running of the household. Our men are our craftsmen who specialize in trade skills."

"What do the wives do, then?" Jack asked as he poked the fire with a long stick.

"They manage the finances their hasanas earn. They negotiate raises and work place advancements for their hasanas. If they do not yet have a Harasan, they designate the daily tasks necessary to run the House and decide whether they will continue in their current profession or find other work. Our women find apprenticeships for their children and work to arrange good marriages for them. They are our religious leaders and political negotiators with other peoples. They make our laws and carry out justice. Women, unlike men, can rule with their heart, mind and soul. It is very difficult for men to find their souls."

"That's not, like, very fair," chimed Jayson, who had apparently been listening.

Dimitri scowled. Even by firelight, his once twinkling eyes were hard as stone. "Our system has worked well enough since long before you or any great kings were here in Chartile. If I did not know better, I would say you sounded much like a Black Diamond."

"A what?" asked Leo, pushing himself up to sit.

"Ssh!" said Jack as Piper stirred slightly. Dimitri repositioned his arm again and continued.

"The Black Diamonds are a society of men who have been cast out by their families, or have joined in secret for want of greater privilege. They have been trying for years to get a man on the Council. They want to manage their own finances. They want to choose their own marriages." He frowned, allowing a scowl to wrinkle his brow. "All they do is want. They have spent too much time among the elves with their society of equality. They have no respect for tradition."

"You sound like you're a dwarf, Dimitri," Leo interrupted in an attempt to break the argument. He could see Jayson had opened his mouth to speak again, but shut it quickly and folded his arms when Leo intervened.

"My mother was the head retainer and liaison for the Empress before me. She fell in love with a brother of the Empress, and died giving birth to me because the healers would not remove her orenite cuffs. The Empress was very fond of my mother, and since the Empress is not permitted marriage or children of her own, she raised me. I recently took my birth mother's place as head retainer and liaison."

"Wait, so you're half human and half royal dwarf? How does that work?" asked Jack.

"And you're awfully tall for a dwarf," said Jayson raising an eyebrow.

Dimitri sighed. He rubbed his temples with his free hand, and the boys could see the circles forming under his eyes.

"The positions of Princess, Queen and Empress are appointed positions, no different than anyone on the Council. This is why we need Piper. There is a stalemate in— well, it's very complicated." He yawned and stroked Piper's hair absentmindedly. "It is late. Let us rest. You will learn plenty when we arrive at the fortress tomorrow."

The boys sat awake for some time, musing over the thoughts of everything they had just learned. When they had first arrived, Chartile seemed smaller, less complicated than home. Now, life was starting to become more complex in ways they could not understand. Magic existed, but was prohibited. Dwarves were a matriarchal society, and Piper was someone important that the dwarves needed to settle a political matter of state. Piper, who once seemed little more than a sisterly figure in this strange land, was becoming more and more interesting by the day.

Chapter Six

At Fortress Kelsii

Jayson woke with a start. He had drifted off, thinking of the "dangers worse than bumbling mountain trolls." His experience of being carried off by a troll his first day in Chartile had set him on edge whenever darkness came. He wasn't sure what had roused him, though he shouldn't have been sleeping anyway. He had traded shifts with Jack only minutes ago. Or had it been hours? There was a rustling just outside the cave entrance. He must have been sleeping longer than he thought, for the fire had reduced to glowing embers. Something moved again, this time closer to the cave entrance. There wasn't much time to rebuild the fire, but he could hardly see to shoot with his bow.

Jayson moved as slowly and quietly as he could, adding a log to the fire. He fanned the flames with one hand and reached for his bow with the other. The sound was more like scuttling this time, and was closer and faster. He thought he saw the glint of glowing red eyes, but dismissed it as a trick of the darkness.

It all happened at once. A massive, leathery-winged creature flew into the cave, its wings fanning out what little fire had just sprung to life. Jayson cried out and shot the beast with the single arrow he had managed to grab before falling spread eagle across the floor and his friends. The arrow missed its main target, but caught in the animal's wing. It screamed, and everyone was on their feet now, scrambling in the dark for their weapons.

The creature pulled the arrow from its wing with almost human hands and rounded on Jayson. He had lost most of his arrows when he had fallen. His hands shook as he fitted on to his bow string. Before he could notch it, the monster was upon him. Its wings beat around him, and its screeching and screaming was deafening now that it was inches from his face.

"Jayson!" someone shouted. There was a flurry of weapons. Jayson was oblivious to anything but the animal screaming at him. He held his arms around his head, and curled himself into a ball. From beneath his arm, he saw a dark gray face, both human and bat-like, with large, pointed teeth in a wide mouth as it screeched. The creature opened its mouth wider, ready to bear down on him. He closed his eyes, prepared for the pain. It never came. Piper cried out and lunged forward to cover Jayson. The creature sank its teeth deep into Piper's arm. She screamed an agonizing cry as loud as the creature's. It echoed off the small cave walls. What appeared to be lightning surrounded her and lashed out at the creature. It screeched its ear-piercing cry again, and turned tail, taking off into the night.

Jack and Leo followed it, but it vanished into the night as quickly as it had come. Piper fell to the floor beside Jayson whimpering and shaking. He knew this was his fault. If he hadn't fallen asleep, the fire would have never died.

"Piper, I'm sorry, I'm sorry," was all he could say. He couldn't move. He shook so violently he could barely hold his bow. He didn't even notice the tears that streaked his cheeks. Piper was shaking more fiercely now, and her breathing was becoming more labored. The lightning coiling around her body had died away, leaving the shrunken form of a little girl curled in pain at their feet.

Jack and Leo hurried back into the cave to find Dimitri cradling Piper, and holding back her hands to keep her from clawing at the bite wounds on her arm. The flesh around the wound was red and raw as though it had been touched by acid.

"It burns! It burns!" She whimpered weakly, her head rolling from side to side. She screamed again and fell unconscious.

"Piper, stay with me! Stay awake!" Dimitri bellowed. He shook Piper and ran a hand over her face and hair, but she did not stir.

Panic followed. Leo and Jack dropped to Piper's side. They too attempted to rouse her, but to no avail. Jayson curled back against the wall, his arms wrapped around his torso and tears continuing to stream down his face. Dimitri stood, cradling Piper in his arms. She suddenly appeared very small and frail.

"I must get her to the healers. They can help her," he said and hurried from the cave. It was still dark, and the threat of getting lost or being attacked again loomed for another several hours. They could not hold out for morning. Piper could not hold out for morning.

"Dimitri! Wait!" Jack cried. "Let's at least light some torches." Dimitri nodded in agreement, but did not set Piper down. He swayed and paced at the mouth of the cave. He kissed Piper's forehead and whispered quietly to her. Jack and Leo worked as quickly to make three torches from the scant supplies they had carried. Jayson attempted to help by fanning the barely warm embers, but he still shook so violently that Leo eventually took over.

"Please! Quickly," pleaded Dimitri. It pained them all to hear such desperation in his voice. "We still have many hours journey. Why didn't I bring a pony? Oh, by Rashiri!"

"We're almost done," said Jack, lighting the last torch. "There. Alright, I'll lead. You just tell me where to go." Dimitri nodded, and they hurried on.

Even by torchlight, their way was still slow and cumbersome. At first they attempted a slow jog. But after having tripped on rocks and roots, or nearly ending up with a face full of branch, they quickly slowed to a brisk walk. If Dimitri tired of carrying Piper it did not show save for the few times he adjusted her position in his arms. She never stirred the entire way.

Finally, the sky began to turn from black to gray. They found a small spring, and collapsed at its banks in an unspoken agreement of rest. Dimitri gently laid Piper in the moss and grass by the water. Carefully, he cleansed her wound, wiping the blood streaks from her arm with immense care. Jayson dropped to his knees and splashed the icy water on his face two handed. He looked at Piper who was ashen and sweaty.

"This is my fault," he whispered. "I fell asleep. The fire died. Damn it! Why does this keep happening to me? First the trolls, now this? Oh, God!"

"Jayson, this could have happened to any of us. We were all exhausted," said Jack.

"If she dies —"whimpered Jayson.

"She's not going to die," said Leo so assuring, they knew it was forced.

They fell silent, looking at Dimitri, waiting for some kind of reassurance. But it never came. Dimitri never took his eyes from Piper. He softly arranged her red hair against the dark green moss. "Let's keep moving," he said abruptly. He lifted Piper with ease and hurried onward.

The boys suspected they may have been slowing their progress, but they still managed to arrive at Fortress Kelsii just as the sun peeked over the top of the mountain. It illuminated the great entrance in a shimmering array of gems and color. Two carved stone doors stood open before them, at least twenty feet high and each twelve feet wide. They were inset with hundreds of gems, and were as strong as they were beautiful. Six armored guards stood at either side of the doors. The boys were surprised to see they were all very tall, and even more muscular and built than Dimitri. They had the same dark complexion, some even darker. These were not the dwarves the boys had expected.

"Dimitri," said the guard on the right. "Thank the stone you are alright. What is going on? Who are they?"

"There is no time to explain, Imohad. Piper has been attacked, and I believe it was a vampire." The faces of the guards turned suddenly grave. They fidgeted and whispered amongst themselves.

"A vampire? Snap, man, that's what that thing was?" Leo asked, but was ignored.

"Come," replied Imohad. Four guards escorted them inside, their bright, polished armor clanking off the stone walls.

Even in their concern for Piper, the boys could not help but hope they would get another opportunity to explore the grandeur that surrounded them. They hurried along so quickly they were unable to take in everything Fortress Kelsii offered their wandering eyes. Different kinds of rock had been layered and arranged in intricate patterns, pressed and swirled together. The runes were their own work of art. Some had been chiseled into the rock face, while others had been carved from large pieces of gem stone, and had been fixed to the wall above the tunnel entrances. There were Dwarvik runes, Draconian runes, Elven script, and several other kinds of writing. They adorned the walls of the great circular room they entered immediately beyond the front gates. At least thirty tunnels led off the main entrance, each with a different pattern and colored gem at the top of each entrance.

"Someone inform the Empress and Queen!" Dimitri called.

One of the guards nodded and took off at a run toward another tunnel. Jayson, Jack and Leo were panting to keep up. They knew that even if they were separated, Piper was all that mattered now.

Twisting and turning, never ending, on and on the tunnels went. The path they took was smooth and square, and illuminated by jewel-encrusted oil lamps along the way. Finally, they turned down a wide corridor and saw their first door in what felt like miles. The guards pushed it open, making room for Dimitri and the boys to pass through. Inside was a high ceilinged room with white marble floors and walls. There were many small beds along the walls, and the shelves were lined with herb-filled glass pots. A small fountain bubbled forth from one wall, falling into a basin and draining through a pipe to a hole in the floor. It was clean and more advanced than Jayson, Jack and Leo expected.

A short woman looked up from her work at a small counter by the herb shelves. Her hair was pulled back into many tiny braids, each intricately laced through with jewels and stone beads. She wiped her hands on a towel and pointed to the bed to her right.

"Elf. Vampire," panted Dimitri, setting Piper gently on the bed. The woman nodded and hurried back to the shelf of herbs.

From the doorway behind Leo, Jack and Jayson, four more guards joined the growing throng of people in the hall. They ushered in three more women, their hair also beautifully braided and decorated with jewels and beads, but far fewer than the healer. They were otherwise plainly clothed, which surprised the boys as they suspected this was the Empress and Queen Dimitri had called for.

"Hello, Dimitri," sighed the eldest woman. She held out her arms and embraced him. Though her skin was smooth and glowing, her eyes looked old and worn. "How is she?" she asked. Dimitri shook his head.

The healer bustled back to Piper with a poultice, a blanket and a cold compress. Her fingers worked the greenish-gray mess into Piper's wound. Quite unexpectedly, she gave a loud cry and jumped back. No one needed ask why. The lightning that had appeared during their battle with the vampire had returned. It snaked its way around Piper's body again, wrapping her in a protective prism.

"Magic?" whispered one of the guards. The boys had nearly forgotten magic was forbidden and feared throughout Chartile. They had become so used to Piper's magic, or at least the idea of it. They hadn't seen her use it since their first night in Chartile. It had not occurred to them what might happen if others encountered it.

"Out," said the older woman. Her voice turned strong and commanding. "Everyone out. Not you three," she pointed to Jack, Leo and Jayson. Dimitri had not moved. He appeared determined not to leave Piper's side and needed no encouragement to stay.

"Empress, I—" began the healer.

"No. No one is to speak a word about this," the woman said sharply.

Everyone nodded, and turned to leave. The Empress sighed once the door had been closed behind them and rolled up her sleeves. She laid a hand on Dimitri's shoulder. He turned to her, and the once strong, young man looked entirely lost and helpless.

"She does not know she is doing this. She cannot help it. She's—"

"I know," said the Empress kindly. She reached for Dimitri's hands, and carefully removed the orenite cuffs from his wrists. Dimitri looked at her, fear spreading more fiercely across his face. "It's going to take all of us to bring her back." The Empress said.

"Back from where? What's going on?" Jayson asked, his voice shaking.

"Her mind has turned inward, hibernating if you will. To protect her. What she does not know is her magic will soon drain her of all her energy, and she will slowly die."

"What?" exclaimed Leo, "She can't die!"

"She's not going to," the Empress said calmly. "I need you all to do exactly as I say. Even you, Jayson. I have no magic, but I can pray to Rashiri to guide us, to guide her."

Jayson, who had been staring grimly at Piper, jerked around at the mention of his name. "How do you know who I am?"

"I have been consulting with the oracle much lately. I will explain more at a later time. Please, we must all join hands around her."

The humming of the lightning that continued to envelope Piper sent the air into a buzzing, static frenzy. The boys could feel the hairs on their bodies standing up. The Empress began to chant in a strange, growling language, and everyone's palms tingled.

"Dimitri, I need you to call her," she said, her eyes still closed in concentration. "Bring her back to us. Now, everyone, place a hand on her. And whatever happens, do not break the connection. Rashiri…"

They all placed their hands on Piper's arms. The Empress stood at Piper's head, her fingers on the girl's temples. She began chanting again, and nodded toward Dimitri.

"Piper. Piper, can you hear me? Piper, please come back to us. Listen to my voice. Follow my voice, please, Piper."

There was an intense electrical sensation as the lightning moved faster. They all winced, but no one dared release from the strange spell. Magical, religious or both, they could not say, but Jayson, Jack and Leo would do anything to bring Piper back.

"I know you're scared. I know, I— I should have protected you. Please come back to me." Dimitri whispered.

The lightening flashed wildly, blinding them all, then ceased. Piper took a deep breath, as though breathing life back into her lungs again. She still remained unconscious. The boys felt drained. Even more exhausted than their day long trek up the mountain. The Empress released her hands from Piper's temples and smiled.

"Well done," she whispered. She applied more of the herbal poultice to Piper's arm, and laid a cool, wet cloth on her forehead.

"Why isn't she awake? What's wrong with her?" Jayson asked. He looked frantically between Piper and The Empress, and back again.

"She is tired, dear. Her body is still fighting the venom. She will be fine, with rest and medicine. Dimitri, please call our friends back inside."

Dimitri hesitated and swallowed hard. He looked for a long moment at Piper before resigning to do his Empress's bidding. He nodded covered the length of the room as quickly as he could. When he opened the door to the hallway, he hurried back to Piper and stroked her hair. The guards, healer, and the two other ladies waited anxiously outside.

"Please take Piper to the Sapphire Quarter. I want her as close to me as possible," said the Empress. "And please find rooms for our guests as well. The Emerald Quarter should do nicely." The crowd bowed to Jack, Leo and Jayson, and then to the Empress, their hands flat on their thighs. Two guards stepped forward to carry Piper away on a wooden stretcher the boys had not noticed hung on one of the walls. Dimitri looked to the Empress, and the woman nodded with a smile. Dimitri followed close behind the guards that carried Piper. The boys hurried after them, leaving the Empress and the ladies alone with the healer.

Chapter Seven

Of Law and Limestone

The boys waited anxiously in the room they had been assigned in the Emerald Quarter. Leo bit his nails. Jack stared at the door, lost in thought. Jayson paced frantically in circles around the sofa and chairs in the middle of the room. The room was large and just as grand as any of the halls they had passed along the way. But they were too on edge to take notice.

Two bedrooms led off on either side of the common room area with two beds each, complete with gosling stuffed mattresses and tapestries on every wall. The common room had several carved high backed wooden chairs with soft green cushions, and a green fainting couch. There were murals on every wall, and even the ceilings, depicting what they assumed were scenes from the history of Chartile. The founding of Mount Kelsii, the gifting of the Draconian Runes by the Dragons to the Dwarves, and something to do with a griffin nesting atop a mountain.

All of this was being completely ignored. Jayson, Jack and Leo had hardly noticed the emeralds and jade around the door frames, nor the stained glass in the windows overlooking the mountainside. Piper was all they could think of at the moment. Piper and what had just happened. The thought of her lying unconscious somewhere unknown scared them. Without her, they were lost in this strange land. Without her, they did not know what to do.

There was a knock on the door. They jumped at the sound, coming back to reality. Jack rose from his chair, and crossed to open the door. He turned the intricate handle, his hands trembling. Before him stood the Empress, but she was not alone. Four guards had escorted her, and a pretty young girl Jack thought he recognized from the healer's room stood against the far wall in the hall beyond.

"Greetings," The Empress said. Her voice was gentle and reassuring. "I am Empress Nefiri. Might I have a word?"

Jack nodded and opened the door for the Empress to enter. To the boys' surprise, she closed the door behind her, leaving her entourage to wait in the hall again. The guards seemed unalarmed at this. Leo wondered if meeting with guests in private was a common occurrence with the Empress. Jayson didn't seem to notice. He sat on the couch, then stood again, and resigned to leaning against the wall. Jack wondered who the girl waiting in the hallway was.

The Empress glided across the room, and perched herself on the edge of a chair. She arranged her skirts neatly around her and folded her hands on her lap.

"Now, I am sure you have questions. Shall we begin?" she asked matter-of-factly.

At first, no one spoke. The hundreds of questions the whirled through their minds were not so easy to make sense of.

At last, Jayson spoke. "How is Piper? What the hell just happened? Was that some magic ritual or something? Is Piper going to be okay? Dimitri said that thing was a vampire? Is that true?"

Nefiri held up a weathered hand to silence him. "One question at a time. I will do my best to answer them all." She sighed deeply, fidgeting with her skirts, then continued. "Piper is still unconscious though we are confident she will make a full recovery. Based on Dimitri's description, it does appear it was a vampire that attacked you. This matter will need to be looked into further. Many believe vampires to be nothing more than myth, and those who do believe in their existence agree they haven't been seen since the days of the old kings. They are called The Lost Legends for a reason. Right now there are matters of law and war that are more pressing than myth at this time.

"Now, as for your questions of magic. No, it was not a ritual. I am a Priestess of Rashiri, our patron Mother Goddess and protector. I have the ability to direct her life energy toward the subject of my prayer, if it is Her will. This is different than magic, because, in the end, it is Rashiri who controls the energy, not I. I know some rumors of you three from my informants in Outland Post." She smiled at them. "I took a chance that you are what we believe you to be. You were unharmed and Piper was safe."

"Wait," said Jayson, "Are you saying that if it wasn't for us doing…magic…that Piper wouldn't be okay?"

"Actually, I want to hear more about these informants of yours," said Leo. "No one is supposed to know where Piper is in those mountains except her grandma." He folded his arms before him, and raised a suspicious eyebrow. "Have you been spying on her? On us? Why?"

"There are rumors that say you are the reincarnated souls of the old kings, sent here to right the wrongs that have occurred. Is this true?" Nefiri asked. Leo sighed as it was clear the woman had dodged his question by asking another. He rolled his eyes and opened his mouth to answer, but Jack got there first.

"Well, that's what everyone keeps saying," said Jack. "But honestly, we aren't anyone important where we come from."

"So how did you come to be here?" Nefiri continued, folding her hands once more upon her knee.

"We're not sure, really," said Leo. His voice was calmer. "There was this weird light, we blacked out, and woke up here just before Taraniz tried to attack Outland Post about two weeks ago."

"So you have no proof that you are the old kings?" Nefiri asked.

"Well, we did all have this weird ability to use these weapons we've never used before." Jack shrugged.

Silence fell, and Nefiri nodded curtly. "Very well," she said. "Then shall we move on to the matter of why I have asked you here?"

Jayson, Jack and Leo nodded, though they seemed to have more questions now than answers.

"In five days' time, there will be a meeting of The Council of Elders. The Council is made up of representatives from each of the quarters in Mount Kelsii and the Tutarian Mountains. The Elders are elected by the residents of each quarter, and the elders then appoint the Princesses and Queens. When an Empress steps down or passes, returning to the stone, one of the appointed queens steps up to take her place, and her princess then takes the queen's place. A new princess is appointed, and her training begins. I am an Empress of Peace. I was never appointed to carry out such duties pertaining to war. Furthermore, I am old. I wish to spend the remainder of my days carrying out the will of Rashiri, and leave the matters of state behind me."

"So?" Jayson shrugged. "What do you need us for?"

"Queen Isla of the Tutarian Mountains would be the Elders' first choice to become Empress. She has been trained in the ways of war, and her princess, Faeridae, would make a wonderful successor."

"That sounds great!" said Leo.

"Dimitri tells me he has told you that our Princesses, Queens and Empresses may not wed." The boys nodded at Nefiri's declaration. "And you are familiar with The Black Diamonds?"

"Yeah, but we aren't Black Diamonds," said Leo. "Why do you need us? Or Piper?"

"My informants in the Tutarian Mountains tell me that Isla has been courting a known member of The Black Diamonds. We believe her to be a sympathizer to this rogue organization. Without sufficient evidence however, we cannot commission the Elders to strip her of her position."

"Why do you hate these Black Diamond guys so much?" Jayson asked. "In our world, men and women are equal. Why don't you just give these people some of what they have asked for?"

"You are not Dwarvik, my dears. The abilities of the genders between races are not equal.

Even if they were, I will never allow an organization to have a voice amongst our Elders that finds ruthless methods of sabotaging our mines and killing our innocent husbands a means of negotiation. In the last five years nearly one hasana from every household has gone missing. The entirety of House Sehtvar has disappeared, or was found dead. These people are killers. We fear that Isla will work to get them a voice on our Council if she is made Empress."

"What are we supposed to do?" asked Jack. He bit his lip and shuffled his feet on the floor beneath him.

"Queen Una of Mount Kelsii, though younger than Isla, is trained in both war and peace. She is the first queen in many generations to be trained thus, and it was by her specific request. Though there may be many on the Council that would vote for her, her successor, Princess Gemari is very young. Many would argue that Gemari is not ready for the responsibilities of Queenhood. We cannot allow Isla to become Empress. I need your help to convince the Council of this, and I will agree to continue to train Gemari, as I was Queen of Mount Kelsii before my succession as Empress. It is the only foreseeable solution."

"Why don't you just stay the Empress, at least until after we get this Taraniz situation figured out? Wouldn't that solve everything?" asked Jack.

"I am not trained in the ways of war. This is how it has always been. If you truly are who many believe you to be, then you should have little difficulty in swaying the Council's decision."

Nefiri's face was beginning to look more worn and lined as she continued.

"You do realize we're only fourteen years old, right? I'm on the debate team and all, but this is different," argued Leo. "I don't know how three teenagers who aren't even from around here are going to have any effect on anything."

"But that's it, isn't it?" asked Jayson after a moment's silence. "The way we talk and act is proof enough that we're not from Chartile. So, even if we aren't actually these reincarnated kings, it's not too hard for these people to believe it. I mean, think about it. If aliens came to our planet and they had this technology that was different from ours, it might be thousands of years out dated to them, but we'd think they were, like, super geniuses, just because of the stereo type about aliens. You want to use our existence and presence here to help you."

Jack and Leo tried not to let their mouths hang open as they stared at Jayson. Nefiri looked at the floor, scowling and sighed.

"I think that's the smartest thing you've ever said, Jay," said Leo.

Jayson smiled. "What can I say?" he said. He crossed his arms and attempted to lean against the wall behind him. "This place seems to be rubbing off on me." Instead, he misjudged the distance and nearly fell over.

"Will you at least consider my offer?" asked Nefiri, "I will ensure that your use of magic is never discovered. You would be awarded Ambassador status among the Dwarves. I can find you permanent quarters of your choosing at the Tutarian Mountains."

"We'll think about it," said Leo. He smirked at Jack and Jayson who nodded in agreement.

"I can ask no more," said Nefiri, unable to entirely hide the defeat in her voice. "Do you have any further questions I can answer?"

"Yeah," said Leo, leaning back and refolding his arms again. "Who are these informants, and how do they know about us?"

Nefiri nodded. "I can say only so much. Please understand, as the leader of my people, it is my duty to have eyes and ears everywhere. I have had them watching Piper for many years now."

"Why?" Jack asked quietly.

"If you do not know the answer to that, you will very soon. It is not information I feel is my right to give."

"If you had all these people watching Piper, how come they didn't try to help her?" asked Jayson. His face grew flush as he spoke. "I mean, she was starving out there. If she's so important, why did you let her suffer?"

"She is an elf. Though an admittedly important one, her fate is in the hands of her people, not mine. It is regrettable, but it is the way of things."

"That's bogus," Jayson huffed.

If there are no further questions, I would like to continue to our next matter at hand," Nefiri's voice raised with more enthusiasm. She rose, and headed for the door. Jayson, Jack and Leo remained where they were. Nefiri opened the door and bowed low. The young girl from the hall entered. She bowed stiffly at the waist to the boys, her hands flat against her thighs. Jack, Leo and Jayson hurried return the gesture, if rather clumsy.

"My Lords, this is Princess Gemari, Queen Una's successor. I have charged her with ensuring you are taught the proper etiquettes of our people. She will be your guide in the days leading up to our meeting with the Elders."

"My lords, it is an honor to meet you," Gemari said sweetly. Her eyes locked with Jack, and she blushed scarlet before looking away.

"I have arranged for our tailors to outfit you in the best garments available. Please, rest for today. Gemari will return tomorrow to take you on a tour of the mines, and have you properly garbed. If you have no further need of me, I shall take my leave of you."

Jayson took a step forward as Nefiri and Gemari turned for the door. "You'll tell us as soon as Piper wakes up, right?" he asked.

"Of course," said the Empress before shutting the door behind her.

ৡৰৎ

Piper's eyes fluttered open. The mural on the ceiling before her. Visions a unicorn and phoenix by a golden fountain swirled together and made her dizzy. She closed her eyes again, and concentrated on moving one part of her body at a time. She was stiff and sore, but thankful for the softness beneath her. For a moment, she thought she had died. The pain was horrible, and had given way to terrifying nightmares. Her mind raced with thoughts from the attack, and she sat up quickly. The room spun around her, and she felt instantly sick. A firm hand pushed her gently back to the bed.

She resisted, but the pounding in her ears became overwhelming.

"Piper, everything is alright," said a male voice. A cold compress was placed on her head.

"Dimitri?" she asked. She couldn't focus. Her mind and her eyes were a blur. "What's happened?"

"Piper," said a different voice, this time a woman. "My name is Nefiri. You are at Fortress Kelsii. You and your companions are safe and well. Please stay lying down. You are not yet fully healed."

Piper did as she was bid. She focused instead on grounding the pain that coursed through her. Very slowly she moved first her toes, then her hands. She wiggled her fingers and moved her shoulders up and down. The sharp pangs within each muscle gradually diminished. After several minutes, she removed the compress, and rolled to face the room. So much was still a blur, but she could make out two figures sitting across from her. They sat in the high backed, wooden chairs typical of the dwarves. She could make out light through the small round window over their shoulders.

"What happened?" she whispered. "I remember the— what was that? I fell unconscious. We were at least a day from the fortress. How long have I been sleeping?"

"Your friends brought you here swiftly, and we were able to heal you. You have been sleeping for two days," said the woman.

Piper sat up, though more carefully this time. A cup of broth found its way into her hand, and she sipped at it cautiously. Her stomach wanted to resist, but she fought it. She knew she needed the nourishment. With each sip, the room began to come into focus more clearly. Empress Nefiri sat across from her in a plain wooden chair. The woman watched Piper with her usual stone faced emotion. She remembered the woman from when she was a child visiting the mountain with Gran. Nefiri had hardly aged since then, though such was typical of dwarves.

A man she had never seen before was bent over the hollow stone pillar, stoking the fine within. She was sure he was Elven, but he bore no heraldry of the King or Taraniz. Piper said nothing, but continued to sip her broth until it was gone. The elf straightened the water basin resting on top of the pillar, and resumed his post in the chair beside the Empress. At once Piper recognized his blue gray eyes. Her heart began to pound and she nearly dropped the mug in her hand. It was one of the men who frequently accompanied Taraniz to Outland Post.

"You!" Piper cried and flung herself from her bed. "Why have you brought me here? When did the Dwarves align with Taraniz? You're not taking me to her!" She scrambled for the door handle, her head spinning again. Nefiri stood and stepped toward Piper.

"He is not here for Taraniz, Piper. He is here for the King. He is a friend. I would not turn you over to her if my life depended on it. Please, calm down. We are here to talk, nothing more. There are many things you need to know. May we speak in peace?"

The Empress rested a hand on Piper's shoulder, and the girl stilled. She had finally found the handle of the heavy wooden door. Her thumb pressed the latch. She need only swing the door inward, and she could run. No doubt, though, there were armed guards waiting outside if the Empress was in here. And, if this man had come representing the King, it meant Aramor may not dead. It meant there might still be a way to fight Taraniz— a way that did not have to include her.

She released her grip on the door, and it latched again loudly. She turned, her icy green eyes staring at the man the entire way back to the sofa.

"Let's hear it then," Piper replied. Her firm and commanding tone had returned as she sat. "What news have you that is so important it could not wait until I was fully recovered?"

"This is Valar Marion. He is the head advisor to King Aramor. It was he who came to us first," Nefiri hesitated and glanced at the man beside her. "Well, there is much to tell."

"Then do so quickly. I do not wish to be hampered with nonsense in my condition. I do not understand why this could not have waited until the council hearing." Piper snapped, waving her hand before her.

"Because there is much more than the issues of the council," said Valar. He sighed and rubbed the back of his neck. "Piper, I am sorry to be so direct with you, and I regret if any of this comes as a shock. But we are on limited time, and a decision must be reached." He sighed again and pulled a leather bound book from his pocket. "My lady, it was I who brought you to Outland Post as a child. I brought you there because King Aramor asked me to get rid of you eighteen years ago. King Aramor did so because he could not bear to watch his kingdom be torn apart by feuding twin sisters."

Piper felt tears brim her eyes. She felt her breathing quicken. Her grip tightened on the arm of the little fainting couch as Valar continued.

"King Aramor knowingly married the daughter of a half human, but it was all kept very quiet. Queen Runa was very beautiful and very kind. She was greatly loved by all the people in Chartile, and the marriage made sense. When she became with child, she was unable to control the magic she had suppressed for years. It was believed she had grown out of her magic, or that it simply had dried up for it had not been used for so long. She was locked away in a tower wing of the palace, and the people were told she was ill.

"When she gave birth, she could not control her magic, and she died. No one knew she carried two heirs. King Aramor chose the first born and asked me to get rid of you. I couldn't kill you. Runa had been dear friend, and you were only a few hours old. I took you to Outland Post. Your grandmother was a friend of mine, and I knew her daughter could not bear children of her own. I knew you would be safe there, far away from the palace.

"When she was thirteen, Taraniz began acting… strange. It was as though she were using magic, though there was no evidence of such. We found ourselves unable to defy her, and King Aramor became weaker by the day. I knew your grandmother and parents had raised you with all the proper courtly etiquettes, as the granddaughter of a palace scribe and retainer should. It was I who stopped Taraniz from killing you that day at the rebellion, and it was I who asked the Dwarves to watch you and protect you in secret all these years you have lived in the mountain. I knew this would not be difficult, as you and Dimitri had been close as children, and he was now liaison to the Empress."

Valar stopped. He quickly wiped away the tears that had fallen from his eyes. Piper had staunched hers some time ago. He walked to the window, and Piper stood to face him.

"Please just say it. Please get it over with," she pleaded. Valar looked into the dark green eyes that once belonged to Runa. She was like her in every way from the flowing red hair to the long, thin fingers. How anyone could have mistaken her all these years was a miracle.

"You are the rightful heir to the Elven throne, Piper Romilly. King Aramor is now dead by your sister's hand. Your given name by your mother is Eva Ruani, and since Taraniz has committed acts of treason against the Crown, it is now yours. If you will accept it."

Piper was silent for a long time. She sat. She stood. She paced. Nefiri looked only at the floor and listened. Valar stared out the window.

"What if I choose to walk away from all this?" Piper finally asked, "What happens if I say no?"

"Certainly no one is forcing you to do this, Piper," Empress Nefiri said. "But, I can assure you, you have every quality Chartile needs right now. Look how you protected Outland Post, or what you have done for Jack, Leo and Jayson."

"It all seems so convenient," Piper snapped, the anger returning to her voice. "Quite convenient that there just happens to be another heir who has been perfectly trained to take Taraniz's place. Should I turn out to be a poor ruler will a bastard son suddenly surface out of nowhere?"

"Of course not!" cried Valar. His eyes softened even as his brow furrowed. "I know this is difficult, Piper. You have no idea how hard it has been for me to watch you struggle all this—"

Piper rushed at Valar, and stopped inches from his nose. "Then why didn't you do anything? You waited until it was convenient for you, while I'm living off scrawny diten mice and mushrooms!" She pushed him as hard as the venom would yet allow. Valar stumbled back into the empty chair, and Nefiri covered her mouth with her hands. He wasn't hurt or angry, and he didn't move to stand again.

"I'm sorry," said Piper taking a step back. "I guess I haven't been trained quite as perfectly as you thought."

"There are some rough edges to polish," Empress Nefiri said lowering her hand to reveal a soft smile. "Still, it is part of who you are, and we're not here to change you. We want to give you the opportunity to have what is rightfully yours, if you so wish it. No one ever said it would be easy."

"You know that those on the councils, Elven and Dwarvik, are going to take convincing. What proof are you prepared to offer?" Piper asked, resuming her steady pacing from the couch to the door. She bit at her cuticles as her nails had long since been chewed away. Valar opened the leather bound book he had carried with him. Carefully he laid three pieces of parchment on a table, then sat without a word.

Piper looked from Nefiri and Valar to the table. It was as though a treat she had never been allowed before had been set before her for the taking. No stipulations, no tricks or gimmicks. The hair on the back of her neck rose and tingled with both fear and delight. Her legs wobbled as she approached the table and picked up each piece of paper in turn. She studied them for several minutes then turned to Valar and the Empress.

"This is your evidence? This proves nothing!" she said.

"Runa may have passed nearly two decades ago, but there are still some on both councils who will remember her," said Nefiri in her gentle, consoling voice.

"That's not all," said Valar, rising from the chair, "These numbers in the corner? They indicate the location of the genealogy record associated with each person."

"Why didn't you bring that?" asked Piper and she realized she sounded exactly like Jayson.

"It is missing," said Valar, "I do not know if Taraniz took it or if it was removed when you were born. Without that, this is the best evidence we have."

Piper paced the room again. "There is someone who may know where the records are," she said abruptly.

"We have sent a scouting party to find her," said Nefiri.

Piper looked between Nefiri and Valar. Her jaw had slacked and her eyes darted wildly.

"I don't understand," said Piper. She had attempted to keep her voice calm, but could not.

"Your grandmother has been captured." Valar said frankly. "The people in Outland Post say it was the palace guards that took her. No doubt they followed me, and captured her for the same reasons I went to her."

"We have to send someone after her!" Piper cried desperately.

"If Kaytah was taken to the palace, she has allies there that will keep her safe. Have faith, Piper. You have more friends than you know."

"And what of the information she has? Surely they will kill her for it. If she reveals its location, then Taraniz will destroy it. If not, then no one will have it." Piper could hardly cope with the imagery her grandmother being tortured. The fact the room spun at times was the only thing that kept her from rushing to save Gran that very moment.

"There will be other ways, other things we can use if it comes to it. Piper, Kaytah will be fine." Valar smiled reassuringly, but it did little to sooth the girl's fears.

Piper's eyes closed. Again, she willed away the tears that formed in her eyes. Gran had been kidnapped because of her. No, Gran had been kidnapped because of a secret about her. This wasn't her fault. But no matter how many times she repeated the words to herself, her feelings of remorse, ebbed by those of anger and betrayal still seemed to eat away at her insides.

How many people had known who she was all these years, and had done nothing? She had been lied to, and hidden away like something unwanted. She had been unwanted, she reminded herself. She had been unwanted by the person who should have loved and wanted her the most. No one had cared about her until it suited their own interests. Now that the dwarves were in danger, she was supposed to emerge from the shadows and save the day. If she accepted her role as Queen, her days of roaming the mountains and forests were over. She would spend most of her life repairing the damage Taraniz – or rather, Duke Noraedin – had caused.

She saw Dimitri smiling and running his fingers through his hair as she thought. As Queen, her marriage would be agreed upon by a majority vote within the Conclave of Nobles. They would never allow her to marry the half-Dwarvik-half-human retainer of the Dwarvik Empress. She could not so easily cast aside her friendship, her love for him. He had been her only friend as a child, and she couldn't imagine her life without him. The very thought of it made her stomach turn.

She hadn't realize she had been staring at the parchment on the table the entire time her mind raced. Their contents slowly faded into focus again. Piper sighed and turned to face Valar and Nefiri.

Chapter Eight

Princess Gemari

Jack, Leo and Jayson were relieved they had been given a guide while exploring Fortress Kelsii. After only a few turns, they knew they would have been lost. Leo had droned on for nearly ten minutes about the scientific process of dehydration and starvation until Jayson threatened to shove a hunk orenite in a rather uncomfortable location, and Jack had to pry the rock from Jayson's fist.

Sintori, Harasan of House Geofra escorted them by pony down a magnificent tunnel toward one of the oldest orenite mines in the mountain. Much to Jack's disappointment, Princess Gemari had other duties leading up to the meeting with the Council that afternoon which required her attention.

"It is said, from this mine came the orenite used to create the circlet that was the downfall of Duke Noraedin," said Sintori. The boys were held captive by the man's tales. The architecture and craftsmanship of the mountain added to the wonder his stories stirred within them. The inlaid jewels that surrounded them at every turn dazzled in the firelight of the torches and lamps. Even the stone itself was a masterpiece in its own right. Bright white limestone had been layered with dark obsidian in swirls and stripes all along the tunnel. This was but one of many tours they had taken over the last several days with the princess, but they never tired of the sights and tales.

Princess Gemari was much like Nefiri in her appearance. She was the Empress's niece after all. But her demeanor couldn't have been more

94

different. She was twenty-three in Dwarvik years, but the boys thought she had been the same age as them. She had explained the slower age progression of the dwarves was believed to be in part due to their constant exposure to orenite, but no one was really sure. Gemari was short, only a little over five feet tall. Her amber eyes and brilliant white smile only added to her bouncy and bubbly personality. Although she was very knowledgeable, she giggled a lot. Especially at anything Jack said. She seemed to find him mesmerizing. She stared at him with sappy, doe eyes and batted her eye lashes.

Jack was unsure what to make of Gemari's attempts at flirting. At fourteen, his experiences in the field of romance were quite slim. The more he talked with her, the more comfortable he became. After only a few days, the two were giggling together almost incessantly, much to the disgust of Jayson and Leo.

The two boys had been glad of the break when Sintori joined them. They had wondered if Gemari had been instructed by Nefiri to purposely flirt with Jack in order to sway their decision. They had not yet decided whether to help promote Una to the Empresshood. The decision meant men would still be no closer to having the rights they were accustomed to back in their world, and Princess Gemari would never be allowed to have a relationship. They secretly suspected that even if Queen Isla had done things that defied her own people's law, the changes she would try to instill could be beneficial. But they never spoke it, even amongst themselves.

They had been told Piper had finally woken the day before last and was doing well. Dimitri had been to visit her once, but she wanted to be alone. She kept to her room in The Sapphire Quarter, which the boys learned was reserved for royalty. Only the Empress, Queens and Princesses stayed there, and visiting royalty from neighboring races. Jack, Leo and Jayson wondered even more what secrets Piper held.

Life seemed to be rather peaceful at Fortress Kelsii, despite what the boys thought they would find after learning about The Black Diamonds. The members of the rogue organization seemed to be few and far between, and certainly not much of a threat, in spite of Nefiri's rant and the increased security to protect the visiting Elders. The men they talked to had nothing but genuine, good things to say about their wives. For the most part, they were happy. And the women loved their husbands unconditionally in return. They showed their love by carrying out their duties as wives. It was all very perfect. Almost too perfect, in Jack's opinion. He lived in a home that looked perfect to the outside world. He knew better than to believe the façade these people were promoting to their prophesized kings.

It was the last day of their visitor excursions. The council meeting was to take place later that afternoon. Jack, Leo and Jayson had been fitted with proper Dwarvik attire, and would be attending as honored guests of the Empress herself. As they returned from their tour of the orenite mines, Princess Gemari greeted them at the entrance to the tunnel with a deep bow. The boys still considered it odd as they had yet to see any other women give this gesture to the men, save for the Empress, Queen and Princess Gemari. Gemari had said it was a sign of respect. The dwarves believed those appointed to political statuses were to give thanks to those who put them there. They wore very few treasures and their clothes were plain. They were there to serve their people, not flaunt their power. Although they never wanted for anything— the best food, the fanciest quarters, the most expensive fabrics— everything they owned was almost entirely devoid of the intricate carvings and gem work the dwarves were renowned for. It made the boys uncomfortable when Gemari bowed to them since they could not bow back.

"Sintori, I thank you ever so kindly for taking such great care with our guests. I shall resume my post of them at this time," she said kindly. She bounced slightly on the balls of her feet and flashed her brilliantly white smile.

"Of course, my Princess," Sintori said and dismounted. The boys followed suit, their legs feeling a bit like jelly from the long ride, and Sintori gathered their reigns. "Please, let me know if I can be of any further assistance to any of you." The boys inclined their heads in a small bow as The Princess had taught them was the appropriate gesture. The Princess bowed low again, and the beads of her braided hair brushed against her knees.

"Did you enjoy your time with Sintori?" she asked them. "He's ever so fascinating, isn't he?" Gemari led the way back to the boy's room, two guards bringing up the rear.

"Yes, my lady," said Jack. He had picked up on the tact and etiquette of the Dwarvik culture better than his friends. It was the only advantage Jayson and Leo could think of for Jack spending so much time with Gemari. The constant giggling and fluttering eyes was worth their friend learning what to say and do. Jack had begun taking lead when speaking to the dwarves. Leo and Jayson were happy to remain silent and not worry about offending someone. Jack seemed to have a handle on it for them.

"Are you excited for the pre-banquet?" he asked the Princess.

Gemari cleared her throat. Oh, of course I am," she replied rather unconvincingly. She stopped to bow to a group of men who walked past them in the corridor, then continued onward. "Though, one must admit, the monotony of these council meetings does grow tiresome." She glanced over her shoulder at her guards and hushed her voice even further. "The endless speeches, knowing all the internal relationships... it can certainly drag on after some time." she sighed and smiled sweetly up at Jack.

"Yeah, that sounds exciting," mumbled Jayson. Leo paused and elbowed him in the ribs. "Dude! I just broke that, like, a month ago!"

Gemari giggled quietly behind her hand. When they had reached their rooms, the Princess held the door open for them and bowed as they walked past. They entered the common room area and found a fire had already been made for them in the little fire place along the outer wall. Three tunics had been laid out across the high backed chairs and sofa. Their sleeves were embellished with tiny jewels, and golden threads ran through the entire garment. Otherwise, they were plain, pale grey tunics similar to those the Dwarvik royalty wore.

"Between you and me," Gemari whispered, and handed each boy an outfit, complete with belt, pants and shoes, "My sister would have been the better choice, but she was too old to be chosen" she sighed. She was even pretty when she looked miserable. "There are endless restrictions on everything I say and do. Ketari does not mind rules so much. I suppose I will learn to accept them in time. I have had to fight to convince the elders that Orctkar is only a friend. Our meetings are already frowned upon."

She looked at the floor and played with the beads in her hair. She shook her head, and stood tall again, her smile wide. "But, there are already arrangements made for Orctkar to marry in three years' time. She already has a Harasan, so the House is much respected. He should be able to find work easily, or continue into an apprenticeship." Gemari paused and bit her lower lip. "I should not be saying these things to you. I am sorry. I love my people, and I will be proud to be Queen or Empress one day."

"It's alright," said Leo, waving the hand the held his gem covered shoes. "We won't tell anyone." The entire affair had given him a difficult internal struggle these last few days. His desperate fight not to interfere in anything was becoming far more difficult to do the longer they spent in Chartile. And keeping his friend from courting the Princess seemed nearly impossible at this point.

"Thank you," Gemari replied sweetly.

"Wait a minute," said Jack, "Who's this Orctkar?"

"Oh, I... I met Orctkar last year at a council meeting." She looked at the floor shyly, nudging the corner of a rug with her toe. "He works for the kitchens. He was ever so kind to make me a lovely wild strawberry tea instead of the usual pearl wine. I met him afterward, and he showed me the kitchens, and cooked for me. We often meet in the kitchens. He is just a friend, though. We cannot be more than that. It is the law."

"So, he's not really your... uh, suitor or anything, right? Like, you guys aren't... courting?" Jayson asked. He watched Jack fidget uncomfortable with the hem of his tunic.

"Oh, no! He is only a friend." Gemari's eyes widened in surprise. "Ketari thinks otherwise, but she can be too protective. She is my retainer, and I rather think she believes she is my personal body guard as well." She giggled and crinkled her nose as she did so. Jack smiled and the strange tension in his neck and shoulders vanished. "Yes, I do believe Ketari would have made the better princess, but please do not mention I said such things."

"What's your sister think about that? Does she want to be the Princess instead?" asked Jack. Gemari's eyes widened. She whipped around the check the closed door behind her before turning back to Jayson, Jack and Leo. "It's okay," Jack continued. "Maybe we can help."

"Do you truly believe so?" asked Gemari.

"It's worth a try. What's the worst that could happen? You don't get to be Princess anymore?"

Jack paused a moment and swallowed. "Then you're free to have a boyfriend, right?"

"Well, I suppose— but, no, no. I never should have said anything! Jack, please, I should not say such things. It is not proper of me. Promise me you won't say anything." Gemari buried her face in her hands and began to cry. Jayson ran to her side and awkwardly patted her back.

"Well, now you've done it, Jack," said Jayson.

"Oh, no, it is not you. I— I'm not good at this, really I'm not. I'm always messing everything up," said Gemari through little hiccups.

"Hey, join the club!" Jayson, threw his arm around her and hugged her. Gemari smiled and wiped the tears from her eyes.

"Ketari is both strong and gentle, and when she speaks, everyone listens. She has such a lovely voice. I was selected by the council and started my training as Princess when I was very young. I am sure with time I will learn to be better. And, Ketari will be there to help me." Gemari nodded her head curtly, as if this were final. "Well, we should not keep the council waiting. They have all been ever so excited to meet you! Please, dress swiftly, and I will take you to the pre-banquet."

The boys headed to one of the bedrooms on either side of the common area. Two beds sat side by side, and Jayson flopped down on his before bouncing up again. The other room across the common area was where Leo slept alone. Jack said he snored too loud.

"Jack, what are you thinking?" Leo asked, pulling off his shirt and tossing it to the corner. He was markedly less pudgy these days. The hunting treks through the mountains and fighting practice had left him with a shadow of defined muscle. Though it failed in comparison to his friends' sleek physique, or even Dimitri's muscular tone, it was the fittest he had ever looked.

"What?" asked Jack, pulling off his jeans. They had just gotten their regular clothes back from one of the Dwarvik washers, and were rather disappointed they could not wear them to the banquet. The cotton tunics were very itchy.

"We tried to stop Jayson from interfering when we first met Piper. Now you're doing it. We can't interfere! This isn't our world! Did you think that maybe she's just doing this so we'll vote for her to be the next Queen?"

"Take that back!" Jack shouted. "Gemari would never do that! Have you stopped to think that we don't know how long we're gunna be stuck here? In case you haven't noticed, we're kind of important. We should start trying to use that to make this place better. We're nobodies back home! We have a chance to do something here, even if it's just for one person. Besides, it's not like I can really date her. She might as well be happy with someone if we can get the laws changed."

"It's not just about one person, Jack, or even two," said Jayson. He hiked up his trousers before realizing they were on backwards. "What if Ketari would be a horrible princess? She hasn't been trained like Gemari has. What if the Queen or Empress dies and Ketari isn't ready? All because you decided Gemari should have the right to date some guy, whose name I can't even pronounce? This ain't all peachy-keen just because we might be these king dudes."

"We wouldn't let this happen if it were one of our friends back home. Gemari is our friend. The laws here are totally bogus! Come on! You have to agree with me!" said Jack.

"I do agree with you, man, but we don't know enough about stuff here yet. Not without messing up the whole system." Jayson stepped toward his friend, a sparkly shoe in one hand. He placed his other hand on Jack's shoulder. "Look, maybe we can talk to Ketari and Nefiri. The Empress seems like she would at least listen to us. Deal?"

Jack sighed and nodded. He pulled his gem covered shoe on and opened the door.

"This Orctkar guy better be worth it," Leo whispered under his breath.

The boys reentered the common area. They felt ridiculous with their sparkly shoes and belts fitted over their tunics. But they knew this was simple compared to the clothing of the middle class they had encountered on the days before. Some of the dresses they had seen when meeting with the middle class merchants must have weighed at least forty pounds with all the gemstones. Gemari clapped and giggled as Jack spun in a circle for her. Jayson and Leo rolled their eyes.

"Oh, you look wonderful," she cooed. "All of you! Now, there are a few things I must instruct you in before we depart."

"Great! More etiquette lessons!" Jayson rolled his eyes, and Jack glared at him.

"It's just a few simple things. The pre-banquet is the social time before negotiations. There are to be no matters of state discussed at this time. Though they have been asked not to, some of the Elders may wish to bestow you with gifts and pearl wine. Talk of who you are has spread rampant throughout the mountain. Accept the gifts, but graciously turn down the wine. Those with a sharper mind accomplish more, especially at Council meetings. Avoid the lamb, unless you like raw meat, and remember to smile and bow. My teachers used to put goat's lard on my teeth to remind me to smile. Luckily for you, I couldn't find any today." The boys blinked stone faced at Gemari until she began to giggle and laugh behind her hand. "I am only jesting." She smiled and they laughed, relieved. At times they did not understand Gemari's odd sense of humor. It was unnerving. "Well, shall we depart, then?" she asked.

They all nodded and headed for the door.

"May I escort you, my lady?" Jack asked holding out his arm for Gemari. Jayson covered his face in his hand. Gemari blushed crimson beneath her dark complexion and giggled.

"It is very thoughtful of you, Jack, but as Princess, I must walk alone."

Jack nodded, and held the door for her instead. She smiled coyly at him as she exited, and Leo promptly smacked Jack on the back of the head as he walked past. At the entrance to the Emerald Quarter, two guards stood waiting. Gemari bowed to them and took the lead.

"The Crystal Quarter is reserved specifically for entertaining guests, and when the Council of Elders meets," Gemari explained as they walked.

She tried to catch Jack's eye, but he stared at the ground, determined to ignore her.

"How many elders are there?" Leo asked, trying to break the awkward tension.

"There is one Elder for each Quarter, but as we have grown, so have the number of Quarters," Gemari replied, and she began ticking the quarters off on her fingers. "At Mount Kelsii, there is the Emerald Quarter, the Ruby Quarter, the Amber Quarter, the Obsidian Quarter, the Topaz Quarter and the Sapphire Quarter. That is where the Queen and I reside, and the Empress, of course, when she is visiting. At the Tutarian Mountains there is the Amethyst Quarter, the Cobalt Quarter, the Moonstone Quarter, the Garnet Quarter, the Citrine Quarter, the Opal Quarter, the Carnelian Quarter, and the Diamond Quarter, where the Empress, Princess and Queen of the Tutarian Mountains live. Queen Isla and Princess Faeridae just arrived today."

"So, the residents of each Quarter get to pick their elder?" Jayson asked. He already knew the answer, but was desperate to keep the conversation going in any direction other than one that involved more sickening moments between Jack and Gemari.

"Correct," said Gemari. "The elders appoint our Empress, Queens, and Princesses. We are selected by the age of five to be trained. We leave our families to live with the Queen and Empress."

They passed tunnel after tunnel, door after door. Each was beautifully decorated with faceted gems, or polished smooth to create murals that continued nearly an eighth of a mile. They passed one of these along the way, and Leo slowed to admire the craftsmanship. A golden fountain beneath a tree bearing golden apples. As he examined the detail, he discovered behind each fist-sized gem were smaller carved gems that portrayed a different scene. The technique was fascinating since the entire piece was completely flush with the wall. Leo ran his hand along the completely smooth surface and stopped. Jayson, Jack and Gemari were gone. They must have continued on without him. He listened carefully, hoping to hear their echoing voices or footfalls in the distance. The tunnel was as silent as stone.

Leo felt his heart begin race and his breath quicken. Now alone, he remembered he was miles beneath the earth, under thousands of tons of rock. He couldn't remember the last time he had seen the sky. Or felt the air against his face. His breath caught in his chest. He felt claustrophobic for the first time in his life. The stone walls seemed to close in around him.

"Don't panic," he whispered to himself. He tried to slow his breathing as he hurried in the direction they had been travelling. He came to a tunnel decorated with pearly white stone. Was this the way to The Crystal Quarter? Or perhaps this was the Moonstone Quarter. But The Moonstone Quarter had been at the Tutarian Mountains, right?

Leo couldn't see the usual oil lamps or even torches. He wasn't sure if the tunnel simply turned and he just couldn't see it. He stood, debating whether to take the dark tunnel or continue the way he had been going. In the end, he chose to stay where there was light, and turned down the first tunnel with lamps he came to. He always said the horror movies had it all wrong. It was human instinct to stay in the light when people were scared. Not that he was scared.

He walked for what seemed like miles. The last lamp he had passed was at least five minutes back. The darkness was pressing in around him, and the air was becoming stuffy. Leo stopped and leaned against the rock wall to collect his thoughts. He could simply turn around. He knew the tunnel gave way to light again if he went back the way he came. He couldn't understand why being alone seemed to bother him so. How he wished there was a fast way out!

A door clicked open on Leo's right, and a sliver of light shown through. He could hear muffled voices just beyond. He breathed a sigh of relief, thankful he had finally found people. He cautiously stepped through the door, and stopped short. The door clicked closed behind him.

Leo had stopped at the top of what appeared to be an old mine— but a mine it was no more. The winding path that led to the heart of the mine once held a track with carts operated by magnetized hematite. Now, a fence stood between Leo and the straight, vertical drop below. Tiny homes dotted the outskirts of the path, and a make shift market square bustled at the center below.

He stood transfixed by his unexpected find. A firm hand gripped the back of his collar and threw him face first into the dirt floor.

"How did you get in here?" asked a gruff voice. Leo felt his arms pulled behind his back and pinned together.

"I'm sorry! I didn't know!" Leo tried to yell, but his cheek was still pressed hard into the dirt. He dared not struggle against his captor.

"Who are you? An elf-spy for Nefiri? Or maybe a rogue slave trying to run? Eh? Which is it? Spy or coward?"

"My name is Leonardo DeHaven. I'm a guest of Empress Nefiri. I was just trying to get to the pre-banquet. I got lost. I'm sorry."

Rough hands pulled Leo to his feet, his arms still pinned to his back. "Honored guests of the Empress shall be granted the grandest holding cells. This way, my Lord." Leo was pushed forward down the narrow path. Below, faces turned to watch his decent into what he knew could be nothing but trouble. For a fleeting moment, he had a pain of sympathy for Jayson and his run of bad luck.

Chapter Nine

The Pre-Banquet

Dimitri knocked softly on Piper's door. "Enter," he heard her say. He pressed the latch on the door handle, and swung the door inward.

Piper's room was small for The Sapphire Quarter, but one of the most luxurious. Tightly woven linen rugs adorned the floor in an array of blues and grays. The entire ceiling was a many colored mural of some of the greatest scenes in Chartilian and Dwarvik history. The chairs were carved of black walnut with deep blue cushions and embroidered with silver thread. Dimitri sat in one of these and watched as Piper finished tying her hair back with the help of Nefiri's personal coiffeur. Together, they had tamed her curls into a twisted braid set with little green gems. It cascaded around the side of her neck and down her shoulder, setting off her sharp jawline. She turned to the man and bowed, offering him a silver coin. The man smiled, and turned to leave.

Piper's dress was fashioned in the elven style and had been gifted to her from Valar. It was her mother's, and hugged her delicate curves in just the right way. She shrugged and fidgeted with her braid until she nearly stabbed her finger with one of the tiny stones.

"Well?" Piper performed a quick pirouette. "Do I look alright? I have not worn such things since I was travelling with Gran, and they were never so luxurious as this." The thought of her grandmother, however fleeting, immediately took what little confidence she had. She looked at the floor, still fidgeting with her fingernails. She closed her eyes, and willed herself not to cry.

Dimitri stood. He was almost afraid to touch her. "You look like a queen," he whispered, and tilted her chin up to kiss her.

Piper pulled away quickly. "Please don't say that."

"I'm sorry," he said. He placed his hands on her hips and turned her to face him again. Piper had told him what Nefiri and Valar had said to her the day she had woke from her poisoned sleep. Even now he could sense she struggled with her decision.

"Whatever you decide, you know I will always be here for you." His breath tickled her ear and he hugged her tightly.

"No, you won't," she said. A tear slipped down her cheek, and she wiped it away quickly. "If I decide to be Queen, you know we cannot be together."

"I do not care what any council says, Piper. You are my best friend, and I...I lo..." Dimitri's heart was racing. He hoped she could not feel it through his chest. His words caught in his throat and he swallowed. He knew the moment he said those words he could never take them back. He couldn't believe he had never said them to her before. He breathed deeply. He didn't want to take them back.

Piper had been his best friend since the day they met in Fortress Kelsii over ten years ago. Since he was neither Dwarvik nor Human, the other children had shunned him. But not Piper. She was the first to see him as an equal. They had played tag in the tunnels of the Tutarian Mountain, and picked flowers along the mountain path. Their friendship had blossomed into something much deeper three summers past. He had not seen Piper or Kaytah visit Tutaria or Fortress Kelsii for some time. He begged Nefiri to tell him where she was. Nefiri would not say, so he left to look for her on his own. Gran directed him to the little path Piper often took to and from her trips to the village. There he had found her. Alone, afraid and hungry. He had taught her how to hunt and how to fight. She confided in him her magical abilities, and what had happened in Outland Post.

He taught her how to control her magic, and promised her he wasn't afraid. They spent days, weeks together, when he could get away from his duties to Nefiri. One day, beneath their gnarled beech tree, she had fallen asleep on his shoulder. She looked so peaceful, so beautiful. He kissed her. Her eyes fluttered open, and she had kissed him back.

Now, as they stood facing each other, his hands resting on her hips, that moment seemed so long ago. They were older now, even if it was only by a year. There were things far greater than the trivial matters of hunting and fishing that governed them now.

Piper wanted him to say those words. She wanted to feel his arms embrace her forever. She could have it, she thought. She could have everything she had ever hoped for if she left the fate of Chartile behind. She had yet to decide if her happiness was more important than the happiness of the people. Her people. She looked into Dimitri's dark brown eyes, and in that moment, she was not a

111

queen. She was just Piper, and she kissed him, feeling his warm arms wrap around her back.

They broke apart, and Piper smiled at him. She fixed the lay of his neck line, and kissed his cheek. Dimitri held out his arm for her, and she took it, her face still flush and lips still tingling. Since she was Elven not Dwarvik, her status permitted her an escort to the pre-banquet. Nefiri had granted Dimitri the time away to do so. Two guards waited outside the door, ready to escort them to The Crystal Quarter. It was a short walk from the Sapphire Quarter, though both secretly wished it would have lasted just a little longer.

The two double doors to The Crystal Quarter opened into a high ceilinged room. Panels of painted glass and carved gems on the ceiling and outer walls allowed rays of sunlight to pass through, casting a rainbow of colors on the guests inside. The perimeter of the room was lined with tables of food and wine. In the center of the room was a long wooden table with chairs. A slightly raised platform with five chairs stood at the head of the room beneath a giant griffin, carved from sapphires and citrine. The creature looked as if he were breaking through the stone into the room below, ready to pounce on the five smaller chairs that stood in front of the platform and faced the wooden table in the center.

Those already in attendance hushed and whispered in hurried voices and behind hands as the two entered. Piper had been assured that none but she, Nefiri and Valar, and of course Dimitri, knew of her true lineage. She hoped their stares and whispers were from the elders remembering her as a child. She said nothing, but held her head high and smiled. Queen or no, she was still the honored guest of Empress Nefiri, and an important piece during today's negotiations.

From across the room she saw Valar and Nefiri. They waved to her, and she and Dimitri crossed to join them. The room parted before her, and each person bowed as she passed. She hoped such fuss over her would soon end. It was one thing she could never get used to, she thought.

Valar reached out an arm to embrace her, and Nefiri bowed as Piper stopped before them.

"You look just like your mother," Valar whispered in her ear. Piper pretended not to have heard, and accepted a glass of pearl wine from a passing beck-and instead. The little bubbles caught in the back of her throat. She coughed and became instantly light headed. She handed the remainder of the drink to Dimitri, who was still at her side. He winked at her, and finished the glass in one swallow.

"Show off," she whispered to him. He winked again and smirked.

From a throng of elders huddled close by, a thin, wispy haired woman in a midnight blue dress approached them. Empress Nefiri bowed low, her braided hair forming a curtain over her face.

"Lady Piper, allow me to introduce myself. I am Frejah of Tutarian's Cobalt Quarter. It is an honor to meet you, my dear. We have indeed heard so much about you."

"From whom, I wonder, my lady?" Valar asked. His smile was polite, but his raised eyebrow spoke volumes.

"Only rumors, I suppose!" Frejah dodged the accusation. "No one in particular, but we are all wondering—"

"Frejah, dear, none of that. It is the pre-banquet. All in good time." Empress Nefiri nodded her dismissal of the woman. Frejah's smile vanished. She stuck her chin out with a "Yes, Empress," and left back to her cluster of whispering women before Nefiri could bow a dismissal.

Piper looked around and noticed the many pairs of eyes watching her, or looking away quickly. Some whispered behind their hands. Others blatantly pointed at her and whispered to their friends. Whether she accepted the Elven crown or not, Piper realized she would always be looked at this way. She would be fussed over, doted on. Some would even attempt to use her as a pawn. She suddenly felt very lightheaded, and it had nothing to do with the wine.

"I cannot do this." She turned to run for the door. Dimitri stepped in front of her, catching her around her waist with his single free arm. Had she continued to run, she was sure he would have simply lifted her from her feet.

"Yes you can," said Valar, resting his hand on her shoulder.

"You will be fine," Dimitri said in her ear. "You are not here to impress anyone." Piper nodded for Dimitri's sake as she fixed the wrinkles in her gown. She still wanted to run, but stood her ground. She took a glass of pearl wine from another passing tray and took a long drink. This time, she welcomed the small head rush. It calmed her, if only briefly.

The double doors creaked open, echoing around the large room. Jayson and Jack entered with Princess Gemari. Piper wondered where Leo may have been, then realized he had probably stopped to speak with a tunnel architect. She smiled at the thought, and a small bit of relief washed over her as she went to join her friends. The recognition caught her slightly off guard. Friends. They were her friends. She had no friends, save for Dimitri, even as a child. Friends. The thought brightened her, or perhaps it was the sudden consumption of the pearl wine.

"Greetings, my lady—oh! Piper! It's you!" Jayson hadn't recognized her at first. She looked so mature. And cleaner. He threw his arms around her, and squeezed her so tight he lifted her from the ground. She laughed and hugged him back. It was something she never would have done a week ago. "I'm so glad you're okay," he said, "Freak, man, I am so sorry I...well, I guess I nearly got you killed, huh? Sorry about that." He scratched his head, making the hair at the back of his head stand up at an awkward angle.

Piper giggled again, and reached up to smooth his hair. She was thankful to finally be away from the formalities of the elders, Nefiri and Valar. Here, she could be herself.

"Jack," said a sweet voice behind them. They turned to see Gemari smiling her brilliantly white smile at them. "This is my sister, Ketari." The Princess addressed the tall girl standing beside her. Ketari, who seemed much older than Gemari, nodded to them in greeting. Jack bowed low, attempting the proper Dwarvik way, and Jayson

115

followed suit. Ketari could not have been more different from Gemari. She was very thin, her clothes adorned with beautiful blue and amber beads that reflected the gold in her eyes. She stuck her chin out and never smiled. She looked down her long nose at Jack, her eyes sweeping from head to toe and back again. Her golden-brown eyes narrowed slightly, and Jack took a step back.

"So you are the one filling my baby sister's head with rebellious ideas." Her accent caught in her throat with a menacing rasp. "As my sister's retainer, it is my responsibility to keep her from such dangers, but I can see why she fancies you so." Dimitri nearly choked on his pearl wine, and both Gemari and Jack blushed scarlet.

"My lady," Jack stammered, "I...I simply wish to help your sister attain what will make her most happy. She seems to believe you would be far more acquainted to her role than she. Might I inquire as to your interest in such a...uh...venture?"

The group quieted and stared at Jack with varying degrees of awe.

"Goodness, Jack," said Piper. "May I take you on as my head advisor?" She laughed, hiccupped, and took another drink.

"Gemari may be young," Ketari continued. The side grin that had tugged at the corner of her mouth vanished, "but she is the rightful Princess and heir. She may have much to learn, but it is the way of things. And I will be here to guide her. It is my duty." Ketari nodded, and Gemari smiled at her adoringly.

"So, you have absolutely no interest in being the Princess?" asked Jayson, "Even if Gemari were willing to just give it to you?"

"I do not see how this can be done," Ketari said frowning. "Gemari is Princess, not I. Your customs must be written in the clouds that they can be changed with the direction of the wind! I appreciate your concern for my sister's happiness, but I can assure you, she is where she is destined to be."

"And what of Orctkar?" asked Jack.

"What of him?" Ketari asked. It was hard for Jack to imagine the young woman's tone could be more serious and sinister. Gemari stood behind Ketari, and shook her head vivaciously. "They are friends. You would not imply the Princess has been having romantic relationships, would you?"

Gemari's eyes widened and she continued to shake her head.

"As if," said Jayson. "But, let's say she did like him, or someone else. As Queen or Empress, she can't get married. That's so not fair. Doesn't everyone deserve to be happy, and find true love and all that stuff?"

"No." Ketari turned on her heel and glided away, leaving everyone to stare at her back until she faded into the crowd.

"I see what you mean about her," Jack murmured turning back to his friends.

"Jack, you nearly ruined it all!" Gemari shrieked, and gave Jack a shove.

Jack took a step back. "I'm sorry! What did I say?"

"Orctkar! Everyone knows we are only friends."

"I'm sorry, Gemari. I'm really not that good at this stuff, honest!"

"Oh! Look! There he is!" As quickly as she had angered, Gemari's voice brightened back into its high pitched sweetness. She pointed to a doorway in the far corner of the room where a boy could be seen standing and speaking with someone. They couldn't make out his face, but he seemed to be slightly older than Gemari with a muscular physique nearly as strong as Dimitri's.

"He works in the kitchens," said Gemari. "Come! Please meet him. He is my best friend!" She pulled on Jack's arm, leading him through the crowd. Jack turned wide eyed to his friends and mouthed help me. Jayson, Dimitri and Piper stifled laughs as they followed.

They walked across the room, the crowd parting before them. Princess Gemari had to stop often to bow to the elders. She hurried through the throng as quickly as she could, pulling Jack behind her as she went. Jayson attempted to grab as much food as he could along the way, but there were too many elders between him and the tables that lined the walls for it to be of any real success. He dared not interrupt the half intoxicated Dwarvik women in the middle of their gossip.

"Hello, Orctkar," said Gemari sweetly, and tapped the boy on the shoulder. He turned sharply, pushing a pretty young girl behind him, who took off into the kitchens. Gemari was mid bow when she stopped. She stood, trying to peer around Orctkar's shoulder into the kitchens beyond. "Who was that?"

she asked, her voice dropping its sweet demeanor and sounding almost exactly like her sister's. Jack tried to back away, but was blocked by Piper, Dimitri and Jayson. They stood shoulder to shoulder behind him, sipping pearl wine and eating stuffed mushrooms.

"Greetings, Princess. Uh...that was Avantria. She is new to the kitchens. I have been...helping her."

"How kind of you to be so friendly," said Dimitri. Piper elbowed him and half snorted into her glass.

"Orctkar, what is happening here?" Gemari asked. "The kitchen is no place for a woman. She cannot possibly work here."

"It is nothing! I promise, Princess!" Orctkar was turning redder by the minute.

"What do you mean nothing? Isn't that what you said about her?" This time, it was Avantria. She must not have disappeared into the kitchens very far. Jack tried to back away again, but Jayson pushed him forward again. Jack stumbled into Gemari, slipping on the smooth stone floor in his unfamiliar shoes. He reached out, catching Gemari's arm to steady himself. Gemari turned to him, and pulled him to her, pressing her lips to his. Still off balance, Jack had nowhere to go but forward. He pinned Gemari against the wall, still kissing her. Piper nearly dropped her drink as her hand clasped to her mouth. Jayson gasped and tried not to laugh. Dimitri grabbed Piper's and Jayson's elbows on either side of him. He pulled them close to him, keeping their shoulders together to hide the scene from the view of the elders.

Gemari pushed Jack away from her. He stumbled back into Dimitri who caught him, and placed a hand on his shoulder to keep him from running.

"Your untrustworthiness to the Royals and Elders has been noted, Orctkar," Gemari said. She turned swiftly, and though completely flushed, looked exactly like Ketari as she pushed past Jayson and back into the room. Orctkar tried to run after her, but Jayson stepped in front of him.

"Dude, I think you should just refill the wine, okay?" He said. Orctkar looked into the stern faces of Princess Gemari's friends, and turned back toward the kitchens.

"Avantria! Wait!" he called, and the kitchen door closed behind him.

Jack stood frozen, staring at the kitchen door before him. That wasn't the way he had imagined his first kiss. Dimitri pushed a glass of pearl wine into his hand. "Come, Jack," he said and placed his arm around Jack's shoulder. "Believe me when I say this sort of thing happens more often than any elder or royal would care to admit. Especially early in their career. These are the secret matters of state that no one discusses. By the time you've finished that, it will all be over."

"It's all peachy-keen, jellybean!" said Jayson, who had obviously begun to feel the effects of the pearl wine. "Let's go get some food," he said, headed for the table piled high with cream cakes.

Chapter Ten

The Black Diamonds

The gems on Leo's cuffs dug into his wrists as his captor twisted his arms behind him. The glint of a sword hilt caught Leo's eye. He watched it sway back and forth at the man's side. Leo knew if he could get it in his hands, he could fight his way out and escape. Not that it would do him much good. He still had no idea where he was. The dwarves knew their mines far better than he did. They'd have him recaptured in no time. No, Leo needed to be patient. He needed to bide his time. He needed to explain his case, find out who these people were and what they wanted with him. Now he wished he had Jack's gift of words, or even Jayson's sense of humor and wit. He wasn't so sure logical reasoning would get him very far with the dwarves.

A horn sounded somewhere, and the activity in the center square below him ceased. The people below stared up at the new, pale skinned prisoner they had never seen before. As one, they all moved quickly to the houses around the perimeter. Doors slammed shut. Curtains were pulled over windows. Leo wondered which Quarter he had stumbled into. It wasn't anything like the other Quarters he had visited.

For one, these were the first houses he had seen in the entire mountain. The other Quarters were designed more like motels. And, he had never seen anything like a village square before either. The hasanas worked for other merchants who did their trade and work from the common area at the front of their homes. Except for the kitchens. Everyone was supplied with basic food necessities every week. They paid for anything extra or extravagant. Leo thought it was a good system. No one had to worry about being hungry. But the few people he glimpsed did look hungry. They were thin and bony, and their eyes looked sunken in.

The man holding Leo's arms walked him toward a door at the far side of the mine. It opened, and Leo was blinded by the bright light of the outdoors. It had been days since he had seen proper sunlight. Leo stopped and closed his eyes before the man shoved him out the door.

There was a small ledge with a straight drop down to the forest below. Leo realized he was at the far eastern side of the mountain closest to the Belirian Forest. The man pushed Leo into a cage woven from ropes and branches, and locked the door. He watched as the man unwound a rope from a nearby rock, and the cage began to rise and sway as it was lifted up and out over the sheer drop below.

"I swear, I didn't do anything! I'm really sorry! I just got lost!" Leo exclaimed. He clutched at the rickety ropes of the cage, and tried in vain to keep his voice from cracking.

The door to the mountain opened and two men stepped out onto the ledge. Their curly black beards sparkled in the sunlight, decorated with tiny black gems. They did not wear the armor of the Dwarvik guards, but pure black metal and leather. A realization began to form in Leo's mind, and he stopped struggling against his prison. The tallest of the men walked slowly up to the cage, and gave it a gentle turn. Leo could hear the ropes creaking, but stayed his hand from grasping at the bars in panic.

He had to show no fear in the face of these adversaries.

"You look like no elf or human I have ever seen," said the man. His voice was deep and smooth. "Where are you from, and how did you find us?"

Leo swallowed hard and took a deep breath. "My name is Leo DeHaven. I am not from your world. My friends, Jack and Jayson, and me, we…we are from another planet, or dimension or something. We don't know how we got here. There was this light, and we woke up here. We met Piper from Outland Post, and she helped us. We came here with her and Dimitri when Empress Nefiri sent him to get us. I think she wants to talk about Taraniz, but I don't know what that's got to do with us. I was going to the pre-banquet and I got lost." He inhaled again, having spoken the entirety of his speech in a single breath. "You're— you're The Black Diamonds, aren't you?"

The dwarf smiled at Leo. "You are observant, little man. What else do you know that may be of use to me? Speak well, or you may find yourself meeting not with the elders, but a rather agonizing end." He swung the cage away from him and gazed over the edge of the drop off. Leo watched as the man kicked a stone over the side. He heard it bounce out of ear shot as his cage slowly spun.

"What…what do you want to know?" Leo couldn't hide the fear in his voice this time.

The other man, dressed nearly identical to the first laughed a hearty, belly laugh. "Oh, haven't you scared the lad enough, Kylani? Let him down."

"No!" said Kylani. "He may be a spy for Nefiri or Una."

"I'm not! I promise! Please, let me go! I'll...I'll talk to the council on your behalf. I'm on your side, I swear!"

The two men looked at each other, then at Leo. Now he'd done it. Leo swallowed and clasped his hand to his mouth. He had promised to do that which he had sworn he wouldn't: interfere in Chartile. Prophecy or no, he reminded himself – and his friends – constantly that this was not their world. It was not their battle to fight. But there had been an unspoken promise between them. Once they had proven the existence of the prophecy, wouldn't they try to fulfill it? To right the wrongs of the land? And even if the prophecy did not exist, if Leo believed in it, didn't it give him the responsibility to carry it out regardless?

Kylani approached Leo, holding the cage in place. He brought his face so close to Leo's, the boy could see his beard and hair were dyed black. "You would do this? Why?"

"Where I come from, everyone's the same. I don't see why it would be different for dwarves. Plus, I'm sure you have some great ideas to, like, help defeat Taraniz, and stuff."

"And stuff," Kylani repeated. Leo nodded and stared into the man's dark brown eyes.

"Why would we want to defeat Princess Taraniz, when she has promised us the rights we desire if we fight for her?" the second man asked from behind Kylani.

"Brande! Hush!" Kylani glared fiercely at the other dwarf.

Leo was quiet. He was sure this was information that neither Empress Nefiri nor even Dimitri could have known about. If Taraniz had started infiltrating the dwarves from the inside, their downfall would be much easier and faster.

Kylani turned slowly back to Leo. "Well?" he asked, "What say you, little man?"

"Because she's mean?" Leo answered.

Kylani and Brande fell into a fit of merciless guffaws and laughter. Leo's face turned bright red. After several uncomfortable moments, the two men took several deep breaths and wiped the tears from their eyes. The man called Brande moved the cage back to the ledge. He held the door open, but Leo did not move.

"Come, young friend. We believe your intentions to be true. My name is Brande, and this is my brother, Kylani. Let us speak."

Leo stepped unsteadily from the cage. Kylani caught him, and patted Leo firmly on the back. Brande led the way back inside as the guard who had first caught Leo glared.

The dwarves were beginning to emerge from their homes again. They cautiously skirted around Leo, and pulled their children away from him as they went. Although the society of The Black Diamonds seemed mostly comprised of men, Leo was surprised to see a few women as well. The center square they passed through had a number of tents and make shift merchant stands. Everything from food and clothing to armor and weapons was available for sale.

Brande and Kylani led Leo through another door at the far side of the mine. It opened into a short tunnel that turned sharply and immediately opened into another large, abandoned mine. This mine consisted entirely of the little wooden homes that dotted the edges of the first mine. Side by side, some leaning awkwardly, others straight and nearly perfect, there had to be at least a hundred little houses within, creating a unique cityscape with walkways between rows of homes, and poles with hanging lanterns.

Leo stopped in the doorway. His eyes gaped at the scene before him. Brande clapped him on the back with a chuckle and urged him forward through yet another door. This one opened into a small, dusty room. A table and chairs sat at the center, each with a large black diamond the size of Leo's fist fixed at the top and center.

Brande pulled three black chalices and a glass decanter from a cabinet by the door. He poured the golden liquid into the chalices, and dropped a pearl-like sphere in each that began to bubble.

"Pearl wine?" he asked Leo. The boy hesitated, then took the chalice. There was a high chance he could be imprisoned again after this meeting. This might be his first and last time having an alcoholic beverage. He raised the cup in a small gesture of a toast and took a sip. The wine was thick and tart, and the pearl-like mineral created tiny bubbles that rose up into Leo's nose making him cough and choke. Brande and Kylani laughed again and patted his back.

"You take this black diamond thing for real, huh?" Leo asked. He raised the black chalice in his hand, attempting to steer the conversation away from his embarrassing splutter. The two men took their seats across the table.

"And why not?" asked Brande.

"Do you know what a diamond is, Leo, my boy?" Kylani set his chalice on the table and leaned forward.

"A clear mineral...uh...carbon, I think, that....when put under immense pressure in the right conditions forms a lattice-like structure. That's what makes them so strong."

Brande nodded with a smirk and replied, "Diamonds, though extremely rare, are absolutely perfect. There are few other minerals that can penetrate its lattice work."

"Sometimes," Kylani continued, "a rogue mineral does penetrate it, and a beautiful, even rarer mineral is created. Black diamonds, though more fragile than their pure white form, are just as beautiful in their own right, if given the chance."

"But the world can't be divided into just black and white. Think of all the other colors that can be created when you mix the two together." Leo sipped his wine. The tiny bubbles rose into his nose again, reminding him he was not absently drinking water. He attempted not to make a face as the tannins spread across his tongue.

"An intriguing point, lad," said Brande. He raised his chalice in salute and drained it. "But if you only see the world as one color, and someone gives you the opportunity to make it so, would you take it?"

"You mean Taraniz, don't you?" asked Leo, pushing his chalice away from him.

"She is planning to attack Mount Kelsii within the month. By bringing the Dwarves under Elven rule, it will also bring us under their law, where men and women have more equal rights." Kylani drained his chalice, too. He slammed it on the table, making Leo jump. "We are tired of not having a voice on the council! There are plenty of men who have found their souls. They will not give us the chance to prove it!"

"I don't understand," said Leo. He remembered Dimitri had said something about souls as well. "What do you mean your souls?"

"There are three Levels of Understanding," said Brande, holding up three fingers. "Your Mind is what you know, what you reason to be true, just and moral. Your Heart is your instinct, what you have never learned, but have always known. Your Soul is your emotion, your ability to show compassion or mercy. It is believed that men cannot, or have difficulty, finding their souls. This is why we are not permitted a seat on the council. An elder must be able to show balance in all three Levels of Understanding. Princess Taraniz does not, however, understand our religion in this regard. By aligning with her, we gain rights to sit on the council, but we lose the right to practice our religion. The Elves find our ways too magical for their tastes, though this is not true. Dwarves cannot do magic. We never have and we never will. It is not in our blood. Our council would become more like the Elven Conclave of Nobles."

"So, if I speak to the council for, you won't fight for Taraniz?" Leo folded his hands on the table before him. He wasn't sure if it was all the philosophical talk of souls and understanding or the wine, but he was becoming light headed.

"Not just speak, Leo. We want a negotiated seat with the elders," said Kylani. "The Black Diamond Quarter has the right to a voice. Even if the rest of the dwarves do not wish to follow our ways, we all have the right to protect each other."

Leo grabbed his head. This was all very confusing.

"We knew who you were the moment you came to Fortress Kelsii," said Brande. "Not all of us are in hiding here. We have infiltrated every aspect of the Fortress. Guards, miners, tailors, priestesses. We have a person in almost every conceivable position and within nearly every household and guild." He paused and waited for Leo to sit up again. "And not just here. We have begun to reach The Tutarian Mountains as well. There are members on the council who are loyal to us. Even Queen Isla. I refuse to believe that you finding us today was a mere coincidence."

"So it's true, what Empress Nefiri said. Queen Isla's been working with you. Is it true she's also got a boyfriend who is a Black Diamond, too?" asked Leo.

Kylani stood slowly. He stared down at Leo, his black eyes glistening with tears. "My dearest Isla has been one of us since before her ascension to Queenhood. You are King Florine, returned to us as the prophecy foretold. Right this wrong. We do not want to kill our people."

There it was. The weight of an entire race had just been put on the shoulders of a fourteen year old boy. The chance to interfere, for good or ill, had been laid upon the table, ripe for the taking. Leo had thought he had been fighting it tooth and nail. Now it seemed he had no choice. He was backed into a corner. To refuse would mean he had been a bystander to the murders of hundreds, probably thousands of people.

Leo remembered back to a video game he had played with Jayson and Jack last year; so very long ago now. As the king in the game, he could choose whether to negotiate with the enemy or send his people to war. Jayson wanted to choose war. There was better armor and weapons. Jack said he should choose to negotiate because there were more level ups to intelligence and persuasion. It was at that moment, the rain outside had ended and they decided to go to their fort. The video game was never touched again— a decision still waiting to be made.

Leo stood to meet Kylani's gaze. Brande stood with him. They looked at each other across the table, tense, unmoving, black-brown eyes meeting blue eyes.

"I'm sorry," said Leo, "I can't do it. I'm just a kid. If this is what you guys want, then you need to come out of the shadows and, like, fight for it. And not by killing people and stuff, either. That's not going to do anybody any good. You have to prove you deserve to be there. You can't put this all on me."

Chapter Eleven

The Meeting of the Elders

Jayson was enjoying some sort of strange, spikey fruit when Leo placed a hand on his shoulder.

"What is that?" Leo asked, his nose crinkling as Jayson turned.

Jayson nearly choked. "Dude! Where the heck have you been?" Jack, Dimitri and Piper turned to see Leo shoulder through beside Jayson to join their circle.

"I got turned around. Ended up in some abandoned mines." he replied and reached for a small stuffed mushroom.

"You are lucky you made it here at all then," said Dimitri. He popped a mushroom in his mouth with one hand, the other rested comfortably around Piper's waist. "Most of the abandoned mines are on the other side of the mountain, and are quite dangerous. There is a reason they are no longer used. It is rare their veins are dried up. It is more likely to do with the stability of the cavern."

"Well, here I am! When is this thing supposed to start anyway?" Leo asked. He seemed too giddy. He bounced on the balls of his feet, and swung his arms to his sides. His friends wondered if he had been given a glass of pearl wine when he entered. No one said anything. The thought was too unlike Leo. After the incident with Jack and Gemari, they were looking for any reason to be cheerful. The dread and anticipation of the council meeting seemed to be breathing down their necks.

The activity in the room seemed to bubble into a chaotic frenzy. Council members flitted back and forth amongst their small groups, whispering to each other anxiously. A horn sounded in the far corner of the room. Guards filed through the large doors to stand around the perimeter of the room. The council members took their seats at the long table. Nefiri, the Queens and Princesses made their way to the plain, tall backed thrones in front of the raised platform. Valar emerged from somewhere amongst the bedlam of the elders and their retainers. He touched Piper's shoulder. She jumped, and the color drained from her face as she turned to him. Valar nodded and smiled. Dimitri kissed her cheek, then hurried away to stand behind Nefiri's throne.

Jack, Leo and Jayson looked at each other. They seemed to be the only still figures as the occupants of the room flitted wildly around them.

"No matter what happens," said Jayson, "we have to stand together." The wonder of their adventure was beginning to fade, and a heavy weight seemed to be settling on them with each council member that joined at the long table at the center of the room.

"Agreed," said Leo and Jack nodded. "I need you guys to just follow my lead, okay. Please just trust me." They did. They trusted each other unconditionally. They had to. They had been through too much together not to believe in each other. They turned to take their seats beside Piper and Valar on the raised platform behind the royalty. The horn sounded again, and silence fell.

The kitchen staff continued to bustle back and forth, filling chalices with pearl wine and water.

The boys noted that while there were both humans with orenite cuffs on their wrists and dwarves, there was not a single girl or woman among them. Leo shifted uneasily in his chair as one of the elders stood to address the council.

"This Council has been called to decide the succession of Empress Nefiri of the House of Auldfr and the involvement of the Dwarves in the civil war of the Elves of Chartile." The woman sat and yielded to Nefiri. The Empress stood and glided a few steps forward to address the table of elders before her. The boys craned their necks to look at her over their shoulders. Piper caught their eyes, and shook her head only once. They immediately faced forward again and tried to not fidget.

"Good Elders, Royals and honored guests. It has been my privilege and honor to serve as your Empress these past sixty-seven turns. I now find myself beginning to tire, as the stone does under the beating winds. I have felt the calling of our Lady Rashiri, and wish to spend the last of my days in service to our Goddess. Though I may depart from this throne, our people shall never fade!" Nefiri paused, and spread her arms wide. "Strength and stone!"

"Strength and stone!" The Council echoed her and raised their glasses in a toast.

"Who now will speak on behalf of Queen Isla and Princess Faeridae of the Tutarian Mountains?" the same woman as before stood again and asked.

An old woman, her beaded braids flecked with gray stood. She had attempted to paint her skin to appear less weathered, but the affect was quite the opposite. "I am Ulfwyn of the House of Hallvor of the Cobalt Quarter. I speak for Queen Isla of the House of Arnkatla. Queen Isla has served the people of the Tutarian Mountains for over seventeen turns. She succeeded Queen Carendeil of the House of Esjamourn when she went home to the stone and our Lady Rashiri too soon. Queen Isla is trained in the ways of war, and has been a valuable asset in training our army in the Tutarian Mountains. She would be instrumental in protecting our people during this time of upheaval amongst the Elves, should she so choose our involvement. I vote that Queen Isla succeed Nefiri of the House of Auldfr as Empress of the Dwarves of Chartile."

Ulfwyn sat, and there were many smiles and small gestures of toasting, but nothing more. The boys dared glances at each other. This was going to be a long meeting.

A younger woman rose from her seat to address the council. She was Lady Ulfwyn's opposite. Her hair had been brushed straight without the traditional beads. Rather, a pattern of gold runes and symbols had been painted down her long plait and matched the gold painted around her eyes and lips.

"I am Ygdalla of the House of Dryfinal of the Amethyst Quarter of the Tutarian Mountains. I speak for Princess Faeridae of the House of Gudvor. Faeridae was made Princess when our Queen Isla unexpectedly succeeded Queen Carendeil. She chose to be trained in War like her Queen before her, but has also shown a great aptitude for negotiations amongst the elders and wisdom beyond her years. If Queen Isla succeeds as Empress, Princess Faeridae would indeed complement not only our new

Empress, but work well with Queen Una and Princess Gemari of Mount Kelsii. I vote that Queen Isla succeed Nefiri of the House of Auldfr as Empress of the Dwarves of Chartile." Jack Leo, and Jayson saw Ygdalla flash them a quick smile and a wink as she sat. She had the air of a woman who knew her beauty, and knew how to use it.

The elder who had first spoke stood again. "Thank you, Elders. Who now will speak on behalf of Queen Una and Princess Gemari of Mount Kelsii?"

Another elder stood to address the Council, and the boys' shoulders drooped. As nervous as they were, their attention was waning. Or the feast prior to the meeting was beginning to kick in. The elder was the same wispy woman, Frejah, who had approached Piper earlier at the pre-banquet. She still looked as though a single sneeze could knock her to the floor. But her voice had turned unexpectedly firm and commanding.

"I am Frejah of the House of Berkhildr of the Carnelian Quarter of Mount Kelsii. I speak for Queen Una of the House of Ulfra. Queen Una is the first Queen in over five appointed Queens to Mount Kelsii to apply herself to the study of both peace and war. Her skills will come as a valuable asset to our people in this time of uncertainty. I vote that Queen Una succeed Nefiri of the House of Auldfr as Empress of the Dwarves of Chartile."

Elder Frejah sat. She was winded but still threw back a glass of ale. She snapped at the passing human to refill her glass as soon as she set it back on the table. It was the first time Jayson, Jack and Leo noticed the symbol on the woman's sleeve. A rose crossing a sword. Gemari had told them it was the symbol for the warrior class of women. Only Empresses could be granted this special privilege after being succeeded by an Empress of peace. Nefiri must have succeeded Frejah and asked her to command the armies as Nefiri was trained in peace, not war. A recommendation for Empresshood coming from a previous Empress would surely make this a cut and dry case in Una's favor, the boys thought.

Nefiri stood again from her throne. This time, she did not step forward. "I am Nefiri of the House of Auldfr and Empress of the Dwarves of Chartile. I speak for Princess Gemari of the House of Jetari. Gemari was chosen as our Princess after Princess Thora was called back to the stone too soon. Though young in years, Gemari has shown wisdom beyond her age. She was instrumental in the negotiations concerning the reopening of the Eastern mines of Mount Kelsii for their refortification and the safety of our patrols. As an emeritus Empress and priestess of Rashiri, I vow to this council that I will take it upon myself to continue to train Princess Gemari until such a time that she ascends to Empresshood, or the council deems my instruction no longer necessary. I vote for Queen Una to succeed me as Empress of the Dwarves of Chartile."

Nefiri sat. Dimitri stepped from behind her high-backed throne and handed her a crystal chalice. She sipped daintily and stared hard at the elders. The elder who had opened the council meeting stood again.

"Now that the representatives of the candidates have spoken, the floor is open for any who wish to speak on behalf of Queen Isla, Queen Una, Princess Faeridae or Princess Gemari."

Whispering ensued amongst the council, but no one stood. The boys could feel Nefiri's eyes on the back of their heads and the hairs on their necks stood up. Neither Piper nor Valar made a move to stand. Jayson and Jack half expected Leo to stand and address the council. Follow my lead, he had said. Jack had prepared a small speech in favor of Una and Gemari, but he held back, waiting for some signal from Leo. After several moments, the elder spoke again, "If there are no further favors to be heard, then we shall move to vote. Those voting for Queen Isla please stand." The chairs shuffled and scraped against the stone floor and over half of council members stood. They waited until one of the elders had finished counting and recorded her notes before sitting again. "Those voting for Queen Una, please stand." There were fewer council members. At least four fewer, the boys noted, and they began to feel sick. "Then by the witness of this council and Mother Rashiri, I am pleased to announce the succession of Empress Nefiri by Queen Isla of the House of Arnkatla. The Rite of Passage shall take place at the nearest sunset after this meeting."

"NO!" someone shouted. Their voice echoed off the high domed ceiling and brought the council to a dead silence. "I will not stand for this!" It was Queen Una. She rose from her throne, her face red even under her ebony skin. "I will not allow someone who has been meeting in secret with The Black Diamonds to sit on the throne of the Empress!

We have intelligence that Isla has not only been meeting with these dangerous people, but is also in an unauthorized and illegal relationship with one of its leaders! Elders, I implore you to reconsider!"

"Isla, is this true?" asked one of the elders. The frantic whispering that had followed Una's words stopped. Isla looked at the women before her as they waited with baited breath for an answer. She stood, and, to Jack and Jayson's surprise, so did Leo. They joined him, though unsure of what plan they were about to execute. They had to leave their weapons in their rooms, but there were far too many guards to attempt any kind of hand to hand combat anyway. They dared to look at Nefiri. Her eyes were wide, almost maddening with anger. Gemari was on the verge of tears.

Isla reached beneath the neckline of her tunic and pulled out a small but unmistakable amulet of a large black diamond.

"It's true," she said. The council gasped and immediately began arguing amongst themselves. Leo looked at the man at the door while everyone watched Isla. He nodded. The doors swung open, and in marched a string of warriors. They were clad in the black leather and sparkling black jewels of the soldiers of The Black Diamonds. The elders ceased their arguments. No one moved. Not the guards, not Leo, not even Isla who had been caught off guard herself. Soldier after soldier marched into the room. Their footfalls echoed as one, creating a drum beat that shook the hearts pounding wildly in everyone's chests. Some of the council members rose to stand beside Isla, also bearing the amulet of The Black Diamonds around their necks. Ulfwyn and Ygdalla were among them. Retainers and kitchen staff left their posts to stand beside Isla as well, unafraid to show their black diamond bracelets, rings and necklaces. Kylani, Brande, and a few other members of the Black Diamonds joined the throng of people surrounding Isla and Faeridae.

When the last of the soldiers had filed into the room, the doors were closed. Six Black Diamond soldiers stood guard against it. Leo descended the steps from the platform. He bowed in perfect Dwarvik fashion to each of the Queens, Princesses and Nefiri. The fire and rage in the Empress's eyes was even worse than before. Leo gulped and turned to address the remaining council members at the long table.

"Good Elders! I am Leonardo DeHaven, the reincarnated soul of King Florine. I present to you, your future."

Chapter Twelve
Foundations Shaken

Leo's speech had sounded much cooler in his head, but he was no Jack. Regardless, the entire room's attention was fixated on him. Queen Una had sat back on her throne when the Black Diamonds had marched in. She whispered frantically to Nefiri who remained stone faced and emotionless to Una's words.

The Black Diamonds had filed into the room and covered the entire perimeter at least two deep. As one, they drew their swords with their right hands and touched their left shoulders with the hilt in a kind of salute. There was a unified clank of hilt against armor, then quiet. The silence was as tangible as the effects of the pearl wine.

A frail and fierce old woman finally whispered against the stillness. "Wh-what is the meaning of this? What in Verika's good name is happening here?"

"Is it not obvious, Imohan?" asked another silver haired elder a few seats from the first. "We are being threatened to change or die. Apparently, the traditions we have worked so hard to keep strong have been undermined and thrown to the wind under our very noses."

"Lady Jarvae, please, that is not our aim," said Faeridae sweetly from behind the boys.

"Isn't it?" shrieked Jarvae. She stood from her seat so swiftly, she nearly knocked her chair over if the woman beside her had not caught it. "The Black Diamonds have been after us for years to put a man on this council. Now it appears we have no choice. We have been surrounded, quite literally in fact. We surrender to this new regime or die, I suppose."

"Hear me, good elders," said Isla. The boys turned to see her unwind her fingers from Kylani's as she stepped forward. The gesture was noticed by several of the elders as well. "We are an organization of the people. Your very presence upon this council is proof we govern not ourselves or our people, but that our people govern us. Since my rise to Queenhood, whispers in the shadows have reached my ears of the pleading of our people for change. For equality. Not just our men, but our fellow women have joined in secret and taken up support of a new era for the Dwarves. An era in which our hearts, and souls are not governed by the gender bestowed on us by Rashiri, but by our actions. The people have cried out for change, and we have stood idly by, unwilling to move beyond the laws that are comfortable and familiar, not necessarily the ways that are right and just. Within every Quarter, every household, every caste from the elders to the miners, we have listened to our people and have grown. Your men and women have not been killed and kidnapped. They have run away to live amongst their fellows as equals in the mines that Princess Gemari so very graciously reconstructed for our use. Unbeknownst to her, of course. We are great in number. Your people have spoken, and it is our right as the leaders of our people to do the bidding of those we have been called to represent, regardless of our own personal aims or beliefs."

"How can you expect us to simply give up what has taken us centuries to create? You are asking a great deal, Isla," said Imohan. "Might I add that the actions you have admitted to this day disqualify you from succession to the Empresshood."

"Only if you let it be so!" protested Isla, the fear rising in her voice. "Elders, there is a war raging at our heels, outside our very doors. Sooner or later it will descend on us. Unless we fight back and take our stand before it's too late."

"Our intelligence tells us Princess Taraniz is planning to strike Mount Kelsii at the end of the month," said Kylani. He stepped forward to stand beside Isla, and several of the elders sneered. "Our forces in the Tutarian Mountains may not come to us in time. The force of soldiers stationed here will not be enough to hold back the Elves and Taraniz's allies."

The elders narrowed their eyes and flared their nostrils. Their disgust at being spoken to as an equal by a man was obvious.

"What allies are those, I wonder?" spat Jarvae. "Do not think we haven't heard about the Black Diamonds joining with Princess Taraniz."

"It does not have to be that way," said Kylani.

"So you admit it! You admit you have turned your back on your own people to gain what you seek! You would have us all dead or under Elven rule. You may be free to make decisions without a wife if you succeed, but the name of Rashiri will never be spoken again, I can guarantee you that." Jarvae sat abruptly. She folded her arms before her and nodded to those around her.

"Everyone makes mistakes." Eyes turned to Jack who stepped off the platform to join the crowd around Isla. Jayson glanced at Leo. Leo raised his eyebrows and shrugged. They both stepped from the platform to join Jack. "What's important is we need to band together now. Change isn't easy. Like, in our world, we've had a lot of changes. At first there were civil wars, and fighting, and stuff like that. But, in the end, there was peace. Change is totally scary. We've been through that. We were brought here against our will and we've had to change the way we live every day just to survive. If change is what your people want, then give it to them. Especially if that's what it takes to save them."

"If it doesn't work out, you can always go back to the way it was before," chimed in Jayson with a shrug.

The council broke into conversation once more. Jayson, Jack and Leo looked at Piper. She smiled proudly at them. They had grown so much in such a short time. She no longer doubted they were the Kings of old. But, that could only mean one thing. As soon as the boys turned away, her fear returned.

"Fine!" shouted Jarvae above the crowd. "If this is what it takes to save our people, then so be it. However, Isla and Faeridae, you shall be placed on probation and await trial for your actions. If you are found guilty of conspiracy, regardless of this permanent or temporary change in our ways, you will be stripped of your titles and banished outside Dwarvik territory for the rest of your days. Nefiri, will you agree to remain Empress until this matter is resolved?"

143

"I will," said Nefiri coldly. She glared at Isla and Faeridae.

"There still remains the dilemma of who will take the throne once Princess Taraniz has been killed or captured," said Ulfwyn. "To our knowledge, there are no other heirs to the Elven throne. With no one to claim the throne, the Elven territories will fall to civil war. Noble and commoner alike will vie for the crown. Usurping Taraniz may end one war and launch Chartile, and us, into another."

"I believe I may be able to assist in this matter, elders," said Valar, rising from his seat. He approached the council with a leather bound book and a stack of papers.

"Many of you remember our Queen Runa, late wife of King Aramor. What few knew was her grandfather was human, and she inherited his magic. For this reason, she was hidden away when she came with child. The populace was told she was ill, but truly she was locked away in a tower. She was unable to hide her magic any longer while carrying. Orenite cuffs were made for her, and she was often chained to the walls of the tower. Our Elven council will say it is because she was prone to sleep walking, but this is untrue. King Aramor believed the now deceased Head of the Elven council, Taervane. He claimed Runa's magic during pregnancy had made her mad and unstable. He said it was for the protection of all that she remain sequestered away in the tower. I visited Runa and can say she was far from mad. She was disheartened and afraid, and though her belly grew, she withered away before my eyes.

"I tell you this as only a few of us were present when Runa gave birth. Aramor and the physicians feared removing the orenite cuffs during this process. As with Humans, there was the risk of injury to those present if the orenite was removed. But the risk to her health was more severe. Keeping the orenite cuffs intact was to her demise. She died in childbirth. Yes, it could have been prevented. The decision was made to cut the child from her dead body, and it was discovered she carried twins."

A muttering moved like a wave up one side of the table and down the other. Valar waited several seconds before continuing.

"The first child was given to Aramor. I watched him cry as I never have before. The second child was thrust at me by the physician. Aramor paced the room for several hours. Runa's body lay on the bed between us. Both children screamed and cried, but he would not look at the one I held. Finally, Aramor asked me, "Is it a boy?" I answered him no. He told me to be rid of the child. He refused to have his kingdom torn apart by feuding sisters. He gave the first child back to the physician and left the room.

"I could not kill the child. It had not asked for this. I had a friend, Kaytah Chaudoin, a palace scribe, and her daughter and son-in-law, who lived at the very edge of Elven territory. I knew they had not been blessed with children, and were likely not to be. I decided to leave the child in their care. She would grow up as far away from the palace as possible. Several years later, I confided in Kaytah the true identity of her granddaughter. I revealed to her that my intentions were never to use the child as a pawn to gain the throne. Kaytah was furious with me, and we spoke little afterward. But, I began to see the child accompany her on her trips to the palace, and even here to Mount Kelsii."

"You knowingly disobeyed your king and assisted in raising an heir in secret?" asked one of the elders. "Circumstances seem awfully convenient that Princess Taraniz has started down a path to her own ruin, and you are the only one able to guide this new heir."

"With Runa's magic becoming so strong during her pregnancy, I knew nothing good could come of such omens," said Valar calmly.

"How do we know anything good will come of this new heir?" asked another. "If she is of the same blood as Taraniz, will she not be like her?"

"Your story is all good and well, Valar, but you know this council cannot make a decision based on your word alone," said Jarvae. "What proof do you have? Where is Kaytah to support this? I know Kaytah well, and I remember the child she used to bring with her. I know exactly whom we are speaking of, Valar."

Valar stepped forward. He laid the small stack of papers in the center of the table before the elders.

"As many of you know, each year, a portrait is taken of each member of the royal family as part of our genealogical records. I have here the last known portraits of King Aramor, Queen Runa and Princess Taraniz." He stepped back and the elders passed the parchment between them. A few, including Jarvae looked at Piper as they studied the portraits. Some leaned in to their neighbors and discussed a facial feature or two before passing the papers on.

Piper rose from her chair and took Valar's outstretched hand. "Elders, I present to you the heir of King Aramor and Queen Runa, Princess Eva Ruani."

"What?" cried Jayson. Jack had to stop him from running to her, though they were all breathless with shock. Their minds raced with questions and scenarios. It was hard to believe this rough and unkempt young woman, who had been their only protector in a savage and unknown world, was the secret heir to the Elven throne. They fought to stay alert as Piper stepped from the platform. She smiled weakly and winked at them as she passed by.

"Valar, these portraits cannot be the only evidence you have to prove that this child is Runa's daughter." Frejah said standing to face him. "I believe we can all agree that Piper looks almost exactly like Runa, but…" She trailed off, looking to her fellow elders for support.

"This is not enough," said Ygdalla firmly. "If this is truly the granddaughter of Kaytah, we are aware she frequently companioned her during her travels. That does not mean this child has any experience in diplomacy or making decisions to govern an entire race."

"This is also not our decision to make, Valar," said Nefiri, her voice calm once more. "Why are you not presenting her to the Elven council?"

"The Elven council has been corrupted by Princess Taraniz. Though she has not shown the same signs of magic as Runa, I believe she has some form of power over those people close to her. There is no other explanation as to how she has been able to control the entire Elven army and most of the council before Aramor's death."

"Yet you were spared," Una sneered.

"A few others as well that I have been able to confide in these past three years. We have all spent much time away from the palace. We believe it is for this reason that her influence is not as strong over us." The man's eyes became glassy and distant, and his voice turned to a whisper. "When you are with her, you can feel a weight on your mind, and a tightening in your chest. She is forcing her will upon you. She is unpredictable. Three years ago, she was gregarious, intelligent, if haughty at times. Aramor's deterioration occurred when Taraniz began having incidents of panic attacks and anxiety that quickly turned to anger and downright madness at times. I believe she has a magic in her she cannot control. And unless we can find a way to dispel her of this magic, she is lost to us. If Piper has the support of the Dwarvik council, then her case to the Elven council once Taraniz has been dealt with, will be a much easier fight."

"Cannot the heir of Aramor and Runa speak for herself?" asked one of the younger elders who had not yet spoke. She was short and stern, and crossed her arms before her in defiance.

Piper looked at Valar and he nodded to her. Piper unhooked her arm from Valar's and walked the length of the long table. She held her chin high, and glided across the floor so unfamiliar to the boys. She turned to face the elders and royals, and Jack, Leo and Jayson saw that the Piper they knew had changed.

"I will speak true and say all that has been presented to you today was only told to me a few days ago. I admit, I grew up in a small village believing myself to be only the stubborn daughter of a blacksmith and healer. I believe Valar with all my heart, even if I doubt myself. You are right, all of you, to question my ability to rule. I question myself. But the day a ruler believes themselves to be all righteous and without fault is the day our people will fall. I have studied the laws of my people, played court to learn the ways of the Elves in high society with my grandmother, and I have an advisor willing and ready to guide me the rest of the way.

"I do not know if I will be worse than Taraniz, or as wonderful as Runa. But, as I stand before you this day, I vow to uphold the laws I believe to be true and just, to govern the Elven people of Chartile with humility and strength, and I will stand before the tides of life not as Eva Ruani, but as Piper Romilly, for that is who I am. I ask for your support as we work together for the good of our peoples, and the strengthening of all of Chartile. Will you have me as your Elven Queen, good elders? Will you stand with me as an equal to forge a better tomorrow?

"I ask you now, friends and strangers alike, no more fancy words, no more talk. Let us settle this and be done. For the good or ill of my future as Queen, I implore you to make your decision so we may begin the necessary preparations for defending our future together."

149

Chapter Thirteen

Lessons

Jayson, Jack and Leo lounged in the common area of their quarters after the council meeting. Several bottles of pearl wine and trays of herb stuffed mushrooms, cheeses and some sort of roasted mountain groundhog littered the floor and tables around them. The council had almost unanimously decided to support Piper, though they all agreed they had little choice. The meeting dispelled thereafter, and the boys hurried back to their rooms. The thought of being cornered and questioned by anyone was too daunting, and Jack didn't want to see Gemari try to hold back the tears any longer.

They ordered as much food and drink as they could think of, and attempted to put the stress of the day behind them. Since there were no age restrictions on alcohol in Chartile, Jack, Leo and Jayson were quite drunk soon into the evening. They recalled their tales of the day with far more vigor and guffawing than was really necessary. Leo told them about his encounter with the Black Diamonds, and his meeting with Kylani and Brande. Jayson and Jack drilled him for over an hour about the mines looked like. Leo took another swig of pearl wine and forced them to change the subject.

"Jack finally kissed Gemari," Jayson blurted.

"It's not what you think," said Jack when Leo's mouth fell open.

Jack launched into the story until Leo fell out of his chair, and rolled on the floor, kicking his feet with laughter. Jack was not amused and sent a piece of cheese flying at his friend's head. The night became a blur of stories and tales from their past, laughing and drinking until at least two empty bottles of wine rolled on the floor among the empty food trays.

The laughter died away, and silence hung in the air between them. They looked at each other, sipping their alcohol and watching the moon rise outside their window. It was almost the same moon that shown down on them their first night in Chartile. Their heads spun and their minds raced. They looked at the empty bottles in front of them. A tingle ran up their backs, and a knot formed in their stomachs that had little to do with the wine.

Jayson set his chalice down. He re-corked the wine bottle that sat on the table and placed it in the cupboard by the window. Neither Jack nor Leo stopped him. They would be attending a battle strategy meeting in the morning, followed by the responsibility of acting as liaisons between The Black Diamonds and the Council afterward. Leo and Jack poured the rest of their wine into the stone basin sink. They did not look at each other, but quietly headed to bed.

They wanted to believe the events they had experienced and helped to shape these past few days had made them grow up. Yet they couldn't shake and uncertainty that grew inside them. They doubted themselves, and they doubted each other. They had tried to suppress it, but the pearl wine sitting heavy on their stomachs made it far more difficult. Try as they might, they couldn't deny they were still just three kids from Swansdale, Ohio. They really had no idea what they were doing.

❦

Someone was using a sledge hammer in the next room. It woke Jayson from his staggered sleep. He had gotten up in the middle of the night to relieve his heaving stomach, but that was the last thing he clearly remembered. He found himself face down on the cold common area floor and tried to push himself up. The room swam before him, and there was still that pounding. He couldn't focus. He laid back on the floor again, but he could not seem to figure out what was going on. He tried to push himself to his knees again, and suddenly felt sick. He ungracefully sprawled back out on the floor, the side of his face finding comfort in the cool marble. He had to decide whether to stay still so as not to aggravate his dizzy head, or run for the chamber pot beside his bed to relieve his stomach again.

The pounding lessoned. Jayson heard a sharp click. The door to the Emerald Quarter opened, and someone with heavy footfalls walked into the room. The stranger stopped beside Jayson, surveying the scene of the room. Two bottles of pearl wine lay empty and rolling on the floor beside Jayson who was covered in vomit. Jayson was too weak to lift his head to look at the towering figure beside him. He listened as the stranger carefully stepped over him and headed toward one of the bedrooms where Leo slept. The last Jayson remembered, Leo had been sitting upright in bed with his back against his headboard and a pitcher, assumingly full of sick, on his lap between his legs. Jack had been able to hold his liquor, but still managed to fall out of bed, and lay on the floor in a tangle of white linen when Jayson had hurried from the room some hours before.

Jayson heard the stranger walking through their rooms. His heart raced. His mind told him he should investigate who it was. Not everyone they had met yesterday at the council meeting was a friend. But his spinning head and queasy stomach told him otherwise. He felt the vibrations of the footsteps draw near to him again, and two strong hands gently lifted him. "Come on, you little drunkard," said Dimitri's soft voice. "Let's get you cleaned up."

Dimitri changed Jayson's clothes, and cleaned up the pool of sick in the common area. He handed Jayson a nasty tasting herbal tea he had ordered to be brought up from the kitchens. He instructed Jayson to sip it slowly, then went to work on Leo and Jack. An hour later, all three sat in the chairs in their common room, mugs of steaming hot tea in their laps, and their heads firmly held in their hands. The pounding had subsided a bit, as had the blurriness, but the feeling of having to puke hadn't yet left them. Dimitri chuckled quietly at them.

"How does my dad do this every weekend?" asked Jack, lifting his head. There were dark circles under his eyes, and his perfectly handsome hair was a tangled mess.

"Remind me never to drink again," said Leo through his hands.

"Remind me of this at my bachelor party," said Jayson into his tea. "If I live that long."

"Did no one warn you about the pearl wine?" Dimitri asked, attempting to stifle a laugh, "It is very strong."

"No kidding," said Leo. He finished off his tea with a look as grotesque as the herbs tasted.

"The reason for my visit was to inform you I spoke with Nefiri and Valar. They have agreed to let me train you in magic." Jayson, Jack and Leo looked up at Dimitri, pushing their headaches aside.

"Really?" whispered Jayson.

"But, we haven't really shown any signs," said Leo.

"When you helped Piper, it was proof enough that you have magical abilities. As much as the dwarves wish to fight it, our religious methods border on the mystical. And more, as Nefiri's unofficial adopted son, I have been allowed certain privileges with my abilities. The day we helped Piper was not the first time my orenite cuffs have been removed. Though I would highly recommend not speaking of this. It was I who taught Piper to control her magic several years ago when she was first banished. Or rather, we taught each other. It was a time of trial and error and learning from each other's mistakes."

"Why doesn't Piper want to teach us herself?" asked Jack. "I'm complaining that you are. It's just, well, I guess we've been through more with her, and she's taught us so much already. It's like she's afraid of it."

"Do you know why Piper was exiled from Outland Post?" asked Dimitri.

"You mean the riot?" asked Jayson. "She was just trying to do what she thought was the right thing. She can't blame herself for that forever."

"Unfortunately she does." Dimitri sighed. "And for the deaths of her parents." He sighed and leaned forward, clasping his hands together. "They were trapped in their home when it caught fire. They were unable to escape, as were many other people in the village. It was not a natural fire, and Piper was the one who started it. I believe part of her has taken on this role as Queen to make up for the lives she feels responsible for taking. It will take her some time to come to terms with her abilities, if she ever uses them at all."

Jayson, Jack and Leo sat silent. Their stomachs churned, and it wasn't from their hangovers.

"But she didn't mean to," Leo said quietly.

"Yeah," said Jayson, "It's not her fault. It was an accident."

"Until you have blood on your hands, you cannot know the struggle she faces every day, the nightmares and the screaming. She was only your age when it occurred. Can you say you would handle being responsible for the deaths of so many any better? People whom you had grown up with and cared for?"

Leo shook his head, and Jayson and Jack remained silent. They sat quietly, sipping their tea or rubbing their temples.

Finally, Jack spoke. "Why are we getting magic lessons? Does the council want us to use magic during the fight or something?"

"No," Dimitri stretched his arms above his head and leaned back in his chair. "Valar believes Taraniz may remain at the castle during the battle. The dwarves will attempt to hold her forces off as long as possible, as this is a proper fortress. If the elves are able to break through the defenses, the

155

dwarves will draw her forces out to The Great Plains between Mount Kelsii and the Belirian Forest. And, if Taraniz does remain at the castle, then we will have only succeeded in delaying her takeover of the dwarves and temporarily diminishing her forces. Valar is right that we need to either kill or capture her. There will be no negotiating while she has the upper hand."

"I know my head is killing me right now, but what's that got to do with us?" Leo asked. He still had one hand pressed firmly against his forehead. "I feel like I've said that a hundred times! Why can't you people just explain stuff?" He now understood why hangovers made people so irritated.

Dimitri chuckled again. "Have you heard of the orenite circlet that was used to kill Duke Noraedin?" The boys nodded. "You have also heard that we believe Taraniz to be the reincarnated soul of Noraedin?" They nodded again. "Valar wants to send a small party into the Elven palace during the battle to search for the circlet. We can then use it to kill her, just as it was done with the Duke centuries ago."

"Is killing her really necessary, though?" Jayson asked. "I mean, can't you just do an exorcism or something and get rid of his soul?"

"I have heard of no such thing." Dimitri's brow furrowed. "One cannot remove a soul the same as someone can remove a possessing spirit from the mind, if that is what you are suggesting. A soul is the essence of a person, who they are. If you remove a soul, you will be left with an empty shell that is unable to accomplish anything beyond the basic instincts of life. There would be no emotion, no growth as a person. No, it would be far better to kill someone than allow them to live such an existence."

"I mean, do we have to kill her? Maybe we can figure out a way to turn her good or something," suggested Jack.

"To risk her escaping? She is also controlling the soldiers and Elven Conclave. If she remains in naught but a holding cell, and is not stripped of her magic, she will still be able to manipulate those people under her control. Chartile will never truly be free of her, or rather, of Duke Noraedin, if she is allowed to continue to live. If she has truly lost control of herself as Valar has said, then there is nothing we can do to save her."

"Maybe only little, but not nothing," Jayson snapped, "Weren't you just talking about what it's like living with killing someone? Now you want us to do it? That's bunk, man."

"We refuse to be part of this — this secret special-forces task group thing unless we agree we'll at least try to save Princess Taraniz. Not just kill her. It's not the way our world works," said Leo. He crossed his arms defiantly, but still squinted from the pain pounding in his head.

Dimitri sighed and rose from his chair, running his fingers through his jet black hair. "I will speak with Valar. I would not have been able to train you in your current condition today anyhow. Speak to no one about what we have discussed here today. I will meet you here tomorrow morning. Until then, drink plenty of water and rest. You will need it." He smirked and gave the boys a short nod. He headed for the door. His footfalls still louder than they should have been, pounding in the boys' ear. He turned, winked at them, and closed the door behind him. Jack, Leo and Jayson sat in silence once more. It was a situation they were beginning to experience far too frequently.

"I don't want to have to live with what Piper goes through every day," Jayson whispered. "I don't want to have to kill anyone."

"Dimitri said he would talk to Valar about trying other options," Leo pointed out, pouring himself more tea.

"Yeah, but just because they say they are going to do it, doesn't mean they will," said Jayson. "How many lies have we found out from these people since we got here? How do we know they'll keep their word? You think they'll ask a bunch of kids what to do with Taraniz once she's captured? Like, they won't ask us what we think about it."

"That's true," Jack added quietly. "I'm sure Taraniz will be brought before the Elven and maybe even the Dwarvik council for judgment. We won't have a lot of say then. We really didn't have a whole lot of say yesterday. Things just kind of worked out that way."

"These people believe we are the reincarnated kings! They have to listen to what we say!" Leo argued. He glared at Jack and Jayson. He was frustrated at something he couldn't pinpoint other than the pain in his head.

"Not if we keep acting like we did last night!" shouted Jayson, jumping to his feet.

"Hey, I wasn't the only one getting wasted," spat Leo. He leapt to his feet as well. His mug of tea clenched in a white-knuckled hand.

"I did say we, doofus. I'm not blaming all this on you. I'm just saying, if we want these people to respect us, then we need to, like, earn it." Jayson exhaled loudly and sat back down.

"Why not? Haven't we been through enough already? Freaking trolls and vampires. I haven't used a proper toilet in over a month, man!" Leo raised his voice in a way his friends had never heard before. He wasn't the first of his friends to lose his temper or his nerve.

"Leo, I'm sorry," said Jayson. He stood to meet his friend's gaze. He reached out and placed a hand on Leo's shoulder. "I'm right there with you, dude. I want to go home as much as you do. It's kind of the thing that keeps me going. I don't want to think about home too much, because if I do, I...I get scared. More scared. God, I'm scared all the time! Every night I go to sleep and hope that when I wake up this would have all been a dream. But it's not. It's real, and that scares me to death! I keep going because I'm starting to think this might be my new home, and I don't want it turning to crap like my last one. So, can you just try to see where I'm coming from for a minute?" Jayson's voice cracked, and the tears he had been holding back began to fall. They were tears he often cried at night, but never in front of his friends. "We have to grow up, okay?" he said through sobs. "We have to be the people they want us to be. And maybe, someday, we can go home and then we don't have to worry about things like toilets anymore."

Leo smiled through the tears that also trickled down his face. He nodded, and sighed before patting Jayson hard on the back. "You're right, I'm sorry."

"It's okay, man," said Jack, his eyes were red too. "We're in this together, no matter what, okay? You're not alone."

They refilled their mugs of tea, and headed back to bed, their heads pounding again from crying. They crawled beneath the soft linen sheets that were beginning to become as familiar as their beds from home. They stared at the ceiling or walls, and each vowed to themselves that when they awoke it would be a new start. Chartile was their home now, and they would fight for it together.

∽∾

After the Council meeting, Piper had gone straight to her rooms. Valar had followed close behind. He yammered away about the next day's battle strategy meeting and other obligations she now had as the heir to the Elven throne. Piper opened her door in the Sapphire Quarter, stepped in as gracefully as a Queen aught, and shut the door in Valar's face. She bolted it shut quickly, and leaned against the door relieved. She heard Valar's boots shuffle away down the stone hall, and smiled a little as she sighed. She headed for the bedroom, letting her mother's dress fall to the floor where she walked. She fell into the feather stuffed mattress, and buried her face in the silk covered pillow. No more running. No more hiding. No more sleeping in drafty stone caves or digging in the dirt for mushrooms. She fell asleep still smiling, dreaming of fruit custards and horses whose coats shined like starlight.

She dreamed she was riding along one of the main roads through the Belirian Forest. The Elven Palace towered ahead of her. She laughed as her hair blew in the wind. She looked back and saw Dimitri quickly gaining on her. She kicked her horse to run faster and whooped as they neared the front gates. Too late, she saw the guards on the battlements above the gate. They fitted flaming arrows to their bows and loosed them at Dimitri.

One. Two. Three. A dozen flaming arrows flew over her head and landed in Dimitri's chest. She tried to scream. She tried to turn her horse back. Dimitri fell to the ground, completely engulfed in the fire. The front gates of the palace opened before her, then shut again just as quickly. She leapt from her horse and ran to the closed gates. She cried out for Dimitri and demanded the gates be raised. She pounded against the metal over and over again, until her fists pounded in sync with the sound of a tiny bell.

Piper came to enough to realize someone was ringing the little bell by the main door. She smothered the pillow over her head, ignoring both the bell and the tears that had made her face sticky. The ringing soon ended, and Piper shifted in and out of dream and nightmare.

The smell of fresh bread filled Piper's room several hours later and managed to penetrate through the pillow she still held over her head. She sat up, her hair still clinging to her face, and hurried to dress. She chose a style that was neither Dwarvik nor Elven. The wardrobe held a fitted tunic that had been too long for her. She grabbed this and pulled on the black linen pants she had worn while living in the mountain. She tightened a jewel encrusted belt over the tunic, and hurried to pull on her boots.

She had decided last night that it was too difficult to balance the ways of her allies, the dwarves, with the culture of her own people. And figuring out how her own personality would work with how an Elven Queen was expected to behave would be an impossible task. Therefore, she decided that as a queen, she would do as she liked, dress as she liked and act as she pleased. At this moment it pleased her to be comfortable, and to stuff her face with that delicious smelling bread.

She opened her bedroom door and found Dimitri lounging across her fainting sofa, a plate of golden brown biscuits in hand. He smiled when she crossed the room in three strides to snatch a biscuit from the plate. She stopped, the sweet smelling bread inches from her lips. She dropped her hand and asked, "Wait. How did you get in here? I locked the door."

Dimitri laughed. "I hope your instincts for safety soon override your love of food now that you are the Queen-To-Be, he said. Piper scowled at him. She placed her hands on her hips and sent little crumbs of biscuit scattering across the floor. "Honestly, I picked the lock."

"Dimitri!" Piper scolded.

"As Empress Nefiri's retainer I have been sent on some errands that have required certain…skills is all. I wanted to surprise you. Especially since you were so kind to tell Valar where to stuff it last night. I thought you could use some cheering up this morning."

Piper shook her head and sat on the sofa beside Dimitri. She finally bit into the blissfully delicious bread, and sighed, a smile spreading across her face. "He's angry with me, isn't he?" she asked after a moment.

"Surprised, yes. Angry, no. I believe I heard him mutter something about "Just like her mother" and "a woman of few words." He does wish to meet with you as soon as possible. Before the strategy meeting, if possible."

"You been speaking to Valar without me? What is Nefiri up to, Dimitri?" Piper moved on to a second biscuit. It was as tasty as the first. Soft, and subtly sweet with its honey glaze and buttery center. She took another bite and sighed again.

"Nefiri is, to be forthright, furious at Jayson, Jack and Leo. She was bent on forcing them to live with the Black Diamonds. I was able to talk her out of it. I cannot say I blame her. It is hard to dismiss the grudge you have had for so long in a heart's beat." He ran his fingers through his black hair and shrugged. Piper had forgotten how much she enjoyed his company and his little quirks. He always fidgeted with his hair when he was nervous.

"Well, I do thank you for that. Though their methods may at times be rather unusual, I do believe it will be best for everyone in the end. Now, exactly why does that matter in regards to you speaking with Valar?"

"Seeing as you and I have been friends for so long, Nefiri has asked if I would be the liaison between you four — I suppose five if you were to consider Valar — and the dwarves. After you shut yourself in here last night, Valar asked to speak with me. He thought I could coax you out of your shell and convince you to meet with him. He has an alternate plan regarding Taraniz." Dimitri pulled the last bite of biscuit from Piper's hand and tossed it in the air, catching it in his mouth with a smug smile. "Have I succeeded?"

"Succeeded in what? Annoying me? Yes." Piper's voice was firm, but she smiled as she spoke. Dimitri leaned in, pushing her tangled mess of hair out of her eyes.

"Have I succeeded in coaxing you out of your shell, you uptight little fireball?" He did not wait for a response. He kissed her warmly. He pushed her back into the corner of sofa and wrapped his arms around her back.

Piper kissed him back. She allowed herself to become lost in the familiarity of him. She felt his strong, knotted muscles encircle her, and felt his breath in her ear. He moved to kiss her chin, and she leapt from the sofa.

"Dimitri, this has to stop," she said, her voice shaking. "I told you, now that I will be Queen, we cannot be together. My — my marriage will be arranged by the Elven Council. There is nothing to be done about it." She turned back towards her bedroom, ready to shut herself away once more. Dimitri's grabbed her wrist, and instinct over took her. She twisted, stepping on Dimitri's foot, ready to elbow him in the stomach. This was a trick he had taught her. As soon as her foot came down on his, Dimitri spun her around. He pressed her back against his chest and crossed her arms in front of her.

"Let me go!" she cried. She fought the tears ready to slip down her face as much as she fought against Dimitri. Dimitri said nothing. He simply held her there. She struggled against his body, but it was no use. Eventually she gave in. She gave in to his strength and to her tears. She slumped to the floor, holding her face in her hands. He still held her, more gently now. He let her cry and let her hot tears splash against his arm like he did three years ago beneath the beech tree. Finally, her crying subsided to little hiccups, and he wiped her face with his tunic sleeve.

"I do not care what any council says," he whispered to her. "I am never going to stop loving you. Stop fighting this. You know we're—"

"I don't want to lose you," she breathed through her hands. "If anything ever happened to you because of me, I—" Dimitri pulled her hands away from her face. Even when she cried, she was beautiful. He wiped the tears from her face again. "Dimitri, you are my dearest friend. I love you more than anyone I have ever known. I cannot bring myself to let you—"

He pressed a finger to her lips. "That is a burden for me to carry, not you. I will never force you to do anything against your will. But you cannot stop me from loving you." He kissed her fingers softly, and left the room, leaving the empty plate of biscuits sitting on the sofa.

୨୧

The sun outside the boys' window had begun to turn the sky from black to dark gray. Shades of red and gold streaked through the clouds, diminishing the grandeur of the Dwarvik gem murals. Jack, Jayson and Leo had slept through most of the day and night. When they awoke, it had still been dark. They sat in the common area, playing checkers with a strange board game they had found in one of the cabinets as the sky outside their window grew brighter.

"Hey, let's go visit Piper!" Jayson cried, startling them out of their bored stupor.

"Yeah!" Leo cried. Then his face fell as quickly as it had brightened. "Uh, does anyone know where her room is?"

"Gemari told me how to get to the Sapphire Quarter a few days ago. I'm sure there are enough people around that could help us too," said Jack.

Jayson and Leo nodded in agreement and hurried off to their respective rooms. They dressed quickly in the original clothes they had arrived in. Jack was thankful to wear jeans again, but he still kept the boots Piper had traded for them. Soon, they found themselves walking the familiar corridors and tunnels of Fortress Kelsii. Word had spread about the boys' involvement with the Black Diamonds. The news seemed to have made the citizens nervous. They moved aside and turned their faces away as they walked past. Some even turned the opposite direction to evade an encounter all together.

Jayson, Jack and Leo spent fifteen minutes wandering the tunnels aimlessly with no help from passersby. They slumped against a nearby wall, looking rather defeated and considered their options.

Cassandra Morgan

"Well, that didn't go according to plan," said Jack. His shoulders sagged and he began fidgeting with a hole in his jeans.

"I guess we aren't exactly the most popular at the moment. I didn't think about that," said Leo.

"Hey, I don't know what their mad at Jack and I for," Jayson leaned forward to look at Leo who sat on the other side of Jack. "It was your idea to conspire with the enemy." Leo glared at Jayson, who laughed and nearly hit Jack in the head as he tried to punch Leo in the arm. "I'm kidding! I'm kidding!" he chortled. "Looks like we're in this together whether we planned it that way or not."

"Yeah, anything one of us does, it's like we all did it," said Jack. He leaned away from Jayson who was still recovering from his laughing fit.

"I guess I didn't think what would happen after the council decided," said Leo. "I just assumed everyone would get along and work together. I guess even adults from another world can't grow up sometimes."

"Hey, they got the job done. Mostly," said Jack. "And you did that, Leo. Believe me, I wouldn't have had the guts to do what you did, man. That was definitely righteous!"

"Word!" Jayson agreed, giving Leo the rock and roll sign this his hands. A middle aged man passed by and stared over his shoulder at the boys before hurrying on. They all started laughing into their hands.

"What do you think will happen after Piper's Queen?" Jayson asked, still giggling and rubbing his chin. After seeing the dwarves' magnificent beards, he had been determined to will his facial hair to grow. So far, he had only managed to make his chin itch when he went to bed at night.

"I thought maybe we'd keep trying to find a way home," said Leo. "But I'm worried people will start to think we're a threat if we stay together."

A large group was making their way down the hall. Leo stopped talking when he saw them. Jack and Jayson turned to look. The party did not shy away as the others had. They walked determinedly forward, their footfalls almost perfectly in sync. It was Nefiri, Una and Gemari with an armed guard. The boys scrambled to their feet. Leo and Jayson attempted a proper Dwarvik bow until Jack elbowed them in the ribs. Commoners did not bow to royalty. It was an insult that put them on the same level as everyone else. The troupe slowed as Nefiri narrowed her eyes at them.

"My Lady," whispered Jack. Nefiri broke from the group and the soldiers stopped. Una rolled her eyes, and Gemari refused to look at them at all. "I—we…we wanted to visit Piper. Could someone show us to her room?" Nefiri squinted at the boys a moment longer, then nodded to one of her guards. The Empress gave the smallest of bows to them, and the group continued their trek down the hall.

"Follow me, if you please," said the guard. His tone was polite, and a smile pulled at his lips beneath his dark brown beard. He led them down two long tunnels then stopped before of the magnificent bejeweled doors. "The Lady Piper," he said, and winked before walking away. Jayson, Jack and Leo stared after him for a moment before pulling on the little bell string beside the door.

"That was weird," Jayson whispered.

"Guess Nefiri must be pretty mad," said Leo.

"You could say that," Piper said, opening the door. The redness in her cheeks and eyes said she had been crying, but she smiled warmly at them. "Please, come in." She stood aside, and they paraded inside, each hugging her in turn. "I apologize I did not stay to celebrate with you," she said. She glanced at the fainting sofa then took a seat in a chair across the room.

"You didn't miss much," Jayson lied, "We — uh, we've pretty much slept all day."

Piper nodded. She looked from the floor to the window, and took no notice of Jayson's forced tone. "I am sorry I have been neglecting you." she said, and began twisting her hair between her fingers.

"Neglecting us? What do you mean?" asked Leo. He picked up the biscuit plate beside him and ate the remaining crumbs.

"I have shut myself away. I was afraid. I see that now. You needed me, and I have not been here for you. You are…my friends, like my brothers, and I have been thinking only of myself. I should not have left you alone for so long. I am sorry."

"It's okay," said Jayson. "Dimitri took pretty good care of us."

Piper smiled weakly. "Yes, he is good at that."

An awkward silence fell between them. The only sound came from Jayson shuffling his feet and the whistling wind outside Piper's window, indicating a storm on the way.

"Alright," said Jack breaking the quiet. "If we're your friends, then you're gunna talk. That's what girls need anyway, right? Talking?" The silence that followed was even more uncomfortable. Jayson and Leo looked at Jack confused, and Piper refused to look at him at all.

"That's what we're doing, Jack," Leo raised his eyebrows at Jack and shrugged.

"No!" cried Jack. "Isn't it obvious she and Dimitri just had a fight or something?" More silence. "Seriously, am I the only one that notices this stuff?"

"Did you guys have a fight?" Jayson turned to Piper, and Leo punched him in the ribs. "Hey! I broke that, ya know!"

"How long are you going to use that excuse?" Leo rolled his eyes.

"For as long as I can," Jayson whined, and his friends laughed. "Okay, but seriously. Did you guys fight? Is Dimitri like, your boyfriend or something?"

"Dimitri and I have been friends for many years," said Piper. "He— he came to me when I was first banished. He taught me my magic. He wishes to be more than friends." Piper continued to study the floor.

"So?" said Leo shrugging. "We already thought you guys were. What's the big deal?"

"I cannot risk putting my truest friend in danger because I will be Queen. The Conclave of Nobles will decide my marriage. Our relationship would be secret and put him at grave risk." She rose from the chair and began pacing the room. "This is ridiculous." She laughed. "I should not be discussing this with you."

Jayson and Leo looked at Jack. They shrugged, encouraging him to continue what he'd started.

"Well, I mean, if you guys are friends, and everyone already thinks you guys are a couple, wouldn't that put him in danger anyway?" asked Jack.

Piper whipped around. Her green eyes were wide and wild. "What do you mean?" she asked.

"Well, if some group of people is going to decide who you have to marry, you probably aren't really going to love that person, right?" Piper said nothing. She remained still, her green eyes piercing Jack as he continued. "And if you really do love Dimitri, regardless of...well... just regardless of anything you decide... they could still use him against you."

"What are you implying?" she asked, her eyes narrowing as she carefully calculated Jack's words.

"You're making this way crazier than it needs to be," said Leo, "Either you're his girlfriend and then you're both happy, or you're not his girlfriend, and you're both miserable. People will use him against you anyway."

"So, just suck it up and...stuff," Jayson shrugged.

The bell rang at the door. They jumped. Piper covered the length of the room nearly at a run, and opened the door. It was Valar. She was both happy and disappointed it was not Dimitri. She stepped aside to allow him through. He smiled at seeing the boys already gathered.

"Fantastic to find you all here!" Valar beamed a wide smile at them. "I do not believe we have properly met. I am Valar, head advisor to our late King Aramor, and now unofficial advisor to Queen Eva Ruani." He bowed to them in what the boys presumed was more of the Elven style. They attempted to return the gesture, but were mostly unsuccessful.

"I prefer Piper," she said, closing the door. She headed for her bedroom and brought out another chair.

"Yes, well, names and titles can be discussed once the battle is won. Speaking of which! I shall send word immediately for the rest of our group to meet here at once." Valar ran to the door and all but ran into Dimitri in his attempt to call for a messenger. "Dimitri! Wonderful! Now, I only need to find—"

"Your meeting will need to wait, Valar," said Dimitri.

"But we cannot delay much longer," said the man. "We have little time to prepare."

"And I still have to train these boys how to use their magic. We were delayed yesterday." Dimitri looked at Jayson, Jack and Leo. He smiled and winked before turning back to Valar. "Nefiri wants to move troops to the base of the mountain in a week. Scouts have reported elven troops gathering to the south. Brande and Kylani have said this was part of their plan. The elves will attempt to enter through the abandoned mines as was planned, but we have a chance to draw away at least half of their forces before they strike. Oh, I'll let her explain it later. The point is, I am taking these three to the

Cassandra Morgan

temple. You can stay here and explain things to Piper while we're gone."

"I think I would like to join you," said Piper eagerly. She swallowed and replied more cautiously, "I could always brush up on my own skills."

"I have meetings for the rest of the day," Valar replied in defeat. "We must promise to meet tomorrow morning before any other training. What good is training without a plan?"

"Agreed," said Dimitri. "We will meet here after sunrise."

Valar nodded. "Until tomorrow then." He bowed to Piper in the Elven fashion and swept past Dimitri, his elven robes billowing behind him.

"Geez, is he always like that?" asked Jayson.

"No," said Dimitri, "I believe he is excited for something to finally go according to plan after so long." They laughed as Dimitri led them down the winding tunnels and halls.

They passed the healer's quarters and entered an area they had never been before. The room was as large as the Crystal Quarter room, possibly bigger. Two of the four walls faced outward and held huge slates of stained glass that filled the chamber with a rainbow of colors. There were pews, much like a cathedral, but they faced toward the center in a spiraling circle, broken only by the small aisle that ran from the great double entrance doors to a stone altar in the middle. Jayson, Jack, Leo and Piper stopped mid-step, and Dimitri nearly ran into them.

"The Hall of Rashiri is one of our greatest accomplishments. The Tutarian palace likes to boast

173

about its grand architecture. Mount Kelsii was originally founded for trade, not for politics, so it lacks much of the splendor that Tutaria holds." Dimitri beamed proudly. "This is our masterpiece."

He led them around the perimeter of the great spiral, and headed toward one of the many rooms off the main area. Clouds of billowing incense filled the room. Four plush cushions were placed on the floor and faced a large copper bowl that held a crackling fire.

Dimitri closed the door behind them, and walked to the rear of the room. He pulled an extra pillow from a cupboard and handed it to Piper.

"Are you sure you want to do this?" he whispered to her. "I know you said you would never —"

Piper smiled at him and cupped his chin in her hand. "I can't be afraid anymore," she said, and sat on her cushion beside Jack.

Dimitri pulled a tiny key from the pouch on his belt and moved to the other side of the fire bowl. "The first thing you need to understand about magic," he said and began removing his orenite cuffs, "is that everyone has it. Most people simply do not realize they do, and there are certainly varying degrees in the amount of skill one has. Magic is nothing more than the manipulation of the energy around you. However, you need to learn to manipulate the energy within yourself before you can attempt to manipulate the world around you. To do this, you must attain a greater sense of self awareness and deep concentration. You must discover your fears and rise above them, your faults and accept them, your dreams and make them so.

You must do all of this to understand who you truly are. When you know yourself, then you can know how to change your own energies. Once you have learned to manipulate the self, you can begin to study and manipulate the world around you." He pulled out a small drum and held it between his feet. "I am going to walk you through a reflection exercise. It is a practice our elders use to keep balance amongst their three understandings. Please, close your eyes, and listen to the sound of my voice. Breathe deeply. Relax. Follow wherever your mind leads you."

The drum pounded like a pulsating heart, and their own hearts began keeping time with it, slow and steady. Dimitri's voice was distant. They could barely hear him. They sat in the trance-like state for what felt like hours. The smoke from incense swirled about them, and the fire before them made the room stifling hot. At first, they fidgeted, unsure of what to do. Occasionally, one of the boys opened an eye to peek at his neighbors. They half expected to see each other surrounded in a light or floating a few inches off their pillow. This, however, never occurred. They relaxed. Every muscle in their bodies released its tension, and their breathing slowed. They no longer fought the smoke and incense, but breathed it in, welcoming.

The darkness gave way to a hazy image that formed before Piper. She faced three doors, and they opened as one before her. Behind the first lay a golden crown. The second revealed a world with unrestrained magic. Here, Piper saw herself as the leader of her people, guiding them into an age of fortune and happiness. The last door opened to

Dimitri. He smiled that brilliant smile, and held out his hand to her. Your fears, your faults, your dreams, she heard his voice in her mind.

Leo stared into the mouth of a cave. A lion slept peacefully at its center. He could wake the lion, risking his life and the lives of those faceless people who accompanied him. He could find a formidable ally in the lion if he kept his cool. He could also walk away. He gripped the sword hilt in his hand so tight, his knuckles turned white. He didn't know if he had become the leader everyone thought he was, or if he was still playing a game. He knew he would have to decide soon as he watched the lion begin to stir.

Jack could hear the drum beating in his ears. It was like the pounding of broken glass shattering against a wall...his bedroom wall. His father stood above him, both afraid and dangerous. "Help me," his father said, then turned to smash the lamp beside Jack's bed. Jack reached out for his father. Mr. Mitchel slammed his fist into the wall, and Jack retreated back to the far side of his bed. "Leave me! I don't need anyone!" his father screamed, and turned to race out of the room. Jack was frozen where he sat.

Jayson knelt on the floor. A sword lay on the ground before him, covered in blood. Blood drenched his hands, and pooled around the gaping wound of the man he had just killed. The blood on his hands oozed down his arms, a warm, thick trickle, dripping onto his legs. It was spreading fast, covering his entire body. He grabbed his head, and hunched to curl into a ball. But the blood continued to spread. It covered his hair, down his head, tickling his temples and stinging his eyes. He screamed. He tried to run, but the pool of blood was too slick. He fell and felt the warm, sticky blood seep through his shirt. He screamed, but he could not hear.

The drumming stopped, and everyone jumped. Jayson sat in a cold sweat. His breathing came in short, shallow breaths and he clenched his hands into white knuckled fists.

"Jayson," Dimitri called gently to him. The boy's eyes shot open. He looked at his trembling hands. They were free of blood. He wiped the sweat that poured down his face with his shirt and attempted to slow his breathing.

"You alright, Jay?" Leo asked. Jayson did not answer.

Dimitri approached him, and placed his hands on Jayson's shoulders. A cool wave of calm surrounded Jayson and pushed itself into the far reaches of his mind. He began to relax. Dimitri looked at him with raised eyebrows. Jayson nodded.

"I want you each to practice this meditation every night before you sleep, and every morning when you wake. Practice it until you can find that place of calm focus in an instant." he paused. "Then, we shall move on." Dimitri leaned the drum back against the wall.

"Really?" asked Jack. "That was it?" The experience hadn't been as exciting as he had hoped.

"What if it takes us too long?" Leo protested. "We don't have a lot of time to learn this. The army moves out in, what, two weeks, maybe a little more? That can't be enough time."

"I do not believe you will have any problems," said Dimitri. "Come, we shall break for a time. I want to show you to the armory." He extinguished the incense in the sand of the thurible, but left the fire burning low. "You can spend your free time training there." He led them out of the room and back up the temple aisle. Jayson lagged behind. He stared at his feet as he walked, and kept looking at his hands. Piper doubled back to walk with him as they emerged into the stone halls once more.

"Jayson, are you sure you are well?" she asked. "May I ask what you saw?"

Jayson was silent for a long while as they walked. He slowed his pace, and attempted to put some distance between himself and his friends. "I— I killed someone. I don't know who he was. I was covered in his blood, completely covered. I tried to scream, but I couldn't make any noise. I don't think I realized it 'til now, but... Piper, I could kill someone. I could kill a lot of people. Even if they agree with Taraniz, they still have families and lives and souls and stuff. I don't know if I can do this anymore. I know I told Leo that we all needed to grow up. I said we need to be the people everyone expects us to be, but..."

Piper stopped walking. She put an arm out to stop Jayson. Dimitri, Leo and Jack stopped as well, but Piper urged them on with a wave of her hand. Dimitri nodded, and continued on with Leo and Jack.

"Jayson, I do not know where I should begin. I suppose with apologies, but it seems trivial to say. I have been putting so much pressure on you as our returned kings. I often forget you are younger than I am, and I am so very confused and frightened. You must understand, you cannot be the person that others want you to be. You must be yourself, and only that. Any changes you wish to make, for good or ill, need to be made for you and no one else. You should not feel obligated to be involved in this in any way. This is not your world, and no one can fault you for staying out of matters if that is your desire. I have nothing but the highest respect for you all in everything you have experienced and the way you have handled yourselves. You have developed a grace far beyond your years. You should not continue to press yourselves to grow up too quickly. If you ever need to talk, well, I am not Leo or Jack, or even Dimitri, but," she stared at the floor and sighed. "I know what it's like to have blood on your hands. I will help you in any way that I can."

Jayson laid a hand on her shoulder. She looked into his eyes and saw his fear and turned to compassion. She held her arms open and embraced Jayson as a sister. He did not recoil or attempt to pull away. He leaned his head against her shoulder, and welcomed the genuine comfort and compassion. He hadn't realized he missed it from his old life. His parents may have been busy with Jessica, but they still loved for him. No matter how old he was, how old he tried to pretend be, Jayson knew empathy and camaraderie were what made them all the same.

Chapter Fourteen

Secrets

Jayson followed Piper along the stone corridor, a weight lifted from his shoulders. The armory was not far from the Southern entrance where they had first arrived at Mount Kelsii, but it was still a trek from the Hall of Rashiri. When Jayson and Piper entered the armory, Jack, Leo and Dimitri had only just arrived.

"Leo, my boy!" a voice called from across the room. They looked up to see Kylani wave to them from amongst a cluster of men. They donned both Kelsii soldier and Black Diamond armor. Leo beamed at the man. He hurried past the other soldiers. They glared at the group, and tried to seem intimidating as they practiced with their swords, throwing knives and arrows.

"How are ya?" Leo asked, holding out his hand for Kylani. The man took Leo's outstretched arm and squeezed it tightly at the elbow before gesturing back to the center of the ring the onlookers had made.

"Fantastic, dear boy, fantastic! Brande is giving a lesson in hand to hand combat. Care to join us?"

Street fighting wasn't exactly something Leo had considered as a useful combatant skill. It didn't seem quite as dignified somehow. He watched Brande flatten a Kelsii soldier to his back with a carefully placed foot and shoulder. Leo had to admit this rather roguish technique might indeed come in handy. The ring of bystanders clapped as Brande helped the solider to his feet. The soldier shook his head and rejoined his fellows, who slapped him hard on the back.

"Leo!" Brande called when he noticed the boy beside his brother. "Care to help me with my next demonstration?"

"Uh, I think I'll pass," said Leo. The crowd laughed, and Leo felt several hands pat his back in agreement with his decision.

"A wise decision, my young friend," said one of the Black Diamonds beside him. "Brande is one of our best fighters. His skills have helped us out of a number of scrapes for certain."

"Incidents that would have never occurred if you had not decided to break the law and kill our families," said a cold voice behind the crowd. They turned to see a man who had stepped away from the nearby archery ring. He still held his bow and arrow at the ready, pointed at the floor.

Kylani's fists clenched, and his already dark skin grew flush with a sudden wave of anger. Brande moved quickly to stand beside his brother, and strategically placed his right foot between his brother's feet, ready to hold him back if necessary.

"We have all made mistakes we regret," said Brande. "Wiser words have never been spoken from the lips of one so young." He nodded toward Jack who blushed and looked at the floor. "Let us move forward civilly and help each other to defeat our common enemy. We can work out our differences another time."

"An enemy you were working with until it no longer suited your needs." The man spat on the floor. "For some vagabond traitor illegally cavorting with the Queen, you throw your words out rather nicely. Or did she teach you those pretty phrases as she screamed your name in the filthy mines you call home?"

There was less than a second of calm before chaos erupted in the room. Most of the soldiers had completely abandoned their weapons, coincidentally resorting to their fists instead. Dimitri pushed the boys back against the wall, and attempted to pull one of the soldiers off a Black Diamond who had been pinned to the floor. Even Piper looked lost in the sudden pandemonium. She watched as Dimitri received a nasty gash to his forehead. She wanted to run to him. She wanted to protect Jack, Leo and Jayson. She wanted to pull the soldiers apart and stop the madness.

Brande was caught in a two on one fight, his assailants inching him back against the wall. He swung, and caught the first man on the wrist as he blocked the attack. The second Kelsii soldier took advantage of Brande's distraction. He pulled a knife, and Leo's heart hit his stomach. The boy felt a surge of energy rise within him. A sword that lay abandoned amongst the fallen soldiers leapt out of its scabbard and into his hand.

"Brande!" Leo shouted and jumped forward into the fray. He knocked the knife from the man attacking Brande and stepped between them.

"Leo!" Piper screamed, and bolted into the fight. A Black Diamond stumbled back to keep himself balanced in his fight. Piper was knocked to the floor, disappearing amongst the boots and armor of the soldiers.

"Piper!" Jayson shouted. He lunged forward, but Jack held him back. "Dimitri!" he called, hoping the broad young man could push his way through in time to save Piper. Dimitri, however, was preoccupied. He fought a Black Diamond warrior with a two handed great sword. Jayson pushed past Jack and jumped into the mess of bodies in the last place he had seen Piper fall. He saw her, trying to stand. She pushed and kicked at the legs of those around her, Black Diamond and Kelsii soldier alike. Jayson grabbed her wrist and pulled her to her feet.

"Let go of me!" she cried, not realizing who had come to her aid.

"It's me!" said Jayson, and he pushed her toward Jack before being enveloped by the crowd. Jack reached for Piper, and pulled her behind him. More and more of the fighters were finding weapons from their fallen comrades or along the walls in the weapons racks.

"We have to stop this," said Piper with a panicked whisper.

Jack felt his stomach drop. He watched as Leo and Brande, were pushed back to back. They were completely surrounded, and a fallen Kylani lay unconscious at their feet. The visions of Jack's father during his meditation rushed into focus in his mind. For the first time, the fear and anger he had bottled inside him collided with his new found strength.

"STOP!" Jack screamed. His voice echoed off the stone walls and seemed somehow magnified. The entire room dropped their weapons, some falling to their knees, their hands clenched their over ears as the boy continued to scream. The air around Jack warped and moved, rippling like heat on stone.

His friends looked on in fear, and Piper wondered if Duke Noraedin was not in Taraniz after all.

Jack's knees hit the hard stone floor, and he held his head in his hands. "Stop fighting!" The scream that had continued to reverberate throughout the room slowly faded. Jack fell forward onto his hands. He was out of breath, and his head spinning. Piper rushed to him, catching him just before he hit the floor unconscious.

"He's burning up," she whispered as Dimitri, Leo and Jayson pushed their way through the crowd. Dimitri lifted Jack across his shoulder and headed for the door.

"Dimitri," said the Kelsii soldier who had first confronted Brande and Kylani. "You keep those unnatural little brats away from us, you understand? By Rashiri I'll-"

"You'll what?" said Jayson. The adrenaline still rushing in this veins had him ready for another fight. "You'll all kill each other? Because you know that's what would have happened. Then who's gunna be around to save you from Taraniz?"

Leo put his hand on Jayson's arm. "Jack needs us right now," he said. Jayson glared at the man then turned and followed Leo.

Dimitri headed into a room across from the armory. It was small, and full of bows, arrows and knives. He laid Jack gently on the floor, and removed the boy's shirt to cool him more quickly.

"What happened, Dimitri?" Leo asked. There was an edge of anger in his voice.

"He must have used his magic somehow," said Dimitri. He wadded up Jack's t-shirt and placing it under his head.

"As what happened to me," said Piper. "His magic began pulling from his life energy."

"Is he going to be okay?" Jayson asked. He knelt beside Piper and looked franticly between her and Dimitri.

"Of course," said Dimitri. "But Tagrin is right. There are too many who both love you and hate you. You are not from Chartile, and yet you are the returned souls of our ancient leaders. That is a threat to everyone."

"We didn't do this on purpose, Dimitri," Leo snapped.

"I know," said Dimitri. He nodded, and a sympathetic smile tugged at his lips. "Still you are the unknown in all of this. It was you who united the dwarves. You who are the reincarnated kings of old. You are both courteous of our ways and unpredictable when you do not understand them. You are extremely dangerous to any race here in Chartile because you have no race to call your own. You have been blessed with the magic of our ancestors, and yet you are only children. This makes you both vulnerable and perilous."

"What are you saying, Dimitri?" asked Piper. "You would not have them —"

"No! You are my friends. But I say this as your friend, so long as you remain in Chartile, you will never be safe. You will be welcomed and hunted wherever you go. Order and chaos will both follow you, and there is nothing you can do to stop it."

"Dude, you're over reacting a bit, aren't you?" asked Jayson, "Look at all the good we've done so far!"

"Look at the fear you have caused in our soldiers because of this one act of uncontrollable magic!" snapped Dimitri, indicating Jack who still lay unconscious between them all.

"You said we would learn this fast. You said our magic wouldn't be a big deal." Leo stood.

"It's not," said Piper, attempting to ease the tension that still lingered from the fight. "I think I understand what you are saying, Dimitri. We need to train in private. We are not dwarves. Even though I am of Chartile, I have not yet proven myself as a ruler to the elves. And I am certainly no dwarf. We are all outsiders here."

"But you still work for Nefiri," said Jayson. "I know she's kind of mad at us, but she'll come around in time. Won't she? Have you tried talking to her?"

There was a strained silence broken only by Jack's deep breathing.

"I no longer serve my Empress," said Dimitri, staring at the stone floor beneath him. "There were... discussions. I had to choose: Nefiri or Piper. Here I am."

"I thought you were our liaison," said Piper, her voice strained with confusion.

"I told Nefiri I would still do this for her, but I have been officially dismissed from her service." Dimitri hung his head. "I...I do this because she is my mother, but..."

Jack took a ragged breath and opened his eyes. His head had stopped spinning, but he felt exhausted. There was only a small bit of light filtering into the room from the crack in the door. He saw several figures surrounding him, but his eyes

186

wouldn't focus. He tried to sit up, and felt multiple hands push him back down.

"Wh-where, am I?" he asked.

"Sit up slowly, Jack," said Dimitri, and Jack obeyed. Piper, Jayson and Leo also sat on either side of him, concern written on their faces.

"Hey, let's go get some lunch," Leo suggested as the tension in the room heightened again.

"Food would be great," said Jack softly. "But what happened?"

"Well, uh… you used magic!" said Jayson. His smile faded when he saw Jack glare at him. "Okay, so you used more magic than your body could handle. You pulled a Piper, okay?"

"What is that to mean? Is that an official diagnosis now?" Piper grinned as she spoke, and they all laughed.

"We'll work on your magic a bit more tomorrow," said Dimitri.

"You rest today, Jack," Piper insisted, and she tussled his wavy hair.

"Well, we can't practice in the armory anymore," said Jayson. He rolled his blue grey eyes and crossed his arms. "So bogus. Where are we supposed to go now?"

"I think I know a place," said Leo.

༄

The air waned from a warm summer to a cool autumn. The leaves in the surrounding Belirian Forest had begun to change to shades of gold and ruby red. The ripe scent of a strange autumn fruit from the trees filled the air, especially at dusk, as it was now. Five laughing figures entered the Black Diamond's central market square from a small door leading to the outside. Some of the residents who had remained in the mine glared behind their hoods, and moved their children away. Others saw an exploitable opportunity to sell their goods and waved as the troupe passed their carts and stands. Jack took little heed of the merchants today. He had bought a new leather grip for his bow staff earlier that day, and was currently deep in conversation with Jayson.

"I nearly had you that time, admit it," said Jayson as he playfully punched Jack in the arm. His thick red hair was windblown and stuck up at the back.

"As if! My staff was at your throat, dude! There's no way you could have gotten that knife out in time!"

It had been three days since the ordeal in the armory. Word had spread fast. The boys were unwelcome in nearly all circles but those with select Black Diamond members whom they rarely saw except those strangers in the market place. Leo had shown them the way to the old mines and the secret door outside to the East side of the mountain. The steep cliff down to the forest was easily passable via a small path that Leo had not noticed before. Brande had showed them a small clearing a short distance into the forest when they had inquired about a place to practice.

Jack, Leo and Jayson had abandoned their magical studies for the time being, save for their meditations, and had focused on refining their combat skills. They had even begun practicing hand to hand combat with Brande and Kylani's help. Dimitri had been against the entire idea of using the Diamond's 'lair' as he called it from the very beginning. He soon found the Black Diamond's still held true to most of the traditions of his people, and his hatred toward them began to subside.

The light of another day faded into a starry speckled sky. Jayson, Jack, Leo, Piper and Dimitri, exhausted from the day's exercises, barely noticed the small knot of people traipsing towards them up the corridor. Jack flattened himself against the wall when he finally saw Gemari among them. Her eyes landed on Jack, and she nearly stopped in her tracks herself. For her sake, it appeared as little more than a small skip in her step due to her training. She pulled her shoulders back and bowed low when she approached the group.

"Greetings," she said softly. Her voice had lost its squeaky quality since the banquet, and there was a constant forlorn undertone to her once bubbly personality. She paused, taking a moment to look at each of the five in turn. "Jack, may I talk with you a moment?"

"S-sure," Jack stammered. Gemari turned to her guards, and nodded. Reluctantly, they retreated several paces back, each placing a hand on his sword hilt. Jack looked at his friends, and gulped. They only smirked and joined the guards down the hall.

"Gemari, look, I'm sorry." Jack began, but the Princess lifted her hand to silence him.

"It's alright, Jack," she said smiling. "I wanted to tell you I was sorry. Am sorry, for the way I have been."

"What are you talking about?" Jack asked. He leaned his staff against the wall and furrowing his brow at her.

"I have been involved with many council meetings ere of late," she replied, looking at the floor, "and, there are things that have been discussed."

"About us?" Jack asked, and he nodded toward his friends behind him. Gemari looked into Jack's eyes for several long moments. "Gemari, don't try to be all formal, and stuff. It's me. Just spit it out!"

She took a deep breath, then replied very quickly, "Nefiri has dismissed Dimitri from her service because of his involvement with you, and your connection to the Black Diamonds. I do not agree with this, and I am finding myself siding more often with the Diamonds. Jack, this goes against everything I have been brought up to believe, and I do not know what to do!" She blinked the tears from her eyes before they rolled down her cheeks. Jack reached toward her. He wanted to brush the invisible tears from her cheek. He wasn't sure if he liked the new or old Gemari better, but he couldn't deny he had feelings for her. Instead, he placed his hand on her shoulder, and she looked back into his face.

"Talk to Isla," Jack said, "If she gets banished after this is all over, the dwarves will need a strong leader. You can do it, Gemari."

She smiled at him and nodded. "I have. She and Princess Faeridae have both been ever so kind and patient with me. I suppose I was still just so confused. I do not understand why, but... you seem to make everything much clearer for me. Thank you, Jack."

Jack reached for Gemari's hand, and bent to kiss it. She stared at him with wide eyes, and he heard her breath catch in her throat as he released her hand. They locked eyes again, then Gemari bowed to him and continued down the corridor. Jack watched her go, a strange smile on his face as he did so. He didn't notice his friends join him until Jayson slapped him on the back.

"Twitterpated, my friend. This, right here, is called twitterpated." Jayson grinned.

"I see," said Dimitri with a chuckle.

The sound of Dimitri's voice brought Jack to again. "What did you say?" he asked. His friends laughed and they continued toward the Emerald Quarter.

The halls were surprisingly empty as they trudged back to Piper, and now Dimitri's, rooms. They each took turns at the wash basin, scrubbing away the sweat and grime of the day, before tearing into the left over fruit from their lunch earlier that day.

"When's Valar getting here, anyway?" Jayson asked through a mouthful of food.

"He should arrive any moment," said Piper. Though she had appreciated all of his assistance, Valar had been a bit overbearing at times. She had enjoyed his absence these past few days. Rather begrudgingly, Valar had rescheduled their meeting from earlier in the week to today. A messenger had sent word for him to return to his son's estate, and he had left immediately.

"Any idea what this is about?" Leo asked. He wiped fruit juice from his chin then dove in for me.

"I do not know," said Piper.

They sat in silence for nearly ten minutes, chewing their food and relaxing. Dimitri used magic to play with the flames in the hollowed out stone pillar beneath the wash basin, much to everyone's amusement.

There was a sharp knock on the door that sent the fruit juice from Jayson's bite shoot across the room and land on Jack's shirt. Piper rose from her chair and opened the door to a smiling and rosy faced Valar.

"Hello, my Queen," he said, and bowed to her in the proper elven fashion with one hand behind his back and the other across his waist. Piper's shoulders dropped. She rolled her eyes and sighed.

"Hello, Valar," she said in a warning tone. The man entered the room, taking no notice. He bowed to each of the boys before taking a seat in Piper's chair.

"We need to teach him what a hand shake is," Jayson whispered to Leo.

Piper closed the door and latched the extra chain. Dimitri uncrossed his legs as she rejoined them, and she sat on his lap, leaning against the corner of the fainting sofa. Valar blinked at them and stammered for a moment before continuing.

"Well, I…So, uh…I have asked you here today to discuss, um, I have information regarding the upcoming battle that may be to our advantage."

"Do you have any news of Gran, first?" Piper interrupted.

"I am sorry, my lady, no," said Valar shaking his head. "But I am sure she is perfectly safe. Your grandmother had many friends in the palace. Even if she is a prisoner, I am sure she is being well cared for."

"As well cared for as prisoners are," Dimitri murmured.

"Yes, well, if we are successful, that will be of little consequence. We can free Kaytah and all will be well again!" Valar rubbed his hands together and beamed with forced confidence. "Now, onto the matter at hand! It has come to my attention that there is a great probability Taraniz will not be at the battle on the Plains."

"Coward," said Jayson. "She's totally afraid, isn't she?"

"Over confident and self-preserving, in my opinion," replied Valar. "I believe we can use this to our advantage." He paused for dramatics, and his eyes darted from one face to the next. "If Taraniz remains at the palace, she will not be heavily guarded, if at all as I hear of late. We can gain access to the palace with little to no resistance in order to kill her."

"Or capture her," Leo added.

"Yes, or capture her." Valar corrected himself with a strained smile. "However, if Taraniz is at the battle of the Plains, we will still be able to infiltrate the palace and find the royal orenite circlet which we can use against her at a later time."

"You mean, the one they used on Duke Noraedin?" Leo asked. "Why hasn't anyone tried to use it on her before?"

"It is hidden away, or so my sources tell me. If the circlet is truly still in possession of the royal family, it would be within the royal treasury. And since most of her army will be at the Plains, it should be unguarded."

"So, you want us to kill Taraniz with a piece of jewelry instead of a sword because that's so much better." said Jack. "I thought we agreed we would try to help her first. What difference does it make how she's killed? It's still murdering someone."

"Jack, you don't understand what she has done," said Piper.

"Piper, we know she's done some pretty uncool stuff," said Jayson. "But, we said we didn't want to… murder someone if it could be avoided."

"The circlet was used many centuries ago to destroy the magic of the royals at their coronation. Yes, at times it did mean their death, but often it simply dispelled their magical abilities and they were unharmed otherwise. If Taraniz agrees to surrender, we can use the circlet on her to ensure she can never use magic again. A willing advocate has a far greater chance of surviving the magic of the circlet than one who has it forced upon them," said Valar.

Silence hung in the air between them. Jayson, Jack and Leo all felt very uneasy. Their stomachs twisted in knots. Leo's palms were sweaty, and Jack cracked his knuckles anxiously. Piper feared she had little choice but to face the fact that she would very soon be sitting on the Elven throne. The thought made her own stomach drop, and she squeezed Dimitri's hand unconsciously.

"How is your magic training coming along?" Valar asked to break the quiet.

"Uh, slow but, uh, steady," said Jayson with a shrug.

"Excellent. I'm sure you will need some degree of magic against Taraniz. If she is the reincarnated soul of Duke Noraedin, you are dealing with very powerful magic indeed."

"It is not wise to grind stone against the same stone," said Dimitri flatly. "If we put Piper on the throne by using magic, she will have a difficult time winning over her people."

"We are not using magic to put her on the throne, Dimitri," Valar said, his voice curt and he glared harshly at the young man.

"No, but the dwarves haven't exactly welcomed our magic with open arms, either. And if the elves hate magic as much as you've said, they'll like it even less," said Leo. "We need to be careful, is all."

"Indeed," said Valar nodding. "I, unfortunately, have no other news. Will you agree with my plan, then?"

They looked at each other in turn, feeling more uncomfortable by the minute, and less like they had a choice.

"Yes," said Piper quietly.

"Yeah, sure." Jayson shrugged.

"I guess so," said Leo. Dimitri and Jack nodded.

"Good. I have made arrangements for you to meet my son, Valin, in the town of Cannondole. You will leave with the Dwarvik troops so as not to rouse suspicion, and get away under cover of night once camp has been set. We can discuss this in more detail when the time draws nearer. I suppose I shall take my leave of you now." He rose stiffly from the chair, and the others got to their feet as well. "Thank you. Truly, I do sincerely thank you. We will celebrate our victories very soon. I guarantee it." He bowed to them and headed for the door.

Three figures stood in the hallway just beyond, one poised ready to ring the little bell, and Valar nearly walked into them.

"My apologies," said Valar as Piper joined him at the door.

"We are looking for Leo, Jack and Jayson. They were not in the rooms, and we thought they may be here," said a familiar voice beneath a black hood.

"Kylani?" asked Leo. He hurried to the door and peered over Piper's shoulder at the figures in the doorway.

"Good day to you, Valar. We will speak soon." Piper said and ushered Valar into the hall. Valar eyed the new visitors over his shoulder as he hurried on. Piper held the door open for her visitors, then quickly latched the door behind her. The strangers lowered their hoods, and Leo saw Brande and Isla were with Kylani.

"What are you doing here?" Leo asked. He reached out his hand to the brothers as Isla bowed.

"Leo, we have something to ask of you," said Isla. Piper emerged from her room with throw pillows from her bed. The boys took these and sat on the floor, giving their seats to Brande, Kylani and Isla.

"What's up?" asked Jayson. He plopped down on his pillow a little harder than he intended and promptly rubbed his tailbone.

"Sorry?" asked Isla. She looked from Jayson to the ceiling several times, her brow furrowed.

"What can we do for you?" Jack asked.

Brande, Kylani and Isla settled into their chairs and looked to one another before speaking.

"As you are aware, the camaraderie between our two peoples has been tense to say the least." Isla said. She released the clasp on her cloak and it fell across the back of the chair behind her. "It has been difficult attempting to find common ground amongst them, and one leader they all can look to."

"Well that definitely isn't us," said Leo. "You saw what happened in the armory. Neither side has exactly given us a warm welcome since then."

"Outwardly, yes," said Brande. "But in secret, there are more people than you would know that look to you for leadership."

"Really?" Jayson shook his head disgustedly. "They sure have a funny way of showing it."

"Remember, Jayson, they must tread carefully." Kylani smiled and closed his eyes for a moment. "We have all lived in fear of each other for so long that it has become our Heart instructs us to keep our true feelings to ourselves."

Queen Isla stood. "We need someone to lead the charge against our enemy in the battle. I know you have not been permitted to attend the strategy meetings since the incident in the armory, but that can easily be swayed."

"You want us to command units in the army?" asked Leo, and his mouth fell open. "Are you kidding? We don't know the first thing about commanding armies."

Isla turned to face Leo. "Not command, Leo. Lead. We need someone to rally morale and unite our peoples under one banner. No more segregation. No more pointed fingers. We need to be as one."

"Then you need to stop calling yourselves The Black Diamonds," said Dimitri. He looked hard at Brande, Isla and Kylani, though his tone was understanding. "If you want to be as one, you need to act as one."

Brande moved to stand but held his place. "That would mean giving up what we have been fighting for."

"No it doesn't," said Jack. "Look, I've been talking to Gemari. She's on your side."

Isla nodded. "She has come to me in confidence to learn more of how we wish to see our society grow."

"She's a good ally," Jack continued. "Why don't you ask her to go to the Council on your behalf and make The Black Diamonds a temporary Quarter? That's really what you want in the end anyway, isn't it?"

"You believe Princess Gemari would do this?" Brande asked, his eyebrow raised.

"If Jack asks her to she will," said Dimitri with a coy smile.

"I'll talk to her," Jack agreed.

"Thank you, Jack," said Isla. "Now, are you still willing to lead the charge at the battle? I do believe it will still help with morale."

"We can't," Leo said, breaking the silence that had followed Isla's question.

"Leo, no!" said Piper.

"I trust them." Leo nodded at Kylani and Brande. "If you trust me, then trust them." Piper clenched her jaw and Dimitri rubbed her back as Leo continued. "We won't be at the battle."

"What? Why?" Brande, Isla and Kylani asked at once.

"We — we have a secret mission." Jayson said and shrugged.

"There's a good chance Taraniz won't be at the battle," Jack added.

"We — we are going to the Elven palace to capture her," Piper replied. She closed her eyes as the words fell from her lips and sighed.

Brande, Kylani and Isla only nodded.

"Fear not," said Isla, and she nodded reassuringly. "If we could keep the secret of The Black Diamonds for all this time, rest assured your secret is safe with us."

"If anyone asks after you, we will take care of it," said Kylani.

"Thank you," Leo breathed relieved.

The sky outside had turned completely black as another early autumn storm rolled in over the mountainside.

"We should go," said Isla. "I should not be caught outside my curfew."

"You have a curfew? For real?" Jayson nearly laughed.

"As part of my probation," she explained. "I am to have an escort at all times, and I am not to be found out past the ninth hour."

"Where's your guard now?" asked Piper concerned.

"I slipped him the tiniest bit of dreamshade in his tea. He is currently napping in my common room. He will wake soon, so I must return." She stood and bowed to them, then secured her cloak and pulled the hood over her head and face once more.

Piper checked the hall before seeing them out, then again, bolted it behind her. She flopped back into her chair in a rather Jayson-like fashion and sighed loudly.

"What a strange day," she muttered, and they all nodded in agreement.

Chapter Fifteen

A Spy Among Enemies

Leo opened his eyes to darkness, though he knew it must be morning. Every muscle in his right arm and shoulder ached. He wiggled the fingers of his right hand which lay sandwiched between his two large feather pillows. He winced as pain shot through his wrist. He groaned and rolled to face the gem covered ceiling above him. Jack had landed a solid shot to his shoulder during practice the day before, and he wasn't about to move sooner than he had to. He didn't even bother with his morning meditations. Though he and his friends seemed to have certain memories and instincts for fighting, it did not take away from the lack of muscle tone, regardless of muscle memory.

Leo suspected he hurt more than his friends after their fighting practice, but he never voiced such. Every night they went to bed sore and achy, and awoke just as stiff and painful. Piper had ordered they drink a strange, lemony tea to ease the pain, and it did help. But this morning, the storm that had plagued them all day yesterday had left an odd pressure in the air, and made the pain almost unbearable.

Dimitri had insisted they practice in the pouring rain. They were not permitted a break from the deluge until Jack left to meet with Gemari for lunch to fulfill his promise to Brande, Kylani and Isla. Leo didn't understand Jack's fascination with her. He still found her slightly annoying. Jayson had mentioned her nice ta-ta's, but when Jack had pulled a dagger, completely serious about dueling his friend, it was never discussed again.

Leo heard movement and voices out in the common area. He knew their breakfast had been delivered, and sure enough, within minutes, the aroma of those delicious honey-glazed biscuits reached him even through the pillows. His stomach gurgled at the first inhale, and he gave in to his hunger.

"Look who finally decided to grace us with his presence," Jack teased when Leo stepped out of his room, squinting and rubbing his shoulder.

"Shut up, man. You hit me major hard yesterday," said Leo. He grabbed the remaining cup from the tray on the table and drank the lemony tea.

"Here," said Dimitri rising from his chair. He and Piper had already joined the boys and seemed eager to begin their lessons for the day. Dimitri rose and laid his hands on Leo's shoulder. A cool, tingling energy moved down his arm. Leo felt the muscles relax as the magic wound its way through the fibers and into the pain.

"Thanks," said Leo. He stretched his shoulder, and nearly upset his tea cup.

"Seriously, when are we gunna do magic?" Jayson whined through a mouthful of biscuit.

"Today," said Piper with a demure smile.

Jayson, Jack and Leo sat a bit straighter. They looked at Piper and Dimitri with wide eyes and slack jaws.

A piece of biscuit fell from Jayson's mouth before he asked, "Really?"

Piper giggled. "Yes, Jayson. Really."

"We believe you are ready," said Dimitri.

"Can you teach us how to do what you just did?" Leo asked flexing his shoulder again.

"The healing arts take an understanding of anatomy," Dimitri said and leaned back on the sofa, his arm around Piper. "This takes many years. I only know what I do, and that is very little in itself, as Nefiri had fallen ill several years ago. I was her caretaker and learned from our healers. Not magic, but about medicine and anatomy."

"So, what are we going to learn, then?" Leo asked.

"Elemental magic is the easiest," said Piper. "From there, moving objects will be next."

"Like telekinesis?" Jayson was nearly bouncing on the edge of his seat in anticipation. "Oh, that is so cool!"

"One step at a time, my friend," chuckled Dimitri. He tossed a piece of biscuit in the air, ready to catch it in his mouth. Piper snatched it mid arch and popped it in her own mouth with a devious grin. Dimitri tackled her to the floor, and Piper laughed gleefully as he tickled her. They did not stop until she nearly kicked over the cabinet with the forgotten pearl wine.

As they walked to the Black Diamond's mines, they remained more observant to the dwarves they passed as they went. Though most skirted around them close to the walls, they caught subtle hints of what Isla had been talking about. A small smile, a slight incline of the head, lingering eyes or a look over the shoulder. Jayson, Jack and Leo had decided to make an attempt to show the dwarves they were trustworthy. They smiled, bowed, and greeted as many people as they could along their trek in the proper Dwarvik way. Even Piper began to accept her role as the future Elven Queen, and followed suit in respect and greeting. Though outwardly, no one seemed to take heed, they were sure their actions were not going unnoticed. At least, they hoped.

The air was still damp and muggy, but the boys enjoyed their time outdoors. They had spent so much time enclosed in the mountain, the open air and skies were a welcome sight. They walked down the steep path to the forest's edge, and to the little clearing that had become their regular practice space.

The boys lined up facing Piper and Dimitri. Their excitement almost tangible as they fought to keep from bouncing on the balls of their feet or wringing their hands in anticipation.

"Elemental magic is most often associated with weather magic," Dimitri began. "Certainly the ability to cause a sudden rain or thick fog has its advantages against an unsuspecting enemy camp. But these are actions one would use from a distance while safely hidden under cover."

"In situations where you are in hand to hand engagement, however, something far less subtle, such as fire, wind or forcing a stream of water at your opponent is more practical." Piper flinched when she spoke the word fire. The boys nodded their understanding. They were determined to show Piper they were taking their magic lesson very seriously.

"However, both tactics require the manipulation of the energy in the environment around you. Please, sit," said Dimitri. Jack, Leo and

Jayson did as they were bid, but couldn't help but wonder how this would help them throw a fire ball at their enemy.

"If you have been practicing your meditations as instructed, you should be familiar with your own energies now. I want you to sense those energies now. Allow the sensation of your own energies to completely surround you."

They closed their eyes. Immediately they found the calm familiarity of their meditations with little effort. "Now, extend your senses outward. I want you to feel the energy pattern of the person sitting beside you."

They sat for quite some time, concentrating, trying to figure out what Dimitri had instructed. It was not easy. Eventually, they felt a different kind of energy mixing with their own.

"Whoa. Cool," whispered Jayson and a smile pulled at his lips.

"Excellent," said Dimitri. "Now, cast your senses outward even farther. Try to sense the water droplets in the clouds. They will not be the size of the rain you recognize, but they will be there. Raise your hand when you have identified them, but do not break your concentration."

This took even longer than the previous exercise. The rain from the night before had made everything around them wet, and it was difficult to separate the vapor in the sky from what surrounded them. Once they had all lifted a hand, Dimitri smiled.

"Now, bring those energies together, and bring them toward you."

This was not as easy as it sounded. But slowly the sky grew darker, and tiny droplets of water landed around them. Dimitri eyed Piper with a mischievous grin. She sat deep in concentration, her lips slightly parted. His smile deepened as the sky completely opened up. In a matter of moments, they were drenched. Leo, Jayson, Jack and Piper scrambled to their feet and attempted to take shelter under the nearby trees as Dimitri continued to laugh beneath the pouring rain.

By the end of the day, they had gotten wet at least twice more with falling snow and thick, gray fog before drying out beneath the scorching sun. They were exhausted, but the elation the boys felt was hardly containable. They had used magic. They fell into their beds that night with smiles that did not fade even as they drifted into sleep.

The next day was bright and luckily dry. Their magic lesson had not affected the normal weather patterns of the mountains too greatly. Dimitri was glad for he wished to begin teaching the boys to work with fire. He was awed at their ability to grasp the laws and concepts of magic so quickly. It had taken him months of practice to learn what they had in a single day. As they stood before him again, Dimitri stifled his excitement. He had never given much credence to the so called prophecies of Chartile. It wasn't that he disbelieved so much as it didn't play a part in his life. The prospect of being the one to teach the returned kings did not sit with him as a burden or weight. It was unreservedly exciting.

They began the morning with their usual fighting drills. Leo refused to let them become rusty.

"We've been using weapons longer than we've been using magic. If we really need to defend ourselves, well, I think fighting will be more instinctual, ya know?"

As the morning wore on, the monotony of the drills they performed every day passed by in a blur. By mid-morning Dimitri was pacing and fidgeting to move on.

"Alright, let's see how you handle something a bit hotter," he said and grinned mischievously.

Piper took him by the arm and turned away from the boys.

"Dimitri, I would much prefer if I were the one to teach them how to use fire," she said quietly.

"My gem, I believe I can handle a little fire," Dimitri chuckled. He winked and nudged her shoulder playfully.

"I know," she said rubbing her hands together. "But... teaching someone may help me to face my fears."

Dimitri sighed and nodded. "Alright," he said. He kissed her forehead and brushed her hair out of her eyes. They turned back to Jayson, Jack and Leo, shoulder to shoulder.

The boys stood at attention like soldiers, chests out and chins up. They felt the importance of today's magic lesson and were not about to mess it up.

"The first thing you need to understand about using fire," Piper stopped her pacing and stared directly at the boys. "Is it can quickly get out of hand. Of course, it is important to remember the other elements can be just as deadly, but the amount of energy necessary to create such devastation is far greater than for fire. A little can go a long way." She sighed and swallowed hard. "You may not always have a flame available to you from an outside source. Fire needs fuel to sustain itself, and therefore, you may need to feed it your own energy to keep it going. Fire is made from certain components in the world around us, and you will need these as well as your energy to fuel and sustain the flame. I will draw each of these elements to you individually so you may learn their energy patterns. Then, I will have you do the same to me." She paused again and bit her lip. "Once you can call each of these elements from your surroundings to you, compress them into your hand, and surround them with your own energy."

They spent at least an hour working with the individual components. Piper was strict and demanded perfection from them, but the boys did not complain. Dimitri became bored and sat beneath the shade of the trees at the edge of the clearing, pulling up clumps of grass and weeds, and tying them into a knotted chain. He watched as Piper worked with Jack, Leo and Jayson each individually. She stood behind them, holding out her hand beside theirs, and walked them through the steps.

The boys were amused with how each of their little hand-held flames seemed to take on the personality of its creator. Jack's flame danced slow and peaceful like a gentle candle flame. Leo's fire ball was bright, compact and perfectly round. Jayson was sure he had singed his eyebrows when his flame erupted nearly a foot skyward in his rush of excitement.

Once they were all creating their own personal flames, Dimitri rose and painted a number of targets on the flat, smooth surface of the rock face of the mountain. They practiced throwing their flames at the targets, and as their aim grew more accurate, they experimented with different sizes and even the speed of their flames. The formality and seriousness of their training slowly ebbed away. Piper tried to smile and encourage them as they went, but her frequent hard swallows and twirling the ends of her hair did not go unnoticed by her friends.

After several hours of practice, Jayson attempted to light the end of one of his arrows. The shaft instantly caught fire. He dropped the arrow to the ground, stamping the flame in a kind of dance to put it out. Leo laughed then tried to set his own blade alight. He was successful at first, but the metal began to heat quickly. He let go of the sword, and the hilt hit his toe as he shook his burnt hand.

"There are many layers of magic needed to attempt such a feat," said Dimitri. "You need to magically protect the wood or metal from the natural effects of the fire. Draconian runes could help with this, but it would be a very complicated endeavor."

"Bummage," said Jack, and he sent a last feeble fireball toward the targets on the stone. A sizzle and a small plume of steam billowed into the sky as Jack missed his mark, and instead hit the small trickle of water that ran beside the mountain.

The sun was high in the sky now, and their work with the fire had made them all hot and sticky. They welcomed the break to refresh themselves in the little brook. Leo ran inside to retrieve some food for their midday meal and returned to find Dimitri and Jayson had paired off against Jack and Piper in a magical water fight. He left the fruit and bread beside the path and quickly joined in. An hour later, they sprawled on the grass, drying and sunning themselves on one of the last warm days of the season. Change was coming, not only the autumn season.

A strange whistle echoed off the mountain from somewhere beyond their clearing. It was unlike any bird they had ever heard. They opened their eyes, and looked at one another. It sounded again, a bit closer this time, and the boys leapt to their feet. Dimitri put a finger to his lips and motioned them to follow. They crouched low ducking behind the trees, and watched as a dwarf in the ravine below them whistled again. His call was answered, and two elves appeared from deeper in the forest. As they drew closer, Jayson, Jack and Leo saw the same heraldry emblazoned across their gambesons as the soldiers who had been with Taraniz the day they arrived in Chartile.

"What news have you, Maltori?" asked one of the elves. "What could be so important you could not have sent a messenger bird?"

"I dared not risk it being intercepted, sir," said the dwarf. He looked behind him so often, he appeared to have a twitch. "We have sent word to Tutaria via the Great Passage. The Diamonds have rescinded their agreement to help Princess Taraniz. Reinforcements will be on their way within a few days."

Cassandra Morgan

"I know him," whispered Leo, "He's one of the blacksmiths for the armory. He was a spy for the Black Diamonds. Kylani introduced me."

"We will need to move quickly then," said the other elf. He pulled a small bag of coins from a pouch on his belt and tossed it to Maltori. "Thank you for your service. Our lady will be pleased." The elves turned back toward the trees. Jayson fixed an arrow to his bow, and Jack pulled a throwing dagger. Piper, Leo and Dimitri readied fireballs in their hands and nodded to one another.

"There is something else Princess Taraniz may wish to know," said Maltori. The elves stopped, and the dwarf jingled the bag of coins. The first elf rolled his eyes and pulled another purse of coins from his pouch, tossing it to Maltori.

"Speak," the elf said impatiently.

"Another heir has been discovered. The twin of Taraniz they claim. Her name is Eva Ruani, though she calls herself Piper."

The elves exchanged concerned looks, then turned back to Maltori.

"You are certain?" the second asked.

"She was presented to the Council by Valar. He was once King Aramor's advisor, yes?"

"Valar is a traitor. There is a bounty on his head, as well as the girl. What are their chances of capture?" asked the other.

"Piper is never alone. She stays with the returned kings, and is always with the Empress's retainer. Valar comes and goes. He is currently under the protection of the dwarves."

"We will inform our lady at once. I suggest you find refuge outside your mountain. If what you

211

say is true, then Mount Kelsii will soon be under siege. Thank you, Maltori."

The elf had barely finished speaking when an arrow pierced his chest. He cried out, staggering backward. Maltori turned to see the group at the top of the ravine. His eyes caught sight of Piper, and he screamed, "It's her!" Dimitri's fire ball landed squarely in Maltori's face as Jack's dagger landed in the dwarf's thigh. As one, the party hurried down the steep embankment. The second elf ran into the forest. Fireballs from Dimitri, Jack and Piper followed close behind him. Jayson, Leo and Piper stopped when they reached the fallen elf. Dimitri and Jack continued after the other. Between the thickness of the trees, and the smoke from their fire balls, Dimitri and Jack lost the man in short order.

"NO!" cried Dimitri furious, and began swearing in Dwarvik, or at least that's what Jack assumed.

"We have to warn Nefiri," Jack said. They ran back toward the mountain as quickly as the thickness of the forest allowed them. They broke through the clearing to find Piper, Jayson and Leo starring at their fallen foes. Dimitri's fire ball had been more than effective against the traitorous dwarf. Maltori lay charred and unrecognizable in the grass. None of them could look at him. Instead, they crouched beside the injured elf who clutched at his chest and spoke through pained, wheezing breaths.

"Please," he called desperately. "Please help me."

"We have to get him to the healers," said Jayson's shaky voice.

"Absolutely not," Dimitri replied, "He is a traitor. He can die like one." The sneer in Dimitri's voice was unlike what his friends had come to know.

"He might have information that could be useful," said Leo. He bent to examine the wound in the man's chest. The elf coughed, and blood trickled from the corner of his mouth. Leo pulled back quickly, looking rather gray. "I think his lung is punctured."

"It is clear now," heaved the elf, his eyes wide. "I did not know, but she has us all."

"He's in shock, or something," said Jack. "Come on." He reached down to help Leo lift the man. Jayson stepped forward, dropping his bow and quiver and reached a hand under the man's arm.

Dimitri snatched up the bow and quiver and raised an arrow to the string, pointing it at the elf's head.

"I will see him dead before his treacherous soul sets foot in my mountain."

No one moved. Only the sound of the elf's labored breathing broke the silence.

"Dimitri, the boys are right." Piper placed a hand on his arm. "He may have valuable information that could help us in the coming battle. Or possibly a way of breaking into the castle." She had never seen Dimitri so full of rage. She forced her hand not to tremble against his skin.

"Did you forget he wanted to kill you?" Dimitri shrugged her hand off his arm and kept the arrow pointed at the elf.

"His actions do not give us just cause for the same," said Piper calmly. Her green eyes stared at Dimitri, though he would not look at her.

"No, please," said the elf. "I did not know, but, I still— my wife, my son. Send me to them. Let her burn me no longer."

"We can get you help," said Jayson, and he squeezed the soldier's hand, his voice cracking as he fought back tears.

"She will find a way back in." The elf squeezed Jayson's hand back weakly. "My mind is mine again. I must atone for my actions."

"Enough. If it is death he wants—" said Dimitri, but Piper reached forward and snapped the end from the arrow. Dimitri finally turned to her. The anger in his dark eyes meeting the fear in hers. He threw the bow to the ground. "Fine! If this is how you want to do this, he's your kin. I am no elf."

The man closed his eyes, his breathing became slower and forced. Piper knelt beside him, and the boys followed suit. She placed a hand on the man's brow and spoke softly. "What is your name, brave soldier, that I may speak it to the stars tonight and pray you find your way home?"

"Tathias," he whispered.

"Tathias, can you tell us what you mean when you say she will find a way back in?"

Tathias released one long exhale. His hand went limp in Jayson's palm and his body relaxed, all the wrinkles leaving his pained face.

Jayson, Jack, Leo and Piper silence for nearly a full minute, lost within their own thoughts and feelings. Finally, Piper rose, looking down at the elf before her. "Did you catch the other one?" she asked

Jack. The boy shook his head and Piper nodded. "Then we need to report this immediately. Come."

They stood to follow Piper. Jayson bent to retrieve the bow Dimitri had thrown to the ground. He stopped before his hand tightened around his bow. He had killed someone. The arrow that had pierced the man's lung was his. He had meant to aim for the elf's shoulder. He couldn't understand how he had missed. His visions had come true. He had actually killed someone. Jayson ran to the nearest tree. He fell to his knees, trembling, crying and vomiting. Leo, Jack, Piper and even Dimitri scrambled back to him.

"Jay, are you okay?" Leo asked from several feet away.

"Are you hurt?" Jack asked. He stood beside Leo, the two exchanged looks of concern.

Jayson said nothing. He rocked back and forth, his arms clutched tightly across his chest and tears spilling down his face.

Piper pushed past Jack and Leo and knelt beside him. She wrapped an arm around him and he fell into her, his tears almost instantly soaking her tunic where he buried his face in her shoulder.

"It's alright," she whispered, and stroked his hair like her mother once did for her.

"It's my fault," Jayson choked, "I did it. I k-killed—"

"No," said Piper. "No, do not talk that way." But she knew he was right. Even if Dimitri had cooperated, Tathias would not have survived the trek across the mountain to the healers. Jayson had acted out of instinct to the prophecy as a King and what they had been training for. But, he had also

215

been the one that had cut the cord on Tathias's last breath.

"Piper," said Dimitri. His voice had returned to its soft and caring tone once more. "We must inform the Elders."

Piper nodded and turned back to Jayson.

"We will always remember Tathias," she said and held Jayson at arm's length. "His sacrifice has allowed us the chance at the upper hand against Taraniz. We must inform the Elders. If we are able to save more people with this information, then we can right this wrong."

Jayson breathed deeply and wiped his face on his shirt.

"It's what we're supposed to do anyway," he said. His voice was stronger and steadier.

"Only if you want to," Piper reminded him.

"For Tathias," Jayson whispered. Piper hugged him and pulled him to his feet. Dimitri handed Jayson his bow and quiver, an unspoken apology in his eyes.

The group tore back through the door to the Black Diamond's mine. Those in the central trading square looked up as they dodged passersby in a panicked frenzy.

"Jentar!" Jack cried to the man who sold them their weapon supplies. "Where are Kylani and Brande?" They skidded to a halt in front of the merchant. Jayson fell on the smooth floor, but no one took notice.

"I do not know," said Jentar with a shrug. "In the main armory, perhaps?"

"Send someone to find them. Have them meet in the Crystal Quarter. It's an emergency," said Leo. Jentar nodded and the group took off again.

The one time they wished the corridors were full of guards was the one time the tunnels were completely empty. They ran as fast as they could back to the Sapphire Quarter. They hoped to find one of the Royals or Elders currently in residence.

Two guards stood at attention outside Una's rooms. They shouldered out of the way, bewildered when the five stopped before them, panting, clutching cramps in their sides and even coughing.

"We need to speak to Queen Una immediately," puffed Dimitri. "Please, Ketill." The guard looked suspiciously at the faces staring up at him.

"I am sorry, Dimitri. I cannot," he said.

"Please," pleaded Jayson. "There was a spy for Taraniz. We just heard him talking to her guards. One of them got away. They're gunna attack Mount Kelsii before the soldiers from Tutaria get here."

The guards sighed and exchanged looks of regret. Before either could speak, the door opened. Una, dressed in a robe and her hair tied up in a towel, scowled at them.

"What is the commotion out here?" She fell silent when she saw who stood before her and glared. "What are you doing here? Causing more trouble, I presume. I thought the kings were supposed to right the wrongs of our land, not cause more."

"Una," said Piper, pushing past the guards. "You must call a meeting of the Elders and commanders. We have less time than we thought before Taraniz attacks."

"Why should I believe you, elf?" Una spat. "I do not care what Nefiri believes. You are no Queen. Not now and not ever. A title and a crown does not make you a Royal. Go! All of you!"

Una moved to slam the door. Ketill reached past Piper and stopped the door with his spear. Everyone caught their breath as Una looked at Ketill wide eyed.

"Forgive me, my Queen," he said. "I love my people too much to have these words of caution go unheeded. If it is nothing, then we still have nothing to fear and we may proceed as planned."

"I should have you stripped of your titles, Ketill," Una breathed. "You are unfit to live as the second hasana of such a noble house as Aulfr. How dare you speak to me in such a way. How dare you speak to me at all!" She lifted her hand to strike him, but Leo jumped between them.

"Stop!" Leo cried, holding up his hands. "This is exactly what Taraniz wants. The more we fight amongst ourselves, the weaker we become!"

"We?" shrieked Una. A few Elders had unlocked their doors to peek at the uproar in the hall. "You are not one of us, Leonardo DeHaven! You have no right to speak to me in this manner."

"What is going on here?" Frejah folded her arms before her as she approached Una.

"We need to call an emergency meeting," Jayson cried. "Taraniz is going to attack us sooner than we thought!"

"This is absurd. Absolutely ridiculous!" said Una, throwing her hands up.

"I will inform Nefiri at once," said Frejah, and she hurried away. Una stared after her, her jaw clenched tight. She turned on Leo, who still stood between her and Ketill.

"For your sake, I pray this is no trick." She slammed the door behind her, leaving those at her door silent, and the onlookers in the hall whispering amongst themselves.

"Thank you, Ketill," said Dimitri softly.

"She will dismiss me," said Ketill, and he shifted his spear from hand to hand nervously. "I have defied a woman, and my Queen at that. I will be called a Black Diamond for my actions. I will never find work in the mountain again."

"Gemari won't let that happen," said Jack.

Ketill looked at Jack, who stood nearly as tall as the dwarf. Jack nodded and followed his friends up the hall.

Frejah and Nefiri wasted no time in gathering the Elders and Royals. And, thanks to Jack's quick thinking, even Brande and Kylani were present. Una continued to protest against them, but most everyone was in agreement they could not risk waiting for the Tutarian reinforcements to arrive. Plans were made to begin evacuating Mount Kelsii immediately and send them along the Great Passage to the Tutarian Mountains.

Jack, Leo and Jayson had briefly heard of the Great Passage from Gemari. As they ate a small meal before joining the soldiers helping with the evacuation, Dimitri explained further.

"The Great Passage is a tunnel that leads from Mount Kelsii, under the Great Plains, and nearly all the way to the Tutarian Mountain range.

Prophecy

It comes up in the foot hills of the mountains and is about a day's journey from the front gates of the mountain. It is often used as a major trade route between our peoples. It is a straighter and faster way, and we are sheltered from the elements as opposed to travelling above ground."

"How far is it from here to the Tutarian Mountains?" Leo asked.

"If you travelled by The Great Passage I would expect it would be about a week, perhaps two for our evacuees as they will have undoubtedly burdened themselves with unnecessary trinkets."

"Dimitri, you can't blame them." Jack popped a spiced mushroom into his mouth, chewed quickly and continued. "They may never come back here again. If Taraniz is successful, all of this could be destroyed."

"She won't destroy it," said Piper. "It's too valuable of an asset. She may repurpose it, but the mountain will still remain, more or less anyway."

"Let us hope," said Dimitri. He bit off a piece of mountain boar jerky and stared quietly at the wall.

Chapter Sixteen
Change and Stubbornness

The day seemed to fly by in a frenzy of screaming children and absolute, utter chaos. As easy as it should have been for the citizens to pack a few essentials and proceed calmly to the Crystal Quarter for final preparations, it apparently wasn't. The dwarves could not leave their treasures behind, and carried bags full of jewels, paintings, and fancy cutlery in lieu of clothes and blankets. Once a home was evacuated, it was searched by the Kelsii soldiers. Any food left behind was taken to the Crystal Quarter for redistribution or storage for the trip ahead. There would be hundreds of mouths to feed, and many had conveniently forgotten how necessary food was for the long trek ahead of them. Once the quarter had been pronounced clear, guards were stationed at its entrance to ensure no one reentered, and the citizens were escorted from the Crystal Quarter to the Great Passage with considerable more food and far less silverware.

Jayson, Jack and Leo worked through the night ensuring the homes in each quarter were empty. The dwarves had offered them a bitter tasting energy bar of sorts that kept them wide awake. It reminded them of chocolate, and they ate as much as they could until they were positively buzzing with energy. They were assisting in a final sweep of the Ruby Quarter when the door to a homestead Jayson had just searched closed behind him. He tapped Jack and Leo on the shoulder and motioned for them to follow.

Jayson fitted an arrow to his bow and stepped quietly to the door. He listened for a moment then kicked in the door, bow aimed and ready to fire. Jack and Leo stood waiting on either side of him. A little girl, no more than six years old, dropped a stale crust of bread that had been left behind. She ducked behind a table in the front workshop of the home, and the boys all lowered their weapons.

"It's alright," Jayson said putting his arrow back in its quiver. "We're not going to hurt you."

"We didn't mean to scare you." Jack said in the same voice he used to sooth his baby sister. "You can come out. We're here to help."

Bushy black hair and big brown eyes slowly peered over the top of the wooden work bench. She looked at them for a few moments, her eyes darting back and forth between them. Very slowly, she crept from behind the bench and handed Jack the other half of the bread she had been eating.

"I'm sorry," she said, her voice so quiet they could hardly hear her.

"What's your name?" asked Jack. The girl was filthy and thin. She didn't answer, but continued to look at the floor, her arms clasped behind her back.

"Where are your parents?" Leo asked. Again, the girl did not speak. They heard the other soldier coming back from his sweep of the corridor.

"We should check this place over again," said Leo, and Jack nodded. They headed into the main living areas of the home to check for any other dwarves who may have stayed behind.

"I'll take her to the Crystal Quarter," Jayson called after them, but Jack and Leo did not answer. The little girl peered up at Jayson, then quickly cast her eyes back to the floor when she saw him look at her.

"Do you want to carry my bow?" he asked and held the weapon out to her. She didn't move. She stared at the bow, her eyes wide and swayed back and forth. Finally, she reached out a grubby little hand and slowly closed her palm around the grip. Jayson let go, and she quickly caught it with her other hand, a smile tugging at the corners of her mouth.

"It's heavy," she whispered.

"A little," said Jayson. "Are you hungry? I know where we can get you some food." He held out a hand to her. She hesitated, holding the bow closer to her. Jayson suppressed an eye roll but still sighed. The little girl was as shy as Jessica had been before his parents had sent her to Cranbrook. Cranbrook Art Academy was an elite school for gifted children, and it was a two hour drive from Swansdale. His parents drove it twice a day so their daughter could receive the best education possible. Even at five years old, Jessica had been wary and intimidated about the prospect of going to a special school. His parents constantly reminded her how smart and special she was. By the time Jessica had attended her first week of preschool, she knew she was different.

The little girl staring back at Jayson held the same scared yet hungry look in her eyes that Jessica had her first few years at Cranbrook. His heart dropped a little at the thought of his sister and family. He pushed his feelings aside, and knelt down as Jack had to the girl's level.

"I have a little sister at home. She's a little older than you, but she loves piggy-back rides. Would you like a piggy-back ride?" The girl's face lit up and she nodded her head. Jayson smiled and removed his quiver so she had room to climb on. "You're gunna need to hold tight to that bow now," he said.

"I will," the little girl whispered in his ear. She clasped her hands around Jayson's neck and held the bow between them. The wood pushed into his throat. He gently adjusted the bow and slung his quiver into the crook of his arm.

Jayson trudged down the winding corridors of the mountain, trying not to take notice of the bow that choked him or the quiver that beat into his shins. He found himself at the large double doors of the Crystal Quarter, and squatted down again to let the little girl climb off. He saw Gemari flitting between the little clusters of people, handing them blankets. He called to her, and she bowed as she approached.

"Jayson," said Gemari. "Where is Jack? And Leo?"

"He's back in the Ruby Quarter," said Jayson and Gemari blushed slightly. Hey, we found this little girl by herself. I think she might be lost." The girl clung to Jayson, hiding her face behind his legs.

"What is your name, dear one?" Gemari asked. Her voice was soft and quiet as she wrapped a blanket around the little girl's shoulders.

"Lynden," the girl whispered through the fingers of her free hand, her other still clutching Jayson's bow.

"Lynden?" said a woman from behind Gemari. She was dressed in a gown that must have weighed at least ten pounds with all the rubies that had been sewn into it. Her hair was pulled back into a tight bun, held in place with a very large ruby comb, and her lips were painted bright red. She rushed to the girl, nearly pushing Jayson over in her haste. "Is your mother Lynhldr?" she asked.

The child looked at Jayson who nodded for her to answer. The girl nodded in reply, and the woman grabbed the child away from between Gemari and Jayson. The bow dropped from the little girl's hands as she stumbled into the woman's grasp.

"Oh, you poor dear! We have all been so worried about you!" the woman said, stroking the little girl's matted hair.

"Do you know this child?" Gemari asked. Her tone sounded more like her sister, as did the look she gave the woman.

"Her family was murdered and dragged off by those horrible Black Diamonds several weeks ago during the altercation at the home of Lynhldr. She must have escaped. You poor thing. Have you been living on your own all this time?"

"Aerndis?" said another woman behind the first. She was not as magnificently garbed as the first woman, but her clothes still held small touches of flashing red gems. The first woman held Lynden close to her side as she stood to address the newcomer. "Is everything alright?"

"Yes, Aeris," said Aerndis curtly. "Lynden of Lynhldr has been found. I will take care of her."

"Are you sure she has no other family?" Gemari asked. Jayson crossed his arms and joined Gemari in staring at the women in disbelief. He was impressed at Gemari's continued tact.

"No, the Black Diamonds killed them all. She is the same age as my son. I can care for her now," said Aerndis.

"The Black Diamonds did no such thing!" Aeris' hands fluttered in the air before her. "It was our soldiers who had orders to kill them. My hasana told me himself!"

"You and your hasana are Diamond sympathizers! Of course you would believe such lies. You are no longer any sister of mine!"

"My lady," Aeris turned to Gemari. "I have not yet been blessed with a daughter. I knew the family from which this child came. I can care for Lynden."

It may have been his lack of food and sleep the last several hours, or the simple mindless bickering that set him off. Looking back, Jayson wasn't sure. But, in that moment, all he could see was his parents arguing over what was best for Jessica. She stood between them, clutching at his mother's legs as Lynden was now, unable to say what she desired, nor even asked.

Jayson reached down and scooped Lynden away from the women.

"If you're going to stand there and act like children, then neither of you should be raising one," he spat. "The Black Diamonds are our allies now, and whatever happened in the past needs to stay there. I'll take care of her if I have to. At least I've got more sense to find out what she wants." He picked up his bow, handed it back to Lynden, and slung her onto his back again.

"No, wait!" Aeris called after him. "I am sorry. You are right. Sister, please, no more of this. Our King is correct. Lynden, would you like to come with me and get something to eat?"

"I am sure you will fit into my son's clothes until we can find you something," said Aerndis.

Jayson looked at Gemari who nodded. Reluctantly, he let Lynden climb from his back. She handed the bow back to him and smiled.

"Thank you, sir king sir, for saving me," she whispered, and took Aeris's outstretched hand. Jayson and Gemari watched them go as Leo and Jack joined them from their final sweep of the Ruby Quarter with the other guard patrols.

Gemari shook her head and sighed.

"This has to stop," she said, more to herself than anyone in particular.

"What?" asked Jack. He leaned on his staff, exhaustion finally catching up with him.

"It does not truly matter if the Diamonds are made a Quarter or not. There has always been a rivalry from Quarter to Quarter. Ruby, Topaz, Citrine. We need proper unification. The rights of our men are only the first step. If we are to succeed and grow as a people, we must change."

She turned away from the women as the disappeared into the crowd. Her face was hard and distant. She looked at Jack and her eyes softened. "You have opened my eyes to ideas I never thought possible. I see things so differently now. I believe in you. All of you. My Kings."

She reached out a hand to Jack. He took it, and tried to lift her knuckles to his lips. But Gemari squeezed his hand and shook it. She smiled at them, and wandered back into the crowd to continue handing out blankets.

"You sure know how to pick 'em, Jack," said Jayson shaking his head. "Your girlfriend's a piece of work."

"She's not my girlfriend!" Jack said through clenched teeth. "It's not allowed."

"You never know, if Gemari keeps this up," Leo said staring after the princess. "I don't know if this is considered a wrong or not, but we've had some major influence here, and Gemari's eventually going do something about it."

❧

The boys were exhausted by the time they were finally ordered to rest by Frejah. They didn't even bother to change their clothes. They fell into their beds and were asleep almost instantly, their weapons haphazardly strewn around the common area.

Dimitri found Piper leaning against a wall in the Cobalt Quarter. She had fallen asleep with her sword still clutched in her hand. He smiled and brushed a strand of hair from her face. Piper jumped awake, smacking the heavy hilt of her blade between Dimitri's legs. She gasped as Dimitri doubled over.

"Oh, Dimitri! Oh, I am so sorry!"

"It's alright," he breathed through clenched teeth. Piper stifled a giggle as he stood straight again. "This arrived for you," he said, his voice still strained. He handed her a small, rolled piece of parchment that had been tied to a carrier bird. It read noCalnoden.

"It was sent to Nefiri. She believes it is Valar's handwriting, so she had me bring it to you. Does it mean anything to you?"

Piper stared at the writing for several moments, her brow furrowed.

"Are you sure this is meant for me?" she finally asked. "This does not make any sense."

Dimitri shrugged. "Nefiri did not say much. I believe she regrets dismissing me. Still, I will not give her the satisfaction of groveling back to her. Certainly not if she makes me choose between you or her."

Piper crossed her arms and sighed, twiddling the parchment between her fingers. "Dimitri, she is your mother. You need to forgive her."

"No," said Dimitri firmly. "She dismissed me. If she wishes me back in her life, she will come to me."

Piper shook her head. "Did you ever think that she knows how angry you are, and is trying to give you some freedom? Perhaps she is waiting for you to forgive her. Nefiri is not above making mistakes, and she knows this. Dimitri, she is your mother —"

"No, she isn't."

"Well she's as good as! And she did a damned good job raising you, if you ask me. The woman I call my mother did not give birth to me either, in case you have forgotten. Your stubbornness is going to be the end of you, Dimitri. I do not understand why you believe you are better than everyone else lately, but you aren't." Piper tossed her messy red hair and stomped away, leaving Dimitri completely bewildered. It was twice in two days they had not agreed on the situation at hand, and it rather unsettled her.

Piper ignored the guards she passed as she stormed back to her rooms. She slammed the door behind her and headed straight to her bedroom. She threw her boots against the stone wall as she undressed and climbed into bed. She lay awake, staring at the little slip of parchment by candle light. Her body still buzzed with anger, though it slowly ebbed away in the flickering light of the soft flame beside her. She ignored Dimitri as he opened the door and climbed into bed beside her. He hugged her close to him, and kissed her back and shoulder.

"I do not want to fight with you," he said. Piper set the parchment on the table beside her and turned to him. It was as close to an apology as she was likely to get from him.

"I don't want to fight either. Dimitri, you haven't been yourself lately. I do not understand what is going on."

"I do not know," he whispered, and looked at the mattress between them. "I never imagined things would happen this way. I just want to be with you. I do not understand why we cannot simply kill Taraniz and be done with it."

Piper pulled from his grip. "There is nothing simple about killing someone, Dimitri. Though, I admit, it has been weighing heavily on my mind ere of late," she said. "Taraniz has done terrible things, and it is my responsibility to my people to bring her to justice. But..." She turned to stare at the ceiling, her eyes distant as she became lost in the visions that played in her mind.

"But," Dimitri prompted quietly.

She looked at him again and replied, "But she is my sister. A sister I never knew I had. A sister who has not only been plagued with this curse of magic as I have, but who has had it affect her more deeply than any of us can understand. Think of what we could learn from each other. If Gran is dead, Taraniz is the only family I have left. We need to give her a chance." Piper propped herself up on her elbow. Her silhouette stood out against the candle light behind her. All Dimitri could see was the glint of her green eyes. "What do you believe will happen when I become Queen?" she asked. "I know we promised each other we would be together, but, you do not seem as though you wish to be King."

"No, I do not. I could never be a king. Even if the Elder's bade it so, it is not the life for me, Piper."

"Then, where does that leave us?" she asked. She closed her eyes, forcing back the tears she felt sting her eyes.

"What do you mean? I thought this was a simple matter of marriage. You never said anything about me being King."

"No, I did not. I suppose it was implied. I need to have heirs, and I need someone to help me make decisions and govern my people."

"Piper, I was raised Dwarvik. I could not help you in the matters of elven state even if I wanted to." Dimitri sat up, pulling Piper closer to him. He clasped his hands around hers and kissed her. "I think you can guide your people without the help of anyone, and you can certainly do it better than Taraniz." Piper rolled her eyes but a smile escaped her. "I know she is your sister, and I know you worry about being like her, but you are different. That is why I love you. So, let us forget that for now. Let me say happy birthday to you properly."

Pulled away and sat up. "What?" she asked.

Dimitri smiled his cocky smile that made Piper melt. He brushed the hair from her face and answerer, "It is why I was coming to find you. I overheard the elders discussing the sun cycles when I retrieved the message from Nefiri. We have been so busy we have not been watching the moons." He pulled her toward him again, and wrapped his arms around her, kissing her fiercely. "Happy birthday, my darling Queen."

Chapter Seventeen
The Belirian Forest

The last of the warm summer days seemed to fade away overnight. A chill hung in the air the next morning, aided only by the fear and sadness that clung to the hearts of all the citizens of Mount Kelsii. Jack felt it in his heart too. A heaviness, a nagging that sat and festered in his chest. His feelings for Gemari only heightened the sense of urgency he felt to evacuate the mountain as quickly as possible. He felt guilty that he had needed to rest, but Frejah had instead. These were the thoughts that inundated him as he lay staring at the jewel encrusted ceiling above him the next morning. He wondered if it would be there in a month. Would it even still be there in a week?

Jack stretched and quietly climbed from his bed. He tried not to wake Jayson, who lay drooling open mouthed in the other bed. He was usually the first of his friends to rise. It probably came from waking early to check on his family after his father had been drinking. He stopped in the doorway to the common area and leaned against the wall. He couldn't remember the last time he had thought about his family. He swallowed hard, and for a moment he wondered if he would have to decide whether to stay in Chartile or return home.

He closed the bedroom door behind him and crossed to the cabinet with the pearl wine. Some bread and fruit remained from their lunch the day before. Most of the food stores had gone to the evacuees, and the kitchen staff were no longer taking orders or deliveries. Most, in fact, had travelled down The Great Passage that very night. Those soldiers and officials remaining in the mountain were on their own. The kitchens were only a half mile or so away from their rooms, but Jack preferred to wait for his friends. He tore a piece from the half loaf and occupied himself with chewing the stale bread.

There was the shuffling of sleepy feet, and the door to Jack's right creaked open. Leo emerged, rubbing his eyes and affixing his glasses securely in place. Piper had long ago tied string to the arms of Leo's glasses so he would not lose them. It was rather impressive they hadn't broken yet, especially during their fight practices.

"Jay still sleeping?" Leo mumbled.

"Yep," said Jack. Leo joined him on the sofa, and they sat in silence, slowly crunching the bread.

"How much longer ya think it'll be before everyone's evacuated?" Jack asked.

"Maybe another day or so. I was talking with Frejah yesterday. She said none of their scouts can find any evidence of Taraniz's army assembling anywhere. It's got everyone really worried."

"Maybe she changed her plan. Maybe we have more time. That means the refugees will be further along the Great Passage and closer to Tutaria when the fighting starts." And Gemari will be safer, Jack thought.

"They could be using magic to conceal themselves." Leo suggested with a shrug.

Jack shrugged back. He didn't want to think about Taraniz's army or the coming battle. The safety of the dwarves who had become like a second family to him was all that matter. It may have been

Leo who had first found The Black Diamonds, and the dwarves did believe he was the reincarnated soul of King Florine. But Jack had felt he belonged here in the mountain since the day they came to Fortress Kelsii. Or, perhaps he only wanted to spend more time with Gemari. He had never felt this way about anyone before. It was strange. He knew some kids in school who had girlfriends, but they always broke up after a few weeks. Sometimes he heard of the high school kids who had the same girlfriend for three years. Even his Aunt Kiera and Uncle Rob had been high school sweethearts. Maybe finding your soul mate when you were really young was still possible. But, Gemari couldn't be his soul mate. She was from another world entirely. It was all so very confusing.

There was a loud crash from Jack and Jayson's room. Jack and Leo jumped to their feet, hands flying to the daggers that sat on the table before them. The door opened and Jayson stumbled out, the evidence of a fallen tapestry and a broken vase behind him. His friends relaxed and sat back down, shaking their heads.

"They really didn't need all that anyway," Jayson muttered, and joined them. His hair was a complete mess, and stuck up in several different directions. They had discussed having one of the Dwarvik hair dressers give them a haircut a few days ago, but it was the furthest thing from their minds now.

"Leave anything for me?" asked Jayson through a yawn.

Leo handed him the fruit bowl. A few berries sat at the bottom and the last chunk of stale bread.

"Fine dining, isn't it?" said Jayson, and he popped the berries in his mouth in one bite. "Piper or Dimitri been by?" he asked, berry spit dribbling down his chin.

"No," said Jack, and he handed Jayson a handkerchief. "Maybe we should just go find one of the guards. Last I knew the Topaz Quarter and Obsidian Quarter were the last two to be cleared. I'm not sure how much they may have gotten through during the night."

"No way, man. We said we would always stay together." Leo said.

"Yeah, I don't want to do anything without Piper," said Jayson, shifting uncomfortably in his chair.

Jack nodded, swallowed the last of his bread, and headed for the bedroom to change.

They waited for Piper and Dimitri for nearly an hour. After several rounds of Rock-Paper-Scissors, they decided to find them. Mount Kelsii was eerily empty and quiet. They passed a few haggard looking soldiers on patrols who must have worked through the night to evacuate their citizens. They passed door after door in the Amber Quarter that had been hastily painted with a strange symbol. Leo recognized it as the Draconian rune Brande and Kylani had described as meaning 'the way is clear.'

The once bustling civilization, now silent, was unsettling to experience. Jack wondered if Gemari had already fled with her people into the Great Passage, and if yesterday was the last time he would ever see her. His fears were confirmed when every door but Piper's along the Emerald Quarter corridor had been marked with that familiar rune.

Surely Gemari would have gone with the Elders. She was, after all, not trained in War.

Jayson rang the little bell beside Piper's door. The door whipped open before the last chime ended. Leo's hand flew to his sword hilt. Dimitri put a finger to his lips and smiled mischievously.

"Dude, you scared the crap out of me," said Jack as Dimitri held the door wide for them.

"My apologies," said Dimitri. "Piper is still resting."

"We can come back later if you guys wanna sleep in," said Jayson. "We can bring you some food from the kitchens." Dimitri smiled at Jayson's constant thought for food.

"No, I am sure she will wake soon enough." Dimitri filled a cup with water from a pitcher and joined the boys as they took seats in the common area.

"Looks like everyone's gone," said Leo.

"Halil informed me they will have troops stationed at the main gates, and a few scouts in each quarter." Dimitri said quietly and flopped across the chair, his legs dangling over its arm.

"How come our doors don't have that funny mark?" Jayson asked.

"We are neither citizens nor Dwarvik soldiers. Like the Black Diamonds, we are on our own." Dimitri's statement hung in the air between them. The dwarves had been so eager to earn the returned kings to their side, but it wasn't a mutual ally they sought. Jack, Leo and Jayson had never been offered a place among the refugees to Tutaria. Despite the help they had offered, they were very much alone once more.

"What's the plan then?" Jack asked breaking the awkward silence.

Dimitri opened his mouth to answer, but stopped when they heard a shuffling in the bedroom.

Piper emerged wearing several layers of sturdy travelling clothes. Her hair had been tied back as well as it could, but she still managed to look rather pretty.

"Oh, you should have woken me," she said, and cast Dimitri a shy, sideways glance.

"It's okay," said Jayson. "We just got here."

"I am glad you are here," she replied, and began rummaging in an inside pocket of her vest. She pulled out the small slip of parchment from Valar and handed it to Jayson who sat closest to her. "This was delivered to Nefiri and then to me yesterday. It appears to be from Valar, but I do not understand it."

"No-cal-no-den," Jayson sounded out very slowly, and looked at Dimitri. "Is that some Dwarvik word or something?"

"I am afraid not," said Dimitri.

"We believe it may be a code, but we do not know what it means." Piper gazed hopefully between Jack, Leo and Jayson.

Leo snatched the tiny bit of parchment from Jayson, pushing his glasses up his nose and squinted at the wide looping script.

"noCalnoden. Wait a minute. Do you have a pen and paper?"

Piper hurried to the table the portraits of her family had been laid upon the day Nefiri and Valar had come to visit her. She pulled a piece of parchment, an inkwell and a stubby calligraphy pen from the center drawer, and rushed back to Leo.

For several minutes, Leo worked quietly, writing on the parchment, scratching things out, and rewriting. He had never used a calligraphy pen before, and the excess ink began to bleed into his fingers from the nib. Finally, he leapt to his feet and triumphantly held the paper aloft.

"Aha! It was out of order!" he exclaimed.

"Huh?" asked Jayson.

"Look," said Leo, and he pointed to the word at the very bottom of the parchment. It spelled Cannondole. "Cannondole. It is where we're supposed to meet Valar before we go to the castle."

"We already know this," said Piper.

"Why would he send us a message for something we already know?" asked Dimitri, squinting his eyes at the paper in skepticism.

"I don't know," said Leo shrugging. He set the parchment back on the little table in front of him, then immediately jumped back up again.

"Wait!" he said, looking at Jack. "Didn't you say the dwarves can't find the elven soldiers?"

"Yeah," said Jack tentatively, "Frejah said none of the scouts can find anything."

"Dimitri, you said this was sent to Nefiri, right?" Leo turned to face Dimitri, who still lounged across the chair.

"Correct," replied Dimitri, shrugging his shoulders. "Nefiri believed it appeared to be Valar's writing. She assumed it was meant for Piper."

Leo shook his head and smirked.

"I think Taraniz's troops are in Cannondole, and Valar was trying to tell Nefiri." Leo pushed his glasses up his nose again, and nodded curtly.

"Cannondole is only two days from here," said Dimitri. "It is one of the main cities the dwarves trade with. We would know if Taraniz had stationed her troops there."

"Not if she's using magic to conceal them," said Leo, and his smile deepened.

They looked at one another, their eyes slowly widening as the revelation hit.

"We must inform Nefiri immediately," said Dimitri. They nodded, and tore from Piper's room, nearly forgetting to close the door behind them in their haste.

The number of soldiers had dwindled even further, and it took them some time to track Nefiri down. They eventually found her in the armory, calculating the weapon stores with Frejah and some of the other commanders. Brande was there to offer his knowledge of the weapons the Diamonds had within their possession.

Jack, Leo and Jayson burst through the door to the armory, completely out of breath. Piper and Dimitri followed close behind, though far less winded. The Dwarvik soldiers in the armory were tense and staring, some with their hands poised over the hilts of their swords and daggers. Nefiri, Frejah and Brande looked equal bewildered at the sudden intrusion. Dimitri shouldered past the boys and stopped a few feet from Nefiri.

"Empress, we have an important matter that must be discussed regarding the recent message sent to Piper." Dimitri held the slip of parchment in his hand for the Empress to see. She nodded, and dismissed the group around her.

"I think Frejah and Brande should hear this too," said Leo. Nefiri's harsh eyes made him blush, but she nodded, and the two rejoined them, Brande closing the armory door behind the last soldier.

"Empress," said Piper, and she stood beside Dimitri, bowing in the elven style, "The message you gave to me was in fact from Valar, but it was always intended for you."

"How can you know this?" asked Nefiri. Her features remained emotionless, though her tone sounded intrigued.

"My Lady," said Jack turning to Frejah, "You said your scouts haven't found any evidence of Taraniz's army, correct?"

"Yes, this is true," said Frejah. She shifted her weight uncomfortably from side to side.

"However, spies within the elven palace, and the information you yourselves brought to us certainly speak volumes that Taraniz is planning an attack on us. It would take great numbers and much time to coordinate enough power to storm Fortress Kelsii. I do not believe Taraniz to be quite so ignorant to the contrary."

"Look," said Leo, snatching the little piece of parchment away from Dimitri. "If you unscramble the letters, it spells Cannondole."

Nefiri, Frejah and Brande passed the parchment between them, looking at the tiny letters and listening.

"We think Valar was trying to tell you that Taraniz's army is in Cannondole," Jack explained.

"Plus, she's probably using magic to hide them. That's why no one can find them." Jayson folded his arms and nodded smugly.

"I suppose it is entirely possible," mused Brande. "Cannondole is one of the largest Elven cities, and is almost perfectly positioned between here and the palace." He stroked his beard and paced. "They still have to cross the river, but, there are a number of places where the water narrows, and a small bridge could be built in only a few hours. How far have your scouts been looking?"

Frejah answered the man without hesitation. "Cannondole is more than a day away, and I do not like to send my troops too far. The last time anyone would have received reports from so far away would have been before the Council met. This theory is entirely plausible, if we are to believe the rumors that Taraniz, is indeed, using magic." She pursed her lips and raised an eyebrow. "We have such little evidence to support any of this."

"Leo has never steered us wrong before," said Brande, clapping Leo hard on the shoulder. "These are our kings, dear ladies. It is our destiny to trust them."

Leo smiled, though his stomach sank a bit. They were closer than ever to the destiny the prophecy had laid before them – whatever it was.

The two women exchanged looks and nodded.

"You know what this means then?" said Piper, staring at Nefiri.

"It is time." the Empress answered. "May Rashiri watch over you all." She bowed very low to them and held her pose for longer than usual.

"Fear not," Brande whispered to Leo, "I have everything taken care of." He winked and hugged the boy.

They turned to leave, their bodies feeling heavier as they went when a voice behind them called out.

"Dimitri!" Nefiri called. He stopped and looked over his shoulder. Nefiri took a single step forward then stopped. She reset her worried face and sighed. "Please, be careful, my son. I wish more than anything for Rashiri to return you safely back to me."

Dimitri looked at her for a long time. He blinked and followed his friends into the hall without reply.

๛

Jayson made doubly sure that their first stop was the kitchens. It was deserted, and most of what remained were perishable items such as cheeses and raw meats. They scrounged for what they could find that would last them a few days during their travels. They packed their bags and nibbled at the fresh fruits and cheeses as they worked. Jayson stuffed the last of his breakfast into his mouth as they reached the Black Diamonds' mine. It was eerily quiet, and they did not linger. They headed out the door at the back of the market square, and set a well-hidden trap as planned long ago with Brande and Kylani. Any elves who may have been working with the Black Diamonds would have known about this entrance into the mountain, and it meant they may try to use it. When the door was opened, it would set off a chain of cascading boulders and alert someone to the matter, as well as kill a good number of elves in the process.

The food the boys had eaten sat heavy on their stomachs as they walked down the little path and away from the mountain. Their trap also meant the mines the Black Diamonds called home would be destroyed. Once again, these people would be homeless. If permitted by the Council to be called a new Quarter, they would be forced to start over. It was the first time they felt the weight of the necessary evils of war, and what it meant to sacrifice something you loved to protect something you loved even more.

Dimitri led the way, as he was far more familiar with the Belirian Forest having run errands and messages to the surrounding elven cities and to the elven palace. They had long ago decided to stay off the main roads, even though it would take them longer to reach Cannondole. Now that they knew, or at least suspected, that Taraniz was hiding her army with magic, they kept a watchful eye out for anything strange.

"There is nothing worse than stumbling right into the middle of the army of the person you are attempting to bring down," Dimitri had said.

The Belirian Forest was thick with underbrush and brambles, slowing their pace the deeper they went. The trees seemed perfectly spaced to let just the right amount of sun in while keeping its travelers well shaded. Dimitri slashed at the undergrowth in front of them, which did little to ease the way. Piper suspected it was doing more to relieve his frustrations over Nefiri's final words to him.

Unlike when they had first traveled to Fortress Kelsii, they remained rather silent, lost within their own thoughts. They ate their midday meal as they walked rather than stopping to make camp. As it neared evening, Piper insisted Dimitri cease his slashing and bashing of the forest so as not to attract unwanted attention.

"We would be foolish to believe Taraniz has not sent scouts out. She has to suspect I would come looking for Gran once I learned of her disappearance." Piper placed a comforting hand on Dimitri's shoulder.

"Piper, we have to keep moving," said Dimitri, pulling away from her. "We have little time to get to Cannondole and then to the palace before the army attacks."

Piper sighed. "Dimitri, we do not know Taraniz's plans. She could be there now for all we know."

Dimitri huffed and turned away from Piper, slashing at one last bush. "Alright," he said and took a deep breath, stretching to his full height. "But we keep moving for a while longer." He turned, sheathing his sword and pushing his way through the tall grasses and brambles.

Darkness came to the forest faster than any of them had expected, and this slowed their progress further. They agreed to look for a small clearing to make camp when the forest broke away before them and gave way to a swiftly moving river several feet below.

"Is there a bridge anywhere?" Leo asked.

"I am afraid not, Leo," said Dimitri. "I hope you all can swim."

245

Leo looked at his feet and kicked a stone down the steep bank into the water. "Actually, I can't," he said.

In the end, they tied the ends of all their ropes together securing one end to a tree. Dimitri swam easily across the river, and tied the other end to a tree on the opposite bank. Jayson, Jack, and Leo held onto the rope and pulled themselves across the deceptively swift current. It was only twenty yards or so, but it was the longest trek Leo had ever taken in his life. Once, an undertow caught Leo, pulling him down enough that a wave splashed over his head. He spluttered, and nearly let go of the rope. Jack caught him by the collar of his shirt just in time. When they reached the far bank, Piper undid the rope on her side of the river, and they all helped to pull her across. They were all soaked and soon gave up any idea of continuing on until they had dried their clothes a bit.

They had skirted around a small elven village called Serestell to avoid being seen, and this had delayed them a further half day. Cannondole was at least another full day's journey ahead of them yet, and none of them could say they were excited about it. They did not sleep well, and were awake and ready to set out again at the first sign of light.

"I never thought I'd miss sleeping on that weird mattress," said Jayson, stretching his back as they walked.

"Yeah, it was kind of weird sleeping outside again," said Jack.

"I will never complain about my bed again when I get home, that's for sure!" Jayson cried, but his laugh gave way to an uncomfortable silence.

246

A realization had fallen over Jack, Leo and Jayson. In a few short days, they could be home again. If they fulfilled the prophecy, then whatever had brought them to Chartile would surely send them home again. At least they hoped so.

"Piper, does the Elven castle have, like, a library or anything?" Leo asked breaking the quiet.

"Really, Leo?" said Jayson. "What could you possibly want to look up right now?" He rolled his eyes and, not paying attention, ended up with a face full of branch he had not grabbed from Jack as they trudged deeper into the forest.

"There might be some old scrolls or something from the time of the old kings that could tell us how to get home." Leo glared at Jayson and stuck his chin out defiantly.

"Oh," Jayson muttered, and brushed the broken twigs from his hair.

"The largest Elven library is, of course, at the palace, but other nobles and elders may have documents in their personal libraries as well," said Piper.

"The largest library in Chartile is actually in Tutaria," Dimitri called over his shoulder. "It has several Draconian texts as well."

"You could always stay," said Piper. She stopped and turned to look at them. "As Queen, I can give you whatever you desire. I promise you will not want for anything. You are my only friends." Her voice trailed off. She looked at the ground and began fidgeting with her hair.

"What about our families?" asked Jack. "I can't leave my mom and sister."

"Our parents have to be really worried," said Leo, nodding in agreement.

"Guys, it's been, like, over a month now. Our families have probably, you know, come to terms with us being gone and all that. They probably had a big funeral and everything. Man, that's so weird."

"We at least have to try," said Jack. Piper sighed and nodded her understanding. She turned and followed after Dimitri who had waited for them several paces away.

Cannondole's silhouette stood before them as the last traces of sunlight dwindled away. They had no idea where in Cannondole they were going, and decided to make camp and steal into the city at daybreak.

The ground felt harder and more uncomfortable for Jayson that night. It seemed to remind him all too well of the comforts of home, and he lay awake long after his friends had dozed off into silent slumber. Piper and Dimitri lay curled together, entwined in each other's cloaks for warmth. He wondered if they would get married. He wondered if Jack would marry Gemari someday. He knew Leo would be content to research in the libraries for the rest of his life. Maybe Leo would even become an Elder on one of the councils one day.

When Jayson thought of his own future in Chartile, there was nothing. If he had to remain, what would he do? Join the Elven army? Fight for Jack and Gemari? That just sounded too weird. He had never really fit in anywhere. Not on Earth and not in Chartile either. No matter how hard he tried, he would never be free of his vision, his destiny, of killing that man.

Jack woke with a start beside Jayson, sitting bolt upright. He clasped his hands to his mouth to keep from screaming, and breathed deeply through his nose to calm himself.

"Dude, are you okay?" Jayson asked, leaning toward him.

Jack was silent for a long time, trying to catch his breath.

"Yeah," he finally whispered through ragged breaths. "I'm okay. Just a dream."

"I know what you mean," said Jayson, patting his friend's shoulder. He wrapped himself in his cloak and settled in to stare at the unfamiliar clusters of stars through the trees above.

Jack looked at him, unsure what Jayson could have meant. Hesitantly he replied, "I saw my Dad." Jayson sat up and turned toward Jack again. Jack's voice shook as he tried to hold back his tears. "He was drunk again. He hit my mom, and he was trying to come after me. I had my bow staff in my hands, but I couldn't move. I was frozen. I can't believe I'm still so scared of him. I can beat Dimitri on my best days. I know I could easily…" His voice faltered, and he hoped Jayson couldn't see the tear running down his cheek. "It's just… he's still my dad."

Jayson could only nod. He didn't know what to say, and could only think of really stupid stuff that might make Jack feel better. Most likely, it would probably make him look like an idiot.

Jayson shrugged and sighed. His mom would have hugged him, but he wasn't about to do that. They sat in silence for several minutes, wishing there was a fire to take the chill out of the early autumn air.

"Well, g'night, Jayson," Jack mumbled and wrapped himself in his cloak.

Jayson watched him, feeling guilty he hadn't said anything. "'night," he said, and settled into a restless slumber.

Piper was the first to wake the next morning. She lay quiet, curled into Dimitri's warmth as his strong arms wrapped around her. Leo was snoring, and she giggled at the thought of being caught because of this. Fear soon overtook her moment of happiness, and she thought of her very near future. It was only a matter of days before she would confront Taraniz. Days before she would discover the fate of her Gran. Days before she could be Queen of all the elves in Chartile. She squeezed Dimitri's hand. He didn't want to be King. He couldn't be King. Still, he was the only one she wanted at her side.

Her heart pained at the thought of Nefiri, having to choose between what was right for her people and the ones that she loved. Nefiri had dismissed Dimitri from her service because he had decided to stand with those who supported the Black Diamonds. Piper did not agree, but she understood. But she couldn't do that to him. She couldn't cast Dimitri away like that— not how she had been cast away so long ago. Almost exactly eighteen years ago. She would find a way. She was Piper. She could fix anything.

Dimitri squeezed her hand back, and hugged her closer to him. She smiled, and her heart raced thinking she would give anything to wake up like this every morning for the rest of her life.

"You're almost home," he whispered quietly in her ear.

"I know," she said and untangled herself from his grasp. She reached for her rucksack and pulled a small pear-like fruit she had been holding onto since before they left the mountain. It was slightly bruised, but plenty fresh. She offered a bite to Dimitri. He sat up cut off a piece with his knife, tossing it into the air to catch in his mouth.

"You certainly cannot do that at the high table." she teased.

Dimitri laughed and shuddered. "You won't catch me anywhere near those prissy elven banquets."

"What is that supposed to mean?" Piper asked, her hands flying to her hips.

"I-I just mean… they're very… well, there are so many rules, and everyone is always so perfectly dressed and poised."

"I have seen you during meetings and banquets. You look wonderful, Dimitri. You can be very proper when you want to be." Piper replied kindly, relaxing once more.

"Only because I had to be. I never really it. I wanted to join the army, but…. Maybe now I can, since…"

"Dimitri, I heard what Nefiri said. I think she will take you back into her service. It was more of a…" Piper struggled for the correct word. "A political move, I'm sure of it. Now that the council has decided to work with the Black Diamonds, there is no need for this rift between you."

Dimitri shrugged, and bit off a piece of dried meat he had pulled from his pack.

Jayson, Jack and Leo woke shortly thereafter, and shared in the last decadent bites of Piper's "pear-apple-fruit-thing" as Jayson called it.

"If Taraniz's army is in Cannondole, it must be because she knows Valar has been helping us, and expects us to go there." said Piper as they cleaned up their camp.

"She obviously knows what Piper looks like, and they probably have descriptions of what you three look like by now." Dimitri nodded to the boys.

"Our shoes would be a dead giveaway, anyway." Leo indicated the tennis shoes they had changed back to before leaving the mountain.

"Yeah, but they don't know you're not with Nefiri anymore," said Jayson.

"What?" asked his friends together.

Jayson rolled his eyes. He did have some good ideas once in a while.

"Well, nobody knows that you're not working for Nefiri anymore. So, just go in there and pretend you have a message from her for Valin. Then, you can talk to Valin and Valar about the best way to sneak us in."

They all stared at Jayson until he awkwardly shrugged and started kicking the dirt with his toe.

"It is not a bad idea," said Dimitri, and Jayson beamed.

"Taraniz knows that the dwarves have turned on her," said Leo.

"No," said Piper, "I do not believe Taraniz will be with the army in Cannondole. She will remain at the castle, because she knows that's where

I will eventually go. If the messengers we caught a few days ago headed straight to the castle, even by the roads, it would be three days at least. Taraniz would need another two days for any messages to reach the commander in Cannondole from the palace. We may be cutting it close, but I think we may still be able to bank on messages not having been received yet. It is a risk, but it is worth a try."

"It is better that we send me in to be safe." Dimitri looked at Piper and smiled. "We wouldn't want anything to happen to our future Queen and our Kings."

They crept as quietly as they could along the outskirts of the forest line. The boys were thankful for the training they had received from Piper during their hunting lessons long ago on how to 'ninja stealth walk' as Jack had put it. At the forest's edge to the village, they hid in the tall bushes and surveyed the scene. There were elven soldiers everywhere. They had camped along the main road that would have taken them from the elven palace straight to Mount Kelsii. Men flitted in and out of the taverns and huddled around the blacksmith's workshop. The people of Cannondole could be seen peeking out of their windows and walking quickly with heads down from one building to the next. The Chantry of Canna, Mother of the skies and seasons, had its doors shut tight, and no candles burned in the windows.

Dimitri put up his hood, and handed his orenite cuffs to Piper. She tucked them in her rucksack, and hugged and kissed him. "Please be careful," she whispered.

"Yeah, be careful, man," said Jayson, and each of the boys shook Dimitri's hand in turn.

"If I am not back by nightfall, get as far away from here as you can."

"You think it'll really take that long?" Jack asked.

"I do not know," said Dimitri. His face set hard, he stood, and made his way around to the bend in the main road.

Chapter Eighteen
Into Cannondole

Dimitri's heart raced. He loved the thrill of the unknown, especially when Nefiri had sent him to spy on the elders and certain elven nobility. This, however, was different. If he was caught, they would begin looking for Piper and the boys. He couldn't let that happen. He wouldn't let it happen. He had to protect them at all cost.

He walked the main road, his face obscured by his hood, hands clasped together beneath his robes. He began running scenarios over in his mind. He never planned what he would say. The mark of a good spy was his art of improvising. He rounded the bend, and a large wagon came bouncing and creaking down the road beside him. Dimitri smirked, and stepped to the side.

Two soldiers stepped out from either side of the road, and held up a hand to stop the driver.

"State your business," said the soldier to the left. He sounded bored, which meant he was likely not on high alert, and Dimitri's smile deepened.

"Goods from Serestell," said the wagon driver, confused as to the soldiers' presence. "I'm headed to Castielle, sirs."

The soldier on the right looked the wagon over. He glanced at Dimitri, who stood lazily beside the cart. He smiled and nodded to the soldier, and leaned against the wagon nonchalantly. The soldier eyed him for a moment, and Dimitri's heart beat harder and faster. The soldier nodded back, and continued his search of the wagon. Dimitri silently breathed a sigh of relief. Posing as the merchant's son had been a trick he had used before, but never when the dwarves had been under such scrutiny with the elves. The soldier on the left recovered the goods in the wagon with the burlap tarp. Nothing more than woven baskets and mats.

"Move along," he said, and waved the merchant on. Dimitri gave a friendly wave to the soldier on the right as he passed. He continued beside the cart, staying just out of the driver's vision. They rounded another corner by the chantry and Dimitri ducked behind a tree.

The Lord of Cannondole lived in a small estate manor behind the Chantry of Canna, facing the very center of town. Dimitri saw Cannondole was filled with soldiers, but certainly not enough as to be a serious threat to Fortress Kelsii. Valar had been the Lord of Cannondole before his appointment as the King's advisor. His son, Valin, had taken his father's place in running the bustling town several years ago. But, since Valar's disappearance after King Aramor's death, walking up to the front door was out of the question. Dimitri would have to improvise. He stepped back onto the road, his hood still drawn up, and headed toward the town center.

The Glass Lantern was Cannondole's main inn for traveler, and the town's most popular tavern for a pint. It was rumored to have a history of aiding those loyal to the magical arts after the fall of Duke Noraedin, but of course it was only rumor. Dimitri held the hanging wooden sign in his sights for a moment. It might be the perfect place to look for someone foolish enough to help him get to Valin. He stepped off the main road as a group of rowdy soldiers emerged from the inn. The door slammed open, and Dimitri stepped back into the shadows of the building. There was no need, as the soldiers appeared thoroughly drunk. Dimitri stepped through the door before it closed, and allowed his eyes to adjust to the dim light.

There were only a handful of people in the tavern that morning, and the last of the soldiers seemed to have just departed. Dimitri realized he had no coin or anything to trade or barter with. He lowered his hood and approached the bar.

"Evenin', sir," said a pretty young girl from behind the bar block. "Will it be board or booze for yeh?" she asked, flashing a toothy smile. She was a few years younger than Dimitri, but her fingers deftly counted out the coins left on the bar with one hand as she balanced a tray with the other.

"Neither," said Dimitri, and he flashed his sultry smile back at her. "I'm only passing through, and needed a place to rest my feet out of the wind for a bit."

"Aye, sir," said the girl. "My name is Atana if yeh change yer mind. Where are yeh headin', if you don't mind my asking?" She set the tray beside her, and began scrubbing them clean as she talked.

Dimitri hesitated for only a moment, gently stroking the stubble on his chin and replied, "I have a message from the Chamberlain of Duneland to the Lord of Cannondole." The lie rolled off his tongue perfectly. "Simply financial in nature, but…" He lowered his voice and leaned over the bar. The girl leaned in closer, her eyes locked onto Dimitri's. She blushed when Dimitri came so close she could feel his breath on her cheek. "It is a matter he would prefer to keep private. You understand. You wouldn't happen to know anyone who could..." He ran his fingers through his hair and licked his lips. He looked over his shoulder, pretending not to notice as Atana blushed and suppressed a shiver. "Make any sort of formal introduction, would you?"

Dimitri grabbed a grape from a dirty plate behind the counter, and tossed it in the air to catch in his mouth. Again, he leaned forward, resting his elbow on the bar and his chin on his hand. He looked at the girl with his eyebrows raised in an innocent stare.

The girl did not speak for several long seconds. She opened her mouth, then closed it again, swallowing and glancing behind her nervously.

"Meet me in the stables in a half hour." she said and rushed off.

Dimitri stretched and swung his feet onto the chair beside him, and waited, a smug grin spreading across his face.

Atana returned minutes later. She continued to wait on the few patrons left in the tavern, but only passed Dimitri brief, side glances as she worked. At ten minutes before their meeting time, she disappeared again. Dimitri found himself bouncing his knee and playing with a hole in the inside pocket of his cloak. His mind raced with the possibility that the girl could have turned him into the soldiers. He glanced at every window and every door in the tavern before allowing his mind to settle. No, the soldiers would have come charging in without warning the moment they heard the news.

Dimitri knew he could be arrogant at times, and he had yet to forget Piper's words to him about his stubbornness. He was not about to take any chances. He headed for the stairs leading to the rooms above the tavern available for rent. He stepped quietly, making no noise and checking for creaking floor boards. He pressed his ear against each door, and listened. The third room was silent, and the door unlocked. Dimitri opened it to find the bed stripped of linens and completely bare.

He sighed and stepped quietly to the window. The city street below was deserted. Dimitri smiled and thanked Ygtall, Goddess of mischief and gambling for his luck. He swung himself up the eaves and onto the thatched roof. From there, he could see the entire surrounding area. He checked every entrance into the inn, lying flat against the roof. No soldiers. He could see the army had made camp in the large, now empty fields at the edge of the town. Cannondole was known for its summer harvest of hot yellow peppers, and the once lush fields had been picked clean and turned into an encampment. More soldiers had pitched tents and pavilions in the area beside the chantry— right in front of Valin's estate. The side road leading to the small manor house was riddled with tents and campfires. None of the soldiers seemed on edge. They were calm. Too calm for Dimitri's comfort.

Dimitri squinted, staring at the most dense sections of soldiers. Through the early morning fog, he saw a different sort of haze. It hung in the air above the natural fog and shimmered slightly to the experienced eye. Leo had been right. There were more soldiers waiting in Cannondole than what first met the eye, and the people of the town took little heed of the strange occurrence. His skin crawled as he thought of Piper facing such a formidable adversary. If Taraniz was capable of this, what else could she do?

Dimitri climbed back down the side of the building, and found a trap door leading from the roof of the stables to the hay loft. He jumped through, landing in the soft bales, and listened quietly. He heard the voices of a boy and girl arguing in the stable aisle below.

"How do yeh know he's not working for the soldiers, huh? How do yeh know he's not trying to get to Lord Valin to kill 'im? His dad was King Aramor's advisor and he's gone missing."

"Oh, go eat dragon dung, Brock," said Atana's voice in response. "If Princess Taraniz's soldiers wanted to kill Valin, they'd just storm the manor and do it by force."

"She knows there's a lot of people who…are…" the boy named Brock lowered his voice so Dimitri could barely hear him, "Yeh know — against what she wants to do. Maybe she's tryin' to be more subtle now."

"And maybe you're just a coward, Brodrick Garrison."

"He has a point," said Dimitri dropping down from the hay loft in front of the two. They started, and Atana made a small squeak of surprise, but they did not run. "I very well could be working for those soldiers." He leaned toward them, his eyes widening. "But, I will tell you a secret. It is not your Lord Valin or Valar that Princess Taraniz wants. If you can get me to see your lord, I will tell you who she is truly after."

Atana and Brock looked at each other wide eyed. They couldn't have been much older than Jayson, Jack and Leo. Dimitri had indeed found a fool to help him get to Valin, but it wasn't the fool he had expected. Brock turned to Dimitri, his chin pushed out and his eyes narrowed. He looked Dimitri up and down. He folded his arms and sighed.

"Alright," he said, "I'll help yeh see Lord Valin. But!" The boy held his finger up to Dimitri's face, and Dimitri bit the inside of his cheek to stifle a laugh, "If yeh try anything funny, you'll regret it."

Dimitri nodded, and bowed in the proper elven fashion to Brock. The boy took a step back and looked at Atana surprised. Finally, he returned the gesture rather clumsily, and forced Dimitri to hide his amusement in the form of a sneeze into the sleeve of his cloak.

Atana smiled. "Well, then. I should get back to work." She kissed Brock on the cheek and bustled off, skirts flying as she rushed through the side door and back inside the inn.

Dimitri and Brock stood facing each other awkwardly for a few silent moments. Brock swung his arms at his sides and kicked at the dirt floor with his toe.

Dimitri finally said, "Chamberlain Herodan would like to keep his matters with Lord Valin quiet. How do you propose getting past the soldiers?"

Brock stood still, staring at the ground then looked up at Dimitri, with a smug smile.

Brodrick Garrison was the son of a local vintner in Cannondole and volunteered for various other merchants and peoples in the city to make his coin. He helped with the horses at The Glass Lantern and even delivered medicines for Lady Delia's apothecary on occasion. Brock also helped the Sisters at the chantry. Mostly he dusted down the libraries and cleaned the dishes, but sometimes the Sisters asked him to take messages to the other Sisters living in the Chantry apartments. There were twelve Sisters living in the small apartments connected to the chapel, and the place was nearly as large as the Lord of Cannondole's estate manor.

Dimitri followed Brock along the road to the chantry. A few soldiers on patrol passed by but took no notice of them. Dimitri exhaled in relief, and Brock dared a side glance at him.

"Look," said Brock, and he stopped in the middle of the path leading to the chantry that loomed behind them. "I'm only doin' this because Atana asked me to. How do I really know you're not gunna, well, I don't know, say, kill Lord Valin or something? I don't want any trouble... but, I want to help."

Dimitri lowered his hood and put a hand on Brock's shoulder. "Your concern and bravery are commendable, Brock. May I tell you a secret? The real reason I am here to see Lord Valin?"

Brock's eyes widened. He nervously looked over his shoulders for any passersby then nodded.

"I am part of a plan to help bring peace back to Chartile, and your Lord Valin is a very important piece in my mission. You want to see these soldiers go away, and not worry about people being killed?" Brock nodded. "Get me to Lord Valin."

The boy narrowed his gaze and nodded determinedly. He puffed out his chest and trudged up the path to the Chantry. Dimitri smiled at him as he followed, and gave a sigh of relief again. Telling this complete stranger about their plans was risky. Very, very risky. Brock could go to the elven soldiers at any moment, and they would all be done for. But Dimitri had a sense about people and when to trust them. It was why Nefiri had entrusted him as her retainer and liaison, even at such a young age. His stomach gave a flop as he thought of his mother. He knew he would have to make amends with her when this was all over.

As they approached the main doors to the chapel, Brock took a small path to the left, and waved to one of the Sisters working in the gardens alongside the building.

"Greetings, Sister Theodora," Brock said.

The woman looked up from her work, brushing a tuft of gray hair from her eyes. Her apron was full of small squashes and a few of the yellow peppers.

"Hello, Brock," she said squinting against the glare of the late morning sun.

Dimitri expected an inquiry to the boy's presence or who his companion was that the woman had surely never seen before. But Sister Theodora bent her head and began plucking up the squashes again.

There was a small door further back along the side of the building. Brock opened it as though he had travelled this route a hundred times. Dimitri reminded himself he probably had. They emerged into a bustling kitchen where several woman, most of them elderly, were finishing drying dishes at a large tub in the corner beside a drain trough.

"Brock!" called one of the younger woman, looking up from the tub. "You've missed the breakfast washing, dear. Who is your friend?"

"This is George. George Potts," Brock answered without hesitation. "He works for one of the merchants from Castielle. Says his master wants him to look in the library for something." Dimitri smiled at the women, and gave a small bow in the elven fashion.

"Sister Marta is in the library if you need any assistance," said another woman, and she dumped a tub of water down the drain with as much strength as any farmer or blacksmith. Dimitri marveled at the women as they hurriedly flitted around the kitchen carrying large pots full of water, or large baskets full of produce hooked on each arm. He had no idea the woman of the Elven faith were such hard workers. It rivaled some of the Dwarvik men he knew.

"My thanks, dear ladies," he finally said, and nearly ran into Brock as he hurried him along behind the boy. "Excellent thinking, Brock," Dimitri said when they had entered a deserted back hallway.

"I'm smarter than I look, Georgie," he said. Dimitri smiled at him and ruffled his hair.

"Good to know. We need allies like you right now."

"Yeh do?" asked the boy.

"Oh, yes," replied Dimitri, though he kept his voice low and his eyes sharp. "Taraniz has allies and spies everywhere, even if most of the elves do not agree with her. She is still the Princess, and soon to be Queen, I am sure."

Brock finally stopped before a skinny door with a rusty handle. He opened it and gestured for Dimitri to follow him inside. Dimitri hesitated, but the boy had been trustworthy so far. He closed the door behind him, and waited for his eyes to adjust to what little light came from around the edges of the door. He could hear Brock feeling along the walls and tripping over what appeared to be buckets and brooms.

"I heard the Sisters talking about a passage to the Lord's estate a few months ago, when some of the other towns were being attack – I mean, when people were being executed for their crimes. I got bored one day and decided to look for it. I nearly gave up when I accidentally found it. Ah, here it is!"

He pulled aside a wooden panel along the back of the closet. It swung toward them as if on a hinge. Brock stepped in and lit the lantern that hung from a nail along a narrow, drippy passage.

"It comes out in one of the bedrooms. One of the Lord's bedrooms, not here," said Brock. "I know. I followed it." He handed the lantern to Dimitri. Dimitri held the tiny lantern up to inspect the passage. It was made of packed earth and crumbling stone walls. It was clearly not Dwarvik made, and he had to hunch nearly double to fit.

"Can I do anythin' else? You know, to help? I just want everyone to be alright again and all. I'll do whatever you need." Brock shrugged and looked from Dimitri to the floor and back again.

Dimitri turned and placed his hand on the boy's shoulder again. "You have already done a great service, Brock. Not only to your Lord Valin, but to all of Chartile. What I need is for you not keep silent. You mustn't tell a soul about this. Not even Atana. If all goes well, in a few days, you will hear the good news of our success. I am sure Queen Piper will make you a soldier one day if you so wished it." He ruffled the boy's hair again, then headed into the passage.

"Who's Queen Piper?" Brock whispered excitedly.

Dimitri stopped and closed his eyes. He had spoken too much, but what was done was done. Words could not be taken back once given voice. He sighed loudly.

"She is Princess Taraniz's sister. Piper is going to make everything right again. But, you mustn't tell anyone, Brock. If Princess Taraniz finds out, she will kill Piper."

Brock's eyes widened and he nodded his head vigorously. "I won't tell anyone. Not ever!"

"Good. Good bye, Brock. And thank you," said Dimitri, and he turned once again up the passage.

There were no other torches or lamps of any kind save the one Brock had handed him when he first entered the passage. It was difficult to see, even by the lamp light for Dimitri had to crouch so low, but the crumbling stone walls looked to be hundreds of years old. He was more positive than ever these were not Dwarvik made. Still, they must have been sturdy enough to have withstood all this time. He hoped anyway. It wouldn't do anyone much good if the tunnel suddenly decided to collapse on him.

No sooner had the thought entered his mind than Dimitri found the tunnel sloping upward. Dimitri crouched even lower, nearly on his hands and knees. The passage ended at a winding stone staircase, and he could finally stand straight again. He took a deep breath and tiptoed quietly up the stair. He assumed he was now inside Lord Valin's estate, and Brock had suggested, and was heading to an upper level.

The staircase concluded at a small six foot room. A plain wooden wall with an ornately carved stone lamb in its center barred his way. Dimitri brushed the string of dusty cobwebs from the lamb. He knew this must be the way to enter the manor, and if Brock could figure it out, so could he.

Dimitri hung his lantern on a nail beside a dusty, unlit torch and set to work. It took him far longer to figure out the lock than he anticipated. Each of the legs had to be turned in a particular pattern so the lamb appeared to be running. When the pattern was correct, there was a soft click and a plume of dirt and dust erupted in Dimitri's face. He fanned it away, and, cautiously, pushed the swiveling wall open.

Light poured in and nearly blinded him. He blinked and found himself in a simple, yet cozy bedroom. He stepped out from behind a fireplace so large he could nearly stand up in. There was a luxurious four poster bed beside a large window to his right, and a small sitting room just beyond. He took a few careful steps forward, and heard the hidden door snap shut behind him, and the stone legs of the lamb slide back into place. A feather duster sat atop the mantle, and he brushed the dirt from his shoes and the floor.

He entered the sitting room, and found no one. He heard voices in the distance, and followed through the private wash room to a small library.

One man sat behind a red oak desk, bent over several books and documents. Another, older man stood over him, also bent and pointing at the book in front of them.

"These pages were removed some time ago. It could not have been Taraniz," said the older man.

"We have no way of knowing if it was Kaytah who did so," said the younger man. "I believe this is wishful thinking, Father. If Taraniz had these documents, she would have destroyed them by now."

"Then we must find different evidence, shall we?" Dimitri walked into the room and lowered his hood.

The younger man at the desk stood up quickly, and the chair he sat in fell to the floor with a loud crash. He reached for the hilt of his sword at his hip, but the older man set a hand on his son's arm, smiling at the would-be intruder.

"Dimitri!" Valar smiled. The young man beside him let go of his sword, and looked suspiciously from this father to the mysterious young man standing before him. "Where are the others?" Valar asked, worried.

"They are hiding in the forest. We saw the soldiers and did not think it wise to attempt entry without finding you first. I came alone. We need to move quickly. I told them to head back to the mountain if I did not return by nightfall." The sun was already high in the sky, and judging by the shadows, was just approaching midday.

"How did you get in here?" Valin asked, his brow still furrowed.

Dimitri smiled. "A young boy named Brodrick Garrison. He is very loyal to you, if a little naïve. He was lucky I was not a spy for Taraniz."

Valin seemed to relax at the mention of Brock and nodded. "Yes, Brock is a good boy." He righted his chair, and sat down heavily, pulling a flask from inside a desk drawer. He threw back a mouthful and asked, "So, how do we get the rest of you here?"

Chapter Nineteen
Lord Valin of Cannondole

The sky had begun to turn a many colored array of grays and pinks. Jack leaned against the tree trunk behind him, sprawled out on a large limb looking up at the sky. Jayson gave Leo a gentle kick from below as he had begun to snore, and Piper dozed beside him.

There had been a joyous ruckus from the town some time ago that had not yet ceased. But that was not Jack's concern. Dimitri had left them in the early hours of the morning. He told them to leave if he had not returned by nightfall, and night was fast approaching. Dimitri should have known his friends would never leave him, and they had discussed several strategies for stealing into the town if he did not return by dark. As the darkness slowly fell, Jack's nerves were more on edge than they had been in a long time. If there were ever a time they could be caught, this was it.

A thick clump of bushes some thirty yards away moved. It was too much to be any kind of rabbit or fox. Jack snapped his fingers three times, and Jayson looked up at him. Jack pointed, and began climbing down toward Piper and Leo as Jayson stood to guard.

Jack shook the two awake, pressing his finger to his lips. They nodded and scrambled up the tree. Jayson saw his friends climb to safety and quickly joined them as the rustling came closer.

They had only just settled into the boughs of the tree when a figure broke from the brush. He carried no torch and wore a thin, tattered traveling

270

cloak. He stopped and surveyed the clearing, studying the ground and underbrush surrounding the area. His hood fell away from his face, and they breathed a sigh of relief.

"Dimitri!" Piper called, and she nearly fell out of the tree in her haste to climb down. She leapt into his arms, and Dimitri stumbled back. "We were beginning to worry," she said and kissed him. Dimitri was not wearing his usual clothes. He looked washed, and his hair brushed.

"I found Valin and Valar by midday, but returning to you was not as simple," he explained. "We were lucky, however. Earlier today, one of the soldiers received word his wife had given birth. Valin ordered a celebration. The bakery presented a large cake an hour ago, and Valin distributed the wine from his personal stores."

"I hope it's not twins," Jayson mumbled, but no one laughed.

"The distraction should be enough to get you in without being noticed, though we must hurry. The Sisters are waiting for us."

"Sisters?" Jack asked.

"There is a secret passage that runs from the chantry to Valin's manor. The Sisters are loyal to him and Valar, and whatever cause they have to usurp Taraniz. Come." Dimitri took off into the growing dusk, and Piper followed close behind.

Jack, Leo and Jayson exchanged worried looks, then took off after them, praying to whatever deities that may or may not rule over Chartile that their way would be uneventful.

They reached the edge of the forest and crawled on their bellies across the open fields to the rear of the chantry. Sister Theodora met them and led them to the passage. The boys were beginning to grow more uneasy when the wall with the stone lamb swung open before them and there was a real bed before them.

Valar stood near the sitting room area and ushered them in, beaming.

"It is so good to see you all safe again," he said and embraced Piper, though she struggled against his grip.

"Where is Valin?" Piper asked warily.

"He attended the celebrations so as not to appear untrustworthy," replied Valar.

Piper nodded and looked behind her as the door to the secret passage clicked closed.

"Come. We have made sleeping arrangements for you all. You can wash up, and we have fresh clothes for you as well." Valar led them out of the sitting area and down a long hallway. There was a room with one bed and three soft looking mattresses on the floor that smelled of charcoal and frankincense. Leo suspected they had come from the Sisters in the chantry. He felt guilty realizing the poor women had likely given up their beds for the comfort of the prophesized reincarnated kings. His stomach lurched slightly.

"The gentleman will sleep here. Piper, Valin has insisted on giving you his quarters. Not to worry," Valar added seeing the apprehension on both Piper and Dimitri's faces. "He will be staying with me in my quarters. Now, I know this has been a long journey for you all. Please rest for tonight, and we will discuss plans in the morning." Valar bustled off down the hall and disappeared down a flight of stairs.

The party stood silently facing each other until Jayson spoke. "Look, I'm not going to say no to something that isn't the ground."

"And warm water sounds amazing," added Jack. The three boys entered the small bedroom and headed straight for the wash room.

Dimitri turned to Piper and kissed her on the cheek. "I will look after them," he said. "Get some rest."

"You're alright with this?" she asked. They had not spent a single night apart in weeks.

"We should be respectful of our host. I trust Valin. And Valar. Besides," he pulled her closer to him, wrapping his arms around her waist. "As much as you detest it, you will need to get used to being pampered sooner or later."

He kissed her again and turned for the door way. Piper caught his wrist and pulled him back to her, kissing him hard. They broke apart, and Piper eyed him fiercely, a mischievous grin spreading across her face. She turned back to Valin's quarters and shut the door quietly behind her.

Piper leaned against the study room door and exhaled. Even the grandeur of the towering bookcases throughout the room could not ease her mind. She was yet another step closer to confronting Taraniz, to meeting her sister for the first time. She had a thousand questions for her. The pained realization that she would undoubtedly succumb to killing Taraniz or imprisoning her before she could get any answers made her stomach churn.

She walked across the room to the bed chamber, her soft leather boots making little noise on the wooden floors. As an extra precaution, she moved a nightstand in front of the door and a small cabinet dresser in front of the entrance to the secret passage in the fire place.

She undressed and scrubbed herself in the warm water provided for her in the washroom basin. She found a linen chemise hanging on the back of the door, and hoped it had been intended for her. The bed was warm and comfortable. It cradled her back and relaxed her better even than the luxurious Dwarvik beds. She reached over out of habit to grasp Dimitri's hand. She closed her hand on cold air, sighed, and drifted into uneasy sleep.

෨෨

There was a loud thump at the bedroom door. Piper bolted out of bed and grabbed the sword she had laid unsheathed beside her. She nearly tripped on the bedcovers as she crept towards the door, cursing the creaky wooden floors and wishing for the stone of the Dwarvik mountains.

The door handle jiggled violently against the top of the night stand, nearly jostling the top drawer out of the stand entirely. There was quiet conversation on the other side of the door. A woman's voice spoke softly to a man who replied in return. Piper took the opportunity to quietly lift the nightstand out of the way and moved it to the far side of the door.

With a loud crash, the door was shouldered open, and a man in sweeping robes stumbled into the room. He fell to the floor, and Piper snatched him up, resting the tip of her sword in the tender crevice above his kidney. The woman behind him screamed. Piper turned to face the woman who stood holding a tray of tea and biscuits.

"Piper, it's me!" Valar said through the strangling of Piper's arm. She dropped the sword and released Valar quickly. The woman with the tray stood in the doorway, trembling so much the pottery clanked. Valar dropped to his knees and rubbed the back of his neck.

"Forgive the confusion, Krista," Valar said to the woman in the doorway. "Please leave the tray in the study, thank you." The woman nodded, curtsied, and hurriedly set the tray in the other room. She picked up her skirts, and bustled from the room as quickly as she could.

Valar sighed and rose from the floor. Piper sheepishly sheathed the sword and laid it on the bed.

"Did you think we did not place additional securities with you and the boys here?" Valar asked, a bit angrily.

"I am sorry," said Piper, fidgeting with her fingernails.

Valar sighed again and placed his hand on her shoulder. He forced a smile and replied, "A queen is never sorry." He showed her to the door of the washroom, where her traveling clothes had been washed and hung on the back of the door. He left her, still rubbing the back of his neck.

Piper dressed quickly, the smell of freshly baked bread taunting her out to the study. When she entered, Valar stood waiting. A young man perhaps a few years older than Dimitri, sat regally behind the desk. The sight of him made her stop in her tracks. She tried hard not to stare at him, or blush too fiercely as she took the seat across from him and beside Valar.

He was gorgeous. There was no other word for it. She could see the similarities from Valar. The light brown hair, the shape of his nose, even the curve of his jaw beneath the scruff of a beard. His eyes were what held her the most. They were the most piercing and icy blue she had ever seen, framed by full, dark lashes.

He rose when he saw her, and bowed, reaching out a hand.

"My Lady," he said in a voice very unlike his father's, and kissed her hand.

She blushed scarlet, and silently cursed herself for tying her hair back. Instead, she smiled nervously, and inclined her head in respectful acknowledgement.

"Lord Valin," she said, her voice shaking far more than she intended. "Thank you for opening your home to us. I do wish to apologize for the misunderstanding this morning."

"You have not lived the life of the Royal that you were meant to be," he said gently. "It is understandable. I am only glad Krista did not drop the tray! Please, eat." He motioned toward the tray.

Piper's stomach was attempting some form of acrobatics. She was no longer hungry, but she knew neither Valin nor Valar would eat before she did. She reached for a piece of the steaming bread and took a small bite.

"Where are the others?" she asked.

"They are taking their meal in their room," said Valar. "I wished to speak with you privately."

Piper's stomach gave another lurch as she swallowed the bread. Private conversations with Valar had yet to yield any good omens, and Piper was far from optimistic.

"Well, I have learned there is little point in attempting to be drawn out and diplomatic with you, Piper," Valar began. "You are well aware that as Queen you will be expected to choose a Royal advisor even before your crowning ceremony."

Piper nodded.

"And, as I am sure you are also aware, since I was Royal Advisor to your father, I am no longer permitted to retain that title. A new advisor must be chosen with each new ruling King or Queen."

"Are you suggesting Valin?" Piper asked, and nodded toward the man sitting across from her. Though she dared not look at him. She was too afraid she's blush again.

"In a manner of speaking," said Valin. "As the only child to the Lord of Cannondole, I had no choice but to become the new Lord of the town when my father became Advisor. I was too young at the time, and my mother helped a great deal before she passed. I have only taken on the role in a full capacity in the last several years. I take pride that I have run the town with great success, but it is not what I ever truthfully wanted."

"There is also the matter of marriage," said Valar bluntly.

Piper sat straighter in her chair, her hands trembling more and more with each passing moment.

"I know you and Dimitri are..." Valar trailed off, searching for the words, "Well, you know it is just not possible. He is not Elven, and half Human. Chartile needs order and reassurance, not revolution."

"So you wish me to marry Valin to appease the people?" asked Piper. She looked between Valin and Valar and could feel the anger begin to rise inside her. "What about what I want? Aren't I already giving up all of who I am for the sake of everyone else? Am I not permitted this one happiness?"

"When you chose to be Queen, you gave up every right!" Valar cried and slammed his fist on the desk.

Valin stood, silencing whatever retort Piper was about to throw. He leaned in to his father, who turned away from Piper and breathed through his nose. "Let me speak with her," Valin said. He turned to Piper, pleading with those bright blue eyes. "Please."

Valar nodded, and left the room, slamming the door behind him. Valin pulled a decanter and two small, crystal glasses from the shelf behind him. He poured a splash in each glass, and offered the first to Piper.

"The finest brandy in Cannondole. Made by the father of the young man who helped Dimitri find me, I might add." He grinned and drank the thick, luscious liquid. Piper took a sip. It was like nothing Piper had ever tasted, and its effects were nearly as instant as the Dwarvik pearl wine.

Valin refilled his glass and leaned against the bookcase behind him. "I had rehearsed this conversation much differently," he admitted. Piper remained silent and sipped at her brandy. "There was supposed to be mention of my father attempting to remain your advisor before any talk of marriage."

"You forget I have the returned kings at my side," Piper replied icily. There was more edge to her voice than she had expected, and she hid her face in her brandy glass.

"Yes, and they are children who know nothing of our laws and customs." Valin said more kindly back. "They are nothing more than symbols of hope. Though, admittedly, that is much of what Chartile needs at the moment."

"I have promised myself to Dimitri, Queen or no. I can do as I please." Piper placed the crystal glass on the table.

"I do not wish to come between you two. Not in that way. If he is where your heart truly lies, then I will not force myself to you. I only ask that you consider our proposal so that my father may still act as your advisor from a distance. So long as there is both a King and Queen, a Royal Advisor is not required."

Valin drank the rest of his brandy in one swallow. He walked to the desk and pulled a small box from one drawer. He stood before Piper then bowed to one knee. Her heart beat wildly in her chest, and she shook visibly from both fear and confusion.

"Piper, I will treat you with the respect I know you deserve. Not just as a Queen, but as the lady you are. I will not push, I will not pry. I will be whatever you need me to be when you need it. I love the people of Chartile as much as you, and only want the best for them." He opened the box and a brilliant sapphire necklace dazzled in its depths. The stone was as large as a quail's egg and caught the morning sun like a thousand stars. "This was my mother's, and I promised her I would give it to my future wife. All I am asking is for you to keep it until you have made your decision." He reached for her trembling hands and placed the box between them. He closed her hands around it and kissed them gently. Then, he rose, bowed, and left the Piper in silence.

ৎৡৡৢ

Leo lay awake staring at the wooden beams of the ceiling above him. His friends had not yet stirred, but he could hear the sounds of early morning birds outside the shutters of their window. He had not slept well, despite the mattress the Sisters of the chantry had so graciously donated. Their conversation with Piper about life in Chartile after the ordeal with Taraniz had left his mind buzzing.

You could always stay, she had said. I can give you whatever you desire.

But what Leo desired most was to go home. He wasn't a fighter like Jayson, or a diplomat like Jack. He had no place in this world, or much less so than his friends believed. He never wanted to be part of this prophecy, and he still wasn't sure if he believed it. He still held to a strange hope that he had perhaps fallen out of their tree fort and was lying unconscious in a hospital somewhere.

Everyone seemed to expect so much of him. His parents, his teachers, his friends, even himself. And he had always delivered. But he knew things about his world, about Earth. He was like a fish out of water in Chartile, and he didn't like it. He had never felt so helpless, despite the sword beside him and his ability to conjure a flame in the palm of his hand.

The prophecy said four kings would return to right the wrongs. Well, this was wrong. All of this. This should never have happened, he knew it. No matter what anyone said, it would still fall back on him to fix everything. Leo always fixed everything. The ability to get them all back home where they belonged was his responsibility alone. And the only way he could do so was to be involved in the murder of Princess Taraniz. Jayson may have had visions of killing someone, but Leo didn't want blood on his hands any more than the rest of them did.

There was a quiet scraping outside the door, and then a soft knock. Leo rose, dagger in hand. He reached for the door handle and felt a hand on his shoulder. He turned to see Dimitri behind him, a finger pressed to his lips. The boy hadn't heard him move from the bed.

"It is our breakfast," Dimitri whispered in Leo's ear. He opened the door, and removed a tray from a folding table outside the door. Another small table held a pile of their clean and laundered clothes. Leo grabbed the clothes, thankful for clean jeans once again, and closed the door behind him.

Jack sat awake on his mattress, rubbing his eyes from the light pouring in the door. Dimitri set the tray of food on a small table beside the door. Leo passed out their clothes, dropping Jayson's directly on the still sleeping boy's face.

"Should we wake him?" Jack asked, stifling a yawn.

"No, let him rest," said Dimitri through a mouthful of apple.

There was a scream down the hall toward Valin's quarters. Dimitri grabbed his sword, dropping the apple, and rushed down the hall.

Valin was already a few paces ahead of him. A woman bolted toward them, frantic and shaking with fear. Valin caught her in his arms.

"Krista, what is it?" he asked. The edge in his voice betrayed the fear he attempted to hide.

"The girl!" she cried. "She attacked Master Valar!"

Valin released the woman and continued his course down the hall. Dimitri and Leo followed close behind, and they could hear Jack bringing up the rear. Valin rounded a corner in the hall and up a very short flight of stairs. He threw the door to the study open, and found Valar closing the bedroom door. Dimitri, Leo and Jack charged into the room, weapons out and ready.

"Father," said Valin concerned. "Krista said—"

"I am alright," Valar reassured his son. "I suppose she was only acting out of habit. She does not trust easily. We will work with her."

Dimitri gave a small laugh. "I wish you luck in your endeavor." he said. "Piper will change for no one."

"She will have to if she is to be Queen," said Valar sternly. He raised his hand to silence Dimitri's rebuttal. "Let her finish dressing in peace. We will send for you when we prepare to discuss further plans."

"We always eat together," Jack protested in a small voice.

"Today I need to speak with Piper alone." Valar nodded curtly, and ushered Dimitri, Jack and Leo to the door. Valin strode to the desk and sat. Dimitri glared at him and stormed back down the hall.

Once back to their room, Dimitri dropped to the bed, ignoring not only the plate of food, but a rather confused Jayson who sat on the floor, rubbing his eyes.

"Where'd you guys go?" Jayson asked sleepily.

No one said anything at first. Jack and Leo kept glancing at Dimitri, looking away quickly.

"Valar surprised Piper, and she attacked him on accident," Leo finally said.

"Everyone's okay," Jack added, taking a piece of cheese and passing the tray.

Dimitri grunted. He shook his head and gathering his clothes in a huff, heading to the washroom to change.

Several minutes later, a knock on the bedroom door made them all jump. Dimitri, who had returned from the washroom much calmer, rose from the bed.

"Who is it?" Dimitri asked gruffly through the closed door.

"Krista, my Lords," said the timid voice of the woman who had rushed from Valin's quarters earlier. "I am Lord Valin's servant, my Lord. He and

Master Valar have asked me to escort you to the morning meal."

Jayson leapt from his seat on the floor and pushed past Dimitri to open the door. "You mean there's more food?" He asked.

Krista's eyebrows furrow, and she nodded at the strangely dressed, young boy before her.

"Yes!" Jayson exclaimed. Jack and Leo joined him at the door.

"This way," said the woman, and looking slightly confused at the entire situation, led them down the hall.

At the bottom of a magnificent, sweeping stair stood Valar dressed in his usual stately clothes. He smiled at them, and ushered them into the next room.

Piper was already waiting with Valin, but the boys hardly noticed. The table was piled high with fruits, biscuits, and suckling pork, which was about as close as Jayson, Jack and Leo were likely to get to bacon in this world. Their mouths watered, and it took all their will to remain poised and polite as they walked to their chairs, respectfully allowing Krista to pour them drinks from a water pitcher.

Dimitri took the seat beside Piper, who sat at the head of the table. She smiled weakly at him as he kissed her on the cheek.

"Are you alright?" he asked. He did not bother to hide the glare he aimed at Valin as the man sat across from him on Piper's other side.

"Yes," said Piper softly. "I thought someone was trying to break into the room." She gave a small laugh. "I suppose I am not used to such things. Servants and being Royal."

"It will come with time," said Valar, taking the seat at the other end of the table. He accepted a plate of pork from Jack as he spoke.

"So, speaking of royal and all that," said Jayson through a mouthful of food. "How long are we staying here?" He had forgotten how much he missed having a meal at a table, or having a familiar meal at all. The Dwarvik food had tasted well enough, but he missed meat, and meat was not something one easily came by when living at the top of a steep mountain.

"That is in part why we are gathered here this morning," said Valin politely. "We will be leaving at nightfall back into the forest."

"Do you have a plan so we will not be seen?" Dimitri asked.

Valin nodded through a sip of wine. "To a degree. I have been closely monitoring the schedules of the soldiers surrounding the manor. I know precisely when and where their guard duties are changed, and which soldiers we can more easily slip past."

"If you knew all this, why did we not use this way to get into the manor in the first place?" Dimitri asked, his tone growing more hostile by the moment. "Why did you not tell me of this before when I went back to get Piper and the boys?"

Valin looked at Dimitri sternly, his face set and his icy blue eyes reflecting the chill within. "I did not wish to use this way so as to draw suspicion in attempting to use it two days in a row. Simply because these men seem controlled by Taraniz in some way does not mean they have lost their wits. They continue to act ordinary and outwardly appear themselves. I distracted them last night. Tonight, we need a new distraction, and I am open to ideas."

"What happens once we get to the castle?" Leo asked. "Valar said you were going to help us sneak in there."

Valin nodded. "You are quite correct, my King." Leo looked back at his plate and blushed at the address. He tried to form a protest, but the words would not come, and Valin continued on.

"When my father returned here, we began discussing plans. I have, over time, procured Royal tabards, including three from the squires of the Lords of Aerandale, Willowford and Stratford. Once we reach the palace, we should blend in, at least more easily. In this way, we can search for the orenite circlet, and hopefully not be found."

"Fantastic," said Dimitri, and his sarcasm was palpable. "We can discuss how to get into the castle once we know how to get out of here. It has not passed my notice that Valar, whom I might add is currently at large, is not trying to hide, even within the walls of this home. You talk of our plans in front of your beck-ands! How do you know we won't be walking into a trap?"

Krista slammed the pitcher of water down beside Dimitri's plate. He had not heard her approach and jumped unexpectedly.

"There are more of us loyal to the cause of replacing Princess Taraniz than you may believe, Master Dimitri." She refilled his glass and walked stiffly back to stand at the wall of the room without another word.

There was an uncomfortable silence for several moments. Only the sounds of the boys devouring food broke the quiet.

Leo's face suddenly brightened. He swallowed his mouthful of food and spoke. "Hey! I've got an idea!"

Chapter Twenty
Cadenceberries

The soldiers in Cannondole stared at the sky above them. It had been clear with a bright, golden sun all day. But a massive storm had suddenly rolled over the town and was threatening to bear down on them. The soldiers scratched their heads and tugged at their beards. It appeared the very center of the storm hung directly over Lord Valin's manor.

Inside, Jayson, Jack, Leo and Piper sat on the floor staring out the large bay window in Valin's bedroom. They had been concentrating all of their will at the sky for hours and into the growing storm cell that now hung above the manor.

Dimitri stood close by watching. There was something about Valin he couldn't trust. He refused to let his guard down while Valin was anywhere near Piper. He didn't know what had transpired between them earlier that morning, but whatever it had been, there was an unease in Piper Dimitri could sense all the way from Tutaria, and he didn't like it.

The abrupt down pour of rain against the glass broke Leo's concentration and he looked up at the candelabra burning low across the room from them.

"Guys," he whispered. "I think it's probably close to time."

Piper glanced at the candles and nodded her agreement. "The storm is strong enough to hold its own for a while."

They rose from the floor, stiff and sore and rubbing at their aching muscles. Valin, who had been sitting at his desk, stood and offered a helping hand to Piper. She took it and smiled her thanks warmly at him. Dimitri rushed in, shoving a piece of bread into her hand.

"You need to replenish your strength," he said. Piper smiled and kissed his cheek.

Within a few hours, the sky was pitch black. No moon or stars could be seen through the thick torrent of cloud cover that swirled and beat down upon Cannondole. The townsfolk had long since taken refuge in their homes, and great plumes of smoke could be seen pouring from the chimneys as they tried to stay warm. The soldiers were not so fortunate. Their fire pits were flooded, as were their tents and boots. They were miserable, and hunkered down beneath what blankets they could find. Even the makeshift lean-tos they had erected at the edge of the forest leaked, and the torches would not light. Leo smiled as he surveyed the scene out a back kitchen window.

"Brilliant idea," Jack said, patting his friend on the back.

Leo smiled. "Thanks. I just figured we might as well use the magic we've been taught, ya know?"

"It was a very good idea," said Valar, handing the boys their packs. They were newly laden with clean clothes, food, flint and their stolen tabards for when they reached the palace.

"Of course it was!" said Jayson joining them. He was dressed for travelling, like the others, a heavy hood and woolen cloak trailing behind him. "It's Leo."

"Hey, is Valin okay?" Jack asked Valar. "He seemed, I don't know, kind of uneasy about us using our magic."

Valar sighed and laid a hand on Jack's shoulder. "You must understand, magic is still outlawed and feared by most. The very man who changed the way we think of magic now resides as the soul of Princess Taraniz. We were all once peaceful, the Elves, Dwarves, Merfolk, Humans, even Dragons. Then, Noraedin decided to use his magic for ill, influencing the way we all thought of ourselves and our powers. Neighbors turned on each other. Brothers killed brothers out of greed and power. Chartile has never completely recovered from the wrongs you are working to make right."

"So, no pressure," said Jayson. Valar surprised them and laughed a deep, hearty chortle, his eyes brimming with tears.

"What did we miss?" Dimitri asked sternly as he and Piper joined the group.

"Just Valar laughing at the pressures of society on young kids these days," said Jayson waving his hand nonchalantly.

"Are we ready, then?" Valin asked, pushing his way to the front of the group. He cast a nervous glance at the sky above. "They will be changing the watch in ten minutes. We need to leave before the new guards come. Their eyes will be fresher, and less weary. The current guards have been in your storm for the past several hours."

They all nodded, and hoisted their packs onto their shoulders. Dimitri grabbed Piper's hand and squeezed it hard, not letting go.

"Let us hurry," said Valin, and he rushed out the back door. The group of friends stood watching his back for several moments before Jayson took off after him. Jack and Leo followed suit, pulling their hoods up against the pouring rain. Piper made to follow, but Valar called to her.

"Wait," he said and laid a hand on her shoulder. He pulled it back, and looked at her sadly.

Piper stopped, looking at him confused. Dimitri peered over his shoulder, watching as the figures of the boys and Valin disappeared further into the darkness. "In case I never get the chance to say this again, your father loved you, and he regretted every day that he sent you away. He died knowing you were alive, and that alone made him happy. Please, be careful." Valar hugged her tightly, stunning the girl, until she hugged him back.

"Come, we are losing them," said Dimitri and reached to grab Piper's hand again.

"Take care of her," Valar said to him, and they disappeared into the rain.

Still holding her hand tightly in his, Dimitri led Piper in the direction he had last seen Valin and the boys. His eyes were more adjusted to the dark having spent so much time in the dim light of the Dwarvik mountains. With their heads bent against the storm, they found their way to the small party, now taking refuge behind a large tree at the edge of the forest.

"I thought we had lost you," Valin said to Piper.

"We're fine," said Dimitri curtly above the roar of the storm. "What is the plan now?"

There was a small shelter area some fifty yards. Two soldiers huddled inside, their cloaks pulled up against the storm.

"There is a small trail the soldiers use for hunting just past their shelter there. If we had a diversion—"

"Leave it to me," said Piper. She stepped from behind Dimitri who had been shielding her from much of Valin's view. She leaned her back against the tree and closed her eyes, whispering quietly to herself. Valin glanced nervously at her, and scanned the darkness with an uncomfortable twitch. They heard movement in the boughs of the tree above them, and a sudden rush of wind sent a slosh of water pouring down on the shelter, collapsing it.

The soldier's shouts were audible, even from the distance from which they stood. Jack, Leo and Jayson stifled laughs as curses and insults were heard over the down pour of the rain. Piper continued to concentrate. Then, the soldiers gave a different cry, and fled from the shelter, away from the party hiding in the shadows. Piper's eyes fluttered, and she slid down the tree. Valin caught her, and much to Dimitri's displeasure, lifted her in his arms with the same ease as he could have.

"Come," Valin whispered, and took off toward the now empty shelter.

As Valin had described, a small trail led from the point of the lean-to into the forest. They left the path after nearly a half mile, relying only on the eyes of Valin to lead the way. They pushed through the brush and brambles with difficulty until Valin stopped. Piper stirred in his arms, raising a hand to her forehead.

Valin set her gently on the ground, and Dimitri rushed to her side, pushing them all aside.

"Piper," he said, both lovingly and accusing. "What did you do?"

Her eyes were still closed, but a smile began to creep across her face.

"Skunk," she whispered.

"A skunk?" asked Jayson, and he, Jack and Leo began laughing.

"Awesome," said Leo through tiny snorts of laughter.

"No, it is not awesome," chided Dimitri. Even in the darkness, the boys could feel his glare. "The manipulation of the elements and weather is child's play compared to the energy and skill involved to control a complex being such as an animal and bend its will against instinct and nature. It is practically impossible."

"She must be very powerful," said Valin, a tinge of fear in his voice.

"Yes," Dimitri snapped. "She is, but that does not mean she needs coddled."

Jayson rushed forward and stood between the two, or what he guessed was as close to between them as he could find in the darkness. "Okay, okay. Let's just try to move on. We have a long way to go."

"We should not venture further with Piper in such a condition," Valin replied, and nodded toward Piper who still lay on the ground before them.

"Then I will carry her," Dimitri answered, the anger in his voice continuing to rise. "I have done it before."

"I can walk," said Piper weakly, and she attempted to push herself onto her elbows. "Just give me a moment."

"You are in no such state, my lady," said Valin, kneeling before her. "You truly should rest."

"We cannot rest this close yet to the edge of the forest!" Dimitri nearly shouted, and Leo hushed him sharply.

"We have little choice, seeing as our future Queen has gravely exhausted herself," replied Valin.

Dimitri pushed Jayson aside and charged at Valin. Jack caught Jayson as he stumbled back.

"I told you, I will carry her," seethed Dimitri, his face inches from Valin's.

"You treat her with little care or respect. She needs rest, and bouncing in the arms of some idiot half dwarf is not sufficient."

"Stop it!" Piper said feebly, but her voice was drowned out by the continued arguments of Dimitri and Valin.

"I can handle your insults for myself, but Piper is not the delicate flower you seem to think she is. Do not try to treat her as such! You know nothing of her!" Dimitri pushed Valin, and he slammed into the tree behind him.

Valin bounced back as if the tree were made of rubber, and puffed himself up against Dimitri's bulk.

"Perhaps you have been treating her wrong all these years. A flower, no, but she is a lady worthy of adoration and care!"

"I care more about her than you will ever know!" Dimitri whispered coldly before throwing himself at Valin once more.

It took several minutes for Jack, Leo and Jayson to pull the two apart. Eventually, it was seeing Piper push herself from the ground and stand with her hands on her hips before them that finally ended the argument.

"I agree we should move deeper into the forest," she said. "If for no other reason than to put some distance between us and Cannondole." She straightened her traveling clothes and hoisted her pack back onto her shoulder. Dimitri pushed Jayson and Leo off him, and turned to Valin with a glare and half smirk. Piper glared back at Dimitri. "I am not concerned about getting our bearing straight. We will worry about that when it is light out." She stepped between Dimitri and Valin and began walking deeper into the darkness.

"As you wish, my lady," said Valin, shrugging Jack off him and following after her.

They continued on for another half hour, but it was growing more difficult by the minute. Like the darkness of the mountain, the forest was so thick in places, they could barely see the back of the person in front of them, and had resorted to creating a chain in order not to become lost. When Jayson tripped and fell, sprawling on the ground, and Leo and Jack tripped and fell over him for the third time, they decided to give up for the night.

They found three large trees standing close together, and climbed into the branches to sleep as best as they could. Though they had rope to keep them from falling, they did not rest well. There was a mix of gratitude and annoyance when the first rays of sun peeked through the canopy above them. They ate their breakfast as they walked, chewing in silence, unsure how to break the uncomfortable tension that had not yet subsided. Jayson, Jack and Leo hoped their journey to the palace would not take long. Fighting against an army of trained soldiers had to be easier than being in the middle of whatever was going on between Piper, Dimitri and Valin.

෨◌ᕲ

Piper sat awake the next morning as the dawning sun cast rays like spotlights through the tree tops to the forest floor below. She and Jack had been on watch, but the poor boy had fallen asleep shortly after Dimitri and Leo were relieved from their duty. She had let him sleep, welcoming the solitude. She hadn't realized how much she missed her time alone.

She quietly climbed down the tree she shared with Jack, and walked some distance away into a patch of wild flowers. She could see the petals begin to open as the sun hit them, and their aroma was sweet and relaxing. She sat down in the very center of the little patch of flowers, and let their scent calm her mind.

She glanced at the others, still asleep in the boughs of the trees, and pulled a small box from her pack. Cautiously she opened it and touched the brilliant sapphire gem with gentle fingers. It reminded her of the trinkets her Gran would bring home from her excursions to the dwarves. She missed Gran desperately. Once Piper found her, Gran would know what to do about being Queen. And what to do about Valin and Dimitri. Perhaps Piper would ask Gran to be her advisor, and that would solve everything.

"What's that?" asked a voice behind Piper. She jumped and reached instinctually to her boot for a knife. "It's me," said Dimitri as she turned to him.

"Dimitri," Piper breathed, clutching at her chest. "You scared me to death."

"You are still plenty much alive," he laughed, and tossed her a large cadenceberry. Piper caught it in the jewelry box, and quickly plucked the fruit from atop the gem, stuffing the box into her bag once more.

"So, what was in there?" Dimitri asked, his mouth full of berry. He pointed to where the box had disappeared back into Piper's bag and popped another handful of berries into his mouth.

"A gift," said Piper proudly.

"From Mother?" Dimitri asked and raised an eyebrow.

"No," said Piper. "From Valin."

Dimitri swallowed hard. "From Valin?" He shook his head, clenching and unclenching his fists. "Piper, he is using you."

"For what, Dimitri? Can a queen not accept a gift from one of her subjects?" She tossed her braid in a mocking gesture, and rose, heading back for the trees. Dimitri grabbed her wrist and pulled her back to him.

"He is using you to become King. I am not as naïve as everyone seems to believe."

Piper yanked her arm free, and looked at Dimitri with stern green eyes. "What if he is? You do not wish to be."

"So that's it then? I cannot be your King, so you are going to throw me aside? Royalty seems to suit you well."

It was Piper's turn to grab Dimitri as he turned away from her. "Do not tell me you can't when you know the answer is you won't."

"Piper, if I knew that is what it would take for you to marry me, then I would do it! By Rashiri, I would do anything for you, do you not know that by now?" He shrugged. "It does not matter." He looked at her bag where Valin's gift lay hidden in its depths. He pulled his sleeve free of Piper's grasp, though there was little strength behind it now, and sulked back to the trees.

"You never asked me," she snapped, but Dimitri ignored her.

She followed him back to the clearing of trees and watched him put an end to Jayson and Jack's argument about who would start the fire with magic. The logs erupted in a great spire of flame that nearly singed the boys' eyebrows as Dimitri strode past. Jack and Jayson leapt back with screams. Piper rushed forward and quickly decreased the size of the fire.

"That was dangerous," Valin scolded. Dimitri spun around and grabbed the front of Valin's tunic, pulling him close to his face. "Do not start with me. I know your game."

The last thing Dimitri saw were ice blue eyes boring into his then he lay sprawled on his back. Jack stood over him, saying something about a sharing circle. Jayson was being held back by Leo and yelling at Valin. Dimitri felt someone kneel beside him and a warm energy wash over his head. The throbbing in his eye subsided, but only slightly.

He looked up to see Piper scowling at him.

"You are an idiot," she said getting to her feet. A strange kind of whirl wind encircled the camp fire and doused it within seconds. She pushed Jayson and Leo aside, meeting Valin's blue eyes with her green.

Valin quickly dropped his gaze apologetically.

"My Lady, I—" Then he was on the ground as well, covering his left eye with his hands.

Piper looked over her shoulder at the boys, her voice cool and calm. "There is a bush full of cadenceberries somewhere around. Why don't you go look for them?"

Confused and slightly afraid, Jayson, Jack and Leo walked off in the direction of the wildflower patch, occasionally looking over their shoulders as they went.

Piper looked between the two men lying on the ground spread eagle before her. She spoke with the voice she had used when addressing the Dwarvik Council of Elders. She was so angry, she hardly noticed.

"We are here to confront Taraniz and to rescue my grandmother. Nothing more. Once my future has been established, I will decide where each of you stand in it, no one else. Until that time, both of you will continue this undertaking, focusing strictly on the task at hand, and taking care of Jayson, Jack and Leo. If you are unable to do so, then you will leave immediately. I am not asking you, I am commanding you. My words and orders are clear. Now, decide."

Piper stood staring at the two for several long seconds. Valin still held a hand over his eye, and Dimitri would not even look at her. She meant to turn and walk away with great dignity and grace, much like she hoped a queen would. She turned, and found her way blocked by the boys who had returned with handfuls of berries.

"I tried to tell them, the birds weren't eating those, so they must be poisonous," said Leo, who was holding the cadenceberries she asked them to find. Jack and Jayson showed her their collection berries. They were a pale gray with a single black spot at the base of the stem.

"I thought I saw a bird eat one," said Jayson defensively.

"There's definitely more than enough to go around for all of us," Jack replied, his face beaming.

Piper hung her head, trying to let a smile wash over her face. "Leo is correct," she said softly. Jack and Jayson dropped the berries as though they were on fire, and wiped their hands on their shirts and jeans. "Those are black-eyed berries. One of the first symptoms of their poison is your pupils will dilate. You become sensitive to the light and your head begins to pound. Wash your hands thoroughly, and please pick as many of Leo's berries as you can find."

She heard Dimitri and Valin slowly move to their feet behind her, but she did not turn around.

"I want to leave soon," she said loud enough Valin and Dimitri could hear her. "No fires. It could draw unwanted attention. We eat as we go, and rest only at night."

Jayson, Jack and Leo nodded. They chanced glances behind her at Dimitri and Valin who held their heads in their hands and stumbled to their feet.

"You… wanna come pick berries with us?" Jayson asked Piper tentatively.

Piper nearly laughed. "Alright," she chuckled, and followed them to the cadenceberry bush.

స్య

Piper walked at the head of the group using the compass Valin had packed to navigate. Jayson walked between Piper and Valin as Dimitri refused to have him anywhere but where he could see him. Valin remained silent as the party continued, except for an occasional warning against a low hanging tree limb or root along the way. He stumbled more than the rest of the party as his left eye was almost completely swollen shut. He had declined Piper's offer for healing, insisting she needed to save her strength for the journey ahead of them.

That night, they found another cluster of trees to sleep in. These were much larger than the last ones they had rested in the night before. The trees here were so large and close together that only small spots of sun could break through the canopy, leaving the ground below rather barren. This had the added benefit of making the way more clear with less underbrush to hamper their way. But Jayson, Jack and Leo soon discovered why it was almost impossible to avoid the main road through the forest.

"It is how the Elven palace remains hidden," Valin explained to Jack. "You are wandering through the Belirian Forest and the next thing you know, you've walked straight into the Royal Gardens!"

"Don't they have some kind of outer walls, or a moat or something?" Leo asked, adjusting his glasses.

"Of course they do," said Dimitri and sighed. "If it were so easy to get into the palace, do you think we would have the tabards?"

"In our world, we have trees that are thousands of feet tall, and hundreds of feet around!" said Jayson, throwing his arms wide.

"You mean sycamores?" Leo asked. "The tallest are about thirty feet around, Jayson, and only a hundred and twenty feet tall." He paused. "Now, redwoods grow to about three hundred feet tall and are about seventy feet around."

"Spoil sport," Jayson whispered, and stuck his out tongue at Leo. "I wonder where the biggest one is."

"The throne room of the palace," said Piper. "It has been carved as the King's throne and still grows a bit each year. Our scholars believe it was the first tree in Chartile, and it was where the ashes of the Great Phoenix fed life into the earth." She smiled at Jayson as she came to walk beside him. She put an arm around his shoulders and gave him a small hug, her mood lightening as the forest darkened.

"Who's the Great Phoenix?" Jack asked.

"Ssh!" said Dimitri, and they froze. A rustling in the distance made them stare wide eyed as they watched a bush sway and move. A fox jumped at a mouse hole, then scurried off after the little creature in an attempt at a before bed time snack. They exhaled the breath they hadn't realized they were holding, smiling at each other before continuing.

"We are less than a day from the palace." Dimitri cautioned them. "We must to be more careful."

They nodded to each other, and did not speak for the rest of their trek that day. They walked in silence for only another hour or so, as darkness fell faster so deep in the forest. Once again, they could hardly see the person in front of them, and the tripping over roots and tree limbs began again at a steady increase.

"This is nuts," Jack snapped and he fell face first onto the ground. Valin reached down and lifted Jack easily.

"Perhaps it is time to set in for the night," Valin whispered.

They climbed as high as they could in the trees off the main path. They did not bother setting a watch, hoping to get as much sleep as possible before dawn. They tied themselves to the giant tree limbs, and settled in, their dreams turning as dark as the forest surrounding them.

It was still dark when Jayson woke to movement in the treetops above him. His unlucky encounters with trolls and then vampires had his heart pumping wildly the moment his eyes shot open. He reached for his bow, but a stone, or something hard, hit him on the head.

"Oh, I am so sorry, Jayson," Piper whispered, climbing down beside him.

"It's okay," he whispered back to her. "What are you doing?"

"Just — going to water the bushes. That is what you boys call it, correct?" asked Piper tentatively.

Jayson blushed and was thankful Piper couldn't see it in the darkness. "Right," he said.

"Go back to sleep," she murmured, and continued on down the tree. "I will come from the other side when I come back. I won't wake you."

Jayson shrugged, hugged his bow to his chest, and fell back into an uneasy slumber.

"Piper! Piper? Where are you?" a panicked voice called from the ground below. Jayson started awake again. It had seemed like only seconds before that he had closed his eyes. Spots of light filtered down through the tree tops, and the small clearing below was cast in a soft gray. He hurried down the tree ready to sting his bow.

When he reached the ground, Jayson was nearly knocked off his feet. Dimitri grabbed him by his shoulders and shook him. "Where did she go? She was in the tree with you!" he screamed in Jayson's face.

"I don't know," Jayson said, and his voice trembled. "She had to go to the bathroom. I went back to sleep, I—"

"You let her go alone?" said Valin from behind Dimitri.

Dimitri dropped Jayson, and turned to Valin. "Do not begin to act as though you care about her!" He raised his fist.

Valin caught his arm, and swung Dimitri around, twisting him at his shoulder. "Do not lay the blame with me, Dimitri. You started this by turn her against me!"

It took all three of them to pull Valin and Dimitri apart again.

"This isn't helping us find her!" Leo finally shouted.

"She took the compass," said Jack. "I checked all the packs."

"She must have gone to the palace on her own," said Jayson, and he released his grip on Dimitri's arm.

"Why would she do that?" asked Leo. "I thought we were all in this together." He looked sadly at Jack and Jayson, his face revealing the hurt they all felt.

"Some of us haven't been very team oriented, lately," said Jack, his arms crossed. He, Leo and Jayson turned to Valin and Dimitri, glaring fiercely.

"I may be able to track her," said Dimitri more calmly.

"I can help more once we get a little closer to the palace." Valin inhaled deeply. "I know my way around the areas within its walls."

"Then let's go as fast as we can," said Leo. He grabbed his pack and straightened his glasses with a sniff. "She's got several hours on us, but she couldn't have moved that fast in the dark."

Prophecy

They agreed, and headed out in the direction they had been travelling. For the first time, Valin and Dimitri worked together. They studied the ground and underbrush for traces of a human trail to follow, and consulted with each other as they went. Slowly, the surrounding area began to take on a faint gray look as the sun rose, which made looking for signs of a recent trail much easier. They were quiet, except when pointing out a foot print or broken branch. They didn't know if the growing pit in their stomach was drawn from concern for Piper or the fear that they would be confronting Taraniz any moment.

Chapter Twenty-One
Shadows of the Past

The gleam of a spear point caught Piper's eye. Sentries stationed mere yards away would have caught her had she not seen it. She flattened herself to the ground behind one of the many butterfly bushes the Elven palace was famous for. She was thankful she had extinguished the small flame she had created for light as soon as there was the faintest bit of sun for her to see by. It may have slowed her up a bit, having to squint at the tiny compass in her hand, but she didn't care. Piper knew she had several hours on her companions and was not worried about them catching up to her. She knew they would discover she was missing soon enough and come after her, but she would already be in the castle by then.

Pangs of remorse ran in waves up and down her spine when she thought of them. She felt guilty for leaving them behind. She had promised the boys she would always be there for them, and worse, the last words she had spoken to Dimitri and Valin had been in anger. She clenched her jaw and pushed her feelings aside. This was her task to do. Gran was depending on her yet. And then there was Taraniz – her sister. She had to find her and speak with her. She had to know. She had so many questions.

The soldiers turned to speak to each other, and Piper reached into her pack, feeling around for the tabard. It wasn't there. Panicked, she dared to sit up, and emptied the pack of its contents on the ground before her. She must have forgotten it in her haste when leaving the campsite. She glanced at the soldiers through the butterfly bush, wondering if she could sneak to the dungeons and work her way up through the palace from below. She had to chance it. It was the only way.

The magic she had once feared only weeks ago was now her greatest asset. She took a deep breath and closed her eyes. She shifted a tree limb several yards away, but the guards continued their conversation. Piper rolled her eyes, and flicked a small spark at a passing bird. It chirped and dropped the seed it had been carrying on one of the guards. This time, they looked up. Again, Piper made the tree limbs sway and rustle, and lifted several large stones, allowing them to fall to the earth again.

She had never been to the dungeons, even as a child, but she recalled the map she had studied in Valin's library the day they left Cannondole. If she remembered correctly, the door she now faced led downward into the dungeons. The map had labeled only the perimeters and the inner gardens of the palace. Once she was inside, she was on her own.

The guards headed toward the sounds. She used compact balls of air to create the sound of footsteps hurrying away.

"Do you hear that?" one of the guards asked, looking in the direction of the sound.

Piper made a distant butterfly bush dance as though someone had hidden behind it.

The first guard looked at his comrade, who nodded. Their spears lowered, the two men slowly approached the bush. Piper took a deep breath and steadied her trembling hands. Silently, she moved behind them towards the door. Her hand touched the heavy iron latch. The guards were almost at the bush. She pressed the handle with her thumb, and it creaked with age. The door swung wide, pulled by gravity, and it creaked even louder.

The guards whipped around, their eyes wide with surprise.

"Stop!" one cried, and they charged her. Piper barely had time to pull her sword from its scabbard, but instinct over took her. She commanded the wind with ease, and knocked the two men to the ground.

They shook their heads, dazed, and the second guard cried, "It's her! It's her! Send the warning!"

The first guard glanced at a pile of kindling mixed with a blue powdered mineral that Piper had not noticed at first. It was a signal fire. It would send a cloud of colored smoke into the air. Taraniz had known all along she would come. Piper was closer to the kindling than the soldiers. She scattered and pile and rubbed it in the earth. One of the soldiers grabbed her, forcing her arms behind her back. Fire erupted from her hands at the guard's waist and caught his gambeson ablaze. He jumped back, beating at the flames franticly. The other guard raised the butt of his spear toward Piper's head, but she was faster.

She swung her sword, slicing the man through his stomach. She turned, and knocked her pommel hard into the still flaming soldier's forehead. Both men fell to the ground, and the burning gambeson was smothered under the soldier's weight.

Breathless, Piper dropped her sword. She felt sick. These were her soldiers. Men who would soon pledge themselves to protect her. And she had killed them. She had killed them for doing their job. She thought of Tathias and wondered if these men were at peace now that they were free from the magic she knew Taraniz was using on them.

Piper moved their bodies behind the butterfly bushes, tears pouring down her face. She wiped her eyes and hurried through the dungeon door.

The smell hit her in the face as hard as a kick in the gut. The stench of human waste and decay wafted up the stone steps from deep underground. Piper wondered how she hadn't noticed it before. The dungeons were certainly not meant to be a place of luxury, but as she descended the stair, the unhealthy conditions of the prisoners loomed at her out of the shadows of the flickering torches lining the walls.

Some of the holding cells had only standing room. In one, a body lay at the door, its face covered by a ragged cloth. Piper knew he must be dead, placed there by his fellow cell mates, waiting to be taken by the guards. The young queen-to-be felt tears sting her eyes again. Whether from the odor or the heartbreak of the deplorable conditions, she did not know. She wiped them away, and began searching the ragged faces for Gran.

Eyes caught the torch light, looking her, then hiding again in the shadows. "Kaytah," she whispered in the dark.

"New here, eh?" said a middle aged man to her left. He looked cleaner and more bright-eyed than most of the prisoners. "We don't see many pretty faces among the guards here. What's your name, lovey?" He leaned against the bars of the cell door, a smile on his face and playful mischief in his eyes.

Piper narrowed her eyes at him a moment, trying to read his intentions. "I am looking for an elderly woman named Kaytah. She was brought here several weeks ago."

The man frowned and shook his head. "I have been here for longer than that, lovey. No old ladies come through here."

"You look rather well to do compared to the others," Piper noted, a cold edge to her voice.

The man shrugged. "This ain't my first time round, darlin'. I know the guards. Know who to bribe and who to take care of when I get out. Though ain't no one getting outta here no more. They shove you in and throw away the key now. No more trials or hearings. No pardons or punishments. They just forget about you and drag out the bodies when you're dead."

Piper blinked at the man in disgust. "How is that possible? The Noble Conclave would never allow such a thing!"

"Ah!" The man smiled again. "Now I know you are an intruder! Everyone knows the nobles have no power anymore. The Princess tells them what to do, and they jump. The ones that stay the longest, ask how high."

"What do you mean?" Piper pressed.

The man's eyes darted back and forth. He looked over his shoulder at his cell mates huddled in the corners. He beckoned Piper closer.

Reluctantly she obeyed, breathing through her mouth instead of her nose to keep her stomach from churning.

"They say she's got magic on them," he whispered.

Piper retreated a few steps away. "Has anyone seen proof of this?"

"No need, lovey. All the proof you need is right in front of all our noses. Aramor was stabbed in his bed. The cells are over flowing because of petty crimes. Princess Taraniz ain't taking any chance of a rebellion against her."

"If she has magic, then why doesn't she just kill everyone who opposes her? Why keep you locked up?"

"Because the magic has driven her insane," he whispered, tapping his head with a dirty finger and smiling.

There was a commotion to Piper's right toward the entrance to the castle. She looked along the line of cells, hoping for a sign of escape.

"Around the corner," whispered the man and nodded to his right. "There's another entrance. Pull on the torch to the left of the wall. It will take you straight to the noble's quarters of the palace."

Piper looked at him doubtful, but he nodded reassuringly to her.

"Thank you," she whispered, and took off as quickly.

"Wait!" called the man. Piper stopped in her tracks, praying whomever had caused the uproar at the main dungeon entrance had not heard. "I didn't get your name, lovey. Seeing as you're probably the last pretty face I'll see before I rot away in here."

Piper slowly turned to face the man. She held her head high, the light of the torches making her red hair appear as flame in the darkness.

"My name is Piper Romilly. I am Princess Taraniz's sister, and I will make this right."

She left the man staring, his mouth hung open in awe. He turned to his cell mates as Piper rounded the corner he had indicated. It ended at a dead end wall, framed only by two torches. The sounds of footsteps were coming closer. She thought she heard the man in the cell shouting for the soldiers' attention, and she vowed she would pay him back the favor of aiding her escape. She raised a hand to the torch on her left. It would not budge from its bracket. She pulled hard, and heard scraping. The bricks of the wall moved slightly. The uproar of the prisoners increased, and she saw a group of five soldiers run passed her, drawing their swords, and paying no mind to her. She breathed a sigh of relief, pulled the torch with all her strength, and squeezed through the small opening it had created. Moments later she heard the scraping sound again as the torch and its bracket returned to its normal position and the wall slid back into place.

Piper found herself in a small alcove. To her left and right was an enormous, golden hallway with the trunks of trees carved as great columns in the center of the hall. She looked up and saw the branches of the canopy above had been woven together over time, creating a ceiling that would keep any weather out. The sight was somehow familiar to her.

The hall was quiet and deserted. This only made Piper more on edge. She kept her hand poised over the hilt of her sword as she went. Torn between looking for Gran and wanting desperately to find Taraniz, Piper wandered the halls, lost in strange memories. She had visited the palace with Gran on numerous occasions, but it did not seem to help her remember her way through the winding corridors.

Ghostly figures materialized before her down the hall. Piper recognized one as Gran, but from many years ago. Her hair was flecked with honey brown, and she wore it in a knot at the base of her head as Piper remembered when she was very little. The ghostly images faded, and Piper hurried after them.

She wandered the hallway, looking side to side at one closed and locked door after another. She did not have Dimitri's gift of unlocking doors, and she dared not try wasting her time to pick the locks. Instead, she continued through the halls, growing increasingly more uncomfortable with the lack of people.

The noble's wing was where members of the royal family, the Conclave of Nobles and select ambassadors kept their rooms and quarters. If an army was ready to march on Mount Kelsii, the noble's wing should have been crawling with dignitaries, noble messengers, beck-ands, and palace guards. But not a soul stirred in the vast, echoing hall. Piper was certain she could have heard a feather land on the golden tile floors.

The ghostly image of a dress train disappeared through a door toward the end of the hall. Piper ran full out toward it. She did not care how much noise she made. She stopped in the doorway, and saw the ghostly figures of her Gran, an old man she did not recognize and herself as a child.

The figures glided over the moss that served as the floor for the elven library. This was one of the original rooms of the palace. The trunks of the trees were carved into towering book shelves. A partial ceiling had been built around the boughs of the trees, but she might as well have been standing in the middle of the Belirian Forest by the palace butterfly bushes. It was the perfect climate for preserving the delicate skins and parchments of the ancient documents.

"I need a favor of you, Raoul," said Gran in a distant, echoing voice. "No one must know." She pulled a piece of parchment from a scroll case she carried and handed it to the man. He stared at it, his expression unmistakably one of shock. He looked at the little girl running her hands and toes through the soft moss at his feet.

"Is she—" he began to ask, but Kaytah held up a hand to silence him.

"No one can know," she said again.

The figures vanished and Piper was left staring at the vast, empty library. She knew she would never find her birth record in the labyrinth of trees and parchment. She would have to worry about that later. She needed to find Taraniz. She needed to talk to her sister.

Movement caught the corner of her eye. Piper darted into the hall and saw two little girls, one red-haired and one blonde meet at the end of the hall.

"Hello. Do you want to play a game?" Asked the little blonde in the same distant, echoing voice.

"Sure!" said the little red-haired girl. She reached a hand toward the blonde's outstretched one. A beck-and bustled up behind them. She lifted the little princess from the floor and brushed at her clothes.

"My lady!" cried the woman. "You will dirty your skirts before the banquet tonight! Come along. Your father is waiting." She grabbed the girl's hand and pulled her away. The little princess looked sadly over her shoulder at the red-haired girl who waved at her and faded away.

A door opened at the end of the hallway. It creaked slowly and stopped suddenly. No one stood behind it. No hand had turned the intricate knob, or pushed it from its frame. Cautiously, Piper walked toward the door and stopped before a winding stone stair. She took a step, and dust plumed around her boots. With her hand still clutching at her sword hilt, she headed up the stair. Higher and high she climbed. The stair held no windows, and light from the door below quickly faded. She thought she was nearly above the treetops when the stair ended at a small landing and a plain wooden door.

She knew she should have been looking for Taraniz. She should have been trying to find Gran. But Piper reached for the handle on the door. The latch clicked loudly, and dusty cobwebs moved aside as she pushed the door inward.

It was a tiny room, untouched by time for nearly two decades. Dust covered the little dressing table, the carved wooden chairs and the four poster canopy bed. Shackles and chains bound to the wall above the headboard hung innocent and unmoving. Piper gasped, realizing at once where she was. She turned to the dressing table and lifted a hair brush with trembling fingers. She pulled a strand of red hair from its bristles and blinked tears from her eyes again.

She let her fingers roam over the back of the chair that sat before the dressing table. Her mother had sat in that chair, brushing her hair and watching her belly grow – watching Piper grow. The latch to the window was rusted shut. Piper could barely see through the glass, but she was well above the boughs of the trees. She ran a hand over the bedcovers and pinched the lacey trim between her fingers. The top drawer to the bedside table sat ajar. The top of the drawer had been nearly wiped clean of the dust and dirt that sat heavy on the rest of the room. Piper pulled the drawer open. At the bottom was a small, leather bound book, slightly brittle and perfectly preserved. She lifted it, running her hands over every delicate edge, and sat on the bed in a puff of more dust.

Her hands shook as she opened the book to the last pages and read her mother's final words.

"The time is drawing near now. I know it has not been long enough, but I can feel it in my heart. They will be here within the week. Yes, they. I say they because I know I carry twins. I cannot say how I know this. Perhaps it is the size of my belly, too many kicks in the night for one child alone, a mother's intuition. I pray my babies will grow up safe and loving, and without magic. This has been like a curse to me, and I can feel such fighting forces of anger welling up inside me – and no, it is not the morning sickness. I have told Aramor I believe I am carrying a boy. We have agreed to call him Taran. If my first born is a girl, she shall be Taraniz. If my second born

is a boy, I wish him to be named Valon after our friend and advisor, Valar, whom has never abandoned me, even after all this time. I care for Aramor, but I can say now that I love Valar, though he will never know. If my second child is a girl, I wish her to be named Eva Ruani, for my grandmother and myself. I know my time is drawing close. My suffering will soon end. I can feel the magic building in my veins, and I am certain I will never survive to see the faces of my beautiful children. I will be at peace once more."

Tears rolled down Piper's face. She wiped them away quickly before they hit the delicate words written across the page. Valar had said her name was Eva Ruani, but she had not known it was for her great-grandmother. A knot tightened in the pit of her stomach, but she pushed it away as she turned the pages, willing herself to continue reading.

"Valar came to visit me today. It was so good to see him again. He had been away visiting Duke Ewan in the Rushing Reeds province. We talked about our childhood today. We reminisced about the times we played in the stables and trees as children. What I wouldn't give now to be picking wildflowers again or climbing a tree. No, not trees, for I have lived too long and too high with nothing more than the birds and boughs for company. But I could not help myself. I could not bear the loneliness any longer. He smiled so warmly, so genuine to me. I kissed him. Damn myself! Aramor, my husband, my king, has abandoned me, and I only long for some kind of comfort. I kissed him, and he kissed me. I had not expected it, and it frightened me. I cried. I told him I loved him, that I think I have always loved him. He said so too, and then he left.

He left me. Just as everyone else I have ever loved has left me. I am alone again, with nothing more than these stone walls for company. If this is the way my life shall forever be, then I will leave them too. If my children do not kill me tonight, for I can feel the discomfort of child birth paining me as I write this, then I shall do it myself. I will not be left alone again, and all those who ever loved me will know my pain."

Piper slammed the book shut. Her tears were gone, replaced with a hot anger that rose inside her. Even if Aramor had not sent her away, she never would have known the love of her birth mother. Runa would have left her, the same way everyone had left the Queen in her tiny tower prison. Runa would have selfishly taken her own life than live to love her children. Piper threw the book on the floor. It slid the length of the room and stopped in the open door way. A pair of embroidered shoes stepped forward, and long, delicate fingers lifted the book from the ground. Piper stood, her hand flying to her sword hilt. The figure pressed the book to her chest in a lovingly.

"Hello, dear sister." The voice was calm and sweet.

Chapter Twenty-Two

Sisters

"There should not be guards in this area," Valin whispered. They had reached the edge of the elven palace. Valin had recognized the outlying gardens, and abruptly halted their way when he saw two guards on patrol. They doubled back behind several Belirian trees, and peered out cautiously at the guards beyond.

"They must know she is here," Dimitri said. His tone spoke of worry, but his face was set hard.

"How are we supposed to get in now?" Jayson asked.

Valin pulled the tabards from his pack. He handed one to each of them, explaining which lord and area he represented.

"Piper would have gone to the dungeons looking for Kaytah first," said Dimitri.

"If she did, that way's probably less guarded now. They aren't going to put more guards in places she's already been," said Leo.

"But if she didn't go there first," Jack whispered, "It could be crawling with soldiers waiting for her to look for Gran."

"I believe it is our best chance to begin," Dimitri replied. They nodded and followed close behind Valin.

They skirted around the same area Piper had followed. Dimitri pointed out a similar set of footprints to those they had been following. They ducked behind the butterfly bushes and nearly tripped over the bodies of Piper's victims. Jack and

Leo looked sick. Jayson couldn't look at the men at all.

"This must be Piper's handy work." Jack's face was ghostly white as he spoke.

"She killed her own people," Valin murmured, closing the eyes of one of the men.

"She likely had no choice," Dimitri said in defense.

"She could have just knocked them unconscious instead." Leo was as pale as Jack. The shock of what Piper had done washed over him with a wave of unease.

"We don't know what happened," Jayson snapped, "We weren't there. We can't blame her."

Jack and Leo exchanged looks and nodded. Valin and Dimitri still appeared uneasy.

"Come, then," said Valin, and they crept toward the dungeon door.

Jack, Leo and Jayson gagged as the stench of the dungeons hit them when Valin opened the door. They pulled their tabards over their noses and coughed.

"You are squires of some of the greatest lords of Chartile," said Valin, his eyes narrowed in distain. "Remove your tabards in that manner."

"We can't help it," Jayson choked.

"We need to blend in," Dimitri replied more empathetic. "You must try. For Piper," and he led the way through the open door. Valin gestured for them to follow. The boys reluctantly lowered the collars of their tabards and followed close behind. Valin brought up the rear and closed the door behind them.

They were instantly plunged into darkness. Many of the torches that had burned when Piper entered hours before had been taken by soldiers searching the cells and surrounding areas for the intruder. Dimitri grabbed one of the remaining torches from its bracket and followed the main corridor past the cells.

It appeared some of the prisoners had caused a riot. Dead bodies had been carelessly kicked to the side of the walk way, and many in the cells were helping each other nurse wounds to the best of their abilities.

"Oy! You're with that red hair girl, ain't yeh!" called a voice from a cell behind them.

They spun around, looking for the voice in the dark. A man, his left eye puffy and swollen shut, leaned against the cell door. He spat a mouthful of blood on the floor and readjusted the arm hanging in a sling. It seemed to have been made from the bottom half of his tunic.

Valin pulled the pack from his shoulder and knelt to extract ointment and bandages.

"You look like you've seen the wrong end of one of them guards' fists," said the man, pointing to the black eye Piper had given Valin the day before.

"What happened here?" Valin asked, ignoring the man's probe and instead dabbed at a cut on his eyebrow.

"Some girl came in the back. Don't know how she got passed the soldiers outside." He shrugged with his good arm and accepted another cloth with ointment from Valin. He passed it on to a woman behind him with a gash across her forehead. He put it in her hand, raised it to the wound, and patted her shoulder before returning to the onlookers outside his cell. "She asked me some questions about the Princess, then the soldiers came lookin' for someone. She said she was Taraniz's sister. I had no reason not to believe her." He shrugged again and leaned on the cell door. "I told her how to get into the palace, and then told the others that Taraniz's sister had come to save us. They – well, we really – we started making a commotion to distract the guards."

"Where did she escape to? Where did you tell her to go?" Dimitri reached through the bars and grabbed the man's tunic. Valin pulled him away, and Dimitri glared, wiping his hands on his pants.

The man smiled and spat another mouthful of blood on the floor. "So it's true, eh? I wasn't sure at first, but any reason to give these damned guards a little hell, and I'm game."

"Where is she?" Dimitri repeated.

The man backed away from the door a bit, but still continued to smirk. "Around the corner there. It dead ends. Pull on the left torch bracket. It takes you to the noble's quarters."

Dimitri took off without a second glance. Valin grabbed his pack and hurried after him, Leo and Jayson close on his heels.

"Thank you," said Jack. "We'll do something to fix all this. I promise!" Jack bowed to the man and hurried after his friends.

Jack skidded around the corner and watched Valin pulled the torch bracket at the dead end wall as the stranger had indicated. The secret door slid aside with a deep grinding noise, and they hurried through, hands at the ready on their weapons.

"This way," Valin whispered, and motioned them toward the library.

Dimitri pressed a finger to his lips emphasizing caution to the boys.

"Where are we going?" whispered Leo at Dimitri's shoulder. Dimitri ignored him and continued to look side to side, his entire body tense with anticipation of an attack.

The door to the library was open. Valin pressed himself against the wall outside the door, breathing shallow and listening intently. Nothing stirred within, and he dared a peek around the corner. It was empty.

"Let's split up," said Dimitri. "We can cover more ground this way."

"No!" cried Jayson, and his voice echoed in the great golden hallway. "We have to stay together. We promised."

"Piper did not heed that promise, did she?" Dimitri snapped.

Jayson looked at his feet, a lump forming in his throat.

"Well, we aren't splitting up," said Jack, standing beside Jayson and placing a hand on his shoulder.

Dimitri sighed. His shoulders drooped and he rubbed his forehead.

"So be it. You three search the library. She may be looking for the birth records," said Valin. "Dimitri and I will continue to look for the circlet." He looked at Dimitri who stood beside him. Though still glaring, Dimitri nodded.

They took off in the opposite direction down the hall, their hands on their sword hilts and their bodies tense. Jayson, Jack and Leo watched them go, and cautiously entered the library. It was vast, larger than they had anticipated, and they stood staring wide eyed in the doorway for several moments.

"Well, this could take a while," said Jack. Leo didn't answer. His eyes ogled at the plethora of information before him, his greed and addiction for knowledge fighting the will to stay on task. Jack gave him a hard push forward through the door, and Jayson followed, his spirits still down cast.

♥≈

Piper's hand flew to the sword at her hip. She drew the blade, but Taraniz held up her empty hands in surrender, tucking Runa's journal beneath her arm.

"Please," Taraniz said again, her voice calm and gentle. It was nothing like the voice Piper had heard her use when commanding her troops against Outland Post. "I only wish to speak with you. I promise."

Piper stared at her skeptically, not daring to move.

"You are free to search me of weapons," said Taraniz, her hands still raised.

Slowly, Piper lowered her blade, but did not sheath it.

"Fine. I am listening, but I want to know how you knew I would be here," she said.

Taraniz lowered her hands, and grabbed Runa's journal, holding it to her chest again. She looked at the floor, silent for some time as she struggled to find the words.

"I knew as soon as you entered Cannondole." She straightened to her full height and took a deep breath. "I could feel your presence through the minds of the soldiers. I knew you were there, in the forest and the manor. Then I lost you for a while, but I knew if you had gone to Cannondole, I just knew where your heart would lead you. I felt you when you entered the noble's wing." Taraniz took a step forward. Piper raised the tip of her blade slightly, and Taraniz, taking the warning, stepped back again. "I do not know how I did it. So much that I do seems that way. I thought it was a good idea. I thought about how I might do such a thing, and then it just happened. I searched your mind for memories, and I used one of mine as well. I made them materialize so you would follow them. I am glad you did."

"You are lucky I did," said Piper coldly. "You should not pry into people's minds, Taraniz. It is not polite for one. Now, where is my grandmother?"

"She is safe. I promise. She is with the nobles of Sparrow's Port. I did not hurt her. I only asked her some questions. I knew you would come here looking for her." Taraniz looked at the floor, her lower lip trembling. She ran her fingers absently over the leather of the journal and looked at Piper again. "I am sorry," she said. "I have wanted to talk to you for so long. Ever since I discovered the truth – but I haven't been able to."

"Not attacking the people of my village would have been a great start," scoffed Piper.

"I know. Piper, I am sorry. I am sorry for everything I have done. I never meant it to be this way." Taraniz dropped the journal. She clutched at her head, grimacing in pain and nearly fell to the floor. Piper rushed forward, abandoning her blade on the dusty bed. Taraniz was panting, her eyes shut tight with pain. Piper touched her shoulder, and almost instantly, Taraniz's eyes opened. She took several deep breaths and rose from the floor. "I'm alright. I am sorry." she said breathlessly.

"What happened?" Piper asked. Her voice was gentle, and her hand remained on her sister's shoulder.

"It is difficult to explain," said Taraniz. "You must understand, I never wanted to conquer Chartile. I wanted to unite our peoples under one banner. I never wanted this bloodshed. When I discovered I had magic, it was — oh, Piper, I cannot put it into words!"

Tears streaked Taraniz's face. Piper reached for her free hand and led her to the bed. She sheathed her sword and sat beside her, holding Taraniz's hands between hers.

"It was as though an evil awoke inside of me. I became two different people, and I could not control it. I cannot control it still. The true me screamed inside my heart and my mind, but it was though a wall had been built around me and I could not escape. I had heard rumors of a girl in Outland Post that had magical abilities, and I thought that perhaps the secret to controlling that… that rage might lie there, with you.

"I wanted your help. Truly I did. But every time I began forming a party to travel there, the evil inside of me would overtake everything and lock me away."

The princess wiped the tears from her eyes, and turned to face her sister. Piper saw the similarities between them now. The high cheek bones she now knew came from their mother, the freckles across the bridge of her nose, which had been from their father.

"Piper, I want you to rule with me. I want us to be equals. We are sisters. We both have an equal claim to the throne, and magic. Teach me how I can control this hate in my heart, and we could be the most powerful rulers in all of Chartile. Think of all the wonderful things we could do for all of the races of our land!"

Piper stared back into Taraniz's blue-grey eyes, and sighed. "Taraniz –"

"It's Ani," said the princess, with a smirk.

Piper smiled back and continued, "Ani, I honestly cannot help you. But I have a friend. I'm sure he has followed me here by now. He taught me so much about controlling my magic. I think, with his help, and the boys, we can help you."

"The boys?" Taraniz asked surprised. "So the prophecy is true?"

Piper smiled at her, and nodded excited. "Yes! This evil in you, it must be Noraedin's soul. Ani, if we can just –"

Taraniz's eyes flashed black. Her smiling face fell, and she stood, pulling a dagger from inside her sleeve. Piper reached for the knife at her back, but Taraniz was too quick. She pushed Piper to the bed, the dagger raised above her face.

Piper kicked Taraniz in her stomach and pushed her to the floor. The dagger flew through the air and smashed against the mirror of the dressing table. Piper ran to Taraniz, who lay face down on the floor.

"Ani," she whispered, pulling Taraniz into her arms. The girl was dazed, and the blackness faded from her eyes as she blinked them into focus.

"Oh, Piper!" she breathed, and began sobbing when she saw the shattered mirror. "I am so sorry! I didn't hurt you, did I? Forgive me!"

"Of course I forgive you," Piper whispered in her ear. "This is not you. The reincarnation process between you and Noraedin's soul has been... compromised. I think he's trying to finish what he started through you."

"Can you fix this?" Taraniz pleaded, looking up at Piper. Her face was pretty, even when she cried.

"No, but I think with returned kings, and Dimitri, we might be able to –"

Taraniz's eyes flashed black again. This time, Piper was ready for it. She pinned Taraniz's arms behind her back, and held her to the ground.

"Leave my sister alone!" she screamed. "Ani, you have to fight this! Come back to me!" A power unlike anything Piper had ever felt surged from Taraniz's body. It exploded through Piper with an audible blast, and Piper slammed against the mirror, shattering it even further.

Taraniz stood, her eyes still black. They flashed back to their innocent gray-blue, but there was no kindness behind them. Taraniz lifted her hand, and Piper flew through the air again, landing hard on the bed. The shackles on the wall snapped around her wrists. Taraniz smiled, and it was very unlike the Ani Piper had just met.

"She is mine," said the voice Piper knew too well.

Taraniz turned and left the room, kicking Runa's journal under the bed.

"Ani, wait!" Piper called. "You can fight this! Come back!"

Her footsteps slowly faded away on the stone stairs. Taraniz was gone.

Chapter Twenty-Three

Sacrifices

Jayson ran his hand over the smooth bark of one of the Belirian tree book shelves in the elven library. He pulled a random book from the shelf in front of him and opened to the center page. It was a record of trading with Harpy's Point, and judging by the fade and smudge of the ink, he guessed it was many years old. He snapped the book shut, and placed it back on the shelf haphazardly.

"This is stupid," he said, not caring to keep his voice down anymore.

"Ssh!" said Leo. He poked his head around the corner and glaring at Jayson.

"Oh, shut up, Leo," said Jayson in anger. "You know Dimitri and Valin left us here to keep us out of the way."

"Jayson, this library is massive," said Jack, his tone more hushed. "Piper could be in here anywhere. We don't want to draw attention from the guards."

"We are the returned kings." Jayson folded his arms across his chest. "We should be out there looking for the circlet and for Taraniz. Dimitri might have magic too, but there are three of us and only one of him. She's not in here. I just know it in my gut."

"Maybe we can find something useful, though." Leo thumbed through a book. "An ancient book on magic, or Piper's birth records."

"I don't think the records are in here, Leo," said Jack. "Taraniz wouldn't have kidnapped Gran if they were."

"But they could be," said Leo. He picked up another book and gingerly turned the pages as though they were made of glass. "If Gran hid the documents in here somewhere, Taraniz might have kidnapped her to torture Gran into telling her where she hid them."

Jack looked at Jayson and shrugged. There was a loud crash outside the door in the hallway, and palace guards materialized from the shadows within the library. They walked toward the boys, swords drawn and their faces devoid of any feeling or emotion.

Jayson, Jack and Leo reached for their weapons and began backing towards the door main door. The guards remained silent, continuing to pursue them slowly and steady. Jayson raised an arrow, ready to shoot. Leo reached out an arm and shouted "Wait! Stop walking for a minute," he said. Jayson chanced a glance at him, his brow furrowed. "Move aside. Away from the door," said Leo. They stepped out of the way and behind a tree trunk.

The guards walked past them, unblinking. Two nearly bumped into them on their trek toward the door. The guards suddenly halted, frozen in their tracks. After a moment, two continued out the door and into the golden hall. A third guard, who had stood beside Leo, Jack and Jayson turned to them. He raised his sword, his eyes blank and staring.

"Can I shoot him now?" Jayson cried.

Jack reacted first. He hit the man in the stomach, then again behind the knees. The guard swung at him and nearly sliced his shoulder. Leo jumped in, swinging for the man's arm. Jack's bow staff knocked into the book case behind him, and parchment went flying.

"The books!" Leo cried.

"Not now, Leo!" said Jayson, his bow still strung. He stepped back and forth in an attempt to get a shot.

"Into the hall!" Leo shouted, and bounded for the door.

"There's more guards out there!" Jack protested, but his back was towards the door and it seemed the only means of escape. He made one last jab at the guard and bolted after Leo.

Jayson groaned, and followed his friends to the main door. More guards swarmed the halls as Jack had predicted, and they converged on the boys as soon as they stepped into the golden hall. Jayson stood in the door, firing his arrows one after another. He made sure to aim for areas that would render his enemies injured but not dead.

He felt a hand grab his shoulder. It tightened, ready to spin him around. Jayson dropped his bow and grabbed for the dagger he kept at his waist. He turned and ducked under his assailant's arm, jabbing him in the neck with the blade.

Jayson's entire body went numb as the guard's hot blood sprayed over his hand. He staggered back, watching as the man's once blank eyes filled with fear. The guard dropped his sword, clutching at his neck. His knees hit the floor, and he collapsed, sputtering and gasping. Jayson backed away. He didn't want to watch the man die, but couldn't tear his eyes from the scene. He looked down at his arm, and saw it was covered in the man's blood. The guard's neck continued to ooze blood between his fingers, and he spluttered and wheezed.

"Why?" the man gasped.

Jayson dropped to his knees, holding his blood streaked arms out before him, and rocked back and forth.

The force of the blood lessened, as did the man's wheezing cries. Jayson knew he was dead when he exhaled one long, gurgling breath. Jayson lost his breakfast on the floor beside the guard. He wrapped his arms around himself, rocking harder, and sobbing uncontrollably.

The guards had somehow regained control of themselves when injured, and had run off as Jack and Leo fought them. The two stood staring at the guard, watching as he took his last breath. It wasn't until Jayson had vomited did they rush to his side. They removed their tabards with trembling hands and tried to wipe the blood from him.

"It happened," Jayson whimpered. "M—my vision. I didn't mean—"

"It's okay, Jay," said Jack calmly as he worked to wipe the blood that had splattered onto Jayson's chin. "He's not in pain anymore."

"He didn't need to die." Jayson was still crying, his words almost incomprehensible. "I didn't mean to. I didn't!"

"We know, Jayson." Leo patted his friend on the back. He tried to wipe the blood from Jayson's arms, but they were clenched too tightly around his body.

Jack and Leo hooked their arms under Jayson's and pulled him to his feet. Jayson staggered upward, leaning on his friends for support. He couldn't take his eyes off the body of the guard before him.

"Hey, hey," said Jack shaking Jayson by the shoulders. "Look at me. Look at me, Jayson!" He turned Jayson's face away from the body. "It was an accident. You were only defending yourself. We have to keep moving. Piper could be in trouble."

It was several minutes before Jayson was able to take the many deep breaths he needed to control his crying and heaving. Leo picked up his bow and handed it to Jayson. The boy clutched it with white knuckles then slung it over his shoulder. His legs felt like jelly as he walked. Before they rounded the corner, he dared one last glance at the guard who lay in a pool of red, sticky blood. He wondered what his name was. Piper had at least gotten Tathias's name before he died.

ভ~৩

Valin leaned against the wall, listening intently. He peeked around the corner into the next corridor, but there was nothing. Dimitri trudged past him, glanced in each direction then hurried on.

"Dimitri, we must use more caution," said Valin. He hurried forward, attempting to lead the way.

"There are no guards here, Valin," said Dimitri, "You are wasting time by checking every opening we pass. We need to find Piper."

"We are no good to Piper if we are captured," Valin said. His voice strained with the effort to remain calm.

"We will not be captured," said Dimitri assuredly.

"How do you know?" asked Valin coldly. He stepped in front of Dimitri, pressing his hand into Dimitri's chest and halting his way. "You are so certain of yourself, Dimitri. Of everything. How do I know you are not working for Taraniz?"

Dimitri threw his head back. A smile spread wide across his face, but he stifled his laugh at the last moment. Instead, he shook his head and pushed Valin aside. "I am the last person who would be working for the woman who has tried to kill my lady for so long."

"Your lady? She will not be your lady when she becomes Queen."

"And how do you know? You are certain of yourself as well that she will choose you over me," Dimitri stopped, meeting Valin's gaze. "After only a few days? For someone who has no desire for power, you are rather bent on bedding her. Well, she was mine first."

"I have only the desire to do what is best for the elves of Chartile! For my people!" Valin cried in a strained whisper. He opened his mouth to speak again, but closed it and took a deep breath. "This is get us nowhere. We will know in good time Piper's decision. We need to find the circlet."

"The circlet? You are not serious. I am looking for Piper. Where are you leading me?" asked Dimitri.

"We need to find the circlet to defeat Taraniz. It is likely in the royal treasury." Valin continued walking, no longer looking at Dimitri.

"I should have left you in the library and taken the boys," muttered Dimitri. "At least they are concerned for Piper."

"Of course I am concerned for her! Why do you think I am looking for the circlet? As a trinket to give her?"

"You seem to have done fine in that endeavor without the help of the royal treasury," Dimitri muttered under his breath, but Valin still heard him.

"That necklace was my mother's," Valin whispered coldly. "I gave it to Piper for her to make the decision for herself."

"I know. I heard everything outside that rickety door of yours," Dimitri lied.

It was movement out of the corner of their eyes that stayed Valin and Dimitri from yet another scuffle. They turned to see a single guard running for them, his sword drawn and ready. His eyes were blank, his lips parted in a slack jaw that gave the dazed impression of sleep walking.

They pulled their swords, shoulder to shoulder, and waited for the charging man to come within range. When the guard was ten feet from them, Dimitri charged and caught the man's arm in his own. He swung him to the ground, pinning the guard's arms behind his back.

"Dimitri, no!" Valin moved behind him.

"Kill the strangers! Kill them!" wailed the guard over and over as he struggled against Dimitri's grasp.

"Where is Taraniz?" Dimitri demanded. He held his belt knife to the man's throat.

"Dimitri, what are you doing?" asked Valin panicked. He attempted to pull Dimitri off the soldier. Dimitri raised his hand and shot a small fire ball at Valin. He narrowly dodged the flame and watched as the fire ball dissipated a few feet away. Dimitri glared at him and returned the knife to the guard's throat.

"Where. Is. Taraniz?" Dimitri asked again through gritted teeth. "Tell me, or that fire ball will find its way down your throat, next." The knife cut into the man's neck and chin. He gasped, and blinked several times. His eyes lost their dull, glassy stare, and his pupils shrank as he became aware of himself once more.

"What has happened?" he asked desperately, his voice no longer gruff.

"Do not play with me!" shouted Dimitri.

"Dimitri, I believe he was under some... influence—"

"Silence!" Dimitri cut Valin short. The knife began to redden with heat, and the man screamed in pain. "Where is she?" Dimitri demanded once more.

"I know not! I know not!" said the guard. "Please! I did not intend – she has us all!"

"What do you mean?" Valin asked more kindly.

"No! No coddling!" Dimitri screamed, and the man fought to remain still against the pain of the burning blade at his throat.

"I swear, I do not know where she is!" he said.

"Then you are of no use to me." Dimitri kicked the man in his stomach. The guard stared up at his captor and watched as Dimitri reached a hand toward his chest, the air in front of his palm moving like heat on stone. The guard clasped his hands to his throat, gasping for air.

"Dimitri, stop!" Valin shrieked. Dimitri glared at him then released the guard from his torture.

"Tell me where Taraniz is," he said again

The man gasped for breath and tried to sit up. Dimitri slammed his boot into his chest, pinning him to the floor.

"The throne room!" he cried in desperation.

Dimitri smirked. "You lie," he whispered and, without hesitation, sliced the man across his throat.

Valin pushed Dimitri away. He did not care if the half-dwarf barbarian used his magic on him. He was stunned at what he had just witnessed and terrified for Piper.

"You did not have to kill him!" Valin cried. He knelt beside the guard, a single tear trickling down his face, and he pressed the guard's gambeson to his bleeding throat.

"We cannot risk him informing someone we were here," said Dimitri, wiping the man's blood from his knife onto his own pant leg.

Valin watched as the man gave one last gurgling breath, then rose and pointed his sword at Dimitri. "You are nothing more than an outlaw," he spat. "Only the Destined may use magic. You have killed an innocent man with it! This is why it was forbidden in the first place!"

Dimitri calmly pushed Valin's sword tip to the side and took a step toward him. His eyes raged with panic and fear, though his face and voice remained calm.

"Perhaps you should reconsider whom you are placing on the throne, then." He turned and walked away, continuing his quest to find Piper.

Valin hurried after him, still attempting to find a promising room in which to locate Duke Noraedin's circlet. They passed hall after hall. The carved tree pillars growing thicker around as they walked deeper into the heart of the palace. Valin no longer tried to check for passersby as Dimitri was now leading the way.

A breeze moved through the passage way, though no open windows were anywhere near them. Dimitri stopped and turned to face the wind. Valin nearly ran into him. He looked around franticly, trying to see what had made Dimitri halt.

"Dimitri," said Piper's voice in his mind. "I'm in the tower… the library… Dimitri…"

The voice trailed off to a whisper. Dimitri turned on the spot, looking at the ceiling and walls like a cat hunting a fly.

"What is it?" Valin asked. He feared more magic was afoot, and knew it could only mean trouble.

"Dimitri, help me," whispered the voice in his mind again.

Dimitri took off, running full out, back up the corridor the way they had come. Valin called after him, but to no avail. Torn between letting this love-crazed young man eventually kill himself with his dark magic, and attempting to stay together for Piper's sake, Valin ran after Dimitri, his foot falls echoing loudly in the grand halls of the palace.

They skidded around the corner into the noble's wing minutes later. Valin stopped when he saw the body of the soldier, and the pool of blood that had begun to solidify around the man Jayson had killed. Fear filled his heart for the safety of the returned kings, and, ignoring Dimitri, he flew past the man into the library.

Dimitri rattled every door in the hall. He used his magic to move the mechanisms of the locks for some of the more promising looking doors, but they only opened into small living chambers for the visiting nobility.

The last door at the end of the hall caught his eye. It stood open by several inches. He raced for it, wrenching it open, and leapt up the stone steps to the tower above. The door at the top was open. The broken mirror of the dressing table was the first thing he saw as he approached the door. His heart began to race faster, and he felt his stomach drop.

"Dimitri!" called a voice, and this time he heard it aloud.

"Piper!" he called back, racing into the room. Piper was chained to a dusty four poster bed. She struggled against her bonds, but her face brightened when she saw him. "I'm here. I'm here," Dimitri said and ran to her.

"I did not know if it would work! Oh, Dimitri! I'm sorry. Forgive me! I love you!" she said, and tears ran down her face. "Taraniz. She used her magic to hold me here. But… She is over taken. She is not evil, Dimitri! We have to save her!"

Dimitri reached out with his magic, but pulled back almost immediately. There was an unfamiliar magic in these bonds for certain, and it pained him from the inside out. Bracing himself, he reached for the magic, willing it to take refuge in his body. When he felt the last of the energy drain from the chains, he forced it toward the ground, and one of the stones broke into tiny fragments at his feet. His face was beaded with sweat. He turned back to the chains, his hands now shaking from the residual pain still coursing through him. The metal shackles around Piper's wrists began to bend and morph. She gasped as the metal dug into her wrists.

"Hold on," Dimitri whispered to her and the cuffs broke free.

Piper sat up and wrapped her arms around Dimitri's neck, kissing him fiercely.

"I'm sorry I left. It was always you. I'm sorry. I'm so sorry," she said through her kisses.

Dimitri held her close, the warmth of her body was the most comforting thing to him. He kissed the top of her head then suddenly held her at arm's length.

"What do you mean Taraniz is over taken?"

"Noraedin," she said. "It is as we feared. She cannot control him. But it is not her fault! Dimitri, he has her now. She is not herself."

"Piper, where did she go?"

Piper looked at the door and her body went numb. The color drained from her face as realization swept over her.

"The boys," she whispered, and leapt from the bed.

୨୦୰

Jack and Leo walked as quietly as they could, one on either side of Jayson. They had already been attacked by two more groups of palace guards and were glad for their magical training as Jayson was now unable to fight. He crouched on the ground, holding his head between his knees as his friends formed a protective circle around him.

They wandered the empty corridors, weapons at the ready for another attack.

"She has to know we're here," said Jack. "That has to be why the guards have started coming after us."

"I think you're right," said Leo. "We need to find Piper. I think it has to be the four of us together."

"Yeah," said Jayson. His voice was dry and shaky, but it was the first time he had spoken since the incident. They stopped, and looked at him with concern.

"You okay, Jay?" Jack asked.

Jayson nodded. "As much as I'm gunna be. It's like, I knew it was going happen. Or maybe it happened because I tried to make it so it didn't happen. I don't know. But, we have to finish what we came here to do, right? Maybe after this is all over, I can find his family and give them money or something."

Leo and Jack smiled weakly at him. Jack pulled him into an awkward hug, but Jayson returned it gratefully. Leo handed Jayson his bow that he had dropped several corridors back, and Jack handed him his quiver. They turned to continue on, when a blast of energy knocked them from their feet and sent them flying through the air.

They slammed into the far wall, and the room spun before their eyes. They hurried to their feet, holding their heads and steadying themselves against the wall.

Walking slowly and determinedly toward them was a tall, young woman. Her blonde hair hung loose to her shoulders, and the air around her quivered with a strange energy.

"You should not have come back," she said. "You should not have been able to come back. I bound your souls in unbreakable ties!"

The boys fell to their knees, and memories that were not their own flashed through their minds. As the images raced before their mind's eye, Jack, Leo and Jayson felt a sense of calm and understanding come over them. The memories were theirs, but from another life. They stood as one, missing pieces from their training and past lives making everything clearer.

"Your unbreakable ties only work in this world, Noraedin," said Leo, but his voice was deeper and more commanding. "You know magic extends past the limits of time and space."

"He won't listen, Florine," said Jayson beside him. But he was not only Jayson Hill. He was King Jenemar from the far western reaches of the Belirian Forest. "He has never listened."

"Noraedin," said Jack, and his voice too was different. He spoke calmly, and stepped toward Taraniz with his arms open wide. "We can discuss this civilly. You are killing that young girl. This is not our time anymore."

Taraniz raised her hand, and Jack was forced back against the wall again. Leo and Jayson ran to his side.

"Enough of your pretty words, Kasmalin! It was all you were ever good for! Chartile is finally mine, and you will not take it from me again!"

Leo and Jayson reacted out of instinct. Somehow, the souls of Kings Florine and Jenemar used the boys to create a barrier between themselves and Taraniz. It was just in time. A streak of blue lightning slammed against the barrier, and they could feel the tingle of the electricity through the air. Jack pulled magic from deep within his core, and released a fire ball that passed through the barrier, aimed for Taraniz.

The girl was too fast. She caught the ball, and seemed to absorb it into her chest, laughing as it disappeared.

"Have you learned nothing, little boys?" she sneered, and laughed maniacally. "You cannot defeat me! I am more powerful than you will ever be!"

One of Jayson's arrows flew through the air and pierced Taraniz through to her heart. Though it had not been Jayson nor Jenemar who had released it. Another, and another was loosed, and they imbedded themselves deep into Taraniz's body. They turned to see Valin, who had found Jayson's bow and quiver as it was lost when they were first knocked back.

"Perhaps not with magic, but the body of the girl you have controlled can still be killed." Valin loosed Jayson's last arrow into Taraniz's heart. The blast of energy was deafening. Everyone clasped their hands to their ears, and ducked as the arrows once buried in the princess now flew through the air.

"Valin! NO!" Piper and Dimitri emerged from another corridor. Piper ran to Taraniz, and she fell into her arms. Dimitri ran to Valin, holding him back from interfering.

"Ani, no, no," Piper sobbed. "I'll save you. I promise."

She raised a trembling hand toward the wound above her sister's heart. Taraniz grabbed Piper's hand, her fingers barely holding on.

"Just let me go," she whispered. "I do not want to hurt anymore. He cannot hurt you if I am gone."

"No," said Piper defiantly, though her voice shook through her tears. "No, I will not let you go, not when we have only just begun. I cannot be a queen without you. I don't know what to do. You cannot leave me like our mother left us."

Taraniz coughed, and a trickle of blood formed at the corner of her mouth. She smiled at Piper and placed a loving hand on her cheek. Piper kissed it and cried. The boys, Dimitri and Valin approached the pair slowly and knelt before the princess. Jayson placed a hand on Piper's knee in comfort, and Jack rested his hand on her shoulder.

"I believe in you," Taraniz whispered more weakly now. "Knowing you believed enough in me to try and save me is more than I could have asked. I am at peace. Now, I must face the judgments and punishments of my actions. I love you, dear sister."

She turned to the boys, her eyes fluttering to stay open. Faintly, her voice nearly inaudible, she whispered, "Take care of her." Taraniz's eyes closed, and she breathed her last breath.

Piper pulled Taraniz close to her and sobbed, her tears falling into her sister's hair. Dimitri hugged Piper, and Leo also laid a hand on her back.

A black shadow which none of them had noticed grew and expanded on the ceiling overhead. Valin looked up, his eyes widening at the sight. The shadow morphed and moved, collecting itself into a solid form and hovered inches above the floor.

"It's not over," Valin said quietly. They turned, their bodies stiffening at the sight of the figure. Jayson, Jack, Leo and Dimitri rose to form a protective circle around Piper. Piper pushed her way through and sent a streak of lighting at the shadow. It bent and twisted as if in pain, and formed itself again into a less identifiable form.

"That was for my sister!" she screamed, and tried to send another lighting strike at the figure. Valin stopped her as they watched the shadow grow blacker before their eyes.

"I require a new vessel," it hissed. Its voice echoed into the far corners of their minds, and they all fought not to clamp their hands to their ears in agony. "You will do nicely." Though it did not have eyes, they all knew it looked at Piper.

"You will have to get past me first!" said Valin. He rushed forward and raised his sword at the figure in challenge.

"Valin, no!" said Piper and Dimitri together. The figure laughed though it sounded more like the creak of an old door. It extended its shadowy form out, wrapping its blackness around Valin's throat and lifted him from the floor. It threw him against the far wall, where he slumped to the floor unconscious.

"No!" cried Piper, and her mind became
flooded with visions and memories that belonged to
King Pasalphathe. She flung her arms out to steady
herself, and felt a warm hand in hers. It was Jayson.
Leo's hand found its way to her other hand and
squeezed it tightly. Jack grabbed Jayson's hand, and
they erected the barrier again.

"He is stronger than all of us, Pasalphathe,"
said Leo in Florine's voice.

"His energy must be dispelled in a way that
it cannot reform," said Jayson as Jenemar.

"The circlet may be our only chance. It is
made of orenite and holds the Draconian runes."
King Kasmalin spoke through Jack.

As the kings continued their discussion,
Dimitri reached into his pocket and pulled out his
orenite cuffs. Piper saw him, and broke free of her
friends. The barrier flickered but stayed intact. She
rushed to Dimitri's side, yanking the cuffs from his
hands.

"No," she said desperately, shaking her
head. "I just lost my sister, I'm not losing you too!"

Dimitri pulled her to him, kissing her
fiercely, and gently pried the cuffs from her hands.
She pulled away and clawed at the air in an attempt
to retrieve the cuffs.

"This evil has plagued us all for too long. I
wish only to see you happy." he whispered and
slipped the cuffs onto his wrists.

"Dimitri, we will think of another way," said
Kasmalin's voice.

"Don't you make me cry again," said Piper
through her tears. "You cannot leave me! Everyone
has left me!"

"We do not know where the circlet is," said Dimitri. "We will never find it in time, and he may kill all of us before we even do."

"Then let me do it," said Piper, pulling at Dimitri's hands, a desperation he had never heard straining her voice. "If someone is going to do this, it should be me. The boys can rule the elves. Please. Please, don't do this to me!"

"I love you more than you could ever know," said Dimitri, and he stepped through the barrier. "I thought you might be tired of being in the body of a little girl," he said mockingly to the shadow before him. "Care to try some power on for size?"

The shadow laughed again and charged at Dimitri. Jayson, Jack and Leo held Piper back as they watched the shadow bore its way into Dimitri's chest. His scream cut through their hearts, and they watched him fall to his knees, clutching at his head as he fought with the soul struggling to take over inside him. His orenite cuffs began to spark, and his body jerked from side to side. He stood, turning to face his friends. He controlled the grimace on his face, and for a fleeting moment, he was at peace. He locked eyes with Piper, and she broke free of Jayson and Leo. The barrier collapsed as she ran to him. Dimitri convulsed violently, blood oozing from his face and ears. Piper cried and tried to hold him, her gaze locked with his. The last thing she wanted him to see was how much she loved him.

Dimitri lurched backward. The orenite cuffs sparked violently, and black dust burst from his mouth. Piper flung herself on him. "Dimitri! Dimitri! Wake up, please. Please."

Leo, Jack and Jayson ran to her, the will of the kings within them subsiding. They dropped to their knees beside their friend and mentor, tears in all their eyes. Valin, nearly forgotten in the heat of the battle, stirred on the floor by the wall. He pushed himself to his hands and knees, shaking and holding his head. He looked up, his eyes focusing on the body some feet away from him. His heart sank, and he hurried to Dimitri as quickly as he could.

"What happened?" he asked. His words were slightly slurred.

"He sacrificed himself," said Leo, tears in his eyes. He removed his glasses and let them fall to his chest on their string.

"How? Why?" Valin dropped to his knees. He touched the cuffs around Dimitri's wrists. They were hot, and he saw burn marks on the skin beneath them.

"He used his orenite cuffs to defeat Noraedin," said Jack softly.

"Piper, I'm sorry." It was all Valin could say. He was at a loss. The guilt that rose in him because he had killed Taraniz made him ill. Perhaps they could have found another way. It was his fault. Deep down, he knew this.

Piper lifted her head from Dimitri's body. His tunic was drenched in her tears. Her eyes fell on Taraniz's body lying several feet away. Agony and anger washed over her. It was as though she could feel it filling her from the inside out.

"I can't!" she screamed, and took off down the hall.

"Piper, wait!" Valin ran after her.

Chapter Twenty-Four

Aftermath

Valin followed Piper back toward the noble's wing. He watched as she leapt up a flight of stone steps and when she reached the top, slammed the door in his face. It wasn't locked, and he could have entered, but the tormented cries behind the door were heartbreaking. He stood silent at the top of the stair, one hand clutched against his heart, the other poised to knock on the door.

"Dimitri," he heard her sob. His hand fell to his side, and he left her alone.

He hurried back to the scene of the fight. Several guards were converging on the boys. They stood back to back, their weapons on the floor in front of them and hands raised in surrender.

"We are the returned kings foretold in your prophecy," he heard Leo telling them. "We mean no harm."

"Gentleman," called Valin as he rounded the corner. There were a few faces he recognized, but none he knew by name. He hoped they recognized him as well. "The evil that has possessed your princess has been destroyed. Princess Taraniz and Dimitri of Mount Kelsii have sacrificed themselves for the sake of us all. I implore you to call a meeting of the nobles immediately. Aramor and Runa's lost daughter and Taraniz's sister has been found. Kaytah Chaudoin of Outland Post will have the records to prove this. She was brought here several weeks ago under Taraniz's orders. We must call off the attack on our brothers at Mount Kelsii, and dispatch messengers and carrier birds at once!"

The guards exchanged looks of confusion and uncertainty. Several looked at the body of Princess Taraniz lying sprawled on the floor before them, and looked at their hands or rubbed their temples.

"Quickly!" Jack urged them. He had nearly forgotten about the attack on Mount Kelsii. Gemari's face flashed before him as Valin had spoken, and fear rose within him for her safety once more. The guards jumped at his voice. Most hurried away as ordered, but others still continued to survey the scene before them.

It took some time to calm and convince all of the palace guards of the events that had transpired. It wasn't until they had persuaded Leland, the Captain of the Elven Guard that plans began to move forward. They found Runa's journal in the tower with Piper. She told them how she had found the tower, and her conversation with Taraniz through unrelenting sobs. Between what they could make of her tale through her tear, and a bit of magic on the part of Jayson, Jack and Leo, Leland was finally made to believe.

Word returned the next day from the lords and commanders marching on Fortress Kelsii. They had marched from Cannondole as soon as Piper had left the town. The soul of Duke Noraedin had known all along. But the soldiers' minds became clear as they battled the dwarves on the Great Plains when Noraedin was finally defeated. An immediate halt was called, and the soldiers retreated to their encampment at the edge of the forest. That night, the elven commanders received messages from Leland, and Leo sent word to Kylani, Brande and Frejah.

Jack had sent a letter to Frejah as well, though his was to be given to Gemari when she returned from Tutaria.

Nobles from all across Chartile began trickling in over the next several days, including with Valar. The trek was too far for many, but they sent messages via carrier bird ahead. Leland and Valin, who had assumed some sort of command in the chaos, introduced Jack, Leo and Jayson to the Barons, Lords and Counts as they arrived. With their minds now free from the manipulation of Noraedin, the nobles saw the boys' magic as a wondrous sign of the fulfillment of the prophecy, and a dangerous power. It was the magic of Taraniz and Noraedin that had placed them all in their current predicament, and it made many even more uncomfortable than Valin.

Gran was found safe at Harpy's Point, and she returned to the palace shortly after her summons was received. Jayson, Jack and Leo ran to her, forgetting their manners entirely. They had grown fond of her during their time in the mountains when they snuck in to see her at night to receive the items she had traded for them. She embraced them warmly and kissed them on their cheeks.

"My dears," she said. "Look how much you've grown!" She squeezed Jayson's chin where his stubble had begun to grow. "I am so proud of you. How are your glasses, Leo?"

"Doing great, Gran," he said, and she hugged him again.

"Where is Piper?" she asked when their third round of hugs had been given. Solemnly, they explained that Piper had yet to come down from the tower. She hardly spoke to anyone, but the boys made sure to meet with her every night and to tell her everything that had happened. She barely ate or slept. She spent most of the time staring out the window and ignored all else.

"Take me to her. At once," demanded Gran.

The boys took off, through the golden halls, Gran keeping up with their quick pace. When they reached the base of the stone stair, Jack held the door for the woman, but they did not follow.

Gran reached the top of the winding stone stair with her knees creaking more than she would have liked. She knocked gently on the door in the manner Piper had once done to tell Gran it was her when she came down from the mountains. She was greeted with silence. Gran pushed the door open, and found her granddaughter a few paces beyond the entrance. Her eyes were puffy and blood shot, and her face pale and drawn. Piper looked up and paused only a moment before she flung herself into Gran's arms.

Gran did not speak. She squeezed Piper as hard as she could for several long minutes. When Piper's grip loosened around her, she led her granddaughter to the freshly laundered bed and stroked her hair.

Piper cried long and hard. She cursed herself for all the times she had done so in the last several weeks, then melted again into uncontrollable blubbering. Finally her sobs subsided to hiccups, and Gran sat her up. She held Piper at arm's length and moved the hair plastered to her cheeks behind her ears.

"I am sorry for your loss, my darling," she said softly. Piper bowed her head, squinting her eyes as if to cry again. Gran put a finger under her chin, and lifted her head. "No one and nothing will ever take away your hurt. I will not tell you that you must forget them, but my darling, you are stronger than this."

"Gran, I wanted to marry him. I'm lost," said Piper, her voice dry and breaking. She reached for her grandmother's hand and squeezed it hard. "And Taraniz – Ani – I never knew she went by Ani. She was kind, and caring. I could have learned so much from her. I cannot understand why everyone I love gets taken away from me. Even the boys. Leo is trying to find a way home for them. Why do they all leave me?"

Tears trickled down her face, and she wiped them away. She wanted to be strong, but she couldn't find the will anymore. Gran pushed her red hair back. She straightened Piper's shoulders, and lifted her chin even higher.

"I do not know, my darling. But what I do know is that life can be cold, and hard and cruel. Only the strong can rise up to overcome those challenges. And a leader must be strong. She must be capable in every undertaking. Steadfast and true. She must be kind, courteous, and eloquent. Your mother and father, Ani and Dimitri will never be gone from you so long as you hold them in your heart, and allow the best in them to shine through you."

Piper hung her head again. She had not been much of a queen to her people lately. She had not been the queen she knew they needed.

"And," continued Gran more gently, "I certainly have no intention of going anywhere."

A week after the death of Princess Taraniz and Dimitri of Mount Kelsii, those part of the Conclave of Nobles who had made it to the palace finally met. It took the entire day, and was well into the evening before the Conclave was willing to make Piper their new queen. Plans for her coronation were put into action immediately, though Jack, Leo and Jayson noticed many of the nobles still cringed and shifted uncomfortably at any sign or mention of magic.

Piper left the conclave wanting nothing more than to fall into bed, but it was not to be. That night, a pyre was made, and Princess Taraniz was returned to the sky by earth and fire. Piper conducted the traditional ceremonies as her first duty as the Queen-to-be and attended to proper receiving and banquet afterward with Jack, Leo and Jayson at her side.

Dimitri's body was escorted back to Mount Kelsii with Empress Nefiri. Piper demanded a full royal elven processional following in honor of his sacrifice. Jack accompanied them as the newly appointed Ambassador to the Dwarves. At first, he had protested, insisting Leo should take the role. Piper held up a hand to silence him.

"There is yet too much controversy surrounding Leo and his involvement with the Black Diamonds," she said quietly. "You have the upper hand, due in part to your connection with Gemari."

Jack blushed scarlet. "It's forbidden," he mumbled, shuffling his feet and fidgeting with his fingers behind his back.

"Not for long!" said Leo, giving him a gentle punch on the shoulder.

"What'd ya mean?" Jack asked.

"Now that we've proven who we are, no one will try to stand up to us," Leo replied with a wide grin.

"Isn't that abusing our power?" Jayson asked, his usual chipper air gone since the battle. He was quiet, and let Leo and Jack make most of the decisions. He immediately looked at his feet, and hugged his arms close.

Leo shrugged. "Maybe. But, Jayson... dude... this man's heart...it's on the line here! There's love in the air!" He gave Jayson a small shove, and a smirk began to spread across Jayson's face as Jack blushed deeper. "Besides," Leo added "I've been working with the nobles to try and find a way to get us home. I don't really have time for all that pearl wine anymore."

The company rode hard to Fortress Kelsii. Nefiri wanted to return to her people as quickly as she could. Now on horseback, and not cutting across the forest terrain, they made the trip in two short days. Trumpets sounded as the procession approached the front gates. There had been no rain recently, and blood stains still littered the nearby rocks along the path to the gates.

The glittering doors were thrown wide to receive them, and the company rode straight into the grand entrance way. Jack dismounted stiffly, grateful the trip was over. He was extremely saddle sore. He had never ridden a horse that long before, and had taken to strapping himself to the saddle so he did not fall from his mount as they hurried back to the mountain.

"Jack!" called a voice behind him. He turned, and saw Gemari pushing her way through the crowd gathered in the main entrance. His face brightened at seeing her. She wore a golden chain with a small diamond pendant around her neck. It was the favor he had sent with his message to her. He had asked Piper for something, and she had obliged with a gift from the royal treasury.

Jack ran to her, and scooped her up into his arms, kissing her. It was only the gasps of those standing by, and the whoops and cheers from the Black Diamonds that brought them to again. They stopped, pulling away from each other, and stared in shock into each other's eyes.

"I suppose some change is to be expected with every new generation," said Nefiri passing beside them. She gave a small smile before turning to the escorts beside Dimitri's body.

Jack and Gemari had little time to spend together, however. There were many dead from the battle, short lived as it was. Among its casualties were Kylani and Isla, who had refused to let her lover fight alone. Jack sent word immediately to Leo, and with Piper's permission, Leo took a small company to the mountain. She sent a few select lords with him bearing gifts of peace to honor the dwarves who had fallen. It was to no one's surprise but Leo's that he was asked to help bear Kylani's body to its final resting place.

No sooner had the ceremonies ended did Jack and Leo return to the elven palace for Piper's coronation. There seemed little time to grieve their losses, though Jack preferred it that way.

"Have you found anything yet?" Jack asked Leo as they rode back to the elven palace. "Anything that might help us get home?"

Leo shook his head. "No. Most of the documents on magic were destroyed when it was outlawed. Brande suggested I go to Tutaria. Their libraries are bigger, and they don't have as much aversion to magic as the elves."

Jack nodded and turned his attention back to riding. They had recently slowed the horses to a walking pace for a bit, and he took the opportunity to tighten the rope around his waist.

"Jayson's doing better," said Leo, breaking the silence once more. "He's been helping Leland and Piper hear the cases of the prisoners, and helping to deal out punishments. He's been suggesting a lot of community service stuff. We need the help anyway."

"I'm worried about him," said Jack, shifting in his saddle. "I didn't think he'd take what happened so hard."

"Jack, he killed someone. What would you do if you killed someone, especially the way he did?"

They rode on in silence, lost in their own thoughts.

Chapter Twenty-Five

Coronation

The morning sun rose warm that day, when all the others had been cool and crisp. Piper sat up in bed, staring out the window of the tower. It was the day of her coronation. In a few short hours, Piper Romilly, born Eva Ruani, daughter of King Aramor and Queen Runa, would be crowned the queen of all the elves in Chartile. She took several deep breaths, and turned to look at the dress hanging beside the newly repaired dressing table. It was her mother's dress that she had worn when presented to the Council of Elders at Mount Kelsii.

Valar had stepped up as her temporary advisor, until she had time to choose his successor, and so Valin could return to his duties in Cannondole. He had insisted she wear something new for the occasion, but Piper put her foot down. She had declared a period of mourning for her people for the loss of their princess, and since her coronation gown was not a requirement for the mandatory day to day workings of the elves, she refused to make them work on a new dress for her. It was Valin who had convinced her to let only the seamstresses who wanted to work on her dress apply some golden thread and embroidery to the gown. When she saw the eager faces of the young girls, she couldn't deny them the pleasure of saying they had worked on the Queen's coronation gown.

Soon her beck-ands would be up to help her with her hair and beauty paints. The tugging and pulling, and the oils and perfumes were enough to drive her mad. Piper pushed back her bedcovers and hurried to the dressing table. She quickly tied her hair back and pulled on plain traveling clothes and a gray wool hood that fell past her shoulders.

She picked up the bow that rested beside her bed and slung a quiver of arrows over her shoulder. They had once belonged to Jayson, and she was bound and determined to somehow get them back to him. But right now, she wanted to be Piper one last time.

She crept down the stone steps and carefully peeked out into the hall. It was bustling with nobles, guards and beck-ands, all excited and preparing for the day's coming coronation.

Carefully, Piper opened the door to the tower stair, but did not step out. The air around her began to shimmer. She could feel the temperature dropping, and she shivered beneath her hood. She moved slowly and tiptoed quietly into the corridor, keeping to the wall. She made her way into the library and halted immediately. Yet more nobles gathered there, whispering amongst themselves beside the bookshelves. She continued along the outer walls of the library. Jack would have called it a ninja-stealth-walk, and she had to stifle a giggle at the thought. There was a door to her right that led from the library out to the gardens beyond. Piper knew the door creaked horribly. She removed the magic she used to conceal herself, and forced the remaining energy toward a large stack of documents on the table beside the cluster of nobles. The pile cascaded to the floor, and the nobles dropped to the mossy ground to retrieve the fragile parchment. Piper slipped out the door and ran to the training yard.

Prophecy

She fought the urge to throw back her hood as she went, and bask in the warmth of the sun that filled the small clearing. The trees surrounding the elven palace were the largest and tallest trees in the forest. They hid the palace well but did not allow for much sunlight to filter through. For Piper, who had been raised at the base of Mount Kelsii, it was almost as suffocating as a prison cell. She took a deep breath, breathing in the fresh autumn air. It was her favorite smell in the entire world. The heat of the sun warmed the dying leaves, and it sent pleasant chills down her spine.

A few archers had already assembled themselves at the shooting range. Every guard was to be on stand by and at the ready during her coronation, and she assumed these young men were getting in some practice before hand. She took the target at the far end of the field away from the other archers. She stabbed a few arrows from the quiver into the ground and lined herself up. The first few were slightly off, but by her last arrow, she had hit the center target a handful of times.

Setting her bow to the ground, she looked up and down the line to make sure it was safe to retrieve her arrows. The group of young archers turned quickly away, and resumed their stances rather untidily.

"I don't think anyone ever expected their Queen to be such a good shot," said a voice behind her. She turned, ready to deny to whomever this stranger was that she wasn't the Queen-to-be. A familiar freckled face grinned at her slyly. It was Jayson. She smiled and hugged him as he approached.

"I haven't seen you for two days," she said as they both traipsed onto the field to retrieve her arrows. "Where have you been? I admit I was worried you would not be here today."

Jayson twisted an arrow imbedded deep in the straw bale target and smoothed its sharp fletching. "Leland told me about some gossip he heard regarding Brexton Hills, and I've been investigating it for him," he spoke nonchalantly.

Piper stared at him in both amusement and surprise. "I never took you to be the spy type." She smirked at him. "Always a bit too loud and brash for that sort of thing." She gave him a playful nudge with her arm. Jayson smiled, but did not reply. He continued to twist his arrows gently from the target, inspecting each one as he did so. "What sort of gossip has Leland been telling you?" she asked breaking the silence.

Jayson looked over his shoulder at the group of young archers. They had moved closer to their Queen's target, no doubt in the hopes of learning something from watching her.

"I've got it all under control," he said reassuring, and giving an obvious side glance at the archers. "Mind if I give it a go?" He held up the last arrow.

"Of course!" said Piper, thrilled to see Jayson with a bow back in his hands.

They approached the archery line again, and Jayson pulled the string of his bow taunt. He breathed out, letting a calm energy wash over him and released his arrows in rapid fire succession. Arrow after arrow hit the center target every time. When he had shot his last arrow and lowered his bow, the group of archers down the line applauded and whooped loudly.

He smiled at them, and gave a small bow of thanks. Before Piper could insist on him taking his bow and quiver back, a horn sounded somewhere in the distance.

"It's the dwarves," said Jayson matter-of-factly.

"Jack and Leo should be with them," said Piper, and the two took off to meet the Dwarvik royalty and their friends.

They skidded to a halt a few minutes later in the courtyard just inside the main doors of the palace. Piper threw back her hood and walked gracefully forward to stand beside Valar, Leland and the other nobles gathered to welcome the Dwarvik representatives to the Queen's coronation. Valar gave a side long glance at Piper and closed his eyes in exasperation.

Jayson and Piper beamed as Jack and Leo handed the reins of their ponies to the waiting stable boys. Fighting the urge to run and collide in a friendly hug, for they had not seen each other in nearly a week, Leo and Jack walked gracefully to Piper and Jayson, and bowed. Jack in the Dwarvik fashion, Leo in the elven style, and then reached to shake their hands.

"It's so good to have you back," said Piper, and she pulled Jack into a tight hug.

Queen Una and Princess Gemari were helped down from their ponies, and made deep bows in greeting to Piper.

"Empress Nefiri sends her apologies that she cannot be with us today," said Una, her voice almost bored. "She had other duties regarding Princess Faeridae."

Leo gave a discreet grin to his friends and a single nod, as if to say she would be safe. They had nearly forgotten that Princess Faeridae was to stand trial for her involvement with the Black Diamonds.

The formalities for greeting the visitors seemed to last a lifetime. But it seemed only a minutes that Piper sat in the chair at her dressing table, her beck-and's pulling and twisting at her hair as they braided it into place. They laced her into her gown and washed her feet before slipping on her shoes. When Piper looked at herself in the mirror again, she hardly recognized herself.

The beck-and's left her at the base of the tower stair. Here, her large contingent of guards led her through the palace halls to the throne room. Once again, the halls were empty, and the only sounds were the footfalls of the soldiers surrounding her. The eerie quiet was unsettling, and Piper pushed away the nausea she felt as they passed the spot where Taraniz and Dimitri had died. They reached the great, double doors of the throne room too soon, and Piper forced herself to breath slowly. They were shut tight, and she studied the carved red wood to keep herself distracted.

Without notice, the doors were thrown wide. The guards parted before her, and Piper stared down the long aisle. In balconies overhead sat the nobles of the Conclave in their traditional robes of office. The floor was packed with nobles and peasants alike. All eyes turned to her. She set her features into an emotionless stare and stepped forward, walking with the grace and fluidity her Gran had taught her as a little girl.

She had barely started down the aisle when thought her heart would completely jump out of her chest. Then she saw Jayson, Jack and Leo. They stood at the base of the dais to the throne. They smiled at her, and hardly looked like themselves. Jayson and Leo wore the immaculately embroidered tunic and hose of elven nobility, and Jack looked dazzling in his jewel covered Dwarvik attire.

On the first step of the dais behind the boys were Valar and Gran. She saw Gran dab at the corner of her eye with a handkerchief, and prayed she wouldn't start crying herself. When she reached the halfway point of the aisle, Valar's booming voice echoed off the domed ceiling to the populace below.

"Where once we were lost, hope has been restored. Where there was darkness, the light has returned."

Piper kept walking, her chin thrust forward, and her hands clasped elegantly before her. Her guards had remained at the doors, and she walked alone. She stopped several feet from the boys. They all looked ready to cry as well. She knew if they did, she wouldn't be able to stop herself. She quickly looked at the steps of the dais, blinking rapidly to hold her tears at bay.

"Eva Ruani," said Jack's gentle voice, but it could be heard throughout the entire room. The crowd that had stirred moments before was now silent and staring. "Do you swear to uphold the true and ancient elven laws?"

"Do you hereby swear to protect your people against the tyrannies of the world with vengeance and retribution?" asked Leo.

"Do you hereby swear to guide the elven peoples of Chartile with strength and power?" Jayson asked.

Piper ascended the three steps of the dais. She looked at Valar before turning to face the crowded room. This was where she was supposed to say, 'I so swear'. Three simple words. They had even practiced it the day before. She knew what she had to do. What she had to say. She stared at the crowd before her, heart still thumping wildly in her chest.

A smile slowly spread across her face. Piper threw her arms wide and replied, "I so swear to govern the elven people of Chartile with truth, justice, and equality."

The Conclave of Nobles began to stir in the balcony above, and the populace before her whispered excitedly.

"I so swear to protect the elven people of Chartile against misguided thoughts and actions. I swear to guard my people against hurt and harm, but always opting for diplomacy before war and revenge."

One of the nobles in the balcony stood, but his neighbor pulled him back to his seat. The whispering continued throughout the room like an endless wave. The eyes that fixated on Piper yearned for more.

"I swear to guide my people with an open heart, and an open mind. For I am hope, I am love, and I am light. Will the people accept my oaths? Will you accept me? Will you accept Piper Romilly as your queen?"

The silence in the room was palpable. Everyone turned to stare at the balcony above, waiting for an answer from the Conclave. Jayson, Jack and Leo looked out at the room. They tried to keep their breathing steady and clasped their hands tightly together to keep from fidgeting. They kept their faces calm so as not to betray the panic they all felt. Though it was anything but, they tried to show this had been the plan all along.

Finally, the noble who had pulled his friend to his seat moments before, stood. "Hunter's Ridge swears fealty and loyalty to Queen Piper Romilly." he shouted.

"Sutton Low swears fealty and loyalty to Queen Piper Romilly." Another noble stood to join the first.

"Sparrowmoore swears fealty and loyalty to Queen Piper Romilly."

Like a chain reaction, every noble in the Conclave stood and swore their fealty to Piper. The populace on the floor began shouting their family names in loyalty and fealty. It was only when Gran held out box to Valar did the room quiet again. He lifted a golden crown from a green, velvet pillow and held it aloft for the crowd to see.

"Will you ever stay to a plan?" he whispered to her with a smile. Piper stepped to the top of the dais and stood before the elven throne. It was carved from the only tree trunk in the entire room. Like the trees in the library, its boughs spread out across the ceiling, enclosing the room beneath its limbs and entwined branches. "Then in the name of love and light, the elves of Chartile do crown thee, Queen Piper Romilly."

The crown sat on her head, cold and heavy. She felt its weight like the weight of the oaths she had just created. Valar stepped back, and the crowd erupted into cheers and applause. The sound was almost deafening. Piper smiled and breathed a sigh of relief.

She moved to sit on the throne behind her. An arrow struck the arm of the throne through a trajectory where her head had been moments before.

"Long live Queen Taraniz!" someone shouted from the crowd. More arrows rained down on the dais, and the people in the crowd below covered their heads, some trying to run for the great double doors.

The guards who lined perimeter of the room were lost in the chaos of the terrified citizens. Jayson saw movement behind a tapestry to his right. He drew his sword, and ran into the stampeding crowd.

"Jayson!" his friends called after him, but he was gone.

"Everyone, into the courtyard!" Piper called over the screams and cries of her people. "Leland! Take Leo and get the Conclave into the antechamber. There are only two doors in there. Jack, find Queen Una and Princess Gemari, and get them in there as well." Piper turned to the closest guard. "You, find the palace healers. Escort them to the courtyard in case there are any injuries." They all nodded to her, and took off in different directions.

Piper swore under her breath for not having at least a dagger concealed on her somewhere. She hurried down the steps of the dais toward the main

Prophecy

doors. A strong hand gripped her arm, and she turned, ready to give her assailant a face-full of fire. Valar locked eyes with her, and attempted to pull her towards the rear antechamber with the Conclave.

"Majesty," he said. "We must think of your safety first. You are no good to your people dead."

Piper glared at him, and pushed his hand from her arm. "What kind of Queen am I that I run and hide at the first sign of trouble, after everything I have been through? My people are afraid, and they need me."

Valar watched as she took a sword from one of the guards at the door, and pointed to the antechamber. He took off at her request, and Piper consoled the people as they rushed past her. One woman flung herself into Piper's arms, crying. Piper dried the woman's eyes with her sleeve, and encouraged her onward.

"What is she doing?" Valin asked worried as he rushed to join his father.

"She is being the kind of queen we have never had," he replied.

Jayson ran along the dark tunnel he had found concealed behind the tapestry. His suspicions of disloyalty amongst the palace guards had been confirmed, and the time had come for him to make an example of these rogues.

A door slid open somewhere ahead of him, and closed again quickly. He heard the lock snap shut, but it did not slow his pace. He approached the door and reached out with his magic, sensing the mechanisms in the lock. The tumblers slid aside easily, and he kicked the door open, his sword held out at the ready. The hall was quiet, but he knew better than to believe it was nothing. This was the way to the stables. He crept along the passage, skirting close to the wall. His heart pounded in his chest. The sound of pounding hooves raced past the window beside him. He cursed loudly, and ran ahead toward the door to the stables.

"King Jayson of the Hill," said the stable hand as Jayson flung open the door wide. The man was on the floor. His nose had been broken, and his arm had been cut.

"Who was it? Did he say where he was going?" Jayson asked the man frantically. He pulled the man to his feet but did not loosen his grip.

"No, my King, but he took one of the horses meant for the Lord of Hollycrest. It seemed deliberate, sir. A beck-and came a few hours before the Queen's coronation and requested it be tacked and ready for the Lord's departure immediately thereafter."

Jayson nodded and rushed to the grain room. He pulled his old bow and quiver from an empty grain bin and headed for the main doors. He had left it there before leaving for the coronation. His suspicions had been confirmed, and he was grateful for his increased intuition since the incident with the Kings.

"There are healers in the courtyard. Take care of those wounds. Tell no one what you have seen here."

The stable hand nodded to Jayson and took off through a side door that lead across the paddocks.

Once outside, Jayson closed his eyes. He sent a wave of his energy out, searching for the man he now tracked. He could feel the panic of the crowd of people in the courtyard. His heart beat in time with those of the guards patrolling the borders of the palace. There were horses converging to a single game trail nearly a mile away. They seemed to come from all around the palace and carefully avoided the guards as they went.

Jayson opened his eyes, but kept the connection he felt tethered to his stomach. He slung his quiver and bow across his back and opted to hunt his quarry on foot, rather than horseback. With a mischievous glint in his eye, Jayson took off silently into the night.

When the aftermath of the battle with Duke Noraedin had begun, everyone's concern had been for Piper, and rightly so. She was to be the next Queen of the elves of Chartile. She had taken a traumatic blow seeing both her sister and lover die before her eyes. The pain Jayson had felt when he had killed the guard had gone unnoticed. Jack and Leo, who had special connections to the Dwarves, were busy helping with political negotiations and preparing for Piper's coronation. Jayson felt alone.

It had been a lonely night sitting in the little tavern in Hollycrest, a tiny village less than a day from the Elven Palace. Jayson had needed to get away. He needed to think, to find some way to cope. Several young men sat in a dark corner of the tavern. Jayson heard them discussing how they might steal into the palace to kill the would-be-Queen, Eva Ruani. Try as they might, their drunken tongues were not nearly as quiet as they likely thought. They were sympathizers to Taraniz's original cause of uniting all the races of Chartile under one rule. Jayson listened, then slipped away unseen to report to Leland.

Now, Jayson walked the dark path back to Hollycrest. The tiny fireball in his hand guided his way. He hoped that after the weeks of planning and spying, the weeks of torment he had silently endured, his debt would finally be repaid. At least in part. The guard he had killed had only been trying to protect his Princess. Jayson still didn't know his name.

ঙ৯৵

The panic finally ceased once the people at the coronation were in the fresh air and the wounds of their friends tended. There were only a few moderate injuries from the rain of arrows that had descended on them. The rest were minor, and easily treated. Piper had addressed them, and the crowd broke apart, either opting to go back to the quarters of the nobles they served, or to head home. After nearly an hour, Piper marched into the antechamber where the Conclave of Nobles and the Dwarvik royalty were safely taking refuge.

"What in the name of earth and sky is happening here?" demanded one of the nobles before she had even covered the distance from the door. "If this is how you will protect your people, then you have much to learn, little girl. Harpy's Point—"

Piper held up her hand to silence him.

"I thank you for your kind words of wisdom and encouragement," she began, and the noble blushed scarlet. "I can assure you, I knew nothing of this, and wish to defer to my Captain for the answers we all seek."

Leland cast his eyes downward, his shoulders drooping slightly. "I suppose this is what I get for putting my faith in a plan concocted by a child," he replied.

At once, everyone turned to look at Leo and Jack. They stared wide eyed and confused back, and Jack threw his hands in the air.

"Not us, man," he said.

"Some weeks ago, King Jayson came to me having overheard of a plan to kill you, Your Majesty," said Leland. Murmurs and whispers moved up and down the group, but Piper looked at Leland unmoving. Jack and Leo recognized the look at once, and remained quiet. "There are still those who are loyal to Taraniz. They were never under her control, but simply agreed with her ideas. Jayson wished to go after them immediately, but... Your Majesty, it was my idea to wait until the coronation. I thought we might be able to apprehend more of them at once. It was foolish of me. I admit, I haven't had to think for myself in so long, what with Taraniz, or Noraedin, or whomever it was controlling me. I admit that I am not yet fully myself."

"Then you should have never continued as Captain!" someone shouted, and the room erupted into chaos. Piper remained quiet, staring at the man before her. Leland would not meet her eye, and she realized he couldn't have been much older than she was. Leland had mentioned Taraniz had killed the previous Captain for disobeying her orders. His actions were certainly foolish, but she knew her own mistakes in the coming years would be many.

"We all make mistakes," she said to Leland. "This is a new era for us all. No one was seriously injured. We were lucky."

She turned to address the crowd before her, but they did not notice. They argued and yelled over each other. Una sat in a chair along the wall, her arms folded before her and shook her head in disbelief. Piper clapped her hands together loudly, using her magic to amplify the sound. The nobles covered their ears and turned to stare in surprise.

"Thank you," she said politely. "As I said to Leland, no one was seriously hurt. Mistakes will happen. It should be our job now to ensure that any of these rebels are found and brought to justice. I encour –"

"So it's true," breathed one of the nobles close by. "You as well. You do have magic."

Piper looked blankly at the people before her. Once again, Jack and Leo had nearly forgotten that magic was outlawed, and they shifted uncomfortably.

"You will submit for The Cleansing, or be removed from your office," said another noble, more defiantly.

Piper smirked at him. "Who then will take the throne, Allister?"

"As there are no more direct descendants to the throne, your land will be thrown into yet another civil war." Gemari crossed her arms and raised an eyebrow at the elven nobles. "The Dwarves will not back you on this. We have chosen to support Piper."

She shot a warning glare at Una, then resumed staring at the nobles from behind Jack.

"Of course you would," spat the noble from Sutton Low. "Your customs are more magical than you pretend them to be. You have no power or say in the matters of Elven state, dwarf."

"She has as much say as anyone here," said Gran from another chair beside Una. "We are all a part of Chartile. The decisions of one race affects us all."

"There have been many revolutions for the better in our world," Leo said. "Change isn't always a bad thing. It's sometimes scary, but it doesn't have to be bad if you don't let it be."

The discussion went on and on, until the attack at the coronation was nearly forgotten. In the end, Piper stood her ground. The Conclave had no real power over their monarchs. The royals looked to them for guidance, and over the centuries, had allowed themselves to be governed by the Conclave in order to keep peace. Piper was confident that regardless of her magic, it was too soon after the corruption of Princess Taraniz for the nobles to want to cause any trouble.

Soon, only Piper, Jack, Leo, Valin and Valar were left in the tiny room. Piper plopped into one of the chairs along the perimeter of the room. "It is not as difficult as I thought it would be," she admitted. "It's that there are so many of them. It is incredibly draining."

From somewhere, Valin produced a chalice of water, and handed it to Piper. She looked at him surprised, and he smiled at her. She accepted the water and drank deeply as Leo said, "Do you think they'll cause any trouble? With the whole magic thing?"

"I believe it is too soon to know that," said Valar. "However, their next push will be for you to choose an advisor, Piper."

"I thought we had until the winter solstice for that." Jack leaned against one of the tapestries. "Shouldn't we be looking for Jayson?"

"Jayson can take care of himself," said Valin. "He's been working with the soldiers night and day for this mission. He hardly sleeps anymore. Killing that guard rather traumatized him, I believe."

"Well, I hope he didn't go traipsing off by himself," said Leo a cold edge in his voice. "He should have taken guards or someone with him."

They sat in silence for several minutes thinking and worrying about Jayson. Then, Valar gave an impressive yawn, and stretched.

"I am far too old for this," he mumbled. "Majesty, my Kings, if you no longer require my presence, I will retire for the night."

Piper nodded to him, though she seemed lost in her own thoughts. Valar bowed to her, then to the boys and left the room, the door click echoing throughout the chamber as he went.

"Do you want me to tell Una or Gemari anything?" Jack asked Piper quietly.

Piper shook her head. "They were here earlier for the important discussions. They know everything that needs to be known. You and Leo should go rest."

"You, too," said Leo.

"Hmm?" asked Piper dreamily.

"You need to get some sleep, too," said Leo again, raising an eyebrow at her.

"Yes, I suppose I should. I have more prisoners to attend to tomorrow." She rose, and headed for the door, nearly asleep on her feet.

"I'll look after her," Valin whispered to Jack and Leo, and trotted off behind her.

Piper had barely walked across the room when she found herself standing at the base of the tower stair. She couldn't remember how she had gotten there, and she stood there dazed for a moment.

"Are you alright, Piper?" a voice asked beside her. She turned to see Valin, his icy blue eyes kind and concerned.

"Yes," she replied. "I am just very tired. And hungry," she added under her breath. She climbed the stair and Valin followed. He held the door at the top open for her and watched as she headed straight for the bed.

"Majesty, let me call your beck-ands to help you," he said, but Piper had already begun undoing the laces of her dress herself. When she couldn't reach them anymore, she turned to look at Valin.

He crossed the room, and with delicate fingers, finished untying the laces down her back. Before he could turn away, Piper let the dress drop to the floor, exposing her smooth, flawless back.

Valin blinked then turned away quickly and heard Piper climb beneath the blankets of her bed.

"Majesty, if you need nothing further, I—" He dared to turn and look at her. She was resting peacefully, her lips slightly parted, and one arm drawn up over her head. It was hard to believe only hours before she had dared the Noble Conclave by creating her own oaths and calmed her people in the face of certain death. The Queen of the elves was a wildfire, and she needed someone to guide her and help her rule her people.

As he turned to leave, Valin noticed a familiar small box on the corner of her dressing table. He opened it and saw his mother's sapphire necklace within, the symbol of his promise that he would help her if she needed it. He left the box open, and left the room, shutting the door quietly behind him.

Chapter Twenty-Six

Jayson of the Hill

Jayson lay on his stomach overlooking the top of a small hill. The last of the party he had pursued through the night walked into a small tavern on the outskirts of town. The rogue looked over his shoulder, as though he sensed he was being watched. He turned quickly and slammed the tavern door behind him.

Jayson smiled wickedly. The group had decided to make camp for the night, and Jayson was easily able to catch up to them. He played havoc with them all night until they finally gave in and continued on their way. Howling winds, sudden rain storms, falling acorns, and voices in the dark had all plagued them, and he had to keep from laughing the entire time. He never slept anymore, and needed all the fun he could get these days. Ever since the encounter with Duke Noraedin when King Jenemar had made himself known in Jayson's mind, his magic came as easily as breathing. He was sure it was the same for Leo, Jack and Piper, but they had little time for him these days. They were too busy with their own affairs to bother much with him.

As the sky turned a pale orange above the small village of Hollycrest, it was time again for him to work. Who knew how many of these small pockets of outlaws there were in Chartile, but Jayson was about to set an example. He headed for the front door of the tavern, and noticed a small bird perched above the open window.

"Hello, little friend," he said softly to it, and the bird cocked its head toward him. "Will you be my eyes?" he asked it in its mind. The bird puffed itself up. Jayson sent a wave of calming energies to wash over the little bird, soothing it and helping it to feel safe. When the bird had calmed itself, Jayson reached into the bird's mind. It took a moment, but he was able to see through its eyes, even if it was a bit blurry.

The bird hopped onto the window sill. It cocked its head and fluttered onto the empty table beside the window. Jayson could see the group he tracked sitting in the far corner of the tavern. They had extinguished most of the candelabras around them and angrily shooed away the poor barmaid, but not before discourteously groping her rear.

"Thank you, friend. Now hurry and leave this place." Jayson withdrew his mind from the little bird. It chirped and trilled loudly at him, then took off through the window once more.

Jayson wretched the door open so hard it slammed against the outer wall. He threw a ball of fire across the room. It hit the unlit candelabra above the table of his quarry, lighting the candles, and sending small bits of fire raining down on them. He drew an arrow from his quiver and sent it soaring across the room. It narrowly missed the ear of one of the men. They stood, drawing their swords and daggers. No sooner had they stood were they lifted from their feet, and slammed back into their chairs. Their blades turned on their masters, and hovered in midair at their throats.

"I am Jayson Hill, the reincarnated soul of King Jenemar. You have committed acts of treason and attempted murder against Queen Piper. You will answer for your crimes."

A bird trilled franticly from the window ledge. Jayson turned in time to kick a middle aged man to the ground, and pressed his boot to the man's throat. The weapons that hung in the air never faltered.

"Tell your people what happens when they deny the Queen of the elves of Chartile and what becomes of those who still support the tyranny of Princess Taraniz." He glared at the man beneath him. The man nodded, and Jayson released him, turning back to the outlaws.

৵৵

Jack sat in the elven library trying to appear interested in what Leo was reading. Nefiri had entrusted some old documents from the Tutarian libraries to him for Leo's research. Leo poured over the notes, talking to himself, and continually referring to the pages of notes he had made on Draconian runes that were piled high beside him.

"I don't think this one's going to help much," Leo said, setting the scroll aside. "I don't even know why the elder thought that was useful."

"Why not?" Jack asked. He ran his hand over his face and hoped some discussion might wake him up. He always regretted that Chartile didn't have coffee.

"It's some kind of myth about the Dragons and a star bridge or something like that. I don't know. It didn't make a lot of sense."

Jack opened his mouth to comment when the sound of running feet stopped him.

"My Lords, my Kings," said a young beck-and boy. "You wished to know when King Jayson returned."

"Where is he?" Jack asked getting to his feet.

"The dungeons, my King. Captain Leland is on his way as well. My Lord, he has single handedly brought back the outlaws who attacked Queen Piper! Twelve in all!"

Jack and Leo tore from the room, leaving the parchment and scrolls strewn across the table. They took the secret entrance from the noble's wing to the dungeons, and rounded the corner to see Jayson locking a cell door.

"Jayson!" Leo cried angrily. "Where the hell have you been? What's going on?"

Jayson held up a hand to silence him and cocked his head toward the main stair. Leo stared open mouthed at him, but followed nonetheless.

They emerged into the more public area of the palace, and headed for the throne room.

"I had some business to do," Jayson said calmly.

"What business? Jayson, we were worried sick! You could have told us! We would have come with you," Jack protested.

"Would you?" Jayson rounded on them. "Would you have left your precious Princess Gemari, Jack? Would you have left your research, Leo? You two have started to make a life for yourselves here, and I'm still nothing! I'm nothing but a murderer, and I have to account for that. I have to try and make up for it."

"Jayson, that wasn't — it was an accident. You can't bl—"

"I can't what, Leo? I can't hold myself responsible for my actions? I can't try to right the wrong I did? Isn't that what we're here for anyway?" He pushed one of the doors to the throne room open and nearly ran into Piper. Her arms were crossed and she scowled bitterly at him.

"Jayson Hill," she began, but threw her arms around him, and nearly cried in his shoulder. "Don't ever do anything like that again! You were gone for two days! We could have helped you."

"That's what we said," said Jack.

"But apparently, we aren't good enough anymore." said Leo.

"That's not what I said," snapped Jayson. "You're all too important and too busy anymore."

"Let's go for a walk," Piper suggested. Without hesitation, they followed her past the front gates and out into the Belirian Forest.

Summer was very much gone and autumn had clearly set its roots in to stay. The air had a permanent chill to it, and the leaves that fell from the trees were the size of dinner plates. They were glad for the fur lined cloaks and vests they wore, even if it wasn't exactly the latest fashions in Ohio. They were warm and comfortable and matched the color of the falling leaves. Jayson picked up a leaf and began shredding it as they walked. Piper changed the subject to what Jack knew about the Black Diamonds and then to Leo's progress with his research.

They settled into a small clearing and talked for hours. They found an apple tree nearby and munched happily. Jayson forgot his anger, opting instead for his usual humor and tact eventually.

Piper took a bite of apple then suddenly spit it back out, clenching her stomach.

"Did you eat a worm?" Jayson asked teasing.

Piper glared at him and replied, "No. It is more than that."

"Are you sick?" Leo asked, very concerned.

"Did someone poison you?" Jack asked almost panicked.

Piper sat up straight again and pulled a sapphire necklace from beneath her bodice neckline.

"What's that?" asked Jayson.

"This was Valin's mother's necklace. When we were at his manor last month, Valar recommended I marry Valin so Valar could continue to advise me. He may not do so in an official capacity, as he was my father's advisor. If I do not marry, then I must take on an advisor. If there is both a King and a Queen on the throne, then I do not have to choose an advisor. I have decided against asking Gran to do it. She deserves her peace after all she has been through these last eighteen years."

"So, you're going to marry Valin?" asked Jack. Piper nodded. "Congrats! That's awesome!"

Jayson glared at her. "What about Dimitri?"

Piper placed a hand over her belly and sighed.

"He is one of the reasons I have decided to accept Valin's proposal. I believe I am with Dimitri's child. I may be able to convince the Conclave it is Valin's if we act quickly. If not, the child will be given to a wet nurse and raised as someone else's. I do not want for my child that which happened to me."

"You're the Queen. Just change the laws!" cried Jayson. "Dimitri died for us, and you're just going to throw him away."

"It is not so simple, Jayson. I wish it wasn't this way." Tears began to roll down her cheeks. "I still mourn him, but I can no longer think of only myself. My world is too big now."

"Piper, maybe Gran could raise the baby for you. Then you could still see it." Jack shrugged.

"And, we could always be your advisors." Leo offered.

Piper hung her head, holding her belly. "I have already accepted Valin's proposal. You are working so hard to go home, I cannot accept an advisor who could leave me at any moment."

"I won't leave you, Piper," said Jayson. She smiled at him and reached across their circle to squeeze his hand.

"Thank you, Jayson," she said. "But it would not be right of me to ask you to stay. As much as I want you to, you have your own lives back home. I cannot ask you to leave it all behind."

"I guess I didn't think of that," said Leo. "I want to go home, but I don't want to leave you either."

"Maybe Piper can come home with us!" Jack exclaimed.

"Who will care for my people?" asked Piper, and Jack hung his head.

Piper grabbed Jack's hand in her free one and smiled at him as well. "Two months ago, I would have."

"I'm sorry, Piper," said Leo, his shoulders sagging in defeat. "I used to have the answers for everything. Growing up sucks." They nodded and their conversation turned to the coming wedding.

They could just see the noon sun through the empty boughs of the trees above them when their discussions came to an end.

"You know, I guess there's one thing we haven't really tried." Leo looked about thoughtfully.

"What do you mean?" Jayson asked.

"To get home. We haven't tried using our own magic. Like how we concentrated to make that storm. Maybe we could concentrate on home," he said.

"That'd be too easy. There's no way it'd work," said Jayson shaking his head.

"I guess it's worth a try." Jack shrugged. "It's the one thing we haven't done. We're more powerful now since linking with the old kings."

"Then again, when we open our eyes, we may never see Piper again," argued Jayson.

"I think you have done what you were brought here to do. It is time to do something for yourselves for a change." She took Jack and Jayson's hands again. "If it is your will, then I will help you to the best of my ability."

The boys looked at each other nervously then joined hands.

"If this is really it, really good-bye and all, I promise I'll try to find a way back. I don't want it to be good-bye forever," said Jayson. His eyes were wet with the tears he forced himself to hold back. "If we can come here once, I'm sure we can figure out a way to come back."

They all nodded in agreement and closed their eyes. They thought about their tree house, the

Prophecy

sunken loveseat, and the tattered tarp and shower curtain. They thought about their families and school. Leo thought about his dad's egg sandwiches, and how one sounded so delicious at that moment. Jack thought about his mother and sister. He had left them alone with his father. Jayson thought about his little sister and wondered what extra classes his parents had enrolled her in at Cranbrook.

The wind began to blow harder than it had earlier, but they did not shiver. They could hear the wind, but they didn't feel it. They were too afraid to look until the sound died away.

When Piper opened her eyes, the clearing was empty. She opened her empty hands and looked at them. She sat for a long time in silence, thinking of the short time she had spent with Jayson, Jack, and Leo, and fighting the tears that brimmed in her eyes. As she walked back to the palace, she couldn't help but think that, once again, those she loved had left her forever. She patted her belly before walking through the front gates and swore her children would never feel that sting of loss.

Chapter Twenty-Seven

Home

Jayson opened his eyes and saw a lady bug crawling across the knuckles of his hand. He sat up, and immediately pulled the heavy fur cloak from his shoulders. The air was heavy with humidity and heat. He looked around. The trees were thin and ragged looking, and he saw a small creek running close by. He turned and looked over his shoulder. Their tree house was just as they had left it, the shower curtain caught in a small breeze.

He walked to the dilapidated couch and touched the arm. It felt real enough. At his feet were the crusts of Leo's egg sandwich covered in tiny black ants. He climbed to the top of the tree house and pulled aside the shower curtain. The sticks they had used for swords were leaning against the corner, as were the assortment of other odds and ends that had been stashed there over the summer.

"Jayson?" He heard Jack's voice calling franticly from below.

Jayson pulled back the curtain. "I'm here," he said. He climbed down and joined Leo and Jack who sat quietly surveying the scene before them.

"I didn't think it would work," said Leo, ashamed. "It was so simple. I didn't think we'd leave Piper like that."

"Well, we did," snapped Jayson. He scowled and bitterly kicked the base of the tree. "Now what are we gunna do?"

"We still have our clothes from Chartile," said Jack. "How are we going to explain this to our parents?"

"I'm more worried about how we've actually changed." Leo flexed his bicep as he spoke. "Do you think our parents will even recognize us?"

"Well, we're bound to look different for as long as we've been gone," said Jack.

"But we haven't been," said Jayson more calmly. Jack and Leo furrowed their brows at him. Jayson sighed and rolled his eye. "Come here. Look, we haven't been gone very long." He showed them the crusts he had found. Leo knelt to examine them.

"Has anyone tried using magic yet?" Jack asked. Jayson and Leo shook their heads. They took turns attempting to create a fire ball and throw it at the tree. None of them were successful.

"That doesn't make any sense," said Jayson. "We could do it before!"

"Earth must be different from Chartile. That's the only explanation," said Leo flexing his hands.

"If I had known I'd lose my magic, I'd have never come back!" Jayson shouted. He kicked the couch and threw a rock into the creek.

"Jay, calm down." Jack placed a hand on Jayson's shoulder. "We'll figure this out."

"Really, dude? We're just supposed to pick up our lives as if nothing happened? What about Gemari and Nefiri, huh? Leo, what about Brande and all the Black Diamonds? Think of all the people we had a hand in saving or killing, and we're just supposed to start school in a few weeks as if none of it ever happened? I know I sure as heck can't tell my parents. I told you when we first went to Chartile that if this was some kind of government

390

conspiracy, no one would ever believe us, and you agreed with me, Leo."

"I don't think we have much choice, Jayson," said Leo in a small voice. "You're right. We can't tell anyone."

"But we're not going to abandon each other," said Jack. "We were together in Chartile, and we'll never leave each other here. We have to promise we'll always be there for each other, no matter what."

They agreed and sat in silence, side by side on the couch for what felt like several hours. Finally, Leo said, "We can get cleaned up at my place. I think, if we had to explain anything, my dad would understand." Jack nodded, but Jayson shifted uncomfortably before finally agreeing.

They hurried through the subdivision of Swansdale, looking up and down the side streets as they went. They hoped no one was looking out their windows to see them. They must have looked like savages or something straight out of a Mad Max movie. They flew up the Leo's porch steps and ran into the living room. The cool of the air conditioning swept over them for the first time in months, and they were nearly stopped dead in their tracks.

"I was wondering when you'd be back for —" Mr. DeHaven stopped short. He dropped the mug he was drying and it shattered on the floor. "Who are you?" he asked.

"Dad?" Leo hesitated, then rushed into his father's arms. Mr. DeHaven tried to take a step backward, but all three boys had pressed him against the doorjamb to the kitchen in a ferocious hug.

"Leo?" Mr. DeHaven asked tentatively.

"Dad, it's me!" cried Leo, and he looked up into his father's eyes. Realization spread over the man's face, and he hugged his son tight.

"What happened to you?" he asked, his voice muffled as he buried his face in his son's hair.

Leo pulled away from his father and looked at his friend. Jayson shuffled back and forth on the plush carpet and Jack nodded.

"I think you should sit down." Leo led his father to the couch, and launched into their story. Jack and Jayson interjected their commentary nearly as often, especially when it came to events Leo was not present for. It was several hours before they had finished. Mr. DeHaven had made them mac and cheese, and the boys devoured it in moments.

Still stunned, he said, "Why don't you boys get showered and changed."

Showers. They had nearly forgotten what a shower was. The unlimited steaming hot water. The soap. It was practically a fight for who got to go first.

An hour later, they hurried down the stairs, looking far more like respectable young men from Swansdale, even if their hair was still long.

They saw a familiar white Cadillac sitting in the driveway from the stair window as they headed back to the first floor. The man who owned the vehicle sat on the couch as they rounded the banister corner. They stopped dead, staring at him and Mr. DeHaven.

"Boys, this is Mr. Darrow." Mr. DeHaven motioned to the man on the couch. "I need you to tell him everything you told me."

"Are you from the government?" Jayson asked accusingly.

"No," said the man kindly. "I am both above and nonexistent to the government. I knew your parents when they worked with NASA." He smiled. "I'm a scientist and an archeologist. I'm what you might call expert when it comes to the strange and unusual, and I know how they all fit together. Your secret is safe with me, if mine is with you." He held out his hand to them. After a moment, Leo shook it, and began his tale again.

Mr. Darrow was very thorough. He asked many questions that didn't even seem to be related, like what direction the sun set and the color of the fire. He took samples from their clothes from Chartile, and was most interested in scraping mud from the toe of Jack's boot. He took blood samples and hair samples and whirled a cotton swab around their mouths. It was dusk by the time he stood to leave.

"I'll get these to Emily right away," he said to Mr. DeHaven and shook his hand.

"Wait, who?" asked Leo. He stood and pushed his way between the two men, looking back and forth between them franticly.

"Someone I know who might be able to figure out where Chartile is." said Mr. Darrow locking his brief bag.

"You said Emily," said Leo. "Mom's name is Emily." He turned to look at his father. "Is he talking about mom?"

Mr. DeHaven opened his mouth to speak, but closed it again. He swallowed hard and said, "Yes, Leo. He means your mother."

"But... mom's... gone! Mom left us!" cried Leo.

"It was for your safety. It was for everyone's safety." Mr. Darrow grimaced and shrugged his shoulders. "I'm sorry, boys, but what you have experienced is— well, it's hard to explain. Just promise me you won't breathe a word about this to anyone."

"We won't," Jack reassured him, though he glanced side long at Leo who looked as though he were about to have a panic attack.

"Thank you," said Mr. Darrow. "With any luck, I'll see you boys again someday." The front door closed behind him. Jack and Jayson watched as Mr. Darrow loaded his samples into the trunk, started his Cadillac and drove away. Leo stood behind them wiping his glasses nervously on his shirt and sighing.

"Leo, I think we should talk," said Mr. DeHaven, setting a hand on his son's shoulder. Leo turned to look at his father and nodded.

"We'll come back tomorrow," said Jack, and Jayson nodded. They left and headed to their homes, walking the dark streets as though it were any other summer night for them in Swansdale.

ৎৡ৵৵

Jack walked through his front door. The smell of rosemary and pork roast filled the house. His baby sister sat on the floor playing with a bucket of wooden blocks.

"Ja-Ja!" she shouted, and opened and closed her hands for him to pick her up. Jack ran to her, and scooped her up, kissing and tickling her. His mother pushed open the basement door with her hip, her arms full of laundry. She dropped the clothes on the couch then turned to her son.

"Jack, your father's looking for you." she said. The swelling around her eye was even worse. Jack had forgotten how bad it had been. He set his sister back on the floor, and walked to her.

"Mom," he said sternly, "You need to go to the hospital and have that looked at."

She pushed his hand away and shook her head. "I'm fine. But your father is very upset. You weren't here when he came home."

"I was at Leo's! I told Aunt Kiera!" Jack cried.

"I know, and I told him that. Still, you weren't here when he came home."

"He was drunk, wasn't he?" asked Jack, folding his arms and raising an eyebrow in a very Piper-like fashion.

His mother stammered, and narrowed her eyes at her son's newfound boldness. "Yes," she finally said. "Yes, he was. You know what he's like when he expects something."

A truck pulled into the driveway and a door slammed. Mrs. Mitchel gave a small gasp, and attempted to push Jack onto the couch as she ran for her daughter.

"Just do whatever he says," she whispered.

Mr. Mitchel stumbled through the front door. His eyes landed on Jack standing tall before him and he shouted, "Where the hell were you? Damn it, Karla! I told you to tell me when this punk got back!"

"Carter, I—he—" Mrs. Mitchel's small voice was drowned out by the deep huffing and puffing of her husband as he stumbled closer.

"Go," said Jack. He instinctually pushed his mother behind him toward the kitchen.

"Think you're so tough, little punk?" said Mr. Mitchel.

"Jack, no," said Mrs. Mitchel. Jack pushed her closer to the kitchen and she covered her daughter's head.

Mr. Mitchel swung at Jack. His coordination was nearly perfect. Jack grabbed his father's fist, and spun him around, twisting his arm behind his back. He thanked Kylani for their lessons in the mines. He walked the struggling man to the door, Jack's other hand in the small of his father's back.

"We want to help you," he seethed in Mr. Mitchel's ear. "But you have to want to help yourself first. I gotta do what's best for us until you figure that out." Jack reached for the door, and his father broke free of his grip. The man turned to hit his son, but Jack caught his fist again. He looked into the man's eyes and pushed him out the front door. Mr. Mitchel tripped down the steps and landed on the lawn.

"I love you Dad," said Jack, and he slammed the door shut, locking it behind him. Mr. Mitchel beat on the door and tried to turn the knob.

Jack turned back to his mother. She was crying and shaking and clutching at the baby in her arms. "What have you done, Jack? What have you done?" she sobbed.

Jack walked to her and lifted his sister from the woman's arms. She wrapped her arms tight around herself and sobbed even louder as Mr. Mitchel beat more frantically on the door.

Jack placed his hand on her shoulder. "It's over mom," he whispered. "He's not going to hurt us anymore. I won't let him." He hugged his mother and his sister then picked up the phone to call the police.

ভিজ্ঞ

Jayson bounded up his front porch steps, as a truck squealed around the corner. It looked like Jack's dad's truck. He reached to his hip, ready to pull out a dagger and run to help his friend. But there was nothing there. Jayson closed his hand on the loose fabric of one of Leo's cargo pants and sighed. He leaned against the door and sighed.

He opened the door and stepped inside. He nearly forgot to take off his shoes, until he tripped over his sister's Reeboks and stared at the little flashing lights in the heels. He noticed her staring at him intently across the room at the kitchen table. He looked away quickly and began untying his laces. His dog, Jesse, pranced around his feet excited. The dog sniffed every inch of him and licked Jayson's face, knocking him over. Mrs. Hill looked up from her reading on the couch.

"Did you eat at Mr. DeHaven's?" she asked, almost bored.

"Yeah," said Jayson pushing the dog off. "We had mac and cheese." Jessica was still staring at him. He tore his eyes away from her again, feeling more uncomfortable by the minute.

"Okay. Well, there's leftover meat loaf in the fridge if you're hungry," she said. Jayson nodded and headed for his bedroom.

"Oh, Jayson," called his mother. He stopped halfway down the hall and turned to look at her. "I'm going to leave some money on the table tomorrow. I want you to go to Cindy and get a haircut, please."

Jayson nodded again. Turning and nearly tripping over his dog, he walked into his room and shut the door.

Character Biographies

<u>Jayson Hill:</u> Born July 22nd, Jayson is red-haired, freckled, and clumsy. His family has lived in Swansdale for several generations. He uses comedy and jokes as a way to hide his personal insecurities about never being good enough at anything. His life's ambition is to become a fighter pilot.

<u>Jack Mitchell:</u> Born May 10th, Jack is very tall and very handsome with dark brown eyes and dark brown, wavy hair. At seven years old, his family moved to Swansdale from Dover, Arkansas for a fresh start when Jack's father attempted to sober up for the first time. Jack escaped into books as a child when his parents argued and fought. Later, he began using poetry and writing as an outlet for his emotions.

<u>Leonardo DeHaven:</u> Born September 19th, Leo and his father, Reagan DeHaven, moved from a small town not far from Las Vegas when Leo was 10 years old. As the son of two NASA scientists, Leo approaches everything in life with a sort of linear logic. Growing up close to the tourist attractions of Area 51, Leo has secretly always had a fascination with historical conspiracies, and the strange and unexplainable events in world history. At the age of 12, Leo began trying to learn Sanskrit in order to read and decipher the ancient documents he heard about while on a trip to the art museum that supposedly mention extraterrestrial encounters. However, shortly after this, Leo received his first video game console, and rarely looked back. Leo is the spitting image of his father from the messy blonde hair, gray-blue eyes, and slightly pudgy physique.

Piper Romilly/Eva Ruani: Born the 14th day of Ansalvar. Born Eva Ruani, the second daughter of King Aramor and Queen Runa, Piper was raised in a very small village called Outland Post by her adoptive parents, Nevan and Paria Romilly, and her adoptive grandmother, Kaytah Chaudoin. Growing up, Piper always felt different. She looked different from the other elves in her village, and her family required far more from her than the other children she grew up with. Piper accompanied her grandmother on trips across the Dwarvik and Elven territories of Chartile where she learned courtly etiquettes, and even how to read and write the fancy calligraphy styles of the nobles.

When she was thirteen, Piper began showing her first signs of magic. Her parents and grandmother attempted to keep her occupied with more etiquette studies and learning the laws of the land. It worked for some time, until Piper accidentally set half of her village on fire in an attempt to help her mother light the hearth. Piper had stood up to the palace soldiers that came to her village, but her parents forced her to return home, fearing she would use her magic. Piper tried to use her magic to stop the fire she had made that was spreading from the hearth, but only created more. Many people were killed, including several of the children she had grown up with, a few of the palace soldiers and her own parents.

Piper fled to the mountain close by until the villagers of Outland Post sent a messenger to the Palace. Kaytah, Valar Marion, and Princess Taraniz returned to the village with an armed guard, ready to take Piper away. Valar, disguised as a knight, recommended casting Piper into the wild, as she might destroy the forest or the palace on their return as she had Outland Post. Taraniz reluctantly agreed, and Kaytah was able to continue caring for Piper from a distance.

Piper has the same messy red hair and brilliant green eyes of her mother, Runa. She enjoyed working with her hands and making things in her father's smithy. She also learned that she enjoyed archery, and liked to collect pretty stones she found. Piper is tenacious. She doesn't like to ask for help, and doesn't always work well in groups. Even though she doesn't show it, she cares about everyone, even those who have done wrong to her.

Dimitri: Born the 2nd day of Kalqar, Dimitri is the son of Empress Nefiri's youngest brother, Nahari, and Nefiri's head retainer, Dujanah. Nahari, who worked as a Dwarvik guard for his sister, met Dujanah on a trip to Duneland to acquire more human servants. Nahari insisted Nefiri purchase Dujanah.

Several years later, it was discovered Nahari and Dujanah had been romantically involved for some time. As this is prohibited by Dwarvik law, Nahari was put to death. Nefiri refused to allow Dujanah be put to death while she still carried an innocent child. The Council of Elders, however, would not allow Dujanah to live, and did not remove her orenite cuffs during labor. Dujanah died, and Dimitri was protected under Dwarvik law as an innocent. Nefiri raised him as her own.

Dimitri met Piper when she was seven years old while accompanying Kaytah on a trip to Mount

Kelsii. The two became fast friends. Dimitri was permitted to spend time with Piper back at Outland Post for a few days at a time while growing up. When he was seventeen, Dimitri took up the role of Head Retainer to Nefiri like his mother just before Piper was cast out to live in the mountain on her own.

Dimitri was both loved and hated by the Dwarvik society. He was a constant, cruel reminder that even those voted into power made mistakes. But his charm and exceedingly handsome looks gave him an upper edge, especially with the Dwarvik women. Dimitri was not afraid to use this to his advantage.

Secondary Characters

Valar Marion: Born the 20th day of Pasalvar, and the first born nephew of the Lord of Cannondole, Valar succeeded his uncle (who had no children of his own) at the age of twenty-two. Before that time, he lived with his parents in Harpy's Point where his father worked as a tax collector. Valar and Runa were friends as children, but grew apart when she was sent off to marry King Aramor. Runa worked to get her old friend appointed as the King's Head Advisor shortly after her marriage when Armor's advisor at the time decided to retire.

After Runa's death, Valar attempted to be like a second father to Princess Taraniz. When the soul of Duke Noraedin overtook Taraniz, Valar was one of the only people who could help Taraniz overcome Noraedin. As Noraedin's soul grew stronger, Valar soon saw there was little more he could do to save her. Heartbroken, he began working to put plans into motion to help Piper ascend to the throne and usurp Taraniz. His original hope was that Piper might be able to help Taraniz better than he could as he had heard rumors of her magic.

After his son married Piper and took the throne, Valar returned to his role as Lord of Cannondole, and attempted to remain oblivious to the greater political workings of Chartile. He spent his time with Brock's father and enjoyed vinting various sweet wines.

Valin Marion: Born the 10th day of Ansalvar, Valin Marion is the only child of Valar and Aylin Marion. His parents met at the age of 16, and were married shortly thereafter. Valin was born exactly one year later. At only five years old, Valin took up the position of Lord of Cannondole when his father went to work as the Head Advisor to King Aramor and Queen Runa. Aylin governed Cannondole until she passed several years later from The Five Day Fever. Valin was seventeen when he officially became Lord of Cannondole.

Valin had a string of lovers early on, much to his mother's dissatisfaction.

Valin is a lover of music (and brandy), and would often join his fellows at The Glass Lantern for a drink and a song. He is quite proficient at the lyre, and is said to have a lovely singing voice.

Empress Nefiri of the House of Auldfr: Born the 3rd day of Jenqar, Nefiri is the fourth born child of Nefara and her second hasana (later Harasan of Nafara of the House of Auldfr), Madiri. Nefara served as a council elder for 38 years. Nefiri was chosen by the Council at five years old to train as a Princess of Mount Kelsii. At twenty, Nefiri chose to be trained in Peace, and became Princess when she was twenty-nine. Shortly after being chosen for training as a child, most of Nefiri's brothers decided to train in the Royal Guard to protect their sister.

Nefiri knew of her brother's affair with Dujanah before she even bought the human girl for service in Duneland. Being denied love as a Royal had never set well with Nefiri. She was often disheartened by this, and didn't want to deny Nahari true love if he had found it.

Nefiri often found peace and harmony while consorting The Oracle to speak to Rashiri. The Oracle is a tool used by only specially trained priestesses – though Nefiri had specifically requested to be trained in its use – to speak with the Gods. The Oracle is a flat, highly polished piece of obsidian surrounded by running water.

Princess Gemari of the House of Jetari: Born the 15th day of Florinvar, Gemari is the second daughter of Nefiri's second eldest brother, Kehara. She was chosen by the Council at age five to train as a Princess of Mount Kelsii. At age sixteen, Gemari chose to be trained in the ways of Peace, like her aunt, the Empress. By age seventeen, Gemari had succeeded Princess Thora as the Princess to Mount Kelsii when Thora was involved in a tragic cave-in that killed her and her entire guard. Rumor and speculation say it was due to Thora's involvement with the Black Diamonds. Some believe several Council Elders planned the accident, and subsequently blamed the Black Diamonds. However, there is no proof of this.

Three years later, Princess Gemari had worked with the Council of Elders to begin working to reconstruct some of the old, abandoned mines for the safety of the Mount Kelsii citizens, and the integrity of the mountain itself. Unbeknownst to Gemari, these mines were later occupied by The Black Diamonds in secret.

Having been thrust into her position of power and responsibility at such a young age, Gemari never experienced much in the way of a childhood. She felt rather naïve and out of place being the youngest among her peers. Meeting Jack and learning more about the Black Diamonds made Gemari see the world in a different light. She felt the weight of her position in a way she never had before, and went on to become one of the most beloved and well known Princesses of Mount Kelsii.

Queen Una of the House of Ulfra: Born the 13th day of Rhidqar, Una is the second born daughter of Ulfra and her first hasana, Bragrin. Ulfra had miscarried her first daughter, and therefore, put many pressures on Una to be the perfect daughter. Una had only one younger brother who worked as an architect and helped to build new mines and tunnels. At the age of fourteen, Una insisted on being trained in both Peace and War. Ulfra did not believe her daughter was up for the challenge. Una was determined to prove her wrong.

Ulfra returned to the stone one year after Princess Thora's death from unknown causes, leaving Una with the additional responsibility to care for her father and her mother's other hasanas.

Queen Isla of the House of Arnkatla: Born the 6th day of Torhirvar, Isla was born the first child of Arnkatla and her first and only hasana, Esjani. Isla's parents had quite a different upbringing for their children. They believed in equality and love above all else. Secretly, Arnkatla and Esjani were two of the first dwarves to begin working towards creating a coalition that advocated the beliefs of the Black Diamonds. Arnkatla and Esjani groomed Isla tirelessly in hopes she would be chosen by the Council for Princesshood. When she was, they continued to influence her training through her teachers and trusted Elders.

Though few ever knew, not even her own parents, Isla taught herself the traditional ceremonial dances of her people. She loved to dance. She met Kylani when she snuck away to one of the abandoned mines to dance in secret.

Princess Faeridae of the House of Gudvor: Born the 12th day of Pasalvar, Faeridae is the first born daughter of Gudvor and her third hasana, Faerdir. Gudvor and Faerdir were friends of Arnkatla and Esjani, and were soon recruited to the beliefs of equality they upheld. Though they did not raise their children with these beliefs as strongly as the House of Arnkatla, Faeridae and her brothers were certainly aware of the underlying political issues in their society.

Faeridae and Isla, though nearly fourteen years apart in age, were good friends. Faeridae was one of the few who knew of Isla's love of dancing.

At the age of five, Faeridae was selected by the Council to train as a Princess of The Tutarian Mountains. Feeling the growing tensions of the Black Diamonds and the Council of Elders, Faeridae felt being trained in War, like Queen Carendeil, would be wise. Her parents, however, were not happy with this decision, and felt they had failed their daughter by not instilling a want of peace and harmony within her.

Both of Faeridae's parents and one of her brothers, were killed during a raid by the Kelsii soldiers when their secret location within the mountain was discovered. Until Princess Gemari helped to rebuild the abandoned mines, The Black Diamonds were scattered after this attack, and worked in small groups. Faeridae turned to Arnkatla and Esjani for assistance in helping find new marriages for Gudvor's remaining hasanas and a few of her brothers who were not yet married.

Brande of the House of Kymora: Born the 8th day of Kalqar, Brande was the fourth son of Kymora and her first hasana, Bairdir. Brande was denied entry into the Kelsii Soldiers training program at the age of fifteen. Ashamed, he ran away from home and lived on the outskirts of the Belirian Forest close to the mountain for three weeks. His brother, Kylani, found him, and told him about The Black Diamonds. Both brothers worked as miners, and were able to falsify their deaths in the accident that killed Faeridae's parents. After which, they worked quietly to bring more members into The Black Diamonds.

Kylani of the House of Kymora: Born the 17th day of Kasmaqar, Kylani was the third born son of Kymora and her third hasana, Bairdir. Kylani's two eldest brothers were accepted to train as Kelsii Soldiers at a very young age, leaving Kylani to help his father and his mother's other hasanas to care for his other brothers and baby sister.

Kylani showed an interest in medicine very early, and began training under one of the Kelsii healers by the age of twelve. This left him little time to spend at home. He felt entirely responsible when his little brother, and best friend, Brande, ran away from home a few years later. While looking for clues to where his brother may have run off to, Kylani discovered Isla dancing in an abandoned mine. They met secretly every day for over a week, where she taught him about her beliefs and The Black Diamonds. With Isla's help, Kylani discovered Brande was living at the base of the mountain in the Belirian Forest. He immediately went after his brother, and convinced Brande to come back home with the hopes of them joining The Black Diamonds. Later, the brothers apprenticed within the miners guild.

Kylani and Isla's secret meetings continued over the years.

Other Characters

- Parents -

Reagan DeHaven: Reagan DeHaven received his PHD in Engineering with a minor in Quantum Physics from Cambridge University. He moved back to the United States to live with his parents, Marvin and Darlene in their retirement home in Las Vegas. After being forced to teach mathematics at a local community college, Reagan received a job offer from NASA two years later. He met his wife while working on their project, P905-Tes.

Emily DeHaven: The adopted daughter of a successful casino owner, Emily Ward (later DeHaven) was expected to take over the family business. When she decided to change her business major to a degree in Quantum Physics, the family disowned her, and she never spoke to them again. She met her husband thirteen years later while working for NASA on the P905-Tes project. Her family never knew she married or had a child. When P905-Tes was cancelled, and Emily and Reagan were dismissed from work, Emily immediately contacted friends she had in France and found a job at CERN. Heartbroken, Emily left her husband and son behind, hoping to return to them one day.

David Hill: David Hill was a software programmer that worked from home, giving him the ability to take his daughter, Jessica, to her specialty school in Michigan. He later went on to work for Apple Corporation after his children had graduated high school.

Susan Hill: Susan Cancio (later Hill) was a dental hygienist like her mother before her, working at the same dentist's office her mother had years ago. Her family had lived in Swansdale for several generations. She and David did not leave until after Jayson had bought their home from them when David was offered the job by Apple Corporation. It was the first time Susan had ever been out of the state of Ohio.

Carter Mitchel: Carter Mitchel began drinking at fifteen years old after suffering years of physical abuse from his alcoholic father. Carter, unfortunately, followed in his father's footsteps, despite every effort not to be like his dad. Carter found a job at a local gas station in Dover, Arkansas as a mechanic. He met his wife, Karla, when her car was towed into the shop. She had been travelling on a road trip across the country with her friends after graduating from college. Karla and Carter fell in love at first sight, and Karla never returned to her home in Maine.

After losing his job due to his alcoholic tendencies, Karla was able to convince her husband to sober up. They were quite successful for nearly a year. Unable to find good work, however, the Mitchel's decided to move to Ohio where there were more automotive jobs available.

Karla Mitchel: Karla Franklin (later Mitchel) was the youngest of three sisters, and the only one to graduate college. Her family had never supported her endeavors of wanting to waste her money on a college education when she would have been perfectly secure in money and life working at her family's historical Bed and Breakfast. But the tenacious young girl had other ideas.

She graduated at the top of her class, with magna cum laude honors. After which, Karla took off with her friends for a much needed escape. When their car broke down, Karla met her husband, the young mechanic at the small gas station up the road. Two years later, they were married with their first child, Jack, on the way.

Karla knew about Carter's drinking habits from the very beginning of their relationship. However, she refused to admit her family had been right about marrying "that redneck boy", and would not leave him. The one thing Karla hated was to be proven wrong. She put up with Carter's drinking and abuse for fourteen years, despite her family giving her several options to get out of the relationship many times.

Nevan Romilly: Descended from a family of blacksmiths that had lived in Outland Post for generations, Nevan Romilly met his wife, Paria, the granddaughter of a successful scribe and herbalist from The Rushing Reeds Province when Kaytah came to do a census of the village and had brought her daughter along.

Paria Romilly: Paria Chaudoin (later Romilly) was the daughter of a palace scribe and local fisherman, and the granddaughter of a palace scribe and herbalist from The Rushing Reeds Province. Paria was mostly raised by her grandparents. Her father drowned in a fishing accident when she was three years old. Her mother, Kaytah, continued to work as a palace scribe, and traveled all over the Elven territories of Chartile, sometimes bringing her daughter once she was older.
Paria met Nevan while accompanying her mother on a trip to Outland Post. Paria followed in her grandmother's footsteps as an herbalist, and was one of the main healers in Outland Post, due to her knowledge and the little village's isolation.

Kaytah Chaudoin: Kaytah was the daughter of a palace scribe and his wife, a successful herbalist from The Rushing Reeds Province. She decided to follow in her father's footsteps and became a palace scribe when she was twenty-one years old. Kaytah met her husband, Patrin, and had married by the time she was seventeen.

Knowing her ambition to become a palace scribe, Patrin cared for their daughter, Paria, and was happy to do so. Patrin died in a fishing accident when Paria was three years old, leaving his in-laws to care for Paria.

Kaytah's father had lost his hand the year before in a bear attack, and was able to help his wife not only care for Paria, but help her to fill orders as the local herbalist.

Kaytah retired from scribal work after the accident in Outland Post concerning her granddaughter, Piper. There, she took over as the healing woman in Outland Post, and cared for Piper to the best of her ability from a distance.

-Dwarves-

Sintori: Harasan of House Geofra and second husband, Sintori worked as a historian at Mount Kelsii his entire life.

Imohad: Third Hasana of House Alofrah. Younger brother to Elder Imohan of the Topaz Quarter of Mount Kelsii. Imohad worked as a soldier his entire life.

Orctkar: Son of Balla and her first hasana, Otkatir, Orctkar should great interest in working with food from a young age. He worked along the mountainside with some of the farmers when he was an early teenager. Balla soon found him a job working in the kitchens at Mount Kelsii. Orctkar went on to marry Neradah, and became Harasan to her House.

Ketari: Ketari was the first daughter of Nefiri's second eldest brother, Kehara, but was considered too rigid for selection in training toward Princesshood. Instead, she decided she wanted to be a retainer. Shortly after that decision, Gemari was chosen to train as Princess of Mount Kelsii, and it was easily decided that Ketari should be her head retainer.

Ketari often helped her sister make important decisions, but she often did not agree with her.

Frejah of the House of Berkhildr of the Carnelian Quarter: First daughter of Berkhildr, a previous elder of the Carnelian Quarter. Frejah always knew she wanted to be an elder. It took her some time to decide whether she wanted to marry or not. Frejah had 2 hasanas that outlived her. She had 3 sons and no daughters.

Ulfwyn of the House of Hallvor of the Cobalt Quarter: Second daughter of Hallvor and her Harasan, Ulfrik. Ulfwyn never took any husbands. Rumors say she bore one illegitimate child, but it was never proven.

Queen Carendeil of the House of Esjamourn: Queen of the Tutarian Mountains, Carendeil passed back to the stone from the Five Day Fever when she had only recently been made Queen.

Goddess Rashiri: Mother Goddess to the Dwarves. She hears the prayers of the dwarves, and delivers them to the appropriate God or Goddess, who then decides whether to act upon the request. She is the protector of the dwarves, like a guardian angel.

Ygdalla of the House of Dryfinal of the Amethyst Quarter: Ygdalla is the first daughter of Dryfinal and her Harasan, Yngvarr. Ygdalla was an only child for many years, as her mother did not wish to take anymore husbands. Ygdalla was raped by a soldier when she was 17 years old. From that point onward, Ygdalla decided to embrace her femininity, and used the position of power she knew she held only because of her being female to hurt anyone who tried to defy her.

It was Isla who calmed Ygdalla's rage and anger, and showed her that not all men acted in such a way. Ygdalla eventually supported her friend's underground movement of getting a male voice on the Council, but there was still a part of her that wanted this only so she could prove how much better a woman was than a man.

Ygdalla eventually married, but only took one hasana, like her mother. She trusted her husband, and wasn't sure she could ever trust anyone else so wholly without the risk of being hurt again.

Princess Thora: Princess to Mount Kelsii. She passed in tragic cave-in that killed her and her entire guard. Rumor and speculation say it was due to her involvement with the Black Diamonds. Some believe several Council Elders planned the accident, and subsequently blamed the Black Diamonds. However, there is no proof of this.

Goddess Verika: The Goddess of Truth and Law

Imohan: Daughter of Alofrah and her third hasana, Imojarah. Elder of the Opal Quarter of the Tutarian Mountains.

Jarvae: Daughter of Jarlil and her second hasana, Torvae, Jarvae is the elder of Garnet Quarter of the Tutarian Mountains. She took a husband very early in life, and eventually took three more. She was blessed with two daughters and seven sons, which gave her a tremendous amount of power and influence within the Council and the Royals.

Tagrin: A soldier of Mount Kelsii. His brother was killed in a sabotage by The Black Diamonds, and forever held the deepest hatred toward the organization.

Maltori: Second Hasana to the House of Arnfastah. Maltori worked as a blacksmith for Mount Kelsii, often repairing the soldier's armor. He turned spy for The Black Diamonds after overhearing a conversation from two colleagues. He later became an informant for Princess Taraniz when he heard she wanted to bring the dwarves under Elven law. Maltori always placed his bets with the biggest fish.

Jentar: A long-time supporter of The Black Diamonds. Jentar learned his trade as a blacksmith and armorer, then faked his death in a skirmish between the Mount Kelsii soldiers and a group of Black Diamonds. Since that time, he has sold weapons and weapon accessories to most of the rogue organization using the connections he still had to those working in secret in Mount Kelsii. He had begun to expand his reach into the Tutarian Mountains in order to obtain other supplies with some of the travelling merchants, and the Queen and Princess themselves. Jentar never married, but eventually began a relationship with one of the human slaves much later in life.

Aerndis: The first daughter of a wealthy family in the Ruby Quarter, Aerndis had taken 2 husbands by the time she was 31, and the other two followed suit shortly thereafter. She had 2 daughters and 13 sons. She had great influence within the Ruby Quarter, often bribing and manipulating whomever held the Elder seat of her quarter at that time.

Aeris: The second daughter of a wealthy family in the Ruby Quarter, Aeris was nearly the opposite of her older sister, Aerndis. She married late in life, having only 2 husbands, 4 sons and no daughters. Aeris's first husband was recruited to the ranks of the Black Diamonds as an inside source within the Palace Guards early in his career, and confided this to Aeris shortly after their marriage. They quietly supported the efforts of the Black Diamonds, and Aeris worked hard to undermine all her sister attempted to do to further the cause of executing all of the Black Diamonds.

Lynden of Lynhldr: The sole survivor of a tragic altercation between the soldiers of Mount Kelsii and The Black Diamonds in the Ruby Quarter. The incident mostly surrounded the third hasana of the House of Lynhldr discovering his wife and her other husbands had been working with The Black Diamonds. He coordinated an attack on the household, but told the family at the last moment, hoping they could all flee into the Belirian Forest and start a new life elsewhere. The soldiers attacked before they could leave. Lynden hid inside a cabinet during the altercation. She watched her entire family slaughtered through the crack between the doors.

Halil Commander of the Guard: Harasan of The House of Isanorah of the Amber Quarter. Halil was father to 1 daughter and 2 sons. He held his position as Commander of the Guard (giving instruction to all of the soldiers and palace guards in Mount Kelsii) into his 60's, until he finally retired once he developed something similar to kidney stones.

-Elves-

Princess Taraniz: Born the 14th day of Ansalvar. First born daughter of King Aramor and Queen Runa, Taraniz Anirya was quite a normal young girl. She liked pretty things, especially shoes and bracelets, and had a pet cat at one time. Taraniz began having strange dreams when she was twelve years old. She would wake up screaming, and still see images before her that no one else could see. By the time she was thirteen, she had fallen into a great depression, and had become cold and bitter.

Taraniz attempted to confide in her father the voice in her mind and the darkness she fought every day. Aramor was afraid, and shunned her. Taraniz became angry. She felt betrayed and abandoned, as Valar had since left several months before with no explanation as to why. Her fear became anger, and Duke Noraedin's soul within her was able to grow and feed from her anger. At times, Taraniz felt powerful, and longed for greater control over the amazing things the voice in her mind could do with magic.

Soon, however, Taraniz began losing moments of time. She could not remember what day it was, or how she had gotten to a particular place. She could no longer remember what she had been doing even moments before, though it had actually been hours. When the hours turned to days, Taraniz began fighting the voice in her mind with what little strength she had left.

Taraniz came to enough to read several documents the voice in her mind was trying to block her from reading. They said she had a twin sister. Having recently heard of an incident in Outland Post involving a girl her age, Taraniz was determined to discover if this person perhaps could tell her who her sister was by using some form of magic. Duke Noraedin took over her quest after she had called the orders to ride to Outland Post, and she did not come to again for several days until they were nearly back to the Elven Palace.

Taraniz did want to bring the dwarves and elves under one rule. Her hope was that by integrating some of the more "magical" and "mystical" practices of the dwarves into the elven culture, her people would one day become more open to allowing the practice of magic under intense restriction and supervision. It was how she had hoped to rid herself of the darkness in her mind. Had Taraniz lived, she and Piper would have clashed over this point, and there would have been a struggle for the throne.

King Aramor: The only child of the late King Armon and Queen Eleanor, Aramor always knew he would be king. He had no cousins, and few uncles and aunts.

Aramor gave little thought to becoming king until his father died of River Lung (similar to our pneumonia). Having little experience with leading his people, Aramor looked heavily to his mother for guidance.

The Conclave was losing faith in Aramor. Talks of finding Queen Eleanor a second husband to be king were rampant. Queen Eleanor arranged the marriage between Aramor and Runa, daughter of the Lord and Lady or Harpy's Point, in the hopes it would settle her son and lead him to be more responsible. The kindhearted spirit of Lady Runa was well known across all of the Elven territories. It was for the love of Runa that kept the Conclave from mutiny.

Queen Runa: Lady Runa Elisa Vouclaine was the daughter of the Lord and Lady of Harpy's Point. Due to the climate of Harpy's point being so close to a very large lake, it is ideal for growing many of the herbs needed for medicines.

After accompanying her father on a several week long trek for his tournament season, Runa saw the need to get these much needed herbs into the hands of the other surrounding towns and villages.

Runa accompanied her father on his next tournament season, and distributed herbs to ever surrounding village and town she could travel to while her father fought in the competitions. She taught some of the healers how to use some of the herbs they had never seen before, and how to grow them outside of the ideal Harpy's Point environment.

Runa was only seventeen when this all occurred. She asked her mother to commission the Conclave of Nobles for a better road to be built from Harpy's Point to the main road so they could get stored herbs to other towns more quickly during times of illness.

Queen Eleanor was not blind to the great deeds being done by Lady Runa. She arranged the marriage between Runa and Aramor when Runa was 19 years old.

Duke Noraedin: Brother of King Pasalphathe, and one of the most powerful wielders of magic within Chartile at the time. Noraedin was also a great alchemist. Some believe he poisoned his own parents to try at attain the throne. Noraedin was able to bring many elves (and humans) under his banner as the rightful king.

King Florine: One of the last known Dwarvik male royals. Florine helped to establish a basic system of writing that could be used between the races, and a mutual form of justice when dealing with interracial crimes.

King Jenemar: King Jenemar (of Elven decent) negotiated with Duke Noraedin for the meeting to call peace between their warring parties. If a settlement could not be made, it was then discussed to use the orenite circlet to kill Noraedin. King Jenemar, however, did vote against this, but the rest of the Kings of Chartile were in favor.

King Kasmalin: The last known merfolk royal. Little is known about Kasmalin. Many believed he was far more intelligent than his other fellow kings, and had far greater magical abilities. However, he chose not to use his magic often, or in great capacities, and took a stance of neutrality most of the time. Kasmalin slowly faded away into history. There is no known record of his death, or where he went after the death or Noraedin.

King Pasalphathe: The last king of the human race. When Noraedin fell, and order was brought to Chartile once more, Pasalphathe was eventually put into orenite cuffs and faded away into history.

Tathias: An Elven soldier, manipulated by Noraedin to work in secret with the dwarves in order to infiltrate Mount Kelsii. Taraniz (under Noraedin's control) had killed Tathias's family. Tathias was manipulated to do Noraedin's bidding in order to join his family in the afterlife.

Brodrick Garrison: The son of a local vinter in Cannondole. Brodrick did not sit idly by and live off his parent's coin. Brock was always extremely ambitious, even at a very young age. He did odd jobs for the merchants and business owners in Cannondole, including delivering medicines from the local apothecary, and caring for the horses and stable at The Glass Lantern.

Atana: Second daughter of the owners of The Glass Lantern. Atana is much smarter than she appears to be. At first.

Krista: Beck-and to the Lord of Cannondole.

Sister Theodora: One of the Sisters of the Chantry of Canna. She particularly likes to garden.

Sister Marta: One of the Sisters of the Chantry of Canna. She likes to read and write.

Mattimore Roux: A first rate rogue. Mattimore earns his coin at various jobs, and just as quickly spends it away. He has traveled all over Chartile, and has been caught by the local soldiers of several towns for stealing or fighting. His most recent antics of attempting to walk onto the palace grounds rather drunk, with the intention of marrying Princess Taraniz, landed him in the palace dungeons.

Duke Ewan of Rushing Reeds Province: A distant uncle to King Aramor.

Lady Evanora, Runa's Grandmother: Part of Piper/ Eva Ruani's namesake. Evanora had an illegitimate relationship with one of her beck-and's, and pawned the child off as her husband's. Evanora's husband died only a few years later, and the truth came to light with close family only.

Leland, Captain of the Guard: Leland took command of the soldiers of the palace, and the movements of the elven armies when Taraniz (under the influence of Noraedin) killed the previous Captain. Leland was rather young for the position, but did well for himself, especially after Piper took the throne.

-Other-

Mr. Darrow: History unknown

Beck-ands: Short for Beck-and-Calls, the name given to human slaves.

Jessica Hill: Jayson Hill's younger sister. Jessica graduated her school for the arts at the age of 16. She studied acting for several years, but eventually went back to school for a psychiatric degree.

Stephanie Mitchel: Jack Mitchel's younger sister.

Ms. Pince: One of the librarians at the Swansdale Public Library. She dedicated her life to the library, and was constantly passed over for promotions for one reason or another.

George Potts: Alias given to Dimitri by Brodric Garrision.

Uncle Rob: Jack's Uncle. Married to Kiera, Jack's mother's sister.

Aunt Kiera: Jack's Aunt. His mother's sister.

The Council of the Elders: A group of individuals, each representing a different Quarter of either Mount Kelsii or The Tutarian Mountains. Each person is elected by those residing in each Quarter.

The Conclave of Nobles: Each region within the Elven territory of Chartile is represented by a Lord, Duke or Baron. These individuals convene and meet to advise the Royals on matters of State. Though they hold no real power, the King and Queen often defer to what the Conclave wishes to keep the peace.

Chartilian Wheel of the Year

The Chartilian year consists of ten months, most of which are named for past kings and ancient leaders. There are 21-23 days in each month, the longest months being in Winter.

Chartile has a very wet Spring and a long Summer. The change from Autumn to Winter occurs rapidly, leading to high amounts of snow in the month of Rhidqar, followed by extreme cold and ice in the month of Murenvar.

Excerpt from Chartile: Magic

The first thing Charlie noticed was the smell. It was the smell of lush grass, sweet, and of course, his one allergy. He lay there, his eyes still shut, waiting for his body to erupt in a red hot itching rash. But it never came. He dared to open his eyes, wondering where his glasses had fallen to, and found himself in a large clearing in the middle of a dense forest.

The second thing he noticed was that he was stark naked. How he hadn't noticed before, he had no idea. Charlie quickly looked around the clearing. There was no one around. Covering himself to the best of his ability, he darted for a mass of bushes straight ahead. He found a leaf on the ground behind the bushes the size of a dinner plate. He wiped the dirt off, and used this to cover the front of himself.

Now panic was beginning to set in. Was this some sick joke Malcolm's friends were playing on him? He wondered if there were cameras somewhere. Maybe behind him at this very moment. Charlie found another dinner plate-sized leaf on the ground, and quickly covered his rear end. He had to get out of here, and fast. But where was he?

Charlie looked at the trees and bushes around him. Some looked vaguely familiar, but most everything else was entirely foreign. Not a single maple tree anywhere, and Fulton County was notorious for its maple trees.

"Okay, don't panic," Charlie said to himself. He reached up to push his glasses up his nose, and realized they weren't there. How could he see without his glasses? He was practically legally blind without them. His heart was pounding so hard in his chest, Charlie was ready for it to burst out and begin flopping around on the ground in front of him.

Charlie felt a warm, humid air across the back of his neck. The hair stood up, and he turned around very slowly. What he saw was not what he expected to see. Charlie stared into the bright golden eyes of a black panther. It grinned back at him, showing a level of intelligence that terrified Charlie even more than being this close to a wild animal.

"If you were to run," the panther whispered to him, "It would be all the more fun for me."

It took only a second for the realization that an animal had just spoke to subside before Charlie bolted back out into the clearing. The panther threw back its head and gave a kind of laughing roar before taking off after Charlie.

About the Author

Cassandra Morgan was born in a small town in Ohio where she spent much of her preteen and teenage years running through the woods behind her house and playing role-playing games with her friends. She comes from a family of both writers and English majors from both her maternal and paternal sides. The Chartile (pronounced KAR-tyl) series came to be when Cassie was thirteen years old. It is loosely based on some of the games she and her friends would play.

Cassie enjoys going to the movies and hopes to be a famous actress someday. Her favorite food is her grandmother's sweet pickles, based off of a recipe from her great-great-grandmother. Her grandma recently passed the original recipe to her. Her favorite colors are emerald green and royal purple, and she loves all animals.

Cassandra participates in historical reenactment and animal rescue. She holds several animal nutrition certifications, and works as a behaviorist with several of her local animal shelters.

Cassie considers herself a professional dreamer and has never given up the hope of travelling the entire world and experiencing as many cultures as possible.

Made in the USA
Charleston, SC
21 August 2016